Running to Stand Still

ELIZABETH FLETCHER

PublishAmerica
Baltimore

ISBN: 1-4241-4827-8
PUBLISHED BY PUBLISHAMERICA, LLLP
www.publishamerica.com
Baltimore

Printed in the United States of America

Dedicated with love and gratitude to
God, my family and my friends.

CHAPTER ONE

Thank God the day had dawned as clear and beautiful as it did! The idea of flying was bad enough but poor weather would have probably changed her mind altogether. Annie was not usually so easily perturbed, but flying was one subject that not only perturbed her, it scared her to death. She realized her fear of flying was normal: her parents had died in a plane crash. But she also knew that as a professional in the medical field, the one thing you must realize and accept is that you cannot elude death—you can take precautions and care in your everyday activities, but you must not allow your fears to insinuate themselves into normal, everyday occurrences, like travel. Watching her plane taxi to a halt outside the window of the terminal, Annie told herself for the hundredth time that the flight would be smooth and uneventful: Greensboro to La Guardia in little less than two hours.

Once settled in her seat by the window, Annie closed her eyes and smiled at the city and the events that awaited her. The trip had been a long time coming as the benefits, plans, and reservations took nearly a year to arrange. Still, she was proud of what she and the other members of the Triad Heart Association had been able to accomplish. Their fund-raising goal had been met, indeed surpassed, and their chapter was to be one of a select few to be honored tomorrow night at a banquet in New York City. This time last year she would never have imagined that Annie Ryan would ever visit the Big Apple, much less be invited there for an award. The award itself was insignificant compared to the money and the awareness that her chapter had raised; but she had to admit that even an overnight trip was a tremendous bonus since she had taken no vacation during the last four years.

Almost immediately Annie chastised herself for even thinking about a vacation when she knew how tight money was and how totally dependent her grandmother was on her. She chewed at her bottom lip even now, wondering if Gramma Ryan would be all right until she returned for she was Annie's only family now. Remembering how they had clung to one another like drowning people to buoys after her parents' deaths, Annie blinked back the familiar stinging behind her eyes and turned to look out the window of the plane. *Gramma would be fine,* she told herself again and again; *for two days, with Monica Holt staying over until her return, Gramma would be fine.*

Dear Monica, Annie thought with a smile. It had been she who suggested they go into nursing school together, and there was no one other than herself more capable of caring for Gramma than Monica. *Who else but another nurse could care for a 79-year-old blind diabetic?* she silently asked herself. "Well Monica, I certainly owe you one," she whispered aloud.

The plane began moving at that moment and Annie drew in a deep breath of apprehension. Would she always react this way whenever she flew? Again, she reminded herself of the beauty of the day and clasped her hands between the knees of her jean-clad legs to keep them from trembling. The captain's voice welcomed her and the other passengers but she barely heard him, for her mind had wondered again to another flight in another part of the country seemingly a lifetime ago. Closing her eyes, Annie allowed herself to remember their faces; and as had become somewhat of a silent prayer to them, she whispered, "Hello Mother...hello, Daddy" to her vision, the spirits of her parents. As they visited with her again this day, inside her head she heard their voices telling her she had nothing to fear; Daddy smiled and took Mother's hand, patting it with the other as he was wont to when he felt secure and happy. And at that moment, Annie smiled at the vision, thanking them for being with her today when she needed them most.

As if waking from a dream, Annie felt a slight pressure upon her shoulder and looked up to find one of the flight attendants speaking to her. "We are preparing to land at La Guardia, Miss. I was going to remind you to fasten your seat belt but I can see that you've done that already. I thought you were asleep when I saw your eyes closed, but I must have been mistaken."

"Thank you all the same," Annie replied somewhat sheepishly as the attendant turned to one of the passengers in a seat across the aisle. Annie raised warm hands to her cool face realizing it would have benefited no one for her to correct the young woman. She had in fact been asleep since the plane taxied down the runway in Greensboro and had never awakened to unfasten her seatbelt at all.

Upon departing the plane and walking into the La Guardia terminal, Annie stared in awe at the enormity of the structure. Several of the nurses at the hospital had warned her of the size of La Guardia in comparison to Piedmont Triad International, but nothing could have prepared her for the real thing. She shook her head as her eyes scanned the horizon of people: expecting to see mass confusion she instead found the scene more akin to structured disorder, not unlike the hospital when short staffed and short tempered!

Annie thanked some unknown patron for giving her the good sense to bring only her garment bag rather than another piece of luggage; she had also chosen her largest purse in which to pack her best shoes and smaller essentials, making the garment bag a carry-on since it held only her dinner dress and a change of clothing for the return flight home. She smiled as she draped the garment bag over her shoulder remembering the beautiful and expensive dress she had saved so diligently for. The rose-print polished cotton material had been designed with a gently scooped neck front and a low, u-shaped back that was meant to flatter in the most feminine way. Annie especially liked the 3/4 length sleeves and the full skirt, which had wrapped itself around her legs as she danced and twirled in front of her mirror at home. Monica had absolutely forbidden Annie's bout with guilt over such a purchase, choosing instead to reason that she had earned the gift to herself after giving so many hours to their chapter of the Heart Association. It didn't hurt either when, after finally saving the full cost of the dress, she found it had been reduced by 15% the day she went back to purchase it!

"Wear your hair down," Monica had instructed, "and curl it with your curling iron like you did when we were in high school. You won't have lack of time as an excuse for not doing it once you get settled in your hotel room in New York."

Annie smiled at her reflection as she stepped toward the glass doors that led to awaiting taxicabs outside the terminal. "Maybe I'll do just that," she stated to no one.

Once settled in her room, Annie did the one thing she had looked most forward to since reserving her room on the 9th floor: she went to the window for a nighttime view of the New York City skyline. The draperies parted easily enough and she felt relief at finding the window full-length and clean, but nothing could have prepared her for the splendor of the city lights, red and white against the evening blackness. Having lived in North Carolina all her life, and having drunk of the Blue Ridge Mountains and the Outer Banks during family vacations, Annie never imagined she could appreciate anything so immense as this man-made skyline, and yet she did. And she was glad, truly glad for the very first time that she made the decision to come.

* * *

Waking the next morning, Annie jerked to sit upright in the bed, her senses piqued by the queer silence of the morning. She remembered immediately where she was and yet couldn't ease the disquiet within her stomach. Looking at her watch, Annie shrieked in alarm when she saw that it was 9am already, chastising herself for having not been up and about at least two hours before. And, though her late evening arrival had seemed reason enough last night not to call home at midnight, she felt herself wince at the possibility of being given a thorough dressing down from her grandmother; as it was, the frail, elderly voice on the other end of the phone line offered no sympathy whatsoever:

"I listened to *Headline News* all evenin after you didn't call, just expecting to hear that your plane had crashed somewhere between here and New York," she whined. "Monica had to give me my sleeping medicine, I was so upset," she added for good measure.

"Put Monica on the phone, Gramma," Annie murmured worriedly. Then: "How's Gramma, Monica, really?"

"She's *really* fine, Annie…probably better off than you are right now, unless I miss my guess. Her sugars and blood pressures have been normal and she ate well at supper; if she was worried or upset it didn't effect her appetite any," she finished in a whisper, angry again at how the older woman used her illness to get what she wanted. "Please don't worry, and don't let your grandmother ruin this trip for you."

"I shouldn't have come…if anything happens to her while I'm here, I'll never forgive myself," she finished earnestly.

"Your grandmother will probably outlive us all, Annie, and you know it!"

"She's not where she can hear you, is she?" Annie asked in a whisper.

Monica laughed. "She went to the bathroom—don't worry, I'm not stupid. What your grandmother misses in sight, she makes up for with her keen hearing. Woke me four times last night because she 'heard something.' Can you believe it?"

Annie didn't smile. "Yeah, I can…I'm sorry, Monica. I shouldn't have wrangled you into this."

"You didn't *wrangle* me," Monica contradicted. "I volunteered, insisted even, remember? I can't believe *I* did *that!*" she teased.

"Well, I'll be home by noon tomorrow. My plane departs at 9:10 and I'll call you right before I board in the morning."

"Aren't you cutting it a little close? You're gonna wish you'd slept in after you realize New York parties don't end 'till dawn!" Monica teased.

"The parties may last 'till dawn, but this kid'll be in bed by midnight."

"We'll see," Monica laughed into the phone. "You forget: there are several celebrities invited to this thing and the men will probably expect lots of booze and babes as repayment for being spokesmen for the Heart Association during the past year."

"Monica how could you? The people we enlisted were very generous with their time and efforts, some of them donating substantial amounts of money as well. I'm looking forward to personally thanking each and every one of them."

"Uh-huh…well, thank a couple of them for me while you're at it: Eric Nielson and Martin Vaughn for starters," Monica taunted.

"You're insane, Monica Holt!"

"Thanks. If being insane means appreciating the opposite sex, then commit me. You'd do well to go a little insane once in a while yourself!"

"Appreciate, my eye. You just take care of Gramma like she was your own and I'll settle up with you when I get home," Annie quipped. Then more seriously, "I really do appreciate your being there, Monica. I wouldn't have left her with anyone else."

Monica smiled as she balanced the base of the ancient telephone on her hip. "I know. You just try to remember to have a good time, okay? You'll probably never get another opportunity like this to travel…or to meet beautiful celebrities!" *Not so long as Grandma Battleaxe has anything to say about it*, she added silently.

Annie smiled. "I know and I do appreciate it. Wish me luck tonight?"

"Of course, like you really need it. That dress will knock 'em dead!"

"I don't intend to knock anyone dead," Annie replied tersely. "I just want the evening to go smoothly. This is foreign ground for me."

"It will. You'll charm those Yankees' socks off!"

"For crissake, good-bye Monica. I'll talk with you in the morning."

"'Bye, y'all," Monica teased laughingly as she hung up the phone.

11

When at 6:00 Annie stepped into her new dress, it was with a feeling of newfound confidence. She had timed her bath and makeup so that she wasn't in a rush when it came time to do her hair. Turning her head from side to side, she was pleased with the soft curls that laid like tan clouds upon her shoulders.

"Mousy-brown!" she accused the mirror.

"Dirty-blonde," her daddy used to say.

At least it's my natural color and it's all mine, she thought to herself. Glancing at her watch she saw that it was 6:25 and she had just enough time to spray on her cologne before heading out the door and toward the elevator.

When she reached the lobby, the number of guests that had already arrived surprised Annie. The doors to the ballroom were open and a steady stream of tuxedo-clad men and elegantly dressed women were mingling back and forth between the dining hall and the ballroom. Annie nervously chewed her lip, noting how simple she appeared in contrast to the other women: their hairstyles were upswept, many glistening with jeweled combs, whereas her hair lay loose and unfettered. A limp brown mouse, she mused, then cursed her own silent bantering for dealing out a taste of what she was certain she would hear during the evening, spreading out before her now like an endless stretch of highway. *I'm out of my league and I know it,* she finally admitted silently, *only it's too late to turn back and too early to turn in.*

Taking a deep, steadying breath, Annie drew herself to her full 5 feet 4 inches and strode determinedly into the now crowded ballroom, thinking as she entered what a contrast it was to the pleasant little parlor in her pleasant little house. Funny how she'd never thought of her two-story house as small, until now. One could set the entire house inside the confines of this one room, she realized in amazement, the chimney and gables, too. Walking into the reception area, Annie searched the throng for a familiar face: heck, a friendly face would do she conceded, familiar or no! She hated standing alone in such a huge crowd of people; she felt as if she stood out because she was the only one she noticed without a date or companion within arm's length. Thankfully only a few short moments passed before she found the registrar's podium and pen in hand, she signed the guest book.

"Ah, Miss Ryan, welcome! We have a nametag already made up identifying you and your chapter. Please allow me to pin it on for you."

"Of course. Thank you," Annie replied as she leaned a bit closer for the rather round and bejeweled woman to reach her. The woman took great pains to place the identification as near Annie's shoulder as was possible stating,

"We smaller women must cater to the taller in assembly so that perhaps they don't have to bend so far when trying to make our acquaintance."

Annie had to smile at the practicality of the comment. "How considerate you are of the taller folk, Miss…" She glanced at the woman's own name tag. "Miss Wittle. Something about your speech is very familiar: are you from South Carolina, or Virginia, maybe?"

"And I'd hoped no one would notice!" Miss Wittle pouted teasingly. "I've lived in New York almost 25 years now and no one notices my drawl but other Southerners."

"Actually," Annie corrected, "your drawl is in check. It was when you mentioned 'making one's acquaintance' that you gave yourself away!"

"Oh, pooh!" the older woman feigned hurt. "You won't tell anyone will you?"

"Not a soul," Annie promised, smiling at having made a true friend. "Will someone relieve you from your post later on tonight?" she asked in all sincerity. "I'd appreciate your company during the reception if you're not otherwise committed."

Miss Wittle took both Annie's hands into her own. "You can't honestly say you'd rather have this old woman's company to one of those handsome young men parading around!"

She reminds me of Gramma, before Mother and Daddy died, Annie mused, and she closed her eyes on a memory that was almost as painful to her as her grandmother's worsening health. The older woman saw the change in Annie almost immediately and patted the young woman's hands appreciatively. "Perhaps I'll see you later, Miss Ryan but for now, have something to drink and mingle a bit. I'm still on duty and will be for a while."

"Very well," Annie replied, not noticing the concern in the older woman's expression. "I'll be looking for you."

Miss Wittle nodded although she already knew she had no plans to join the pretty young woman. That young lady is lonesome, she thought to herself, and not for some old woman's companionship. Glancing around, Miss Wittle noticed the number of male heads that turned when Annie walked by and she smiled, wondering which one would set his sights on her by evening's end. Ah, to be young (and thin) again!

By ten o'clock most of the speeches had been made and the leaders of the various chapters recognized while nearly everyone in attendance freely sipped champagne and several surreptitiously lit cigarettes. How ironic, Annie thought to herself, that the very people who so stridently fought the war against heart disease were also the ones indulging now in rich food, liquor and tobacco, the major contributors, along with heredity, to the hated affliction. It was one thing to recommend alcohol in moderation and quite another to drink oneself into oblivion, as several in the audience seemed intent upon doing. Soap star Eric Nielson seemed quite content recreating the role of the angry, thirty-something alcoholic of "When Tomorrow Comes," throwing himself into the belligerent role as if it were second nature to him. At first, Annie smiled at what she thought was the actor's brilliant method of attuning the audience's awareness to the characteristics of one who obviously could not hold his drink. It wasn't until he finished slurring his way through his written speech and was turning to leave the stage that Annie realized he was done! There was no reverting back to the warm, solicitous gentleman she had imagined the actor to be from his taped commercials for TV; he was genuinely drunk and the very last person who should have been offering advice, pre-written or not, concerning the negative effects of excessive alcohol use in relation to heart disease.

It was obvious that Annie was not the only person in the audience who was disturbed by the spectacle Mr. Nielson made of himself. Almost immediately wine glasses were inched across linen tablecloths to sit half-consumed beside empty dessert plates, and new bottles were refused when brought out by the servers. Annie cast a curious glance at the half dozen or so tables between hers and the stage, smiling appreciatively that the inebriated actor had gotten the desired effect after all. She wondered if the next speaker would be anti-tobacco with an obvious nicotine cough, or a four hundred pound speaker on cholesterol and the importance of a low-fat diet.

There was a noticeable delay before the final speaker stood up from where he sat at the speakers' table. He rose slowly, glancing from the guest of honor across from him back to the one seated at his right and slid his chair back into place under the table. Annie recognized him immediately and a shiver of delight ran up her spine. There was no mistaking the tall, broad shouldered, dark-haired man for anyone but Martin Vaughn, and Annie felt a thrill that he had chosen to attend the banquet after all; that he was also going to speak was nothing less than icing on the cake.

Annie's was not the only surprised expression in the audience. Vaughn had apparently slipped into the hall during Nielson's "speech," his appearance at the podium causing a ripple effect among the entire assemblage. The chapter guests (most of whom were women) as well as the featured speakers seemed to sit a little taller in their chairs, their attention all on the highly respected actor whose role as Michael Maurer in "The Misbegotten" had earned him an Academy Award nomination, the honor especially sweet considering the movie marked his debut as a leading man in a major motion picture. Lauded as the next Mel Gibson or Denzel Washington or, depending on which reviewer one read, the next Lawrence Olivier or Clark Gable, Martin Vaughn had seemed bemused by the comparisons, amused even that reviewers could be so bold in their appraisal.

"If I thought I was really expected to live up to what you writers say about me," Annie recalled him saying after the Academy Awards ceremony, "I'd go back to loading and unloading boxcars today. I'd be a fool to set such high goals and expectations. It won't be easy to find another part like that one." The comment had touched a cord of sensibility in the minds of several million-television viewers that evening, suddenly making Vaughn an "accessible star," a *real person*, a man's man. The tabloids ate it up and Hollywood managers scrambled to do his bidding while, during the months that followed, Martin Vaughn would learn just how much publicity could be garnered from his estrangement from his English wife Claire, whom the tabloids frequently seemed to confuse with Sybil, the sado-masochistic murder victim of "The Misbegotten."

Drawn back to the present by Vaughn's tentative "Uh…good evening," Annie swallowed once and set her mind to memorizing as much of his speech as possible, for Monica would demand to know everything the actor had to say, in spite of the fact someone else probably wrote his speech for him.

As his eyes scanned the audience from behind round wire-rims Martin swallowed hard, finding it every bit as difficult to address audiences today as himself instead of in a role, as he had that first time four months ago at the Awards. He realized his delay in continuing grew more conspicuous with each passing second, yet he couldn't force his mind beyond the scene he had witnessed from Eric Nielson when he'd entered the hall, and could only pray that he would not make an equal fool of himself. He nervously scratched at some imaginary itch at the back of his neck, finding his voice with a shrug. "I don't have a prepared speech, I'm afraid…I fell asleep during the flight over from London, and…"

His confession was met with good-natured laughter and though he seemed unsure as to why what he said came off as funny, he smiled and welcomed the lightening of the tense mood.

Forget the speechwriter, thought Annie. What we hear is what we get, or words to that effect!

"Well, like I said, I don't have a prepared speech; but then I shouldn't need one when addressing something as important and relevant to each of us as the Heart Association. First, let me say that I'm…I'm tremendously honored to speak on behalf of this organization. I understand that this evening's banquet is a thank-you of sorts for the many chapters throughout the United States, and I'd like to personally express my gratitude to all of you here tonight who have given so much of yourselves to this very worthy cause.

"I um…I have lost my father and a brother to heart disease." He swallowed again and looked down at the empty podium, seemingly arranging his thoughts with as much care as his empty hands afforded him. He reached to grip the front edge of the lectern, then swallowed once more before lifting his eyes to the sea of silence staring so intently back at him. "There isn't a day goes by that I don't wonder if somehow *something* couldn't have been done; then I realize something *is* being done…just as quickly as money is raised and put into research, doctors are doing all they can to find new treatments…"

Martin's eyes touched upon several faces in the audience and the pause grew to an emotional peak, his attention finally drawn to one face at the very edge that seemed to visually express the words that chose to elude him. Annie dropped her prayerful hands from her lips and linked the fingers together in a tight mesh so that she might calm their shaking. For just an instant she imagined he was looking straight at her, then realized she was probably too far away to appear as anything more than a shadow against the wall. And yet, it was Annie that Martin saw, or rather the eloquent sadness on a face that spoke the very words he found so difficult to say.

He drew empathy from that shared sadness and knew somehow that this woman had shared an equal grief as he. Instantly, she drew herself straight and strong, defiant almost as she silently willed her encouragement to him. Martin drew that reassurance in with a breath and broke the eye contact only after the accidental ring of silverware against crystal gave him back over to the audience.

"If what each of you has done helps save just one life, that alone is reason enough to continue…that one life may be a father, or a brother…or your child." He let go a long breath and again his eyes dropped to the pedestal, a muscle twitching in his jaw in time to Annie's heartbeat. "Thank you again for your support of the Heart Association, and thank you for being kind enough to include me in tonight's ceremony." His eyes rose then as if relaying a silent apology for having stared too long at the podium and he smiled at the audience luminously, nodded once, and closed with "Good night."

Before Martin had fully turned away from the podium, the hall erupted in applause and the audience stood almost as one, so moved were they by the few sincere, well chosen words that spoke what was in each of their own hearts. Martin was met at the stage edge by the president of the New York City chapter, his hand clasped in a show of great appreciation for not only delivering such a moving speech, but for saving the remainder of the evening as well. Though no formal receiving line had been planned beforehand, the audience commenced to form one long line of well wishers who passed in procession before the stage in order to thank the guests of honor as well as the host city's chapter president.

Though several dozen people would eventually shake his hand before the evening drew to an official close, Martin was as generous with the sixtieth person as he had been with the sixth, taking an extra moment to share a comment or two whenever a handshake and thank you were not enough. Standing in line, Annie decided that she liked this Martin Vaughn very much and would usher Monica out to a theater as soon as possible to see "The Misbegotten" herself, knowing Monica wouldn't pass on seeing the movie again, especially if Annie paid her way. She smiled to herself, picturing Monica's wagging finger under her nose and her pouting lips teasing, "I told you so!"

When the procession drew near to the end, Annie found herself one person away from meeting Martin Vaughn in person. She searched through the half dozen comments she had thought up while standing in line; her mind went completely blank however, and she came up with absolutely nothing to say as her hand reached out to shake his.

"Ah, my friend," Martin murmured, his eyes going from Annie's face to her name tag and back again. "I see the face has a name."

"Excuse me?" she stammered in a shaky whisper.

Martin smiled and gave her hand a gentle squeeze. "Ann-Elise Ryan, I presume?"

Glancing over at the badge, Annie realized suddenly it must appear she was having to check to recognize her own name; in actuality, she hadn't noticed before that it read 'Ann-Elise' instead of 'Annie.' She swallowed convulsively. "Yes…I mean, no…I mean, actually it's just Annie but…" She felt like a blubbering idiot.

"It suits you, I think, Ann-Elise," Martin broke in appealingly, his brow drawing together thoughtfully. The way he said her name made Annie wish she had his voice on tape, for never before had anyone said it that it didn't come out sounding like 'Anna-lease' or 'Annie-lees,' the enunciation from which she had been given the nickname.

Annie smiled appreciatively, and "Thank you" was all she managed to say before the woman behind her none too gently nudged her ahead and took Martin's hand into her own. Annie dropped her eyes as a wave of embarrassment swept her from her toes to the top of her head. Venturing a glance back over her shoulder, Annie saw that Martin was moving to straighten himself from a too-enthusiastic bear hug and she smiled at the surprised and disconcerted expression on his face. At that moment, he lifted engaging eyes to her own and returned her smile, studying her for a long moment as if he might have wanted to say more. Feeling content at having shared a moment of humor with such a special man, at last Annie turned and walked away. Monica would have enjoyed this, she imagined smilingly.

At half past eleven, the last of the guests were being squired away in limousines and taxis to several private parties which usually followed such an evening as this; *those* are the parties that last until dawn, Annie realized thoughtfully, and that was fine with her. A hot shower and a cool bed—ah, the thought was glorious!

Walking through the corridor that led from the ballroom to the hotel lobby, Annie looked one last time for her friend Miss Wittle and felt somewhat at a loss for not having encountered her again during the evening. As she entered the glass elevator with several people she recognized from the banquet, Annie leaned her head back against the crystal wall and silently confessed that it was in fact Martin Vaughn who had left her feeling at a loss: a loss for words, a loss of what little sophistication she could claim, a loss of control over her fragile emotions. "The face has a name…" he had said; then he *was* staring at me during his speech she reasoned silently and with a sense of childlike giddiness, and she smiled. Monica would never believe it, she decided logically, stepping slowly from the elevator when it opened at her floor. "And now…?" She let her whispered question go unanswered as she unlocked the door to her room, stepped inside, and closed it back again slowly, regretfully, as if to shut the most exciting evening of her life away as one would a souvenir. She had kept her program of the evenings' events and rather wished she had thought to ask for Martin's autograph; after all, she could hardly have appeared less sophisticated than she already was!

As she moved slowly across the elegant room toward the lovely armoire that housed the television planning to check the weather for the next day, she noticed that the message light on her phone was blinking. Frantically she picked up the phone, imagining that something must have happened to her grandmother. But instead of a message from Monica, she was asked to call another room in the hotel "no matter how late she came in." Annie could only assume that it must be Miss Wittle, regretting they had not found one another during the banquet and possibly wanting to arrange to meet another time. Too bad she would be leaving so soon, Annie thought to herself; she would have enjoyed getting to know the kind, older woman.

Listening as one, then two rings at the extension she had been told to call reverberated back to her, Annie suddenly heard a deep, masculine voice answer, "Vaughn," and she very nearly dropped the phone from where it was cradled between her ear and shoulder. "I...I must have dialed the wrong extension," she began and started to return the phone to its base.

"Hello, Miss Ryan?—Yes, I'm glad you got my message. Thank you for returning my call," he began sincerely.

"I thought I was calling someone else," she replied absently, and Martin chuckled.

"Should I let you go, then?" he asked only half jokingly. "I just realized I'm still on London time, and yet it's probably late for you..."

"—no! I mean, it's not that late really, I'm just...surprised," she offered as she lowered herself to sit upon the bed. "What can I do for you?"

Martin chuckled. "May I ask if you have plans for the rest of the evening?"

"Plans?" She had somehow expected him to address their joint participation in the Heart Association and his query took her by surprise. "I don't understand..."

"—you see," he interrupted, sensing her confusion, "I missed the meal at the banquet and since I really hate to eat alone, I wondered if you might join me for a walk through Greenwich Village; maybe we could find a sandwich or something," he paused for a moment and Annie had to smile at the enthusiasm she heard in his voice: "I really *am* starving!"

Annie had to laugh then. "I'd love to join you Mr. Vaughn, though I honestly can't remember the last time I did a sandwich run at midnight!" Nor could she imagine why Martin had decided to ask her to join him then decided she didn't care why. It was thrilling enough that he had. "Shall I meet you in the lobby?"

"That would be fine, just wear comfortable shoes and be prepared to walk," he teased. "After all, this *is* the city that never sleeps!"

As Martin had said to dress casually, Annie hurried into her jeans and a beautiful silk sweater she had bought at one of the many factory outlet stores that dotted the North Carolina countryside. The Spring-like mid-March weather was lovely: cool enough for a light sweater, but not cold enough for a coat.

A few minutes later, Martin watched as Annie stepped out of the elevator and walked toward him through the lobby. He thought how like a Siamese cat she looked with her small triangular face, ash-blonde hair, and tanned skin; she gave the same impression of fragility and strength, and her vivid blue eyes really made the resemblance striking. She even had a slightly husky voice.

"Ann-Elise..." Martin nodded a welcome then added, "May I call you that?"

Annie shrugged almost indiscernibly. "Of course."

"And you must call me Martin. I thought we'd take a cab to the Village, then walk around and see what we might find. How familiar are you with New York City?" he asked, recognizing her voice was definitely NOT of the Northern persuasion.

"Not at all," Annie replied regretfully. "My visit here is for only a couple of days; I wish I had time to see everything."

"That would take you about five years, *if* you devoted all your time to it," he laughed, delighting in the gentle lilt her very Southern voice held. "Maybe we can find a few special sights if you don't mind missing your sleep?"

Annie's private opinion was that any woman who would choose sleep over seeing the sights of New York with one of America's must glamorous men, had to be dead or crazy! However, all she said was that she thought she could survive without one night's sleep.

Martin and Annie had walked only a few blocks when she realized New York really was a city that never slept! The big stores and the office buildings were dark, but little shops and restaurants, street vendors, and art galleries were open, and throngs of people were walking through the Village as though it were midday instead of after midnight. Annie was surprised to see that the majority of the people in the Village would not have drawn a second look, even in conservative North Carolina; then again, there *were* some unusually dressed and peculiar-acting individuals who would definitely have been considered odd. Since Martin seemed to know where he was going, she asked him if he knew the city well.

"I studied acting here," he replied, "and was in several off-Broadway shows- that mercifully stayed off-Broadway! -before I moved to the West Coast."

"Was that when you loaded and unloaded boxcars?" she asked demurely.

"Oh no! I'll never live down that remark!" he laughed, his deep laughter causing Annie to smile. "You'd think that should have taught me to follow the script when I speak in public but, as you saw tonight, sometimes I don't even have a script, much to my embarrassment." He seemed suddenly reminiscent, shaking his head before he spoke again. "Yeah, I did my boxcar-loading stint in California, waiting for a chance at a good part."

"Well, you can't complain about the part you did get," Annie offered. "For your first leading role to earn an Oscar nomination, it was certainly worth waiting for."

"In a way, that's just the trouble," he replied thoughtfully, "because it's a hard act to follow. Think of all the rotten movies Gable was in after 'Gone With the Wind'...not everything he did was bad, but after Rhett Butler, it all seemed anti-climactic. And what about Anthony Perkins? The poor guy was typecast as a weirdo after 'Psycho,' even though he was a good enough actor to play almost any role...it can be death to an acting career to play any part that is too memorable before your reputation is established. People start seeing you as the part you played first because that was the role that gave them their initial impression of you." He paused for effect. "How many 'Misbegottens' do you think are out there?"

"I see your point," she replied, having read the book and thinking at the time that she didn't think people wrote books like that anymore—not in a day and time that promoted The New South as having stepped away from the antebellum era and onto the plane of the 21st century. Antiquated or not, the characters of the Old South still appealed to her- and many others it would seem -as 'Misbegotten' became a best seller as well as a box-office smash.

As they talked and nibbled their way through the Village, Annie comfortably followed Martin's lead: having a hot dog on one street, sharing a pretzel on the next and a sausage sandwich followed by cherry ices in Little Italy, and espresso in several coffee houses. If she had any inclination to be sleepy, that strongest of coffees would have taken care of it! Annie was amazed that no one seemed to recognize Martin and finally assumed that it was part of the New York sophistication she had heard of, which gives anonymity to anyone in the city.

Annie was equally surprised that she and Martin seemed to have so much in common, but came to realize sometime during the night that his upbringing in an English village was not so different from hers in a small country town in the South. He seemed to have the values that go with a country upbringing:

a contempt for facade and an appreciation of reality—two virtues Martin admitted he'd found all but absent in Hollywood. They talked until nearly dawn, although how anyone could tell dawn was approaching since the tall buildings and artificial lighting had made the night seem like day, was difficult to discern.

"Now," Martin said, turning her to face him, "there is one tourist-y thing you absolutely have to do, and that's ride the Staten Island Ferry at dawn; it's an experience never to be forgotten. And," he teased, "I've cleverly planned our expedition so that we'll arrive at the ferry landing at just the appropriate time!"

Laughingly, Annie allowed Martin to clasp one of her hands with his own as they hurried toward the ferry; as they rode out, they stood by the rail and looked out over the rippling water at the brilliance of the city in the distance and she was again awed by the manmade splendor of it all. Eventually, the ferry passed the empty space where the World Trade Center once stood, and a chill shook Annie at the memory and horror of September 11, 2001. Thinking he saw her draw close against the growing coolness and the breeze that swept their faces, Martin put his arm around Annie and held her close, noticing only then the single tear that fell down her cheek.

"You're remembering 9-11...I didn't think to warn you, Annie...I'm sorry."

Annie simply shook her head. "I don't think anything could have prepared me for seeing Ground Zero...I'm suddenly very, very cold, Martin..."

Slipping his free hand around Annie's waist, Martin drew her closer against him. Seeing the emotion on her face and feeling her tremble within his arms, it was like he was seeing the emptiness for the first time as well, and he let go a long, thoughtful breath. He was glad that she had not been made to visit the area alone and murmured soothing words against the crown of her head, drawing as well as giving of their physical warmth—and perhaps something more.

It was then that Martin's memories of another Annie and another time taunted his thoughts, and he questioned the possibility that she night be the same girl he'd once known as a child...a whole other world ago. No, it wasn't possible: he was simply letting his imagination get the best of him...

Sensing the easy closeness with which they both seemed so comfortable, Annie ventured to rest her head upon his shoulder thinking that at this moment in time, life could hold no more. In the next moment, however, she found that it could indeed hold more gladness and contentment than she had ever imagined: as Martin turned to stare down at her very serene face, he slowly, timorously slipped a wisp of hair from her cheek to behind one ear while his eyes seemed to silently ask a million questions at once. The slight parting of Annie's lips stopped his mouth from putting voice to those queries as he gently, almost reverently clasped the side of her neck, tipping the base of her chin upward with his thumb as his mouth lowered to meet hers for a kiss that was thorough, and thoroughly unsettling.

Martin looked as surprised as Annie felt when they finally drew apart; quickly realizing the void their separation caused, he caught her back to him with tightly restrained desperation, his voice barely a whisper as he found himself confessing, "I feel like I've known you forever, Annie Ryan…and I don't want to let you go…"

Closing her eyes, Annie suddenly felt as though she were on an emotional roller coaster for the physical warmth and desire Martin stirred in her all but kept her from being able to think clearly…and she definitely needed to be thinking clearly! Her mind was a mass of confusion for never in all her 26 years had a man's kiss alone made her body want for intimacy; it was absurd and wonderful and scary, but as confused as her emotions made her feel, she was equally certain that she wasn't ready for any of them to end.

As the sun strained to show from behind a low morning cloud, Annie suddenly realized that she only had about three more hours to spend in New York before catching her return flight home; and though she might allow herself to fantasize about how she would like to spend them, it would definitely not be a good idea, the more logical mind reasoned. She didn't know if Martin made a practice of picking up frustrated females, she thought wryly, or if he could somehow tell how starved for love and affection, and how vulnerable she truly was: neither of those ideas appealed to her for one was as bad as the other!

Martin stood silent with the woman drawn against him: his mind was anything but! He had been taken aback once he realized he knew the name Annie Ryan from his past. It didn't register immediately in the packed ballroom, but slowly he realized that he may have once known her, or a younger version of her, he corrected. He had been seven when his parents left Mount Airy, North Carolina—his father's transfer to the other side of the world a turning point in all their lives. A young Daniel Martin was made to leave everything and everyone he had ever known that summer some twenty years ago, but he never forgot the little girl who lived two doors down and with whom he shared many a childhood memory. Annie Ryan had definitely grown up, he mused, and she was still the sweet, friendly girl he remembered. Their meeting again after all these years was a fluke: there was no other explanation for it, he reasoned, for the Annie Ryan he remembered could not know her playmate Daniel Martin became Martin Vaughn when he enrolled in acting school. He supposed he should tell her the truth, but he wasn't sure how to even begin.

Annie felt Martin's arms tense around her waist and she clasped his hands beneath hers as if to reinforce their closeness. Was there a chance he might somehow feel as she did, she mocked herself—that there was something special about their meeting and that it would inevitably lead to its inevitable conclusion? *Get real* she silently chided, realizing that he'd probably be all for the conclusion, but that it would be just another one-night stand for him where she'd found his kiss alone to be incredible. Of all the people in the world to fall for, she chastised herself sternly, why did you have to pick someone so totally out of reach? Maybe out of reach was the wrong term, she thought hastily as Martin drew her even closer into his arms.

The decision as to what would follow the ferry ride was never Annie's to make, for once the boat had at last docked, Martin led her back in the direction from which they had come and hailed a taxi to return them to their hotel. He never spoke any indication as to what his intentions were, but when drawing the two most likely from her own mind, Annie realized that one was as terrifying to her as the other. She had no doubt that the time they had spent together had been as meaningful to him as it had been for her; and though her knowledge of the male mind wasn't extensive, she could read his expressions well enough to understand the subtle undertones of his words. What worried her was whether he would want to follow their very limited time together through to an intimate end, or if he saw a furthering of their relationship as all but impossible- as she did -and would be wise enough to conclude their final moments together from the hallway side of her hotel room door. As much as she might have wanted their time together to last, she knew she would not invite him in. It was for the best.

"I enjoyed showing New York to you, Ann-Elise," Martin began, breaking into her thoughts as they began the ride up in the elevator. "I felt like I was seeing the city for the first time, looking at it through your eyes." *Looking at it through your child-like eyes,* he corrected silently.

Annie smiled at the sweet sincerity in Martin's voice. "You were a wonderful host, Martin," she replied as they stepped from the elevator, their fingers interlocked in a vice-like grip. "I can't remember when I've enjoyed myself more," she admitted almost too honestly.

Martin smiled at the expression on her face. "I'm glad," he replied just as earnestly.

"I have a feeling I'll sleep the whole way home," she mused. "Those last few blocks to the ferry landing were exhausting."

"I guess I 'pushed it,' huh?"

Annie laughed. "I'm glad you 'pushed it,' really! I wouldn't have missed the ferry ride for anything."

There was a heavy pause as Martin felt Annie's hand leave his to reach into her pants pocket for her pass card. "Would I be pushing it if I asked to come in?" he whispered huskily.

Drawing a deep breath, Annie made herself turn away from Martin, praying for the strength to keep her promise to herself as she took the plastic card and slid it into the slot beneath the door handle. *As much as I might wish otherwise, if I DID let him in, nothing could ever come of it* she reasoned with the Practical Annie of old: *I have to tell him no.* "I don't think that would be a good idea," she murmured to the space between herself and the door, grasping the door handle with her other hand and giving it an unsteady turn. "My plane leaves around nine...and I have just enough time to shower and change before I have to leave for the airport."

Martin straightened at her refusal; he could not believe she was sending him away! "There will be other flights; you could reschedule if you wanted to."

She still refused to look at him. "As much as I might want to, I can't stay. I...I have obligations."

Martin winced at how simple she made saying good-bye sound. Then he remembered another good-bye many years before and how the little girl had said, *"You can't just go away, Daniel. You can't just say good-bye and go away!"* But he had, and some part of him remembered anew the hurt of that day so many years ago. His next words expressed his frustration. "Of course...I imagine the hospital you work at must be completely lost without you," he murmured slightly sarcastically.

Annie turned about then and squarely met his eyes. "I'm not talking about my job!" she defended somewhat heatedly. "I have responsibilities, people who depend on me."

"What could be so damned important that you can't put it on hold one more day?" he pressed. Annie dropped her eyes then and Martin immediately stiffened. "You've a husband."

Without looking up, Annie shook her head. "No, Martin."

"A lover, then?"

Another long pause "No..."

Though he felt an ache for the pain that one word brought to her voice, Martin's sense of relief at finding her unattached was greater: it surprised him how much. "I won't say I'm sorry for that."

"I can't imagine why you should care," she returned bitingly. "Besides, I have enough going on in my life that I really don't miss being in a relationship."

Clenching and unclenching his jaw until a muscle throbbed in his temple, Martin felt the first pang of humiliation in a wave of heat that ran the very length of his body. Of all the responses he might have prepared himself for, rejection wasn't one of them. "You're a very bad liar, Annie," he taunted scathingly.

Annie's face blanched as she drew herself to her full height and met his angry stare straight on. "And you are very ill-mannered to say so," she whispered, swallowing hard to keep from telling him the truth, to keep from telling him about her grandmother, about her responsibility to the memory of her parents, about everything.

"To quote my soon-to-be ex-wife, I'm an 'EEL-mannered Yankee BAS-stud,'" he corrected in perfect, clipped-English syllables, relaxing a bit then as Annie dropped her head to hide a smile. What on earth made him think of Claire at this moment? Likely the fact that she was always reminding him of his place, reminding him that he would always be beneath her. Annie was the first person in years he felt completely at ease with, probably because she reminded him of happier days, carefree days he could barely remember having known. Reaching above her bent head, Martin pushed the door fully open and took a small step back to let her pass. "At least let me take you to the airport...I'd like to know you got away safely," he murmured without malice.

Annie stopped in mid-stride as she entered her room. "You have your own plane to catch, Martin...to London at three," she reminded without looking at him.

Remembering that he had in fact told her of his scheduled flight back to England he winced, realizing it must now look to her as if he had wanted only one thing from her all along. "I'll have my driver take you to the airport, then!" he pressed, moving to place himself upon her threshold.

Feeling his warm breath upon her neck, Annie turned slowly about and pasted a wan smile upon her lips. Wanting nothing more than for what she believed was a pathetic travesty to end, she nodded her acquiescence as her eyes lifted to meet his one last time. "Alright."

He swallowed and nodded, deciding at that moment he would have his attorney look into learning all he could about her, where she now lived, and what had caused the genuine sadness he often saw in her eyes. With new resolve, Martin smiled as he caught the movement of the door out of the corner of his eye. "God's speed," he offered in a rush and barely heard her whispered, "Good-bye, Martin," as he stepped back for her to close the door between them.

CHAPTER TWO

When the door clicked shut before her Annie stood silent, straining to hear the instant when Martin moved away from it. There was nothing for a long while and she imagined that the thickness of the door between them had smothered the sound of his footfalls upon the carpeted hall. But even as she thought this, she heard his body turn as he stepped away from the door, and the slow cadence of his footsteps as he moved to cross the hall to the elevator. It was another long moment before she heard the ding of the bell announcing the elevator's arrival at her floor, and yet another before the doors opened for its passenger. Only then did Annie release the breath she had held, lowering her forehead to rest upon the cool metal door jamb and allowing her senses one full minute to regain equilibrium. *You did the right thing* she told herself again and again...*you must remember Gramma is waiting at home and she needs you.*

The moment grew to two, and then several, and it wasn't until Annie heard the light brushing of wind against her windows that she realized how long she'd been standing there. Dragging herself away from the door, she released a long breath as she turned and moved toward the bathroom, the thought of a long hot shower suddenly a balm to her weary body. There in the distance however, beyond the windows of her ninth floor room, the movement of white in the wind caught her eye and she stopped just short of the bath's tile floor. It was snowing...*It's the first day of spring, and I have to fly home to Gramma today, and it's snowing?* she wondered in disbelief.

As if pushed into moving, Annie all but lurched toward the windows, her eyes scanning first the skyline and then the street below. *It's just started,* she thought with some relief *and it's early yet...surely it can't worsen so much between now and nine o'clock that it'll delay me!* But even as she thought it, her movements carried her to the bathroom where she quickly stripped and stepped into the shower to bathe.

Lathering her hair, she mentally ran through the procedure for checking out of the hotel; as she rinsed it, she compiled a mental list of what she had brought with her so she would not leave something behind while packing. Her bath complete, Annie wrapped a towel around her upper body and once again stepped to the full-length windows. The flakes were a bit larger than before, and it was falling a bit heavier, but with only two hours before her flight was scheduled to depart, she felt certain it wouldn't be delayed by a mere flurry. And that's what this must be, she reasoned silently. After all, it's the first day of spring!

Once she had dried her hair and dressed, Annie collected the few carry-on items she had brought with her and packed them hurriedly away. Her program from the banquet the night before she rolled up and shoved into her handbag; and the beautiful, costly dress she had saved and scrimped for and that she would probably never wear again, was pulled from the closet in a jerk, her movements such that the plastic name tag Miss Wittle had pinned upon it broke from the material and fell to the floor beside the bed.

Her packing done, Annie gave the room one last quick look and was satisfied that she had collected all that was hers. Retrieving the pass card from where she had placed it on the nightstand, she stepped to the door and opened it, remembering only then Martin's promise to send his driver for her.

"Yeah…sure," she murmured to no one as she stepped into the hall and closed the door at her back. But as she joined an older couple in the elevator, she pursed her lips thoughtfully and realized she would genuinely appreciate such a gesture from Martin, for it would mean that perhaps she had not made a complete fool of herself after all.

The elevator stopped twice more during its descent, and once at the lobby, Annie patiently waited for the others to exit before she did so. One glance at the reservation counter told her she was not the only early traveler this morning and that there would be several minutes of waiting in line before she would be able to check out. Hefting her carry-on bag upon her shoulder, Annie started toward the counter and set her mind to being patient.

"Miss Ryan?"

Turning with a start, Annie nearly collided with the young black man who had called to her. "Yes?"

"I thought so! Mr. Vaughn's description of you was right on the money," he offered smilingly.

"Mr. Vaughn...?" she caught herself immediately. "Of course, you must be his driver."

"Raymond, ma'am," he nodded. "Here, let me get that for you," he offered, and Annie surrendered her carry-on with a murmured thank you. "Mr. Vaughn says you have a nine o'clock flight out of La Guardia."

"Yes..." she whispered as her eyes looked past him to the glass doors.

Noting the direction of her stare, Raymond glanced quickly over his shoulder. "Don't worry, the snow's not gonna delay you any."

"But it's sticking!" she realized woefully. "And it was so beautiful earlier—cool, but not cold!"

"Some low pressure system moved in from the South overnight...it's near freezing out there now," Raymond offered. "I think I heard that the temperature dropped seven or eight degrees just in the last hour."

Annie's mouth dropped open in disbelief.

"Hey, it's really no big deal! It would have to snow three or four inches for the traffic to even slow!" he offered smilingly. "Rush hour traffic in New York waits for no man—or weather system!"

Annie smiled back. "I'll take your word for it, Raymond."

"You sound like Mr. Vaughn!" he laughed. "And I tell him, 'You gotta trust a chauffeur to know his own city!'"

"Okay then!" Annie shrugged. "Let me get checked out and then we can go."

"I'll have the car waiting for you by the door, ma'am."

Twenty minutes later, though Annie was still waiting, she was at least at the counter and being waited on. The middle-aged woman who stood behind the computer glanced over her glasses when she spoke; and though she was obviously trying to work in an expedient manner, the ring of the telephone was a constant interruption, causing Annie and those behind her to expel long, frustrated sighs every time the woman was interrupted.

"Do you wish to pay with cash or credit?" the reservationist asked, her eyes lifting wearily over her glasses again.

"Cash...you've already asked me that, remember?"

Again the eyes lifted, and this time so did the clerk's eyebrows. "Had I remembered, I wouldn't have the need to ask again, now would I?"

Again the telephone rang, and again Annie dropped her head in disgust. "I cannot believe this..." she whispered to no one, glancing at her watch for what seemed like the twentieth time. Ninety minutes before her plane was scheduled for departure and she was still trying to get checked out of the hotel! Glancing back over her shoulder, Annie saw that the snow continued to fall, heavier now than ever, and that thankfully the limousine Martin had arranged for her still waited by the curb.

"Here is your receipt, Miss," the reservationist offered, this time without looking up. "Please sign where I've indicated."

Reaching across the counter, Annie took the paper and did as she was told, returning it with several twenty-dollar bills as payment.

Returning a copy of the receipt with Annie's change, the reservationist offered but the very slightest hint of a smile. "Thank you for choosing New York City's finest for your travel accommodations. We look forward to serving you again."

This time, Annie met and held the woman's eyes with her own. "Somehow, I honestly doubt that, ma'am," she replied coolly, turning without another word to hurry toward the waiting car. She was barely beyond the hotel's entrance when Raymond appeared at the rear passenger door. "You don't get carsick, do you?"

Annie shook her head, a hesitant expression on her face. "No...why?"

"Good. Just sit back and hang on: you're about to get a taste of REAL rush hour traffic!"

"Will we make it to La Guardia by nine?" she asked as he moved to close the door.

"Is there a bigger tip if we do?" he teased, and then smiled as he ran around to the front of the car.

Martin stood by the window of his penthouse room and watched as the snow continued to fall. "Unbelievable..." he murmured to himself thinking only a few hours before, he and Ann-Elise had been walking through Greenwich Village wearing only sweaters, jeans and 'comfortable shoes,' a coat the farthest thing from their minds.

He could not get her out of his.

How many times in his life had he so enjoyed simply being with someone? There was his father, who had loved him as father *and* mother nearly all his life...but he was gone. And his brother John, with whom he had shared every childhood dream and adventure...he was gone as well. There was only Stuart now, his son, his life, and *he* was very close to being taken away from Martin by an act of the courts. "Damn Claire to hell!"

The sound of the telephone jerked Martin's head about and he picked it up on the first ring. "Raymond?"

"Yes sir, we finally got away from the hotel but I'm gonna have to gun it to make it to La Guardia by nine!"

"You're just now leaving *here*?"

Raymond glanced over his shoulder and back to the street. "Couldn't be helped, sir. 'Betty the Bag' was working check out."

Martin winced inwardly. "Miss Ryan must be beside herself."

"Well actually, she's been pretty cool so far...just wants me to get her there by nine, so I told her I would. She *says* she doesn't get car sick but if she does, you'll owe me extra!"

Martin's voice became thoughtful. "Think there's a chance you might not make it by nine?"

"Depends on the traffic lights: you gotta time it perfect or you'll hit 'em all red."

There was a pause. "Then do it."

"Do it, sir?"

Martin drew a long breath and stared out the windows again. "Get out of sync so that you hit them all red."

Raymond pulled the phone away from his ear and looked at it dumbly, then jerked it back to his ear again. "Sir?"

Martin's expression lit with expectation. "Have you heard the weather forecast, Raymond?"

The chauffeur shook his head in full then, completely dumbfounded. "It's snowing! What else you wanna know?"

"I want to know if it's supposed to worsen...and if there's any chance it'll interrupt air travel."

Raymond slowed the automobile for a red light, realizing then the direction of Martin's thoughts: "You don't want her to make this flight!"

"Will that be a problem?"

Raymond shrugged to himself. "Hey, you're the man paying the bills! You wanna keep her from making it to La Guardia by nine, she won't make it to La Guardia by nine!"

"Is the snow sticking?"

"Oh yeah, it's sticking!"

Martin stroked his beard-stubble chin and nodded to himself. "Can you have a break down that will keep you tied up say, another hour or so—?"

"—to give the snow time to start backing things up?" Raymond interjected. "Heh-heh-heh…you've got an evil mind, Mr. Vaughn!"

"I'm not paying you to judge my character, Raymond, only to do what I ask you to," Martin replied. "Do we understand one another?"

"Oh, hey! Absolutely!" Raymond offered eagerly, smiling at the mock-censure in his employer's voice. Having worked for Martin Vaughn for two years, the driver had come to recognize when something was important to him—and this girl obviously was! "You gonna call the weather bureau and have them arrange a blizzard?"

Martin smiled at the teasing tone in his driver's voice. "I suppose we'll just have to keep our fingers crossed and hope that as long as you create the delays, the weathermen will keep sending the snow."

"I think I can handle that"

"Good. Find a weather update on your radio and call me back once you know something more."

"And what do I tell the young lady when she starts complaining about missing her flight?"

Martin's mind immediately pictured Annie's lovely face as she had looked to him on the ferry. There was something about her that made him want to gather her into his arms and hold her forever. "Tell her you're doing all you can," he offered with a smile. "She doesn't have to know for whom."

Annie looked at her watch and looked out the window and looked at her watch again. The snow was falling heavier than ever now, blowing in great drifts against the cars parked along the streets and the buildings where they disappeared into the white sky. She shook her head. It was nearing ten-thirty and not only had she missed her 9:10 flight, but it was growing increasingly doubtful she would make the 11:50 one she had scheduled from the pay phone down the block.

The driver had pulled the automobile to the curb an hour before when it cut off with him, and when he got out to look under the hood, she motioned for him to let her out as well.

"Oh, no ma'am! You—you don't want to be walking about in *this* neighborhood! It's…it's not safe!"

"Then show me how to use the car phone."

"Ma'am, it won't work if the engine isn't running," he lied.

"But I have GOT to call and reschedule my flight! Will you walk with me to a phone booth?" she had pleaded. And so he had, acting all the while as if he feared someone would jump them at any moment, even though there was obviously nothing at all to fear in this very friendly, very Italian district of the city. Annie had rescheduled her flight but was met with the news she had dreaded most: the winter weather was causing delays and in fact, some flights out were being cancelled altogether for many airports down the East Coast had already closed their runways until the snow ceased or at least let up enough for runways to be cleared and planes to *stay* de-iced.

Now back in the limousine, her warmest navy wool cardigan gathered close at her throat, Annie shivered from the cold and the genuine fear Raymond had instilled in her that they may be stuck there indefinitely. He had left her locked in the automobile just long enough to return to the phone booth; supposedly to call for a wrecker or a replacement vehicle to take them back to the hotel. Not surprising, when he returned to the limousine, Raymond told her that weather related accidents had most emergency vehicles tied up or en route. And when she asked why he didn't simply flag down a taxi, he told her he had been trying to all along but that every one that had passed them already had fares.

Raymond realized he no longer enjoyed the role he had been asked to play; while making it appear as though he was exhausting every possible option for getting Annie to her destination, he had instead phoned Martin for further instructions. And as much as Raymond liked and respected his employer, the frustration and genuine worry he now saw on Annie's face made him regret ever agreeing to any of it.

At that moment, Raymond's personal cell phone rang low and seeing Martin's number displayed on the caller ID, he hesitated disgustedly before answering it. "Yes?"

"Raymond, it that you?"

"Yeah, it's me..."

Martin recognized a curt tone in Raymond's voice and offered, "I take it she's becoming impatient?"

Raymond shook his head. "Actually, she's still as patient and courteous and...NICE as she was before this whole delay game started! I would have been cussing me *but good* by now!"

"Really?" Martin pursed his lips. He wasn't surprised, given what he remembered about Annie as a child, and what he had learned about Ann-Elise during their evening together. She was genuine and kind, so unlike most of the women he had known in his life. He smiled. He was glad he had not let her get away.

"So what do I do now?" Raymond pressed impatiently. "She's not gonna buy this much longer, Mr. Vaughn. My excuses are NOT that good, even if they *are* yours!"

"Alright, I get the point!" he replied lightly, appreciating the slight censure he heard in Raymond's voice: Annie Ryan had obviously gotten to his driver, too! "Look, get back under the hood and give yourself, say, fifteen minutes before you try starting it again. This time let it crank and act as surprised and relieved, as I'm sure Miss Ryan will be. Take her to La Guardia and insist that you're going to wait for her to let you know she has a flight out. When she comes back and tells you all the flights South have been cancelled, tell her you'll take her back to the hotel to get her old room back…"

"—and how do you know she won't get a flight out?"

"I just got confirmation that all flights out have been cancelled," Martin answered, a satisfied lilt in his voice. "And to answer your next question, Miss Ryan's room has already been reserved for her, though when she asks if it's still available, Betty will give the impression she is doing her a tremendous favor by working her in."

"She would have done that anyway."

"You're probably right," Martin chuckled. "But as it was, the room had **not** been assigned to another party yet and I simply asked Betty to hold it for Miss Ryan's return this afternoon."

Raymond glanced at Annie in the rear view mirror and shook his head at the pitiful picture she made; there had obviously been something (or someone!) very important to get home to and it made him second-guess his part in the whole mess. "You know, Mr. Vaughn, if she ever finds out what we've done…"

"—she won't, Raymond," Martin cut in, his voice not quite as certain as his words. "As long as you or I never tell her, she won't."

"I hope you're right, sir."

A pause. "Yeah, well…so am I."

*   *   *

When the limousine drew up along the entrance of the hotel, Annie had already grasped her handbag against her breast and was waiting for Raymond to come around to her door. As it opened, Annie heard the bottom edge scrape across the snow that had drifted against the curb, and Raymond was made to

35

jerk the door several times before it had cleared a berth wide enough for Annie to step from the car.

"We've got a good five or six inches, Miss Ryan, and no one's shoveled the sidewalk yet...watch your step."

Annie took the hand he extended and smiled, "Lucky for me I wore boots, huh?"

"Yes, ma'am! I'd say you're good for another couple of inches for sure!"

Annie shook her head at the driver's attempt at humor. "I personally hope this mess will quit entirely before another couple of inches can fall! I could be stranded here for days!"

"Not likely, ma'am," Raymond defended with a shake of his head. "With the snow removal equipment this city has, they'll have the airports up and running again in no time. A city like New York can't afford to be shut down for very long."

"You're probably right," Annie replied, realizing cities in the North were much better prepared for winter weather because they have so much of it every year. "And to think I've prayed for a snow like this all winter long back home..."

"Where's that, Miss Ryan?" he asked as he removed her carry-on bag from the trunk.

"North Carolina...I wonder if *they're* getting any of this?"

"Oh, yes ma'am!" he returned wide-eyed as he led her into the hotel. "It's a weather system *from* the South that's responsible for all of this!"

"Great."

Raymond gave her a bemused smile. "Look at it this way: if you gotta be stranded somewhere, where better than the Big Apple? No finer accommodations anywhere in the world!"

"Yeah well, we'll see...wonder what the chances are of getting my old room back?"

Raymond shrugged although he knew the reservationist was expecting Annie's return and he smiled to know that, for at least one time today, she wouldn't be disappointed. "I'm gonna hang your bag here on the rack by the desk, Miss Ryan, while I'm getting the limo parked. Have someone page me when you're ready and I'll take it up for you."

"That's not necessary Raymond, I can manage, really. You've already done more than I could have ever expected."

The driver swallowed guiltily—she had no idea! "Well, good-luck ma'am. Enjoy your stay."

"Thank you. Oh, before I forget..."

"—no ma'am," he interrupted with a raised hand when he saw her open her purse. "Mr. Vaughn has already paid me in advance. Not that I don't appreciate it!" he corrected, fearing he might insult her generosity, "But I can't take your money. It wouldn't be right."

Annie's expression showed her confusion. "But I feel like I've put you to so much trouble!"

Raymond nervously tried to lick his lips but found his mouth had suddenly gone dry. "No ma'am...the limo, the weather...you couldn't have known."

Annie smiled. "Well, I appreciate all you did just the same."

"Yes ma'am..." Raymond stammered, her kind, Southern honesty almost his undoing. Nodding one last time, he turned and all but ran to the limousine.

Turning back toward the reservation center, Annie saw that the person who had been in line just ahead of her was now stepping away from the counter; and who should still be working reservations but the very person who had checked her out only hours before. She wondered if the woman would remember her.

"May I help you?"

"Um...I was a guest here last night, and now my flight home has been cancelled. Is it possible to possibly, get that room- or a room! -for another night...or two, depending on the weather..."

"—name please, last name first then first name and middle initial," the clerk replied without looking up.

"Ryan, Ann-Elise....with a hyphen...it's one name..."

"—of course," the reservationist replied looking over the top of her glasses, entering information into her computer without once taking her eyes off Annie's anguished face. "Room 918 is still available...isn't that a lovely surprise? How many nights do you wish to reserve it for?"

Annie's brows drew together at the woman's sarcastic tone. "One...?"

The clerk's expression was expressionless.

"Two then, I guess...is there a minimum?"

The reservation clerks' eyes dropped to her keyboard. "You may pay by the night, or at the end of your stay...whichever is most convenient for you."

Remembering that she had brought very little cash with her, Annie did a mental check of what she did have and decided on the latter. "I'd like to pay for just tonight...right now..."

Again the woman's eyes lifted above the rim of her glasses to stare at Annie as she handed her the passkey and receipt to sign. "I presume you wish to pay with cash."

Inwardly, Annie winced. Oh yeah, she remembers me all right. "Yes…cash," she replied, laying the signed paper and the balance of her spending money on the counter. The charge for the room took everything she had but a twenty and four ones.

The reservationist took the receipt and money, her eyes piercing Annie's across the space of the counter. "Check-out is at eleven."

"Yes, I know."

"Thank you for choosing New York's finest for your travel accommodations—again," she smiled.

Annie swallowed—yep, the woman's memory was perfect. "Thank you," she smiled back and turned shamefaced to collect her carry-on. Hurrying in the direction of the elevators, Annie prayed she would not have to look in the woman's direction again. By the grace of God, the elevator doors were open!

Martin had been waiting by his phone for the call from Raymond telling him that Annie was safely back at the hotel. What he didn't expect, however, was the condemnation he heard in his driver's voice.

"Really, Raymond, you have done nothing to feel guilty for! You simply worked with me to insure that Miss Ryan would not leave New York without first having the opportunity to further enjoy all that the city has to offer!" he teased.

"Yeah…right."

"Seriously, my intentions are completely on the up-and-up. She's an attractive, intelligent woman and I simply wish to get to know her better."

"So…why was she in such a hurry to get home? You're supposed to be like, this hunky movie star that could probably have any woman he wants…"

"—thanks for the vote of confidence."

"No man, really! You don't **know** how upset she got when, after all the delays and all the B.S., she gets to the airport and finds there are no more flights out! It's like she was worried about someone, really worried about getting back to them."

Martin chewed at the inside of one lip as he recalled her need to return to her 'obligations.' It made him feel no better having Raymond all but reiterate it. "Did Miss Ryan mention a name, or a place…?"

"—she didn't have to," Raymond broke in evenly. "Her determination to get home to North Carolina spoke volumes. For what it's worth, you better believe the lady would not like it if she ever found out her flights were intentionally interrupted."

Martin drew a long breath. "Yes, you've already told me." There was a pause. "Can you have the car ready by morning, should Miss Ryan still wish to leave?"

"It's ready now except for refueling."

Martin laughed a mirthless laugh. "You don't approve of any of this." It was a statement, not a question.

"No sir I don't."

Another pause. "Good afternoon, Raymond."

"Afternoon, sir."

Annie slipped the passkey into the slot beneath the door handle and remembered with genuine sadness the last time she had done so. As she withdrew the card, she turned slightly about, Martin's presence as real in her mind as if he were actually standing there again. She swallowed hard and turned the knob, chastising herself for allowing him to even enter her thoughts at all. Crossing the threshold, she turned and pushed the door closed, laying the pass card on the nightstand as she walked toward the bed. God, but it looked welcome! Smiling, she bowed to the exhaustion that demanded she lie down and draped the carry-on across a chair back as she sat upon the bed and removed her best-worn boots.

Just as she would have relaxed against the pillows, it hit her that she had not been in touch with her grandmother and Monica since learning all flights out of La Guardia had been cancelled. Drawing herself to sitting again, she reached to dial her home phone, closing her eyes wearily as the line rang two then three times.

"Hello?"

"Hey...me again."

"I figured as much," Monica droned. "News of the 'blizzard' is all over the television and radio. Just tell me you were able to get a room!"

"Oh yeah—they hadn't given mine to anyone else yet, so I was able to get it for another night." She relaxed back against the pillows. "You guys snowed under yet?"

Monica laughed. "Cute. As a matter of fact we are. There's a good two or three inches on the ground and it's still flurrying."

Annie moaned out loud.

"Hey, this is *all* you've talked about *all* winter!" Monica countered.

"I know...but who'd have thought we'd get it in the spring?!"

"You know Annie, you're right! I hadn't realized that today's the first day of spring!"

"I guess Gramma's beside herself with worry," Annie murmured more seriously.

"Yeah, but you know Gramma: she'd worry about you if it was clear, sunny and seventy degrees."

"I know. At least let her know that I'm settled in at the hotel for another night. I don't know if things will clear out enough to fly back tomorrow or not, but if there's any way of getting a flight, I will!"

"Yeah but think about it, Annie: if Greensboro stays shut down after La Guardia re-opens, you're still stuck! Unless you can fly into Raleigh-Durham, or Charlotte maybe."

Annie released a disgusted sigh. "You know I hadn't even thought of that...and here I am down to my last twenty-four dollars..."

"Time to break out the plastic!" Monica sing-songed.

"I detest credit cards."

"I know you do, but sometimes they're a necessary evil. *This* may be one of those times."

"Yeah..."

Monica sensed more than frustration in Annie's voice. "Hey, are you all right? You sound exhausted."

Closing her eyes, Annie told herself it was little wonder. "I am...I feel like I've worked a double shift; but, I'm gonna lie down for a while, maybe order up a sandwich later."

"Well, I won't pester you NOW, but I expect a full accounting of the banquet once you're home. Anybody worth mentioning show up?"

"Yeah, but to even try and tell you about it would take too long..."

"—and you'd rather be sleeping," Monica finished. "That's cool. All that's missing is a roaring fire in the fireplace and a gorgeous guy to snuggle with, huh?"

"That's all?"

"It could happen."

"I don't think so," Annie countered, remembering then that the gorgeous guy had actually been within reach at one time. Closing her eyes, she wondered if Martin had been luckier than she had, perhaps leaving the city in his own private Lear Jet! "Give Gramma a hug for me and please assure her that everything is fine here," Annie offered, silently willing herself to completely forget Martin.

"I will. *You* get some rest—relax and enjoy your time away from everything."

"I'd honestly rather be home. And I know my being away is causing Gramma even greater anxiety than usual."

"If she weren't worrying about you, it would be something else…but, I'll tell her you're fine, the weather's great and you wish we were there!"

"Do that."

"Give a call when you know something more."

"I will."

Monica frowned. "You really *are* petered out!"

"Yep…I really am."

"Then go to bed. You could use a good day's rest."

"I have a feeling once I'm asleep, I'll sleep straight through 'till tomorrow." As if on cue, she yawned.

"Good NIGHT, Annie!" Monica taunted, a smile in her voice because it was barely noon.

"Give my love to Gramma…?"

"I will…bye, now."

Martin stepped from the elevator and walked the half-dozen or so steps that took him to Annie's hotel room door. Looking at his watch, he saw that it was just a few minutes past six and silently hoped she was not so punctual as to have already left for dinner. Lifting his hand to rap upon the door he paused a moment, bringing the thumb of his clasped hand to his lips instead. *Perhaps I should have called first*, he thought, tracing his lips back and forth with the knuckle of his thumb. Just as quickly however, he had decided against it, wanting to be able to see her face when he spoke with her again: the woman's expression, he decided, would tell him with greatest candor whether she was glad to see him again or not.

Swiping a lock of hair from his brow, again Martin moved to rap upon the door and this time followed through with a nervous urgency. He stood for a moment, then two, listening for a reply or her eventual approach to the door; he heard neither. Feeling certain then that he must have missed her, Martin swallowed and drew a deep breath, rapping upon the door once more in an almost perfunctory manner.

41

Before his hand had fully left the door, Annie opened it, a murmured, "Yes, who's there?" dying on her lips when she saw that it was Martin. Slowly he allowed his arm to fall to his side, words of his own forming on his lips but finding no voice, as he simply stood mute before her. Dear God, but she was beautiful! Her hair was mussed wildly about her shoulders and her face flushed pink from sleep. The first three buttons of her sweater were undone to reveal but the swell of one breast; seeing the direction of Martin's eyes, she dropped her head and straightened the sweater upon her shoulders.

"I-I'm sorry, Ann-Elise...I should have called..."

"—no...no Martin, it's alright..." she broke in with a slight shake of her head. "I'm afraid you caught me napping." And half-dressed, she added silently, drawing her hands down from her shoulders to cross her arms in front of her breasts.

He nodded, meeting her hesitant eyes. "Considering you got no sleep last night, I can understand." There was a long pause.

"I guess the snow has stranded you as well?" What a conversationalist you are, Annie silently chided herself: she could just imagine Monica saying, "**Duh**..."

"Yeah...a couple of days at least," he nodded. "My, um...my driver told me that since your flight was delayed indefinitely, you were going to try to get your room back...I'm glad. That you got a room, I mean. From what I understand, given the sudden bit of weather, there *are* no more vacancies."

Annie winced as she drew a hand through the mane of hair that had fallen across one shoulder...she knew she looked a fright and desperately wished that the floor would just open up and swallow her! "I guess I was one of the lucky ones then," she offered weakly, staring at the blinking lights above the elevator doors to try and avoid his eyes.

"Yes..."

Waiting for him to continue, Annie wet her lips with the tip of her tongue, her throat having suddenly gone dry from nervousness. She still avoided looking directly at him, so certain was she of the disappointment she would see in his face. But disappointment was the farthest thing from Martin's mind. Stunned? Yes. Enthralled? Absolutely! And yet, of all the emotions that seemed to hit him in those moments, he was most surprised at his body's complete desire just to hold her full against him again; the agonizingly sweet warmth that swelled in his abdomen and lower was a longing he hadn't felt in a very long time. Her sleep-softened lips, the blush of her cheeks, and the scent of her warm body aroused him as she stood before him, still clasping the door handle with nervous hands. And any misgivings he might have had for using deception to keep her in New York were instantly banished from his mind.

"Martin?"

Instantly his eyes went back to her face, and he realized she had been speaking to him. "I'm sorry…what did you say?"

"It was nothing," she murmured to herself, thinking she had probably interrupted his thoughts of a plan for how to excuse himself from her company. "Was there something else you wanted, other than to see if I'd gotten my old room back?"

Oh yes, he thought to himself, *there is definitely something else I want!*

"I mean, there's probably somewhere else you need to be," she offered. "Even if your flight was cancelled, there must be plenty to keep you busy until you're able to return to London…given the three scripts for new movies you've been approached with, I can imagine you have a lot of reading ahead of you."

Martin smiled and shook his head. "The very last thing I intend to do today is read another boring script…I am not a reader."

"You don't know what you're missing," she taunted. "I read The Misbegotten in an afternoon and evening: I couldn't wait from one chapter to the next to see what new mischief Michael could get into."

Martin had the good grace to blush. "He was quite a character, wasn't he?"

Annie smiled. "I can't wait to see how you delivered him in the film."

"You haven't seen the movie?" Martin asked in disbelief.

"It's…on my list of things to do," she replied guiltily.

"After what?"

The smile left Annie's face. "After I return home, and take care of things there."

He felt the wall going up between them again.

"Thank you for coming by, Martin," she began after a long moment. "I'm glad for the opportunity to thank you for sending Raymond for me. Even if everything sorta went to pot, I appreciate all he went through trying to get me to my flight."

Martin avoided meeting her eyes and simply nodded.

"And thank you for showing me New York. I had a wonderful time…I'll never forget it," she finished in a whisper, dropping her eyes from his face as she moved to close the door.

Martin's palm met the door as he found himself dismissed. "Wait Annie!"

Feeling the resistance on the door, she peered around the edge to find Martin standing on the threshold. "Have dinner with me?" he asked insistently then caught himself. "I'd like to take you to dinner tonight. I can only offer the restaurant here in the hotel, because the roads are impassable."

Annie didn't reply.

"My driver says they make terrific omelet's," he taunted with a half grin.

Annie returned the smile but then glanced down at her clothing. "I don't have anything that would be appropriate to wear, Martin…"

"—what's wrong with what you have on?" He watched Annie's eyes as she weighed his expensive suit against her own outfit, and there was suddenly understanding in his. "I can leave my tie here," he offered in a burst as his hands worked the hindrance from around his neck. He stepped further into the room and laid the tie upon the table by the door, unfastening the first two buttons of the fine linen shirt in the same movement. "Better?"

Annie swallowed and nodded. "Better."

Martin silently enjoyed the spark of feminine interest that caught fire in her eyes. "I'll leave my jacket as well," he announced, shrugging out of it as Annie stood numbly before him. Taking the jacket, she realized he was intent on having her agree to dine with him, regardless of any hesitation she might still have.

"I can't go anywhere looking like this, Martin! My hair is a bird's nest…"

"—so freshen up," he interrupted. "I'll just wait for you…here…in the doorway…"

Suddenly aware how quickly Martin had turned the tables on her, Annie shook her head and reached for him as if motioning to a little boy. "You can't wait there! You're practically in the hallway!"

"You haven't invited me in," he countered too-innocently, then allowed her to whisk him into the room. As she pushed the door closed behind him, Annie realized she'd been had.

"I keep forgetting that I'm dealing with an actor," she taunted then turned to face him head-on. "You'd be great as Alfalfa in 'The Little Rascals Grow Up'."

Martin laughed out loud then, appreciating her sarcasm and the arms crossed upon her chest. "Only if you play the part of Darla! All that's missing is the background music!"

At that, Annie instantly recalled the simple, sweet theme he was referring to and shook her head smilingly. "You are *so* impossible, Martin…I'd almost think you've had absolutely no raising whatsoever."

Martin winced in mock embarrassment and replied, "Ooooh, that cuts!"

"It should," she rebounded, indicating he should take a chair by the window. "I won't be long," she offered in earnest, but then thought better of it. She would take her own sweet time, she decided: he deserved to wait. "I won't be a minute," she murmured a bit too sweetly.

Martin smiled to himself as the expression on her face changed from annoyance to calculation. He decided he liked the somewhat catty inference in her voice as he settled himself into the lounge chair and watched her disappear into the dressing area.

*   *   *

Annie entrusted the ordering of the meal to Martin, thankful that he seemed to understand the heavily French accented English of the waiter; once they were alone again however, Martin confessed that he hadn't understood a word the man had spoken! He had simply chosen the things that sounded good!

Upon the waiter's return, they were treated to fresh slices of various fruits and feather light omelets that all but melted in their mouths.

Annie cast him a curious glance and he rebutted, "So, I lied…I recognized 'omelets'! And, Sauvignon Blanc…are you complaining?"

She simply smiled and shook her head, savoring the delicious meal and the wonderful company that came with it.

"All that's missing now is strawberry shortcake," Martin announced after some moments. "Would you share one with me?" At Annie's enthusiastic nod, he set out to find an English-speaking waiter explaining that he might take chances with a meal, but *never* with dessert!

When several moments later Martin returned to their table, Annie saw that his mood appeared to have changed completely.

He was quiet and withdrawn, preoccupied to the point of rudeness; she wondered that he even remembered she was there.

The waiter appeared with his order yet, where before Martin had seemed to want the luscious dessert, he simply nodded in Annie's direction and had the waiter set the huge portion before her.

"Won't you share this with me, Martin?" she asked, concerned by his lengthy silence.

Martin's eyes rose slowly as he seemed to have not heard her.

"The dessert you ordered..." she murmured, pushing the still untouched plate more toward him. "Won't you join me?"

Martin let go a long breath. "I um, I don't care for any, Ann-Elise. But please, help yourself...I'm sure it's delicious."

Annie swallowed hard and pushed the dessert away to the side of the table, her appetite having suddenly left her as well.

She sat patiently and waited for Martin to offer some explanation for the change in his mood, her heart aching at the sadness and despair she saw in his eyes; after several long moments however, she realized she could endure his total silence no longer and reached across the small table to touch one his hands.

The touch of her hand drew Martin back to the present with a jerk, his head coming up with such a start that Annie held her breath.

For one quick instant, she feared that he might strike her, such was the anger she saw in his expression; but just a quickly as she had seen the anger, it was gone, replaced by a hurt and hopelessness that made her lean across the table and cradle the side of his face with motherly tenderness.

"Dear Lord, please tell me what's wrong, Martin! I can't bear to see you like this...something or someone has hurt you terribly."

Her thumb brushed at a suspicious wetness upon his cheek and he winced that she should see it.

"Please, Martin, I want to help if I can..."

Closing his eyes, Martin drew a long, shuddering breath and clasped her free hand tightly, hurtfully within both of his.

Annie drew her bottom lip between her teeth but never made a sound; she was instantly more aware of his pain than her own. Her other hand continued to cradle his face, her fingertips brushing gentle strokes across his brow and into his hair until slowly, as slowly as the other diners began to empty the enormous dining room, she felt his hold on her lessen until her hand was no longer numb and the one cradling his face lowered to join it.

They sat that way for half an hour until Annie whispered his name, twice in fact before he acknowledged her.

He must have heard the desperation in her uneasy voice because only then did Martin finally speak: "I'm loosing my son, Ann-Elise...because of the claims of a madwoman, the courts are taking my son from me..."

Annie ceased to breathe.

"I've been separated from my wife for several months now, but it was a mutual agreement...we couldn't continue living together hating one another as we do. At first, there seemed to be no problem with our sharing joint custody of Stuart—indeed, I think it was initially *her* idea!" he laughed bitterly. "I should have known better: Claire is incapable of sharing anything. For as long as I've known her, she's had to have all or nothing. I knew when I married her that I could never stay faithful to her. I was so young...too young to be married at all, too young to really know what a lifelong commitment was. I don't think I even knew what love was until the night Stuart was born...I grew up that night, and I lost my heart to a tiny boy with golden hair and eyes the color of my father's.

"There have been other women, Ann-Elise, just as I'm sure there have been other men for Claire, though I've yet to be able to prove it in court. I guess you could say we've failed each other...but I would be willing to overlook her affairs for the sake of our child, as I'd hoped she would grant me the same pardon."

There was a long pause. "But Claire must have all or nothing...she knew she never had all of me, so she's determined to have all of Stuart."

"But Martin, I don't understand! There isn't a court in this country that would allow a man to be raped of his child when all she can charge him with is infidelity! And if you can prove she has been with other men, that should counter any charges she's brought against you..."

"—we're not talking about the courts in America, Ann-Elise. My son is a Briton. His mother is a Briton. The laws I'm fighting are British laws."

"And you're not."

"I was born here in the States—I'm a Yank, in every sense of the word."

Annie's hands clenched Martin's ever tighter as she shook her head in disgust.

"I cannot believe the British courts would deny you so! And it isn't right to deny a child the love of his father! There are too many children already who have been deprived of a father's love and caring...*every* child understands the love of a father, and Stuart knows you love him; to take that away from him would be damnable!"

Martin smiled at the fury in her voice. "You have the same attitude as my attorney, thank God, and he assures me that he's taken every legal measure to prevent Claire from keeping my son from me...I spoke with him earlier though, and he informed me there had been another order presented to the court, forbidding any contact whatsoever with my son...he says the petition is to be heard by the end of the month."

"That's where you were before, talking with your attorney."

"I had missed him earlier in the day because he was in court with her," Martin nodded guiltily, "But I shouldn't have called him tonight; I've completely ruined our evening."

"You haven't ruined *my* evening," she offered sincerely. "I just feel so…angry! This is the twenty-first century, for crissake!"

"British courts are NOT known for having a 'progressive' interpretation of the law."

Annie's face lifted and she met his eyes with her own.

"Have you considered reconciling with her, Martin? Have either of you really tried?"

"Right now, there is so much anger between us, a reconciliation would be impossible."

"But if both of you love your son…"

"—I would likely be provoked to do murder."

Remembering Martin's death grip on her hand, she had no doubt he was serious. "I never wanted to hurt Claire, I don't want to hurt her now," he continued in a whisper. "Hurting his mother would destroy Stuart, and I won't have my son hating me…even if it means letting him go."

Annie offered Martin a smile as she gave his hand a final squeeze. "I don't think that'll happen, Martin. I can't tell you *how* I know but…it's just a feeling I have."

He returned her smile. "Intuition?"

Annie shook her head no. "It's just a feeling."

"Are you often right?"

Her brows lifted thoughtfully. "Almost always."

Martin's face lit with genuine hope. "Are you an angel, Miss Ryan?"

"I don't think so."

"A witch, then?"

She smiled. "No, but sometimes I wish I were."

"Oh? And what would you do if you were a witch?"

Annie swallowed and looked away, her heart thumping at the bedevilment she recognized in his look; she was certain he must be the most devastatingly handsome man she had ever met.

"I'd cast a spell on you so you could be happy again, the way you were earlier tonight. You're a different man when you're scared and hurting. You scared ME, Martin."

Martin sat fully back in his chair. "Damn, but you're honest."

"I don't know any other way to be," she nearly whispered, shrugging slightly when she found his eyes studying her. His stare, it was as if he was taking stock of her, measuring her...against what, she didn't know.

"I think we should go," Martin announced at last, rising from the table and extending his hand for Annie to join him. Though her hesitation was slight, as if she were wary or unsure, Martin felt it and grimaced inside.

They walked in silence from the dining room, neither wanting to say good-bye though both knew the night had already rolled into another morning. It was confusing at best, knowing he would take her to her room and that she would be expected to say good-bye...again. Annie realized as they stepped into the hotel lobby that for now, for this night, she did not want Martin to leave her.

And for once, Gramma never entered her thoughts.

CHAPTER THREE

"The snow stopped just before dusk," Martin commented as they began the ride up the elevator. "By noon tomorrow, La Guardia and the rest of New York should be back on its feet again."

"You must be relieved. I can imagine you want to get back to London as soon as possible."

"No more than you want to get back to North Carolina, I'm sure. You *were* the one out chasing planes all morning," he half teased.

"And I didn't catch a thing!"

Martin laughed then, the full, deep sound of it filling Annie with a sense of longing. Looking up at him she thought she had never met a more handsome man, both inside *and* out; knowing that she might never see him again after this night made her wonder that he'd been brought into her life at all.

"I'll admit I've never seen Raymond more frustrated with a situation," he offered with a shake of his head as the elevator deposited them within a few feet of her door. "Given all you had to go through, you must be exhausted as well."

Stepping from the elevator, Annie noted that Martin still had not relinquished the death grip upon her hand and wondered if what he had said had been more a question of her, for his eyes spoke what he apparently couldn't bring himself to ask. He was offering her an out.

"I'm not at all tired," she began, surprised that it was indeed the truth. "I guess there's something to be said for adrenaline…"

"Is that what it is, Ann-Elise, adrenaline?" he asked huskily.

"What else could it be?" she replied in a small, shaky voice; her whole body trembled and she realized Martin must be able to feel it as well.

While his eyes bored into hers, asking a hundred things of her at once, Annie became painfully aware of the precious moments that were slipping away from them and groped for the one ready excuse that might keep him there, if only for a little while longer. "I was...very rude before, not asking you to come in...would you like to come in now, Martin?"

It was impossible to disguise the flicker of surprise he knew must have lit his face, for hadn't he hoped the entire evening-indeed the entire day-that he might somehow find a way to prolong their limited time together?

Every excuse he had thrown about in his own head had seemed so shallow and yet, she had relieved him of the burden of making the first move by making it for him. She was asking him to stay.

Martin's throat convulsed as he swallowed back whatever it was he had thought to say; wanting to retain their easy camaraderie, Annie followed with the best attempt at light humor she could think of: "You'll need your tie and jacket when you audition for that revival of Alfalfa...I can't very well let you leave without them."

Her timid smile beseeched him to understand.

Martin reached for the pass key she had pulled from her pants pocket and slipped it into the lock of her door, taking advantage of the momentary silence to gather his own wits about him.

"A queer thing, adrenalin," he announced into the near dark silence of Annie's room, drawing the plastic card back out of the lock before placing it on the small table which stood by the door.

"Adrenaline hides behind facades," he whispered breathily, watching the play of emotions that crossed Annie's face before he motioned her into the still-darkened room ahead of him. "Do you know what façade adrenalin is hiding behind at this moment?" he asked, stopping her hand before it could reach the light switch on the wall.

"No," she whispered, her heartbeat quickening at the lie; Annie was certain Martin could feel it where he gripped her wrist at the pulse point.

"You're not a very convincing liar," he murmured as if reading her thoughts, stroking her wrist now with his thumb. "But then, you told me before that you weren't...everything you're thinking is clearly etched on your face, did you know that?"

The only hint of light came from the partially open door and the bathroom light that had been forgotten earlier and yet, it was enough for Annie to realize that Martin's face had become intense, studying her in the shadows as if his question had become a plea for sustenance.

"You're not being fair, Martin…if I were to be completely honest…"

"—I want you to be." Reaching behind her, Martin pushed the door closed with a gentle click and in the almost darkness, Annie realized his stern expression told her he would give her no quarter. "Tell me what you feel: I have to hear you say it."

My God, but I want him she cried unto herself, not brave enough to put voice to the thought.

"Oh Martin…I don't want you to go…and I don't want to leave *you*," she finally burst out in a whispered rush. At that, Annie allowed him to pull her against him and for one long moment, they held to one another fiercely, grasping at that which was so quickly slipping away from them; the warmth of his body was like a poultice, drawing the painful loneliness out and replacing it with a rush of need so great that she felt sensitized, within and without. Martin's strong hands stroked up and down her back coming to rest at last upon the slope of her hips, pressing her so close against his body that the most intimate part of him became hers by touch.

"Annie…there's no way I'll let you go now," he murmured wistfully, his voice oddly hoarse as if he hadn't meant to speak out loud.

Annie raised her head from where it had lain upon his chest and leaned back so she might better see the man who's plaintive words touched deeper than his hands upon her skin. Half of Martin's face was shadowed so it was the other side that taunted one nervous hand from where it lay upon his chest. Lifting her hand slowly, tentatively as if testing its ability to work on its own, she traced the line of his beautiful mouth with two fingertips, lingering an extra moment when she felt just a hint of warm breath upon her knuckles. *He must think I've never touched a man's mouth before*, she mused silently. It occurred to her then that she actually had not, at least not like this, not with this damning need to memorize it, to brand the texture and slope and curve of his mouth for the nights to come when all she would have of him were these memories. Dear God, I will never have anything beyond this night! The realization hit her in the gut, and it hit with all the hurt and anger and frustration that one feels when they learn someone has been terribly wronged. She remembered feeling it when a classmate died on an ice covered bridge at 16, when her grandmother's sight was taken, and when her parents were robbed of their lives on a doomed airplane. Internally she bargained to set the anger aside for another time, closed her eyes, and simply concentrated on tracing every bend beneath her hand. She let it stray upward along the warm plane of his cheek, her thumb finding the straight slope of his nose and then the curve of his brow before brushing feather-soft hair that trailed downward past one ear and onto his neck. The corded muscles tensed within her palm so she cupped his neck full in her hand and began a soothing caress in step with his hands upon her back. When her fingertips again touched the recently barbered hair behind his ear, deeper into its lengths her fingers splayed, cradling his head and clenching his hair, releasing and grasping. Stroke by stroke her hands' movements were mimicked by Martin's larger, stronger ones, straying lower to pull her upward and more fully against him.

"I've wasted a lifetime," Martin whispered, his warm breath teasing Annie's parted lips, "but I'll not waste another moment after tonight…now that I've found you—"

Whatever else Martin might have thought to say was cut off when Annie pressed her palm to his mouth and murmured, "—no regrets, Martin. Please, please don't talk about regrets, not now!"

With a groan, he drew Annie closer and dropped his mouth to the curve of her neck, her hand pinned between them in a fist against one breast. When his mouth opened and she felt his tongue and teeth against her skin, her whole body shuddered, her breath caught, and she released an innocent though provocative sigh at the exquisite, excruciating pleasure to be found in that small expanse of skin between her shoulder and ear. With only the tip of his tongue, Martin traced and taunted and tasted her until she thought her legs would give way beneath her. She freed her fist to wrap her fingers in the folds of his shirt, arching against him just to remain standing. When she thought the last bit of strength had left her, Annie felt Martin's hands under her buttocks, lifting her fully off the floor as if she were weightless. Helplessly looping her left arm around his neck in a desperate attempt to hold on to the man, Annie drew his head close enough that she gained some stability from resting her lips upon his brow. Over and over again she replayed the feeling of his breath against the back of her hand, the softness of his lips, the scent of his throat and the scent of his hair: two different smells, her mind noted. *Remember everything, every second*, she cried silently. *Remember. Remember…*

At some point, Annie realized that Martin had carried her to the bed for she felt him easing her onto it: one knee rose to brace beside her on the mattress as he lowered her gently and slowly to its cool surface. His movements were smooth and sure, as natural as breathing, essential and deliberate and controlled for a man of his size; leaning over her, one elbow pressing into the material beside her shoulder, she felt his body lower to lie beside hers.

For a long, lingering moment, Martin simply looked at her. Lying on one side, his arm bent with the palm of his hand supporting his head at the jaw, he realized he had never wanted any woman as much as he wanted Annie. He couldn't explain it; he couldn't rationalize it. Hell, he didn't begin to understand it…it just *was*. Dynamic, crazy, shameless, just, fanatical: it was everything at once, and better than anything he had ever imagined. This woman, this beautiful, giving, incredibly sensual woman wanted him…for *him*, for the man he is and not for celebrity or the character that he portrayed or the notoriety of saying she had bedded Martin Vaughn. She saw something more in him than People Magazine's favorite cover of the moment, or even the thumbnail black and white photo from the Heart Association brochure. Had he been no one, had he still been Daniel Martin!, she would *still* see the heart of him, the part no one else had ever cared to look for much less touch. She had been his friend in another life, when he was no one special and she was befriending him now.

What is he thinking? What is this intense study of me? Why is he staring at me like he can see right through me? What is he looking for? Annie silently wondered.

Martin wanted to trust her but this was foreign territory, his actually *wanting* to trust a woman. After everything he'd gone through with Claire, this new desire, this new awareness gave the thought of making love a whole other attraction. His expression must have been reflected in his serious study of the woman because she reached to touch his face…

If he would smile or just say something! Annie screamed inside. If he would just touch me again and tell me this hasn't been some game to see how far I would let him go! Her head was spinning with questions and feelings and, the wanting of him! "Martin…?"

Whatever else Annie might have said was cut off. With a low groan, Martin lowered his lips to hers as the full depth of his wanting met hers to ignite feelings that had lain dormant in both of them for too long. Arching against him, Annie felt the tension building in the muscles of his legs where they now lay upon hers and she stroked this head, his neck, the length of his back as if to do so might ease the low, hoarse whispers that seemed to be pleading for something.

Though she lowered her arms from around his massive shoulders, they never broke contact with him. Instead, she brought her hands to press flat against his chest and reasoned his heart was beating as quickly as a man who had been running. She didn't realize she had smiled until Martin lifted her chin so he could look more fully at her face. "Pleased with yourself, are you?"

Her smile widened. "I was just thinking: there's a cardiologist at my hospital who would want a stress test run on a man whose pulse ran this fast in a sedentary position."

Martin pursed his lips; he wasn't particularly pleased that Annie was thinking about another man while in his arms. "This cardiologist, is he a friend or…"

"A friend?" Annie paused for effect and bit the inside of her lip to keep from laughing outright. "Yeah…I guess you could say that."

The expression on Martin's face was anticipatory. And his heartbeat accelerated, if that was possible! Annie loved finding that she could wreak such havoc on this man's emotions; she meant something to him, otherwise he wouldn't care. "Dr. Holt is very dear…probably everyone's favorite doctor…" she continued evenly. Martin tensed somewhat as he clenched and unclenched his jaw.

"She's my best friend's mom, Martin, and she would love to get her hands on you!"

At that, Martin's eyes narrowed for a look that Annie could only describe as priceless, and he rolled over onto his back taking a laughing Annie with him. "You little…witch," he murmured after some thought. "You heartless, devious…delicious witch," he whispered, feeling her fingers playing with a button on the front of his shirt. "So…now that you've gotten your wish, Miss Ryan, what else do you have in store for me?"

Meeting his eyes, Annie's expression became serious then serene, as she lowered her mouth to his. With but the tip of her tongue, she traced the natural boundary of his lips, dipping to where they parted to feel the quick breath that Martin exhaled; it became a desperate battle to retain control over her own body while she lay upon his and she almost wished she hadn't teased him so. Though her experience with men was limited, she knew her own body and she had never felt so completely aroused as at this very moment. And she had never felt more alive! While her fingers again found the buttons of the linen shirt, she drew herself up upon her knees and slowly worked the buttons loose and the shirt apart. One of Martin's hands clasped the back of her head to keep her mouth from leaving his and she met his seeking mouth just as deeply. But when her hands touched his skin, when the warmth and the scent and the dampness hit her senses, her silent assault became a vocal plea, unintentional yet raging, fierce and wanting and confused.

Martin's mouth had muffled the moan but there was no tempering of Annie's searching hands.

She wanted to touch all of him at once and finally drew her mouth free long enough to tell him, "It oughta be a sin for a man to kiss like you do...I swear, Martin, you don't know what you're doin' to me..."

Grasping the bottom of Annie's sweater in both hands, Martin lifted it up and off of her in one movement, smiling when her hair fell from it to cascade upon her shoulders and bare chest. She had worn no bra and her nipples hardened in an instant from the rush of cool air.

Smiling, he clasped her neck and back, pulling her close enough that their bodies fully touched before rolling her over to lay on her back beneath him. "I know exactly what I'm doing, my little witch," he whispered, cradling the sides of her head in his hands. He stroked her temple with his thumbs and seemed to gear down, slowing their pace with long, precisely placed kisses to her brow, her cheeks, her upturned chin. "You're an exquisite creature, Annie, and I want to savor every inch of you," he whispered as one hand moved slowly lower, to lift the hair from one shoulder, to gently circle then cup one breast. Stroking the nipple with the pad of his thumb, he followed a moment later with gentle strokes of his tongue, causing Annie to jerk suddenly. Martin's head lifted and he cast a curious glance that caught Annie's own inquisitive eyes.

"Your mouth is so hot...like a fever," she mumbled, touching his lips with trembling fingertips, not understanding or even realizing how the innocence of her words might further fuel his body's response to her. She instantly cradled his dark head against her chest and pressed her own wanting lips against the crown of his scalp. Another scent, another memory. *Remember, remember...*instantly, a trembling began in the centermost part of her body that wrought such tortuous feelings, she feared she might go insane from the need of him.

Martin heard the throaty desperation of her sighs, pressing her back upon the bed when they unconsciously became moans while her nails dug into his shoulders until he swore he could bear it no longer. Removing his shoes and trousers took him a mere moment and yet, Annie's lips trembled as she rolled her head from side to side, the back of one hand draped in a tangle of hair by her right ear while the other hand lay in a fist upon her stomach. A dozen thoughts assailed him at once: how long has it been for her? How can I contain myself to make it better for her? Who is it that waits at home for her...?

Inside Annie's head she vaguely heard the sound of her jeans being unzipped and then slipped down her legs, her panties silently following. A moment later, she felt Martin's hands clasping her own and lifting them to his neck as he knelt over her upon the bed.

"Grab on to me, Annie...hold on," Martin urged in a voice that was seemingly just above her own lips and in one sure movement, he had lifted her to lie more fully in the center of the bed. The weight of his body as he lay upon her brought Annie back from the surreal world her body had led her senses to and she smiled to know he was resting as fully upon his elbows as possible. Opening her eyes she saw Martin draw back somewhat, his expression at once serious and heady. "Tell me if I'm ever hurting you," he murmured, his eyes serious and intent.

"Oh, darlin'...the only way you could hurt me now would be to turn about an' leave—can't you see that?" She asked in a whisper, her drawl more pronounced than he'd ever heard it before.

"A man would have to be a fool to leave you," he heard himself confess, realizing he'd never before praised a woman so. Her face flushed and she smiled in such a way that he had to believe the compliment embarrassed her. He would enjoy the coming months, getting to know the soul of this woman, as well as every moment of her past since their parting some twenty years before. Closing her eyes with feather-soft kisses, Martin murmured, "Sometimes Annie, time is a man's worst enemy. It would take days to love you as I want to..."

"—then we must make use of the time we have," she interrupted, placing the fingertips of one hand upon his lips as the other reached higher to brush the longish bangs off his brow where they partially hid one of his beautiful olive colored eyes. *Remember his eyes*...from black in the center to deep pine to emerald she noted the silver ring around the outer edge of the iris and memorized those eyes for the nights she would be alone, just hours from now...Annie allowed the fingers at his lips to trail a sensitized path past his chin and down the length of his neck before slowing to gently circle the muscle at one side of his chest; it flexed at her feathery touch as did that part of him that sought to become one with her, and she stayed the circular motion of her hand to press it lower until she touched him—tentatively at first then more completely as she began at the lowest part of his abdomen and continued down the entire length of him with just her fingertips. Annie's expression so boldly reflected her awe of him that she pressed the palm of her hand full against him and breathed a solemn, "Oh Martin..." to which he again met her eyes with the same tender sincerity as before.

"Tell me if I'm going too fast," he whispered, lifting him self so she could guide him into her warmth. "I'll stop if..."

"—don't ever stop, Martin!" Annie murmured as her body bowed beneath him, her eyelids trembling closed as she pressed her head back into the mattress beneath her. A low moan escaped her throat and she drew her bottom lip between her teeth; she was not prepared for Martin to fill her so completely. "I feel you here," she whispered, her right hand drawn into a fist against her navel. "Oh please darlin', don't ever stop..."

Martin was neither expecting nor prepared for the burst of passion that followed his entry, for his hands, lips and tongue explored every inch of her body that he could reach without ever breaking contact with her. Annie moved and responded to his steady, powerful rhythm as she too found herself desperate to explore and taste of him as he had her; for the first time in her life, she felt a building up and centering of all sensations in just their joined, moving bodies, and her mind screamed to her *remember, remember...*

"Wrap your legs around me, Annie...hold on to me," he whispered into her sweat-moist temple as he slipped his hands past her waist to her bottom and lifted her flush against body. He was somehow on his knees and she realized she straddled him just below the waist as she lifted for him to press deeper. Grimacing suddenly Annie let go a moan that stopped Martin mid mid-movement. "Annie, if this isn't good for you..."

"—it's not that Martin..."she murmured, pressing her trembling lips to his cheek and trailing kisses to his right ear. She didn't speak or move for one long moment. She found his left hand and pressed its palm flat against her stomach. "I feel you here, Martin," she whispered, "I feel all of you, darlin'...all of you!"

Gently, slowly at first then faster, Martin moved within her, taking himself to the edge of her body and then pressing fully inside her again. When she felt him tense within her, their rhythm in sync so perfectly, she met him gently then aggressively, slow then quickening, over and over until Annie felt drunk from their loving. At last, feeling the woman convulse around him, Martin pushed himself over and over while great, numbing blows shook them again and again. The contractions within her all but depleted her body of strength until they subsided into slow pulsations that were the very essence of contentment. And Martin, drenched in their sweat above her, allowed Annie to turn and draw him down to the bed beside her; as they lay on their sides facing one another, still joined, their bodies replete and nearly numb. Remembering that this woman had planned only hours before to return to her home in North Carolina, Martin felt certain she would rethink the necessity of leaving so soon. His breathing slowing gradually to normal, his voice a hoarse whisper, Martin put his feelings into words. "You can't leave now, Annie...don't even try to tell me that you weren't as moved as I was, because I wouldn't believe you."

"I couldn't lie about it...my body wouldn't allow it," she conceded in a whisper against his lips. She had never imagined something so sudden could feel so totally right, and she smiled to herself at the contentment of their union...until common sense intervened. "I still don't have any choice about leaving, though—I'm needed at home, Martin."

A warm smile touched Martin's face. "Here I've known you as intimately as a man can know a woman and yet, I know so little about you...where in North Carolina IS home?" he asked. It was necessary, for now, to continue the pretense that he'd never known her before, he told himself; just until he could convince her to stay.

Annie's smile was a bit shy, realizing what he said was true. "Home seems very far away right now," she mused to herself, running the tips of her fingers across Martin's lips as if to forge them into her memory.

"It's for coi-tain you're not from Brookl'n," he offered in nasal tones, tapping her recall of several Brooklyn-accented people they had shared the ferry ride with. Annie laughed out loud for Martin had intoned the peculiar speech to perfection while guiding her through a verbal commentary during the ferry's excursion.

"You're horrible," she chided through lips he had once again claimed in full.

"And you're wonderful," Martin countered when his lips finally left hers. "I don't care where you're from or where you've been or who you were before yesterday. Nothing before yesterday matters in my life," he corrected, "*or* in yours...not anymore."

Annie felt her skin flush and she closed her eyes against the familiar, restrictive feeling. "Oh, Martin...I wish it were that simple, but it isn't—at least not for me."

Martin's expression froze on his face. He could not believe the woman could be so stubborn! There couldn't be one thing in Mount Airy, North Carolina he couldn't replicate for her in New York or Los Angeles or London...he wasn't buying it for a moment. "What could possibly be so important that your plans can't be changed? You've already told me you're not married…and I **know** you haven't had a lover in a long while," he reminded in a tense, sensual tone.

Annie's face blushed scarlet as she gave him a look that clearly spoke her hurt. "You're absolutely right: I haven't had a lover in a long time…and no, I'm not married. I came close once but…" her voice trailed off as she remembered, for the first time in weeks, the plans she and David had made all those years ago…before her parents died. "I…I live with my grandmother, Martin. I lost my parents a few years back and we're all that each of us has."

Martin swallowed hard as a mental picture of Annie's mother came to him. Mary was dead, the woman who had been his mother's best friend in high school and her husband Stephen were dead. He couldn't process it, not right now, not when Annie was again talking about leaving him.

"I'd like to think that just changed," he returned sharply. "For crissake, what am I now? A one night stand?"

Annie's face paled and she moved to draw herself to sitting, taking care to keep the sheet across her naked breasts. She suddenly felt cold and ill at ease, ashamed that Martin had put words to a fact she found she couldn't deny, and which crudely and tersely summed up what so special an encounter must eventually be. "I wish you wouldn't call it that," she thought aloud.

"What would you have me call it?" he pressed in a hushed yet angry tone.

"I don't know! Just not **that**!"

Martin's expression became very solemn. "You never intended for us to go beyond this night." It was a statement, not a question.

"I never *intended* anything," she countered. "But I won't say I'm not glad it happened, either. I won't forget a moment of this, Martin…but I have obligations, and what happened with you doesn't change anything."

"How can it NOT?" he bellowed as he swung himself from the bed to stand stiff and naked over her, taking advantage of her silence to regain his flailing composure. Never had he imagined her or any woman to end a relationship with him so abruptly. This was like some pathetic joke, and the last thing he ever expected from Annie.

"My grandmother needs me to care for her," Annie argued in a whisper, twisting the sheet with trembling hands. "She's like a child, Martin, a difficult child…you cannot begin to imagine."

Realizing that Annie was now refusing to look at him at all, Martin turned from the side of the bed to part the drapes at the window with the back of one hand. For the first time in years, a woman—this woman—had made him feel strong and sure in a way he doubted he ever could again. Where Claire had managed to cut his legs from beneath him with the war in the British courts for their son, making him feel like less of a man with every battle lost, Annie had reinforced him, encouraged him, given him hope it would all work out in the end. He couldn't accept that she might leave him with no more explanation than this. "Would you just not make such a rash decision, Annie? We will think of a way to take care of your—your grandmother." *Just don't throw away what we've found before you've given us a chance*, he added silently.

Annie heard everything that Martin was saying but inside she knew the situation was hopeless. And inside, she was hurting with the same pain she had felt when she lost her parents: the thought scared her for she had never expected to hurt with such intensity again. The hot tears that spilled down her face and onto her breasts were evidence of not only her pain, but her fear as well.

Martin stood tensely at the window's edge, drawing the drapes open to half way so that the city shone silver beneath the full-moon sky. He took Annie's silence to mean she might be considering his words and pressed on. "Perhaps we could put her in a good home…or at least get a full-time nurse for a while. Then we would have some space to make whatever arrangements you think best. It would be entirely your decision," he insisted, turning with a hopeful smile to greet her acquiescence.

Instead, Annie buried her face in her hands and began to sob in huge, racking spasms that so shocked Martin, that he stood frozen for a moment. Then just as suddenly, he was beside her on the bed, holding her close against his chest as if to cushion her quaking with his big body. Finding herself wrapped once again in his arms, Annie grasped the man tight against herself, a desperate, clawing hold cradling his head in her palms and holding him against her with her hands entwined in great clasps of his hair.

"Jesus Christ, Annie…"

The woman's mind half-acknowledged Martin's soothing murmuring and she let him hold her until she felt there must surely be no more tears to cry. When finally she allowed him to lower her back upon the pillows, she turned her face to the wall so he could not see her, so that she would not have to look at him. "You don't understand Martin…even if I were willing to put her into a home and financially able to do it, I would still have to go home…it would take time…there are waiting lists for those places." She turned then to look him in the eyes. "You have someone who needs you as well. Your son needs you more now than at any other time in his life…I would be nothing but a hindrance…I might even hurt your chances in the British courts."

Martin found Annie's love and protectiveness of her grandmother moving, in spite of his frustration. And her consideration of Stuart genuinely surprised him, if only for an instant. He realized he had not himself known such devotion for many years; a part of his mind had led him to believe such had become the manner of all women in this day and time: that their every motivation was self-serving. Hadn't that been the case with nearly every woman he'd ever known, especially Claire? At the thought of his estranged wife, Martin drew back from Annie somewhat to caress her face with gentle ministrations that meant to soothe, to somehow express his appreciation of this sensitive, passionate woman. Instead, his touch became erotic, extending past her lips and throat to her breasts where his lips and tongue teased and taunted, caressed and celebrated. At last Martin found a voice for his emotions and he cradled Annie fully against his body so that she was left with no question as to his wanting of her.

"Somehow, I'm finding it harder and harder to think of home and obligations," he murmured against the nape of her neck. "I promise we'll talk all this out later—on the plane when I take you back home…"

Annie unconsciously held her breath no longer hearing the endearments Martin spoke to her. What did he mean, 'when I take you back home'? *Could he honestly be considering following me back to North Carolina?* she asked herself. This was all happening too fast for her; she preferred for a relationship to build slowly from friendship, or at least she thought she did. This wild, passionate sense of loving she felt was so alien to her…she didn't fully understand it! And yet, hadn't part of the amazing attraction been their awareness of similar emotions in the other person? Thoughtfully, she accepted a small inkling of the truth: for them to meet and immediately become aware that the other was their ideal of the opposite sex, and for Martin to so completely ensconce her into his plans for the future, their feelings must be mutual…and yet, nothing can ever come of it, Annie conceded her more logical mind, not ever.

Martin caught her chin between two fingers and lifted her lips for his direct assault, both tender and insistent at once. Annie slowly allowed herself to return the depth of his kisses with her own, allowing herself the joy from this man's touch…allowing them the few precious hours that remained before she must leave his life forever. The decision made, her lovemaking became more ardent as she strained against him for every ounce of the so sweet passion he evoked in her. *We will have this one final time to love,* she screamed inside her head, certain it was the last time they ever would.

*   *   *

Having finally booked a 1 pm flight to Greensboro, Annie stood at the pay phone and waited for the operator to place her collect call to Monica.

Staring at her reflection in the panes of a mirror that bisected the wall directly across from her, she shook her head at her disheveled appearance.

Her eyes bore dark circles beneath them, her lips were puffy, her face was red from whisker burns, her clothes were rumpled and wrinkled from having been strewn into a heap with Martin's several hours before, and her hair more resembled a bird's nest than it ever had before.

She looked a mess.

"Collect call from Annie, will you accept?" The operator's high, nasal tone broke into Annie's thoughts.

"Of course," came Monica's usual catty response "Let me guess: you can't get a flight."

Annie smiled into the receiver. "Actually, I'm scheduled to leave in just about five minutes. I wanted to let you know to expect my plane to arrive in Greensboro at about 3:30 this afternoon. Will that be a problem?"

"Naah. I took the weekend off so there's no problem as far as getting to the airport." A pause. "Unless of course, you'd rather not have a welcoming party to meet you. Shall I see if Mrs. Adams can come over and stay with Gramma?"

Monica's insinuation was clear: did Annie want her to come alone to the airport so the two of them might talk one on one? How many times had she and Monica confided in one another? Monica had been her best friend since they met in middle school and yet, how could she talk to *anyone* about Martin?

"Annie? Are you still there?"

"Yeah, I'm here. Y-you go ahead and bring Gramma when you come. It'll do her good to get out," Annie offered in her most convincing voice.

"Okay...hey, are you alright?"

Annie heard her flight number being called over the PA system and welcomed the interruption. "They just called my flight to board so I've gotta get off here. I'll see you and Gramma in a couple of hours, Monica."

"We'll be there."

Annie's plane taxied down the runway of Piedmont Triad International Airport and she strained to look out the window. The pilot had said there was four inches of snow in the Triad and she could believe it! With the exception of the runways, everything was still a blanket of white. Stepping through the door to the waiting area of gate 40, Annie hunched her carry-on higher upon her shoulder and scanned the sea of anxious faces for Monica's.

At the far end of the reception area, Annie's friend stood placidly behind the chair of an elderly, white haired woman who seemed to stare into nothingness. Upon seeing Annie's familiar though weary face, Monica leaned to whisper into the older woman's ear and a nod of acknowledgement was Gramma's only indication that she had heard Monica announce Annie's approach.

"Gramma! Monica!"

"Hi stranger!"

The two women wrapped each other in a tremendous hug that indicated closeness not unlike sisters before Monica stepped back and lifted as single, questioning brow as her eyes took in Annie's appearance. Annie pressed a finger to her lips as if to say, *I know I look like hell, but don't let on to Gramma, okay?* before bending at the waist to embrace her grandmother in the same loving welcome.

"Ah Gramma, don't you look pretty today? Monica did your hair and everything!" With an upward glance, Annie mouthed a genuine 'thank-you' to Monica who in return mouthed 'no problem.'

"I wouldn't know about that now, would I?" her grandmother returned sullenly. "Monica had me get on my best dress too, and to come out in this kind of weather…"

"The roads are clear. We had no trouble at all getting here," Monica countered. "Annie thought to have me bring you along because she believed you'd enjoy getting out for a while…"

"—I thought maybe we could stop at K&W on the way home and get something for supper," Annie broke in, noting Monica's chagrin. "I know how much you love their chicken and dumplings, Gramma…wouldn't you like to do that?"

The elderly woman pursed her lips and rocked agitatedly in her seat. "Well, I reckon since we're already out in this mess it won't hurt none to stop. It's the only time I get chicken n'dumplins anymore since y'all won't let me cook…and don't neither one o' you know nothin' 'bout makin' dumplins…"

Annie and Monica each grasped one of the elderly woman's arms and together they lifted her round yet frail body from where she sat. Though her grandmother's verbal barrage continued, neither she nor Monica seemed to heed the old woman's menacing insults as both knew such was her way and to try to reason only spurred her on. An occasional "Uh-huh" or "I know, Gramma" were the only comments necessary as Annie asked herself once again if there wasn't somehow something more she could do to make her grandmother's situation more comfortable.

*　　*　　*

It was late afternoon when Martin found himself coming out of the dreamless sleep that had so enveloped him. His sleep had been so thorough and the awakening so peaceful that he felt lethargic, and oddly at peace. He let his eyes open slowly expecting to be met with blinding sunlight but instead, the room was almost dark as the drapes were now drawn tightly shut. He smiled realizing from the empty space beside him that Annie must already be up and that she had drawn the drapes to allow him an extra bit of sleep.

"Annie," he called into the silence, tuning his ears in the direction of the bathroom, "have you called about a flight out yet?"

Silence.

Martin pulled himself to a sitting position and threw the bedding back as he let his feet drop to the floor. "Annie?" Even before he stepped into the darkened bathroom he knew the woman was not there. Bracing the palm of his left hand upon the upper end of the door jam, Martin drew a deep breath that did little to calm him. He slapped the wooden casing once and then slapped it again before feeling the painful stinging that inched into his awareness. Balling the numbing hand into a tight fist, his fingertips touched the sensitive bones at the base of his fingers but cared little that tomorrow the pain from the bruises would be such it would hurt to merely flex his hand. He could not think about tomorrow, would not think about anything except finding Annie. Two strides placed him back at the bed and he lowered himself onto it slowly, seemingly unaware or perhaps uncaring that he was still naked. He picked up the telephone receiver and dialed the front desk, realizing only after the manager answered that Annie had left the passkey to the room along with a folded note between the base of the lamp and the telephone.

"Um, this is room 918," he stammered as he lifted the flap of the hotel stationery to find his name and several lines scrawled upon it. He didn't allow himself to read any of it before folding it closed again to give his full attention back to the person on the other end of the line. "I would like a...would you send up a pot of black coffee immediately? Thanks." He had wanted to say that he would like a bottle of Scotch sent up but knew that alcohol wasn't what he would need to get through this day.

Replacing the receiver on the telephone base, Martin held the small note pinched between his thumb and index finger, stroking the laid linen texture as if it were Annie's satiny skin instead. At last his right hand joined the left as the folded note was opened and again, he saw his name written in her flowing hand staring back at him:

Martin,
How can I begin to tell you all that I feel? There are not enough words and so little time anyway that I'd rather leave you with the memory of what we shared than try and explain reasons for something I can't even begin to understand myself. I have to go back home and I have to go alone because my first obligation is to my grandmother and she would never accept you or anyone else in our lives. I can't ask you to understand, only accept because the situation isn't going to change. Please don't try to find me. It's for the best that we go our separate ways because sometimes simply wanting someone isn't enough. I know you have a life of your own and you should try to work with it, give it another chance. I will keep you in my prayers.
My love, Annie

Martin repressed the urge to crush the note in his fist and sling it against the wall. As cool and final as her words sounded, they were her words in her hand, smudged in spots by what he could only hope were her tears. As he lay back upon the pillows propped now against the headboard of the bed, he closed his eyes and pictured again how she looked as she had lain beneath him that final time. So intense was her giving and so complete had been their bodies' union...had she decided even *then* that she would leave him? He shuddered. For several moments Martin sat within the darkness behind his eyes, recalling every breath and every movement from Annie's body as if to recall it might somehow place her there again, until the knock announcing room service jarred him to full consciousness and reality.

"Come in!" he barked harshly, noting only then that he still lay naked and now, thanks to his memories, fully aroused. With a growling lurch he bent to retrieve the sheet from the foot of the bed and jerked it into place across his legs and groin a scant second before a pretty brunette in a hotel uniform backed a cart with his requested order into the room.

The pleasant "Good afternoon" had barely left her lips when she stopped halfway in her turn. Her momentary pause and the unconscious sweep of her eyes told him at once that she recognized him, while a becoming blush lit her cheeks. "Hello, sir…um, where would you like this?" she stammered, dropping her eyes to his chest to avoid meeting his eyes and then immediately reversing herself when she recognized her mistake. Her discomfort amused Martin, and he felt himself abruptly relax. Turning her attention fully upon the tray of coffee, croissants and butter, the young woman studied the accoutrements as if unsure what she should do next.

"Thank you…I'll um, I'll help myself to coffee in a bit," he offered in a kinder tone than he'd thought possible this morning. She lifted grateful eyes and smiled, opening and shutting her mouth as if wanting to say something more before pushing the cart to the bedside. Taking a step back from the cart and toward the still open door, she crossed the distance to the door in several smallish steps as if still trying to find voice for her thoughts until finally, she turned with her hand upon the door knob to venture a final glance at Martin Vaughn, the actor who had so completely stolen the hearts of several million women through his role as Michael Maurer, including hers.

"If I may say sir, you were wonderful in 'The Misbegotten.' I've seen it, I know, a dozen times and it's better each time I watch it!" She dropped her eyes again, realizing she had been babbling and yet, dared to add, "My parents were born down South and they said you played the part perfectly!"

Martin's attention piqued when the young woman mentioned the South for it was North Carolina that Annie headed back to right now and he swallowed convulsively. He had to find her.

Realizing he had not answered her, Martin smiled at the young woman and raked his hair back from his forehead in that self-conscious gesture she recognized from his speech at the Academy Awards. God, but he was gorgeous!

"I appreciate your good words, Miss…"

"—Daves."

"Miss Daves. And thanks for the coffee; it smells wonderful."

"Are you sure I can't pour you a cup…?"

"No, I'll get it myself...thanks," he finished with a half nod and smile that indicated she could leave. As she closed the door, Martin shook his head at her comments and awestruck expression. If he lived to be 100 he would never get used to being thought of as a sex symbol and a 'star' for he felt he was the same person he was a year ago, or twenty years ago when he was growing up in 'Mayberry.' He wondered if Andy Griffith, who immortalized Mount Airy in 'The Andy Griffith Show', had ever felt the confusion of wondering where you really belong once you leave the security of home and attempt to make a life half a world away. *You can't go home again* taunted him as he rubbed his eyes wearily.

Dropping his legs back upon the floor, Martin's left knee bumped the service cart and a linen napkin fell from it to land on the floor beside the nightstand. When he reached to retrieve it, he glanced a small white item lying on the carpet between the nightstand and the bed. Twisting slightly he snatched the rectangular plastic placard from the carpet, turning it over as he did so.

ANN-ELISE RYAN
Triad Chapter
North Carolina

It was her nametag. Martin drew a deep breath and clinched the smallish item tightly in his now-sensitive left palm. Ann-Elise Ryan...ANNIE Ryan..."My God," he thought aloud, "is this is all I have of her?" Releasing a breath of frustration, his skin tingled with a chill at the thought of possibly not being able to find the woman. It will be enough, he conceded, bringing the fist gripping the placard to his lips. How many Ann-Elise's can there be?

*   *   *

Leaving Martin in her hotel room had been the most difficult thing Annie had ever done and yet it was the only thing she *could* have done. She realized that now more than ever as she sat upon the sofa studying her grandmother who had dozed off while listening to the six o'clock news. Why did she put up such a fuss to listen to something she always went to sleep on? And why had she complained so damningly about her supper when Annie had had the chicken and dumplings too and found them as delicious as always? Annie just shook her head. Her grandmother had begged off her evening snack completely complaining that what she'd had for supper had caused her to have an upset stomach and that if she tried to eat anything else, she would become sick.

"She's probably full to near popping," Monica commented later when the two of them were finally alone. "Didn't you find it strange that she cleaned her plate of something she swore she hated? She does that all the time, Annie, and you just let her get by with it!"

"What am I supposed to do then, threaten to send her to her room without any supper? She's my grandmother!"

Monica shook her head disparagingly. "That old woman has you right where she wants you girl, and until you get a little backbone about you, she'll make you miserable till the day she dies."

Annie's expression became angry. "How can you say such a thing? She's all the family I have! I'd be completely alone without her!"

Monica's face was sympathetic, wanting to remind her friend that there had once been David and that he had wanted to make a life with her; but David was a sore spot with Annie, as were men (or rather the prospect of a mate!) in general.

Annie felt rather than saw Monica's withdrawal from the subject of the conversation but she didn't pursue a continuance. Instead she took a long breath and broached the subject that had been itching at her since leaving New York City: "Is 'The Misbegotten' playing anywhere now?"

Monica's smile snapped to attention. "Why?" She felt certain she already knew the answer but she had to ask: "Martin Vaughn didn't put in an appearance at the banquet, did he?"

Annie's face reddened. "He spoke toward the end of the evening. I was very impressed by his honesty and directness." The half-truth nearly choked her.

"I bet that wasn't *all* that impressed you!" her friend teased. "Did you get to see him up close? That man is gorgeous! I can't believe he actually showed for the ceremony, I really can't…"

"—and why not?" Annie broke in. "He seemed very sincere when he spoke of his support of the Heart Association. He's lost some of his own family to heart disease."

"I know, I read his bio in People. The man's had a bitch of a life."

"Really?" Annie's voice was a whisper. She caught herself and asked as nonchalantly as was possible, "So…what else do you know about him?"

Monica's face went alight with mischief. "What's this? Two months ago I couldn't pay your way to go see 'The Misbegotten' with me and now…"

"—all I asked is what you know," Annie interjected. "If it's gonna put you out…"

"Hey, I could talk all day about Martin Vaughn, I'm just surprised is all! Too bad a guy around here that you could get your hands on can't stir the same interest," she taunted. Watching Annie turn away to finish the laundry as if suddenly disinterested, Monica decided to curb her quick tongue and enjoy a conversation with her friend about a man for once. "Alright, alright, I'll behave. But it really is impossible to try to tell you anything about this guy until you've seen his movie, and it's not in theatres anymore, only on DVD."

"A lot of good that would do me."

"I forgot you're still living in the dark ages with your VCR! Want me to rent it and bring my DVD player over?"

Annie wanted to scream YES!, but instead simply replied, "If you want. Maybe you can get it for next weekend."

"Not unless we reserve it now."

"Give 'em a call at the rental store and see; the number's on the inside back cover of the phone book." As Monica strolled into the kitchen whistling the theme music to 'The Misbegotten,' Annie silently prayed for her success. Just seeing Martin in a movie wouldn't replace the misery of her leaving him but dear God, it would be something. *Oh Martin, how I miss you…*

* * *

The lobby of the hotel was inordinately crowded for a late afternoon and the two young women who stood just inside the ballroom stared as curiously as the other employees and the numerous guests who had stopped to watch Martin Vaughn step out of the glassed-in elevator.

"It oughta be a sin for a man to look that good," the young Negro woman commented.

"He looks even better in the buff."

"What did you say girl?"

Gina Daves offered a sly, knowing smile. "I took room service up to him earlier and found him still in bed. He had a sheet draped up to his waist but what I got to see was enough!"

"Was he alone?"

"Yeah, and looking rough…jeez Amy, can you imagine a man like *that* not having a woman to wake up with?"

Amy laughed. "Oh, he's got a WIFE, but they're separated."

"Oh yeah? Wish I'd known."

"Like you'd have done something about it!"

Gina smiled and shook her head. "Of course not!" Both women laughed and continued out of the ballroom in the direction of the break area.

"Hey, wait a minute," Amy demanded, turning about to face Gina. "Aren't you working nine?"

Gina shrugged. "Yeah, so?"

"The ninth floor was reserved for the members of the state chapters of the Heart Association. Martin Vaughn shouldn't have been booked in one of those rooms."

Gina's face screwed into a questioning expression. "Maybe he wasn't...maybe he spent the night with someone from that group..."

Amy's eyes lit with delight. "Do you remember the room number?" At Gina's nod, Amy prodded further: "Let's see who was booked in that room!"

Several moments later, Amy had shuffled Gina to the reservation desk where the two of them waited impatiently for Betty to check the previous evenings' reservations on the computer.

"Room 918 was reserved and paid for in advance by a Miss Ann-Elise Ryan...does the jacket you found there look like a woman's jacket?" she questioned over the rim of her glasses.

Both Amy and Gina's faces were void of any misgivings at having created the lie about having found a jacket in an abandoned room; it was worth it to learn whom Martin Vaughn had spent the night with!

"Well, no, now that I think about it, I don't believe it is a woman's..." Amy began, hoping Gina would jump in with a good reason to drop the inquiry now that they had the true information they sought.

"And you know what? It might have even been 819 instead of 918...I'm not altogether certain..."

"—we'll check with the front desk and see if anyone has asked after a lost jacket," Amy offered as she moved to step away, Gina following close on her heels.

"You haven't checked with the front desk yet? C'mon ladies, let's follow procedure around here! You should have checked with them first!" Betty shook her head after the retreating employees. "Where do we find these people...?"

CHAPTER FOUR

Monica's expression gave Annie her answer quickly enough: the DVD was rented out. "They have three copies and they're all spoken for through next Wednesday," Monica explained. "I had them put me down for Wednesday night, if you think you can wait that long."

Annie's face flushed slightly. "It really is not that important," she lied. "I just thought it would be nice to get it for the weekend is all."

Monica accepted another rational answer from her always-rational friend. Then: "You never did tell me what all went on in New York. Start from the beginning and don't leave **anything** out!"

Annie was glad her back was to Monica for there was no way she could have masked her uneasiness. Swallowing hard, Annie continued folding the laundry from the dryer and summoned every ounce of strength she could muster to refrain from relating the story in full. How she wished for someone to confide in, to tell her that she had done the right thing in leaving Martin behind.

"There really isn't a whole lot to tell," Annie began at last. "My flight to La Guardia was fine and from there I went directly to the hotel and to bed. The next morning I called you, attended a couple of seminars, took a nap, got ready for the banquet and went down to the ballroom expecting a semi-formal gathering. Surprise, surprise: all the women had on formal evening gowns and jewels just about anywhere they could stick 'em."

Monica laughed at the description knowing gaudy shows of opulence were as offensive to Annie as they were to her. "So, were there any good looking men there? Besides Vaughn, of course."

"A few, I guess. And in answer to your next question, no, I didn't make a move on any of them, mainly because they were all taken," Annie added knowingly. "Everybody had a somebody hanging on their arm."

"Except you."

"I didn't go to the banquet with anything more in mind than enjoying having our chapter recognized for its contribution to the state Heart Association. And I didn't miss not having a man with me," she lied peevishly; Monica's smile telling her she knew so. "Besides, if I *had* had someone, the way my luck runs he would have probably ended up making as big an ass of himself as Eric Nielson did. Would you believe the guy ended up drunk as a skunk, just like Rob on 'When Tomorrow Comes'!"

At Monica's open-mouthed surprise, Annie nodded. "Slurred and babbled his way through his speech and then stumbled back to his chair. It was horrible," Annie concluded, shaking her head at the memory.

"Was that before or after Vaughn spoke?" Monica asked. Her question had been innocently enough asked but just the mention of Martin's name, Annie realized, was enough to unnerve her.

"He, um…it was funny, watching the others in the room as Eric Nielson stumbled back to his seat. I really thought the evening was a bust; I mean, I half expected someone to take the podium and make excuses for him. But as it was, Martin…Vaughn, he…it was like he appeared from nowhere," Annie recalled, her face changing as she spoke to show an expressiveness Monica had not seen for a long while. Her friend smiled in anticipation, though of what, she had no idea.

"He walked to the podium and just stood there for a moment," Annie recalled almost in a whisper. "I really believe he was embarrassed for what Nielson had done, maybe even a little bit afraid that he would screw up as well. As it was, he didn't even have a prepared speech, nothing! But then, he just started talking, saying how he was honored to have been asked to speak…can you imagine? HE wanted to thank the Heart Association for thinking of HIM!" She paused thoughtfully. "I thought he was gonna start crying, Monica…when he spoke about losing his father and brother to heart disease, I nearly lost it, I really did.

"When he finished speaking, I don't think there was a person in the room that didn't hurt for him; and then I realized what he had so passionately said explained what everyone in that room felt, or else they wouldn't be involved with the Heart Association: it was as if our purpose had some full circle, ya know?"

"Aw, man…what I wouldn't give to have been a fly on the wall! Sounds like something out of a movie!" Monica teased.

"Doesn't it though?" Annie concurred, shaking her head. "I don't think the Association's entire advertising budget could match the awareness Martin alone could raise."

Monica's brows rose. "So it's Martin now, is it?"

"That **is** his name."

"So did you and *Martin* ever get to meet face to face?" Monica taunted.

"As a matter of fact, we did," Annie replied, knowing her friend would no doubt read about the impromptu receiving line in the Association's next newsletter anyway. "He very graciously allowed folks to greet him and shook nearly everyone's hands before the president of the New York chapter ushered him out of the hall. For a lot of us there, it was the highlight of the event, getting to meet a real movie star."

Was her unflappable friend's voice tinged with a bit of awe? Monica had to laugh: "And there you were, the only woman in the room who didn't know squat about him!"

Annie touched her mouth with the tips of two fingers in an attempt to hide the treat of a smile. "Aren't you gonna say 'I told you so'?" she asked at last meeting Monica's taunting expression head-on. "All right, I'll give you this one" she finished without ceremony, hefting the basket of folded laundry onto her left hip.

"Why Annie Ryan! I do believe you're star-struck!" Monica prodded after Annie's retreating form as she disappeared up the creaking stairwell and into the darkness at the top of the stairs.

* * *

Within forty-eight hours of Martin's departure from New York for London, there appeared a photograph of him on the society page of The Times. The caption read:

IN OVER HIS HEAD? 'Misbegotten' star Martin Vaughn takes in the New York City skyline aboard the Staten Island Ferry while wife Claire takes him to divorce court in London. And who, pray tell, is the lovely stranger on his arm…?

Gina Daves placed a call to the newspaper editor and received $500 for the answer.

* * *

Annie fretted with the battery-operated calculator frustrated by its failure to give her the same answer twice for the column of numbers she was attempting to figure. She knew it wasn't the batteries for she had replaced them before even starting her taxes; rubbing her eyes, she also knew her frustration was piqued by lack of sleep. And beyond a doubt, she knew *everything* she was feeling or had felt for a week now was a direct result of what had happened between her and Martin.

Propping her chin upon her knuckles, Annie flexed her fingers and intertwined them to rest flush against her mouth, stifling the yawn that threatened. Her exhaustion was evident in her stilted movements, the dark circles beneath her eyes, and the sudden harshness of her tongue. She winced and rubbed her eyes again at the memory of her grandmother's hurt expression when earlier Annie had told her that their Wednesday trip to the grocery store was off and that no, she wouldn't make a special trip out just for a bag of apples.

"All we need this week is sweet milk and a loaf of bread, and Monica said she would stop for them on her way back from the movie rental store," she had explained.

"When can we go, then? You know how much I look forward to going out on Wednesdays," Gramma asked forlornly.

"I don't know, Gramma, I'll let you know, alright?" Then, realizing the shortness of her tone, Annie had relented. "I'll stop on my way home from the hospital Friday afternoon and get you some apples, okay?" Gramma had pouted the remainder of the afternoon – was pouting still – and Annie felt horrible because of it. From the direction of the driveway, Annie heard the low purr of Monica's Volkswagen and straightened, pushing aside her tax information and calculator before going to meet Monica at the door.

Even before Monica spoke, Annie knew that something was terribly wrong. Feeling her face blanch, she swept the screen door open for the other woman to pass into the kitchen and immediately asked, "What is it, Monica? Something's up…"

"—you're damned right, something's up! Do you care to 'fess up or do *I* tell *you*?" she bellowed, hands planted squarely upon her hips.

"I don't know what you're talking about…"Annie replied, shaking her head at Monica's murderous expression.

"Well now, ain't that peculiar, that everyone knows but YOU!" At that, Monica tossed the latest edition of the 'American Star' onto the kitchen table and it unfurled to display a vivid color photograph of Martin Vaughn on it's cover...and a very radiant Annie Ryan standing at his side.

SOUTHERN BEAUTY DAZZLES MISBEGOTTEN'S MARTIN VAUGHN!

Annie's jellied legs gave away and she dropped into the chair she had been sitting in only moments before. A chill started at the top of her head and seeped through the length of her body before she was able to wrap her arms about herself to ease the quaking. Even so, her lips quivered preventing her thoughts from becoming words.

"You just gonna sit there?" Monica asked incredulously. "Open it up, Annie: there's a center spread of a half-dozen more just like the cover!"

Annie barely heard Monica for the pounding within her ears sounded like the crashing of ocean waves against a rocky cliff. Over and over again in her mind she asked herself how this could have happened: how could photographs of Martin and herself be taken without their knowledge, much less end up on the pages of one of the country's most notorious tabloids?

Slowly her mind registered Monica's words and she thumbed through a dozen or more pages to find a center spread laid out in sequenced, clockwise order: she and Martin standing by the ferry's railing; laughing into one another's faces; his arm around her shoulders; her head upon *his* shoulder; his hand whisking the hair from her face; and finally, a much closer shot than the previous ones: Martin's hand clasping her neck as they stood poised in mid-motion, lips parted and eyes closed, only a fraction of an inch away from what looked to be a very passion-filled kiss.

Slapping the pages closed again, Annie rose without speaking and ran from the kitchen, toppling her chair in flight but never slowing for an instant as her still-tremulous legs carried her from the room.

"Annie, wait!" Monica called but the only answering sound she heard was the slamming of Annie's bedroom door at the top of the stairs.

The ring of the telephone jerked Annie roughly awake and she shook her head in an effort to rid it of the cloudiness. By the third ring she was coherent enough to know that she must reach the phone immediately or risk having Gramma intercept it on the fourth ring, as was their system.

"'ello?" she asked groggily, surprised to find that it was dark outside.

"Hi Annie." It was Monica.

"Uh, hi…what time is it?"

"What time is it? It's quarter of seven…are you all right?" she asked with genuine concern. "You want me to come over?"

Annie swallowed. Her tongue felt thick and her eyes stung from crying. "No, Monica, I'm okay…I um, I fell asleep…I didn't realize it was so late. I need to go and see to Gramma…"

"—hey listen, I'm sorry about before. I had no right to come down so hard on you. I guess I was just shell-shocked; I mean, it isn't every day your best friend has a rendezvous with a hunky movie star and you have to find out about it in the tabloids," Monica taunted half-teasingly.

Annie was well chastised. "I didn't intend to tell you or anyone…what happened won't happen again so it's not like there's this 'budding romance' to keep tabs on. I'd just as soon forget it ever happened."

"Forget it? Oh Annie, what ever *happened* must mean more than you're letting on or else you wouldn't have cried yourself to sleep."

"How do…"

"I waited for an hour for you to come back down so we could talk, and when you didn't, I went up to check on you…I could hear where you'd cried until you had the 'snubs.' When I peeked into your room, I saw that you were asleep across the end of your bed, so I took Gramma into the kitchen and fixed a bit of supper for us before heading home." She paused. "I can be back in five minutes if you want."

Annie smiled into the receiver. "I really don't feel like facing anyone tonight…please understand, Monica."

There was a momentary silence. "I left the movie by the TV…I hooked up my DVD so, it's ready to go."

"What? Oh Monica, you didn't!" Annie clasped her hand over the mouthpiece and choked back a painful sub: painful because her eyes already burned like hell and she didn't think her nose could bear any more wiping. "I wish you hadn't done that…"

"I think you should watch it, Annie. You'll understand why then," Monica implored. "I don't know how far things went with the two of you but, if it went as far as I think it might've, it'll do you good to see him, even if it is on film…I honestly don't know how it *can* be over, not if he's half what he seems. Too, you'll understand why the tabloids have made such a big deal over this…this…"

"—affair."

"Oh Annie," Monica's voice was a whisper. "Oh…"

There was a long pause then as Annie swallowed again, then twice, finally finding her voice through the burning constrictiveness in her throat as the clock by the bed struck the hour of seven. "Listen, Monica…I um, I'm gonna get Gramma ready for bed now, so I have to go. I'll talk with you tomorrow maybe…"

"Alright Annie…you call me, any time of the day or night, you hear? We've meant too much to each other for too long for you to try and ride this out alone."

Annie's smile seemed to reach through the phone line. "I know, and I love you for it, Monica."

"Thank goodness tomorrow's Thursday, huh?"

"Yeah, I hadn't realized it was my day off." She couldn't have gone into the hospital looking more like one of the patients than the nurse she was supposed to be. "Thank God for small favors."

"Yeah. Well, I'll be goin' then. You get some rest tonight," Monica urged recalling the dark circles she'd noticed under Annie's eyes but had given little heed to until now.

"I will. Good-night, Monica."

"Good-night. And Annie: sweet dreams!"

"You are such a tease," Annie murmured, thankful to know she could count on Monica to help her through the next few days. "Bye."

As Annie helped her grandmother step from the shower, she caught a glimpse of her own reflection in the mirror over the basin. She looked horrid and for the very first time since her grandmother had lost her sight, Annie was thankful she could not see, for the haunted look that shrouded her face frightened even her. *How foolish to let a man drive me to this!* she screamed inside her head. I have got to get a grip on my senses; even David's leaving didn't affect me this badly and we were to have been married! Thinking of David, she wondered what his reaction would be when he learned of the story in the 'American Star.' For that matter, what would her coworkers, friends, and neighbors think? They knew her as a quiet and sensible woman who cared for her grandmother in the same old house that had been her father's birthplace.

And what would Gramma's reaction be? *What am I to do?* she pleaded inwardly, as she slipped the warn cotton robe around her grandmother's shoulders and led her into her bedroom.

*   *   *

"I called you over so that we might talk, Marty. *Do* make yourself at home," the lovely blonde woman quipped, a smug expression adding frostiness to her delicate and airy demeanor.

Martin took his time entering the beautiful townhouse. 'Make yourself at home,' she had said. *How generous since this is still my home, at least for a few weeks more*, he thought inwardly though the realization did little to appease him.

"Where's Stuart?" he asked at last when a sweeping glance of the immaculately kept foyer and living room did not reveal his son.

"Always the doting papa..." Claire taunted bemusedly. Then, "Betsy has taken him to the square for the afternoon. I felt it best we have this discussion alone."

"**You** felt it best? How dare you decide for ME what's best for our son!" Martin exploded. "Had I known you sent Stuart away, I wouldn't have come at all..."

"—precisely. Darling, I know you *so* well," Claire broke in too calmly. "You've never failed to show just what a despicable bastard you are and today, I think I'll take advantage of the opportunity to show the same to you."

"What the hell are you talking about?" Martin beseeched, his hands in the air. "I have no desire to fight with you Claire, so just spit it out!"

She laughed then, stepping behind a huge mahogany desk that took up one full corner of the living room. "Do have a seat Marty, and help yourself to a drink; I think you are going to need one."

Martin's sixth sense told him that Claire was exerting an even greater amount of haughtiness than was her norm and it set his nerves on end. "What is this all about?" he asked again, his voice lower and calmer than it had been before.

Claire settled herself comfortably into the massive leather chair, raising a brow in question. "You have no idea?" At his lack of a response she lowered her eyes to the drawer she extended above her lap and slipped one well manicured hand inside to retrieve what appeared to be a newspaper. Handing it across the width of the desk, she offered blithely, "You may keep it...I have several."

Taking the folded newspaper Claire offered Martin was immediately assailed with a hint of foreboding, his brow drawn over wary green eyes that hesitantly dropped from her gray ones to the parcel in his hand. Unfolding the paper, his eyes were immediately drawn to the lips of the woman in the photograph, as if from the photograph Annie might somehow speak to him. Dear God, how he missed her and to see her again like this...He swallowed, masking his reaction as best he could knowing that Claire sat across from him with venomous anticipation; refolding the paper, he laid it nonchalantly upon the desk. "I think the photographer got my best side," he commented offhandedly the double meaning, though not intentional, bringing forth a slew of obscenities from Claire.

"I now have what I've searched almost a year for," she began in a hiss, standing to talk down to him. "With this," she grabbed the paper and slung it into his face, "I'll see you rot in hell before you *ever* see Stuart again."

Martin picked up the paper from where it had landed in his lap; his eyes never strayed from Claire's as he stood, his height making him half a head taller than his statuesque wife. "If that's all, I think I'll show myself out," he returned evenly, deliberately nonplussed. *I won't give her the satisfaction*, he thought silently as he turned to walk back toward the foyer.

Martin had taken but a few steps before stalled by the grasp of Claire's hand where it held fast to a fistful of his hair; jerking him about painfully to face her, Claire's expression was insidious. "Don't you dare turn your back on me!" she screamed with a shrillness that wrecked his senses. "Who is she, damnit? I want to know!"

Gripping his wife's wrist, Martin offered just enough pressure that she was forced to release her hold, slinging her fist away as he turned to continue through the living room toward the foyer. Yet again however, he was besieged by his wife's anger as she thrust the full weight of her attack upon his back and shoulders, pelting and slapping him repeatedly until at last Martin reached the door and opened it to find several neighbors standing across the hall staring as if awestruck by the violent sounds that had come from behind Claire Vaughn's door. "I apologize for my wife's behavior," he murmured through clenched teeth as he turned about to pierce her furious yet embarrassed visage. "It's obvious she's not at all well."

Without bothering to brush his disheveled hair from his brow, and seemingly oblivious to the ripped and torn sleeve of his tweed jacket, Martin bid a hurried, "Excuse me, please," before turning from the unwanted audience to disappear down the richly carpeted hallway. He was never aware of his wife's damning promise to "make the limp-cocked bastard pray for death before this is over!"

Barely an hour later, Martin sat wearily at his lawyer's desk. Having been photographed to prove later the extent of his wife's violent assault, he was now being administered to by the English barrister's Irish secretary who, though well past the age of retirement, welded a spitting tongue as well as a proficiency with first aid. "'tis most horrid, sir, the abuse you received by your wife's hand," she clucked. "These scratches on your neck drew blood, they did…" At Martin's wince and whispered curse, she drew back. "I'm being gentle as is possible sir, but the alcohol, it's got to burn like blazing Hades to help ye…"

"I know, Maggie," he smiled. "Go ahead and finish…I wasn't cursing you."

"Aye, 'tis smart ya are too," she offered with a self-satisfied smirk, drawing another smile from the man.

"I'll admit Martin, this latest bit of news doesn't help our case any," Christopher Taylor murmured as his eyes scanned the center spread of the 'American Star.' "Your timing couldn't be worse or the evidence more damning."

"For crissake, Chris, do you think I tried to find this woman, or that I tried to get us photographed, or that I tried to fall in love with her?" His expression was incredulous. "I had a 48 hour visit, round trip mind you, so the last thing I expected was to meet someone like Annie."

"Annie," the lawyer's brow quirked, "how provincial."

"Her name is Ann-Elise Ryan," Martin returned, his expression black. "And I want *you* to find her."

A long moment passed. "I'm of the opinion you have quite enough, as they say, 'on your plate,'" Chris offered almost flippantly. "You cannot seriously be contemplating yet one more complication…" Maggie's hands stopped in mid motion as she paused to read Chris' intentions. He was goading Martin, testing the importance of this woman in his already complicated life. She smiled at the maneuver.

Martin's expression was pinched, unnerved. "You hire the best investigator you know, and have him or her on the next flight out of Heathrow. I want Annie found by week's end," he demanded. "Is THAT serious enough for you?"

Chris' eyes met Maggie's over Martin's head before returning to his client's green ones. He shook his head disdainfully. "Simply impossible, my friend…I can't just…"

"—what can't you do?" Martin ground out, having leaped from his chair to clasp his attorney's shirtfront at his throat. Maggie's hands went to her mouth and Chris' eyes flashed honest fear, surprised by the passionate anger that shone on Martin's face. *Perhaps my test worked too well,* he thought, swallowing back a choke before Martin finally released him.

Stepping raggedly away from his oldest friend, Martin murmured, "Forgive me, Chris," a muscle working in his temple as he turned to stare out the fourth floor window. "Dear Lord, how I miss her," he whispered, closing his eyes and pressing his forehead against the cold windowpane.

Maggie cleared away the first aid items and discreetly left the office, having been put at ease by Chris' gentle nod. Standing, the lawyer moved to place a reassuring hand upon Martin's shoulder and without a hint of sarcasm implored, "Where shall we begin looking, my friend?"

* * *

Saturday came and with it, Annie's first encounter with someone who had seen the article in the 'American Star'. Mrs. Adams greeted her at the door and ushered her in quickly asking, "Do tell me how you ever came to meet that handsome young actor, Annie-girl! Might we expect to hear wedding bells in the near future?" she prodded giddily.

Annie rolled her eyes skyward. "No, Mrs. Adams. Mr. Vaughn is a friend, nothing more."

"Oh, pooh!"

"Sorry to disappoint you." She really wasn't sorry but it seemed like a good thing to say. "I'd like to get started with your cleaning right away, so…"

"Very well," the older woman replied. "How is dear Emma this morning?" she asked as she slipped on a much heavier coat than was needed just to step next door to Annie's house.

"Gramma's fine. She asked if you would bring your size 10 crocheting needle when you come. She's misplaced hers."

"Why, of course," Mrs. Adams replied, reaching into her sewing basket for her package of various sized needles. "When I find Emma's, shall I lay it on the mantle as usual?" she asked with a wink.

"Yes, please. You know, Gramma really would be lost with out you, Mrs. Adams. There aren't a lot of people who care for her the way you always have."

"I've known Emma all my life. She's as honest as the day is long and has never been anything but good to me," the older woman replied. "Besides,

82

she's the only person 'round who'll listen to me run on about a lot of nothing without trying to shut me up!"

Annie's expression showed her surprise at the lady's candor but then she smiled, knowing the old woman spoke the truth. "Would you do me a favor and NOT mention Mr. Vaughn or that article to her? It's really something that was blown all out of proportion and I'd rather not have to try and explain it to her," she added as off-handedly as possible.

"Why of course dear, I understand."

Annie wasn't sure she really did but what could she do but take her word for it? As Mrs. Adams turned to leave, Annie called out the same parting she always did: "Give a call if you need me for anything."

And as was her usual non-reply, Mrs. Adams simply nodded once and continued out the door in the direction of Annie's house. Hearing the door click, Annie headed toward the hall closet where Mrs. Adams kept her vacuum thinking again how laughable it was that they continued this working exchange, for Mrs. Adams was a neat-nick and her home immaculate. Annie's 'cleaning' consisted of running the vacuum, dusting and occasionally moving one of the older woman's huge potted plants from indoors to outdoors and vice versa. The entire 'cleaning' took about an hour, enough time for Annie to completely turn off the outside world and just think.

She would have liked having the opportunity to study about whether or not to quit her PRN nursing position at the hospital entirely as Gramma's care in itself was becoming demanding enough without the hospital constantly pressuring her to go full-time. Instead, Annie found herself drawn back to Martin and the part he portrayed in 'The Misbegotten.' She had watched the movie twice through the night Monica rented it and, upon returning it to the rental store the next afternoon, drove to the mall in Winston-Salem to purchase her own copy of the film on video so she might have the privilege of seeing Martin-if only on film!-whenever her heart desired.

Plugging in the vacuum, Annie moved about mechanically, missing nothing and yet, seeing only Martin as Michael Maurer and thinking, *that is Martin*...he portrayed Michael as an extension of himself, how Martin might have lived and fought and loved more than 140 years ago. Seeing Martin dressed in the clothes of the Civil War period, his hair longer than it was now and intoning the slow, proper speech of a Southern gentleman had acted like an aphrodisiac, making him seem as close as her own neighbors. He had lent a sensuality to the role of Michael Maurer which would likely have been absent had any other actor she could think of been chosen for the part. She couldn't imagine Kevin Costner's blue eyes when Martin's green ones had darkened to a deep verdant shade in the height of anger. And where Jude Law's features went soft when impassioned, Martin's were fierce when stimulated to painful ecstasy.

While remembering the scene where Michael and "Alex" finally consummate their long denied love for one another, Annie shuddered at the similarities to their encounter: two lovers pushed to the brink by their passions and obstacles beyond their control, who must part too soon to follow a direction they can no more deviate from than the attraction that drew them together. And as Annie studied Martin's lovemaking in the role of Michael, she realized that he *is* the consummate actor for even though she knew the scenes were drawn from a script, he enriched them with gestures and motions that only she could know were his and not contrived to fit a storyline.

Returning the vacuum to the hall closet some minutes later, Annie quickly dusted and checked the small tabletop in the kitchen for any note Mrs. Adams might have left concerning her plants. Indeed, a note lay there, beside a copy of the 'American Star.' Martin's strong yet strangely serene face drew her again to the memory of the ferry ride and their few precious hours that had followed. She wasn't aware how tightly she gripped the top of one of the ladder-back chairs at the table until she felt the tingly sensation of a thousand tiny pin pricks and realized her knuckles were white, her fingers almost numb. Drawing the hand into a fist, Annie pressed her wrist against her brow and closed her eyes against the familiar burning just behind her eyelids. "Dear God," she prayed in a whisper, her other hand resting palm down upon the damning tabloid, "please help me to forget…"

*　*　*

"Mom and Dad said we're going to move across the Atlantic," Daniel murmured sadly.

The little girls' face showed her confusion. "Atlanta, where the Braves play? That's not so far away."

Mary Ryan smiled at her six year old. "The Atlantic Ocean, Annie…remember when we went to the Outer Banks last summer and walked on the beach? You asked where all the water came from and I explained that it was the Atlantic Ocean. Daniel is going to live in a country on the other side of the ocean."

"Why?"

"*Because his daddy's job is sending them there,*" Mary offered, a thoughtful smile touching her lips as she looked in seven-year-old Daniel's direction. "*That happens to families sometimes.*"

"*Well, I don't like it...daddy should tell them he wants to work here and just not go!*" Daniel pouted.

"*You can stay with us, Daniel...can't he Mother? Can't Daniel just stay here with us?*"

Mary smiled at her daughter's youthful rationalization. "*I'm sorry honey but Daniel has to go wherever his family goes...his mom and dad would be very sad if they had to leave him behind, and I believe Daniel would be sad without them, too.*"

"*It's just not fair! All my friends are here, Grandma and Grandpa Martin, Uncle Jeff, everybody's here! I just don't understand...*" the little boy murmured, propping his chin on the palm of his hand, a single tear getting wiped away by those fingertips. "*I won't ever see you again, Annie...dad says Englan' is too far away to drive back and forth, like when we go to Nanna Vaughn's house in Florida. We have to ride over there in a plane...I've never rode on a plane before.*"

"*Daddy does it all the time, don't he Mother?*"

"'***Doesn't he***', honey," her mother corrected. "*And yes, he does, because he works for an airline.*"

"*Tell your dad to come to work for my Daddy!*" Annie offered enthusiastically. "*That way y'all won't have to move away!*"

Mrs. Ryan's face blanched. "*I'm afraid it's not that simple, sweetie...*"

"*I already asked Dad to get a job somewhere else but he said we couldn't afford to. That's so stupid.*"

"*It's grown-up stuff, honey...you'll understand it someday, when you're older...*"

"*—I won't ever understand!*" Daniel interrupted, shaking his head as another tear threatened to fall. "*It's just stupid...*"

* * *

RING, RING! RING, RING! Shaking his head, Martin heard the sound of the telephone but silently wished it away. Rubbing his eyes he realized the dream he'd had was actually a memory he had not thought of in many years, and the clarity of it literally surprised him. Annie had changed very little from the child of 20 years ago: she was still as outspoken and beautiful as the tiny sprite that had dogged his every step from toddler to first grader. Their mothers were close from high school, and living only two houses apart meant *their* friendship was extremely close as well.

RING, RING! RING, RING!

"Yeah! Hello!"

"It's midmorning, old boy. Shouldn't you be up and about?"

Martin laid his head back upon the pillow and drew his free hand down the length if his face. "I was up most of the night reading depositions. Your handiwork, I might add, tends to be a bit longwinded." Two weeks to the day after Martin's encounter with his estranged wife, Claire's attorney had served him with the equivalent of a restraining order that forbade any contact with her or their son. Chris had assured him that the ploy was to anger him only and that visitation with Stuart would be established shortly. "I could use some good news, Chris."

"I wish I could be more forthcoming," Chris began hesitantly. "Your Miss Ryan has proven most elusive, I'm sorry to say. I've had my very best man searching this North Carolina town of Mount Airy you referred us to and he hasn't found the slightest trace of her…of course, we will continue to look, but I must ask if there isn't something more you could provide in the way of information?"

"I told you all I know…she has a grandmother that she cares for. Besides her parents, I'm certain there was no one else…she was an only child."

"That, what town she's from and her name are not a lot to go on, Martin…"

"—how many Ann-Elise Ryan's can there possibly be?!" Martin broke in, his frustration having gotten the best of him once more. "I can't believe one woman can be that difficult to find, Chris! There must be a central registry for the Heart Association…"

"—I'm afraid that information is not available to just anyone." Catching Martin's low expletive on the other end of the line, Chris smiled into the received. "But of course the information will soon be available to us. McDougall has been instructed to spare no expense."

"I never imagined that anything would ever make me a party to bribery Chris and yet, where Annie's concerned, I don't care what laws must be bent or even broken," Martin finished, his voice as raspy as a thirsty man's pleading for water, "I have to find her…"

* * *

Annie stepped from the shower and began to towel herself dry, noticing for the fifth morning in a row the tiny specks of blood on her beige bath linen. She had moved Mrs. Adams plants on Saturday morning and though she recalled the pinching feeling in her lower abdomen, she had brushed it off as muscle strain from moving the plants from indoors to outdoors for the first time this spring. The nurse in her became uneasy, though not overtly so, for her period was almost a week late and never being particularly regular anyway, she silently chided her body for being so damned unpredictable. Still she countered, if she had in fact put some undue strain on her female organs, rationality told her that an appointment with her gynecologist was in order for left unchecked, an internal strain could only become worse, often time by doing something as menial as bending to retrieve a dropped purse.

Rushing through her toilette, Annie checked her watch and saw that it was 6:00 am. It would take about 25 minutes for her to get to Baptist Hospital from her home in Germanton, leaving a few private moments to put a call in to Dr. Clark's answering service before she must clock-in at 6:45.

Half an hour later, Annie smiled to find the nurse's lounge empty and took advantage of the privacy to place her call. "How many of these things have I tossed in the last two weeks?" Annie asked herself aloud, picking up yet another copy of the infamous 'American Star' from the dining table. Offering but a glance of it as she waited for her call to go through, Annie folded the newspaper in half and then folded it again before stuffing it lengthwise into the trash bin an arm's length away. A click at the other end of the line and then a perfunctory "Dr. Clark's answering service," brought Annie's attention back to the business at hand.

"Good morning, this is Annie Ryan. I'd like to make an appointment with Dr. Clark at her earliest availability, please."

There was a short pause. "Actually…Dr Clark had a cancellation for this afternoon at 2:00. Would you like to take that appointment?"

"Yes, that would be perfect!" Annie returned decisively, offering her number there at work in the event Dr. Clark needed to contact her. "Thank you for penciling me in," she finished, returning the receiver to its vertical cradle upon the wall. She was relieved that she hadn't had to enlist the backup tactic of 'I may have an emergency' in order to see the doctor because she didn't really feel that her situation required an emergency appointment; then again, she hadn't wanted to delay treatment for the strain, whatever the form and location, for the usual month's wait it took to get an appointment with her doctor, either. Smiling, she turned and headed toward the nurse's station, swiping her ID badge in the time clock as she passed it in the hall.

As she stepped to within a few feet of the nurse's station, Annie's eyes rolled heavenward at the performance Dr. Barry Roberts was giving the fourth floor staff—and at such an early hour! Though still in his residency, the man had inspired quite a following with the nurses and clerks. That he was married seemed inconsequential; indeed, his reputation with women almost overshadowed his very promising future in obstetrics. As much as Annie had enjoyed working with the nursery staff, she transferred to the children's wing two months earlier because of the doctor's less than honorable intentions. Their history made his appearance on the floor today all the more aggravating for her.

Stepping up to and just behind one end of the huge crescent shaped desk, Annie smiled a 'Hello' to the middle-aged Charge Nurse who was said to run the tightest floor in the hospital. Nurse Bennett in turn gave an almost indiscernible nod of her head, obviously not pleased with Dr. Roberts' presence at her station. "We got in two new patients late last night," Nurse Bennett indicated on her clipboard as she passed it literally to Annie. "Two brothers who were injured in an auto accident off of Highway 66 North—isn't that up in your area?"

Annie read the quickly scrawled message on the yellow sticky-note where it was attached to the top of the clipboard:

Caught Romeo in Rolodex—

Think he copied your phone #

The two nurses exchanged knowing nods before Annie removed the sticky note and balled it into an angry fist. "Highway 66 North? Yeah, that's *very* near where I live. I don't recognize their names, though," Annie answered at last, somewhat taken aback by the meddling of the doctor. Her eyes continued scanning the patient roster a moment longer before handing the clipboard back to the Charge Nurse.

"Well, good-morning Annie! You look especially bright-eyed today," Dr. Roberts beamed as he stepped to block Annie's passage from the nurse's station.

Annie stopped dead in her tracks to avoid a collision with him, her expression offering little more than irritation. "Get real," was all she said before stepping around him in an effort to continue toward the night shift's nurse to get report on the patients on her hall.

"I would think a flesh and blood man a great deal more 'real' than some actor in a tabloid."

Annie drew to a halt in mid stride, her back stiffening with rage at the underhanded remark. It had taken two weeks for someone to attach a taunting comment to the seemingly unending availability of the 'American Star' on her floor and though she had thought to prepare herself for the inevitability, she could think of no better retort than to physically strangle the arrogant bastard where he stood! The doctor appeared quite pleased with himself, as well he should have, for not only had he finally garnered Annie's undivided attention, but that of every nurse and ward clerk at the station as well. *I can either put an end to it here and now, or expect more of the same from someone else,* Annie thought when at last it came to her what she should do.

"You are sadly mistaken, Doctor. I shudder at the thought of YOUR touch...you so sicken me that I fear I may vomit upon your feet," she replied in a clear, succinct voice. "You have a loving, trusting wife at home who would no doubt welcome your advances: wouldn't Karen be devastated to learn what a randy bastard you are away from home?"

"You don't mean to threaten me?" the doctor whispered incredulously.

Annie glanced beyond the man to share the amused expressions of her coworkers who stood some distance away before looking the doctor square in the eye. "Of course not...I'll simply report you to the Ethics Board if you so much as speak to me in such a manner again." Instantly, every head turned back to the work at hand, except that is, for Nurse Bennett who simply offered Annie a wink.

Though his handsome face now showed a scowl that promised certain retribution, Dr. Roberts simply mumbled several choice words before stomping past Annie. Shaking her head, she started once again in the direction of the night shift nurse who still waited to give report, her own smile greeting Annie as she sat down.

Lawrence McDougall was a persistent man who had made his name in the private investigation business by being thorough to a fault. He took great pains to insure his clients' satisfaction and regarded very few things as being outside the law. He had never restricted himself with a code of ethics nor were his moral standards etched in stone; in short, he got things done and was paid well for his efforts.

Sitting back now against propped pillows upon the twin bed in his hotel room, McDougall smiled a satisfied smile at having eliminated 99% of the Heart Association's master list of its North Carolina membership. He shook his head when recalling how difficult the numerous stages of his search had been and fervently wished he had somehow been able to bypass the telephone query route altogether, for it had proven downright maddening. But when one is tapping all available resources, one must be patient and expect to be tripped up from time to time.

Ann-Elise "Annie" Ryan had all but sent him sprawling face first!

McDougall had been surprised to learn what a great expanse of area the 'Triad' region of North Carolina encompassed. There had been the towns and communities that made up the suburbs of the larger cities, the townships and districts that made up the communities, and the intersections and junctions that made up the townships and districts! Each area had differing yet distinct vocal majorities while **all** the population held one distinct notion: bribery money is mute in the small towns and communities of the South. And that was an ideal McDougall found himself dumbfounded by. He was livid at having used up nearly two weeks of time between his luckless searches for Annie in Mount Airy and trying to simply obtain the Heart Association's master list. It had been difficult, at best, to ingratiate himself into the earnest, conscientious communities; and when those communities are Southern and you speak in clipped Irish tones, the folks think your accent is cool but will still ask, "Who's your family?" and you better have one close by or a damned good excuse!

He shouldn't have been surprised then to learn that Germanton lay on the Stokes and Forsyth County line, yet one more hindrance. Too, the place was considered a town though there was once a railway that ran the length of the community, an obvious indication to him that it was more a junction or intersection. What he found most frustrating however, was there was no phone number with the address given for this Annie Ryan: only a post office box number in Germanton and nothing more. McDougall had considered planting himself in the post office lobby after the postmaster refused to give him the street address for this Miss Ryan, but the lobby was very small and he had the good sense to realize a stranger in such a small community would stick out like a sore thumb. That's when he had tried the telephone directory approach, smiling to himself when he found the Germanton numbers so few that they were listed within a section that was barely a sixteenth of an inch thick and which contained three other towns as well! Sensing that his too-long search was drawing to its overdue close, McDougall had skimmed the listing of "R's" and smiled at the last listing: Ryan, Mrs. A.

Dialing the number, McDougall wondered yet again what emergency or scandal could have possibly led an English barrister, London's best in fact!, to search for some elusive American woman in a tiny town in North Carolina. Finally on the forth ring, his call was received.

"Hello?"

"Ah, yes...might I speak with a Mrs. Annie Ryan?"

There was a pause on the other end of the line. "There's no one here by that name," came the haughty, elderly reply.

"No one there...perhaps you misunderstood..."

"—I can hear very well, thank you. Are you a telemarketer solicitin' for somethin', 'cause if you are, I don't want any!"

McDougall was taken aback, but only momentarily. "I most certainly am not! Is this Mrs. A. Ryan's residence, madam?"

"Yes it is...Mrs. Albert Ryan. Just who is it you want to speak to young man?"

McDougall frowned. "Is there an Ann-Elise Ryan there, perhaps?"

The voice on the other end of the line sounded exasperated. "There ain't no one here goes by that name!" With a click, the line went dead. The private investigator sighed and replaced the telephone receiver to its cradle. "I think I need a drink," he announced to no one as he threw on a jacket and stomped from his hotel room.

Laughingly, Annie hugged her grandmother and received a reassuring pat on the back. "You were perfect, Gramma! 'Doctor Love' will have better sense than to ever try calling me again! That's what he gets for snooping through the nurses' Rolodex: Emma Ryan!"

Emma smiled at her granddaughter's lilting laughter. "He had a foreign-soundin' voice, just like you said—sounded like he asked for Mrs. Annie Ryan when I first heard him speak, but then it was hard to understand him to begin with."

"He's from up North somewhere, Gramma, and he talks real fast anyway. I'm just **so** glad I didn't have to talk to him at all, because you handled him perfectly!"

"Well, it's like I always said: men ain't got but one thing on their minds! Remember that, Annie...that and whose granddaughter you are!"

"I'm not likely to forget that anytime soon, Gramma," Annie replied, bending to place a kiss on the elderly woman's soft cheek. "I love you very much!"

"I know you do darlin," Emma replied as she turned toward the living room, feeling her way to the sofa where she sat down to listen to the evening news. Within 10 minutes and as if on cue, she had fallen asleep, her peaceful snores filling the house to make Annie smile.

CHAPTER FIVE

Giving the macaroni and cheese a final stir, Annie smiled again at her grandmother's handling of Dr. Roberts over the telephone some thirty minutes earlier. Gramma's opinion of men was already well known to her, so when she had explained about the arrogant doctor's helping himself to her phone number by snooping in the nurse's station Rolodex, well, Gramma had needed little coaxing to put him in his place.

"Gramma, supper's ready," Annie called several minutes later as she stood on tiptoe to reach a serving bowl for the macaroni and cheese. No sooner had her arm reached upward than she felt a cutting spasm in her lower abdomen that was so severe, she immediately dropped both palms flat upon the countertop, gasping and squeezing her eyes shut against a pain that seemingly ripped through her entire body. Backing herself against a nearby chair, Annie grasped her abdomen with her right hand, the other gripping the edge of the table for support.

At that moment, Monica tapped upon the kitchen door and stuck her head just inside, a musical "Hello! Anybody home?" dying on her lips when her eyes lit upon Annie's grimacing face. "What the…"

"—Monica!" Annie broke in breathless, her head shaking at her friend's worried expression. "Come in and join Gramma and me for supper," she added, darting a glance at her grandmother as the elderly woman slowly felt her way to her chair at the head of the table. Slowly, Annie eased herself back against the chair and expelled a slow, easy breath; Monica's hands perched upon her knees where she now knelt on the floor at Annie's side. Understanding the near-frantic expression on her friend's face, Annie mouthed, "I'm OK," smiling timidly before Monica would believe her.

"I really didn't come to eat," Monica offered as she settled herself into the chair across from Annie, uncertainty still etched across her face.

"But we're having your favorite: macaroni and cheese. I was just about to get a serving bowl when you came in," Annie supplied with a nod toward the cabinet behind her. "Would you mind getting one while I fix Gramma's plate?"

"Oh...sure," Monica replied, standing to place a hand on Annie's shoulder as she mouthed, "I'll get Gramma's plate, too." Her expression forbade anything more than a nod from Annie.

"The weather-boy says it oughta be clear the rest of the weak. I hope it is so we can get in the garden; Annie's got some bulbs that need to go in the ground," Gramma commented several minutes later as she slipped her spoon into the small bowl nearest her hands. "Lord, if you don't make the best macaroni and cheese, Annie-girl!"

"She does that," Monica agreed unconsciously, her plate still empty. "Any chance I could talk you into letting me borrow her for a couple of hours tonight, Gramma?"

Annie's mouth silently asked, "Why?" and she was answered with Monica's "one minute" sign with her raised index finger.

"I don't see why not, Monica," the older woman replied as she took a sip of her sweet iced tea. "I reckon it's up to Annie anyway 'cause I'll be goin' to bed here in about a hour."

"I'll call over to Mrs. Adams' then and have her keep an eye out this way. We should be back by 10:00," Monica finished, still refusing to offer Annie any idea as to what she had planned for them.

Half an hour later the two women were getting into Monica's Volkswagen, Annie still unenlightened as to her plans for the evening. "Are you gonna tell me what's up or do I have to play 20 Questions?"

"I could ask the same thing of you," Monica returned as she eased the car out of the driveway and headed in the direction of Winston-Salem. "What happened to you before, and no hedging, alright?"

Annie looked insulted. "I don't have any reason to hedge. I strained myself Saturday when I moved Mrs. Adams' potted plants outside. Dr. Clark examined me and said it was probably a simple muscle strain and nothing more."

"I'm glad you had the good sense to make an appointment with her. Did she prescribe anything for the spasms?"

Annie shook her head no. "She wanted to get the results on some tests first."

"What kind of tests?" Monica's voice was obviously full of concern.

"Blood tests—a complete profile, three vials worth," Annie replied as she rubbed the bruise in the crook of her arm where the nurse at the lab had drawn the blood. "Dr. Clark had pricked my finger before the exam and found my hemoglobin low, so she ordered up the works to find out why."

"Did you bother to tell her you're running yourself ragged and not getting near enough sleep?" Monica chastised. "You've been pale as a ghost ever since you got back from New York."

Annie turned her head to stare out the passenger door window. "She had seen the article in 'American Star' the same as everyone else; it wasn't hard for her to put two and two together..."

"I guess not."

"And I'm not a ghost! I'm just a little strung out is all," she defended at last, anxious to change the subject. "You never did say where we're going, by the way."

There was a long pause. "It's a surprise," Monica finally offered as she turned onto University Parkway.

Another long pause. "Tell me, Monica."

"If I tell you before we get there, you'll probably have me turn around and take you home," she replied matter-of-factly.

Annie almost laughed. "That makes me feel a *whole* lot better...you know I hate surprises Monica, so tell me."

It was another moment or two before Monica turned her car into the parking lot of a shopping center, pausing beneath the marquee of the twin theatre to put the engine in neutral and pull up the handbrake. The Volkswagen purred softly as the two women faced one another. Monica's head nodded over her left shoulder. "Have you ever heard of the film 'Benevolent Afternoon'?"

Annie's expression was amused. "Hardly...I'm sure I would never forget a title like that! What's it about?"

"It's a rather old movie, an English adaptation of an American novel set during the early stages of World War II. From what I understand, it was filmed about seven years ago and released only in Great Britain, though it put in an appearance at Cannes as well; got pretty high praise for Best New Director or Producer or something like that."

"So...why is it showing up again now?"

"Most of the magazines boast it as being the film debut by Britain's latest sex symbol," Monica shrugged, "though the American entertainment community claims first dibs 'cause he was born on this side of the Atlantic."

Annie gave her friend a knowing look. "Who are we talking about here, Monica?" The other woman couldn't mask the glint in her eye and seeing it, Annie felt the blood rush from her face. "Martin…" The name came out in an exasperated whisper. "Let me guess: it's a low budget masterpiece that ranks somewhere between 'Texas Chainsaw Massacre' and 'Rambo,' right? No thank you."

"Actually, it **was** low budget, but the comparisons have been more toward 'American Graffiti,' thank God." Monica's face lit with excitement. "The catch all is who his co-star is, Annie—I'll give you one guess."

"I don't want to guess, and I don't want to see this movie," she replied emphatically. "You were right when you said I'd want you to turn around…"

"—but we're here! Aren't you the least bit curious about the movie that introduced Martin to the world?"

"It introduced him to Great Britain and a few souls at Cannes. The fact it took seven years for it to come to the States tells me all I need to know!"

"He and Claire Morgan met during the filming of this movie and married before it was even completed. Two co-stars coming together for a lifetime commitment!—aren't you the least bit curious?" Monica asked incredulously.

Annie's frustration was palpable. "The last thing I need, Monica, is to see Martin and his wife, bigger than life and blissfully happy…"

"—aw Annie, I didn't mean for you to take it like that!" Monica shook her head. "The marriage went sour almost immediately: they've been separated and reconciled more times than I can recall! It's just that this movie was made when Martin was only twenty-one…and his co-star and future wife was thirty-three!"

Annie's mouth fell open in disbelief.

"They called her a 'cradle-robber'…wouldn't you love to see Martin when he was just a 'baby'?"

Annie had to smile at Monica's method of persuasion. "You are bad."

"Hey! If he divorces her, then the punishment suits the crime!" Monica offered smilingly, letting the handbrake down and shifting into first gear, moving the Volkswagen into a nearby parking space. "I'll even pay your way in!"

Annie threw up her hands in mock surrender. "Alright! I'm game if you're paying…" *So why do I feel this isn't a good idea?* She asked herself silently, opening the door of the car to Monica's lilting laughter.

*   *   *

Martin and his attorney were not only exhausted but deeply troubled as well, for in addition to visitation of his son bring denied Martin, Chris was unable to give him any positive news from his private investigator, Lawrence McDougall, who was entering his third week in the States.

"When did you last hear from him?" Martin asked as he sipped his steaming coffee, the lateness of the nighttime hour having become almost routine for him since initiating the divorce action against Claire.

Chris's expression was forlorn, his own disappointment at the judge's decision making him feel as if he had let his dearest friend down. Despite knowing he had done everything legally possible to ensure Martin's right to visitation, it didn't make facing his friend any easier. "McDougall called day before yesterday to tell me he had finally gotten the Heart Association's master list—I expect to hear from him before the day's out…Eastern Standard Time," he added, casting a half-smile in Martin's direction, shaking his head at how anyone could drink that bitter black broth, coffee.

Martin looked at his watch. "It's almost ten o'clock in North Carolina," he offered offhandedly thinking that Annie was probably getting ready for bed; it was all he could do to keep his mind from wandering further.

"Shall I call McDougall, then?" Chris offered, noting how Martin's expression suddenly seemed a thousand miles away.

Martin nodded. "Please. I'd rather know than not before I have to go back to my apartment tonight."

Several minutes later, Chris nodded to Martin that the trans-Atlantic call had finally gone through and that the hotel's desk manager was ringing McDougall's room.

"McDougall here."

"Good-evening, McDougall," Chris began in his sternest voice. "I had thought to hear from you before now."

"I've only just returned to my room, sir. I had need of a drink, I did, for there has been very little to go right this day," he replied.

Chris shook his head disdainfully. "Did you or did you not obtain the telephone number for Miss Ryan?"

There was a momentary pause. "I found a number, Mr. Taylor, but the woman who answered denied that Ann-Elise Ryan could be reached there."

Chris's eyes flicked in Martin's direction: "Was this an elderly woman you spoke with, McDougall?" Immediately, Martin set down his cup of coffee and moved to stand nearer the telephone.

"'Aye, sir, and a feisty one! Asked if I was soliciting..."

"—give me that number, McDougall."

"Of course I will sir, though I doubt you'll fare any better. The woman was most unaccommodating," he commented as he passed along the number Chris had requested.

"Remain in your room the remainder of this evening, McDougall; I will be in contact again shortly," Chris instructed as he hung up the phone, turning to Martin as he did so.

"You have Annie's number?" he asked without preamble.

"I have **a** number, Martin. It is a listing for Mrs. Albert Ryan, and according to McDougall, the woman who answered claimed that your Ann-Elise could not be reached there."

"I'd like to try it for myself..."

"Of course, my friend...I think I'll step out for a spot of tea," he offered, looking in the direction of Martin's coffee cup. "Shall I get you a cup as well?"

Martin smiled at Chris but shook his head no. "I like my coffee."

Chris' smirk showed that he found the statement doubtful, at best. "You were born a Yank; what other excuse is there?"

Annie closed the kitchen door as quietly as possible; from the virtual darkness of the house, she imagined her grandmother had indeed gone to bed a good while ago. She closed her eyes and welcomed the feeling of blessed relief at not having to detail the evening; it would have been too much to ask of her this night.

Stepping through the darkened kitchen, Annie paused in the lamplight of the parlor to pull a tissue from the box on the desk by Gramma's chair. *How could there be any tears left in me to cry?* she asked herself, swiping at the wetness that hung on the ends of her eyelashes. Stepping into the hallway, she paused to look into her grandmother's bedroom; finding her sleeping soundly and snoring loudly, Annie drew the door closed so her alarm clock wouldn't wake the woman in the morning and stepped toward the kitchen once again for her nightly glass of juice before turning in herself.

Annie had barely swallowed the last of her drink before the ring of the telephone jarred her so badly, the small juice glass slipped from her fingers to land with a dull thud upon the maple table. Within a second of the offensive sound, Annie was to her feet and reaching for the receiver, lifting it from the cradle before a second ring could be delivered in full. "Hello?" she whispered almost frantically, listening with her other ear to hear of her grandmother had been awakened. After a couple of seconds, she turned her full attention back to the phone, having heard nothing from the direction of Gramma's room or a reply from the telephone receiver. "Hello?" she asked again, somewhat louder this time. "Is anyone there?"

"Hello Annie," came the voice she thought to never hear speak her name again. "Please don't hang up on me."

Slowly, shakily Annie let her body ease down the length of the wall that held the kitchen phone, coming to rest at last in a squatted position, her knees drawn tight against her chest. She gripped the receiver with both hands, so weak was she from the shock of hearing Martin's voice; closing her eyes, she saw his face in her memory and inwardly she smiled. "I won't hang up Martin...but...but how did you find me?"

"You didn't make it easy for me...I've been trying to find you for weeks now, ever since the morning you left...I can't understand, Annie, why..."

"I don't know what more to say," she murmured. "You read my letter..."

Across the width of an ocean, Martin shook his head incredulously; a letter alone could not explain away what the two of them had known. "Your few well-chosen words can't undo what we shared—you may wish to simply forget you ever met me, to forget it all! But I don't want to forget any of it, because what we had was too good...I think it's worth fighting for, if you'll let me..."

Annie could still see Martin's face behind closed eyes, could still feel the texture of his hair and the tilt of his lips...she could smell the scent of his hand pressed against her own lips when she'd kissed his wrist and suckled one fingertip. *Remember, remember*...she shuddered at the memory of how he had so thoroughly loved her...how would she bear living the rest of her life knowing that no other man could fill her so completely? The tears welled in her eyes once again. "You have a wife, Martin, and a life completely different from anything I've ever known; it wouldn't work, I would never fit in..."

"Claire and I have been separated for almost two years, I filed for divorce seven months ago!" he broke in angrily. "As for you not fitting in," there was a long silence, "other than my son, you're the only thing I've ever known that was completely right in my life. I swear I will fight as hard to have you again as I've fought to keep him!"

Annie was crying in earnest now, torn by her love for a man who wanted a life with her as desperately as she with him, and her promise to love and care for the woman who had loved her as her own, and whose dependence on her was absolute. "I can't be with you now, Martin...maybe not ever," she whispered through such sobs of anguish that her soul felt as if it were being torn from her body. "If it were somehow possible, I swear by all I hold dear that I would come to you now—I would have never left you..."

"Then let me come to you! There is nothing, NOTHING!, that can't be overcome if you'll only allow me the chance to try! Please...Annie, tell me yes and I'll be on the next plane out of London, tonight by God! All you have to do is say the word, one word..." his voice was a murmured plea.

Annie's silence was in itself her answer, dragging endlessly through the thousands of miles of telephone lines and cables just as surely as her future without Martin laid endlessly, desolately before her for perhaps the rest of her life. "Oh, Martin..." she screamed into her fist at her lips, the receiver of the telephone pressed against her chest now, "I love..." and she cried completely, hurtfully, hopelessly then until Martin could listen no more. Feeling Chris' hand upon his shoulder, he surrendered the receiver to his friend and buried his head in his hands, crying huge, racking sobs for a loss he had not known since the death of his father some ten years before. Chris put the receiver to his own ear and heard a woman's deep, pitiful sobs, as mournful as those which shook the man who sat at his side. Returning the receiver to it's cradle, Chris moved to leave Martin the privacy of the office, swallowing back the words that burned to pass his lips: *What fools you both are to destroy one another this way...*

*   *   *

Annie sat in the examination room as she waited for Dr. Clark's return, having gotten dressed again as the doctor instructed. Propping her elbow on the countertop beside her chair, she rested her forehead on the knuckles of her right hand, exhaustion from the previous evening's ordeal coupled with the doctor's request to see her again the next afternoon having all but worn her completely down.

Dr. Clark paused in the doorway and stared at the young woman who had been her patient since age 14. For just a moment, Annie had let her guard down and the physician was allowed a glimpse of how physically and emotionally distraught she truly was. Now that there was no doubt regarding her patient's condition, she had the unenviable duty of making Annie aware of all the possible options. She felt a certain dread in the discussion that lay ahead, for she knew without a doubt the decision Annie would make would have to be what the woman felt would be best for everyone else; she always put herself last.

"Annie?" the doctor asked smilingly as she tapped lightly on the door and stepped into the room. "Haven't caught you napping, have I?"

Sitting upright in her chair, Annie offered the usual bright smile and shook her head slightly. "It's been a long morning that looks to become a longer afternoon...I could tell from your expression during the examination that something is wrong. All I ask is that, if there's any way I can avoid being hospitalized, give me a muscle relaxer and a regimen of exercises to follow and I'll be the perfect patient until this...this strain has healed itself."

Dr. Clark smiled. "You'll be relived to know that I don't foresee the necessity of hospitalization at this point, Annie..."

"—thank God!" she broke in as she allowed her head to relax against the wall behind her. "I don't know what I'd do with Gramma, Dr. Clark. I couldn't afford a full-time nurse for her."

"Perhaps you should consider finding an affordable nursing home that more fits your budget; I understand the difficulty of caring for someone who is practically an invalid because I've done the same thing myself."

Sitting forward in her chair again, Annie met the doctor's eyes and followed them as she moved to sit down across from her patient. "Then you understand why I can't do it; she's all the family I have...we've sacrificed a lot to be able to stay together."

Dr. Clark became thoughtful for she was certain the sacrifice had been entirely Annie's. "You may have no choice...for you to continue caring for an adult who is as helpless as a child..."

"—I can handle it!" Annie defended heatedly.

"But can you handle it and carry a child of your own to term?"

Annie's face lost all expression, all color as she sat back fully in her chair again, holding the doctor's eyes with a silent plea she had somehow heard wrong; she was afraid to ask outright.

"You are pregnant, Annie. You're going to have a real child to care for in less than eight months," Dr. Clark offered gently, reaching across the counter to clasp Annie's hands in a show of support and reassurance. "I take it you had no idea..."

"N-no...none," she whispered. Annie's body trembled and she held to the doctor's hands with all her might, needing the physical link to reality when all her words had seemed like part of a dream.

"You realize that you're late..."

"—you of all people know I've never been regular...but I never for a moment imagined that...that I..."

"—you're only a few weeks along," the doctor offered, tipping Annie's face upward with a finger under her chin. "And if I know you, I have no doubt you're certain who the father is. I think you could even tell me the exact date..."

Annie closed her eyes tightly and fought back the crazy urge to laugh. "It was the first day of spring...it snowed on the first day of spring..." she murmured, shaking her head sardonically. Straining then to focus through the blur of unshed tears, Annie held fast to her doctor's steadying stare. "There has been no one since David..." she murmured, barely able to recall the face of her fiancé now four years after their breakup. "Martin was just there, and so kind...and I was so lonely..."

Dr. Clark drew Annie closer, bringing her palms together to form praying hands. "It's alright, Annie. You're not a bad person for needing someone...we all do at one time or another. You're 26 years old, and you've given the last four years of your life entirely to your grandmother...isn't it time to give something back to Annie, now?"

Annie stared at her hands, shaking her head uncertainly: she was unable to hold a coherent thought. "I don't know what I'm supposed to do..." she murmured as if to herself. "I just don't know..."

"—no one is asking you to make any decisions right now," Dr. Clark broke in, realizing that the young woman was very emotionally distraught as well as physically exhausted. "Go home and take a few days off from the hospital so that you can get yourself together. The cramping that brought you here to begin with is not going to be helped any by the stress you're under..."

"—the bleeding—!"

"—you've had very minimal spotting, Annie; I'm not so concerned with the spotting as I am this emotional and physical stress you're continually putting yourself under. Some spotting in the first weeks occurs with some women; given your history of irregular cycles, it doesn't surprise me. Don't let it scare you, but also don't ignore it if it worsens or becomes heavier. I expect the spotting to end completely in a week or so," she offered with a smile. "Until then, no more worrying, no more crying," she wiped a tear from

Annie's cheek, "and absolutely no lifting or straining. Give your body a chance to accept the change it's going through; give your mind the same courtesy!" she finished giving Annie's hands a final squeeze.

Taking a tissue from her purse, Annie wiped the wetness from her face and offered her doctor an expression as steadfast as her words. "I want this baby, doctor…I swear I'll follow your instructions to the letter," she promised, her free hand going unconsciously to her stomach.

Doctor Clark smiled. "I'm relieved, and glad, that you want this baby— I'll admit, I fully expected…" The doctor's pause was brief but telling. "Never mind what I may have thought; you're the most caring person I know, Annie Ryan…I can't imagine anyone who would make a better mother."

I'm going to have Martin's child, she thought to herself, the sense of pride and awe humbling her. "For whatever reason, God's grace has given me a gift," she replied as she stood to leave the room. "I'll do whatever I have to do to keep it."

*   *   *

"You are what?!"

Reaching up to grab a length of Monica's sleeve, Annie tugged upon it as she motioned for her to sit back down, glancing around the restaurant disconcertedly as heads turned and stared in their direction. "I'm trying to have a *private* conversation," Annie whispered, her expression exasperated.

"Well, you can't honestly expect me to take that kind of news sitting down!" Monica defended, her face flushed with excitement.

"I did."

Monica shook her head in disbelief. "I would have fainted dead away."

"Had I not been sitting, I probably would have," Annie reasoned, a small hint of a smile pulling at the corners of her lips. "Can you be happy for me?"

"Then you ARE going to keep it?"

Pursed lips replaced Annie's smile. "Of course I'm going to keep it! This baby is a part of Martin—the *best* part of him, the best of **both** of us…everything that was good and right that weekend!"

"Okay! Hey, I couldn't be happier! It's just not what I'd have expected: you doing something for yourself, for once."

Annie's eyes peered out from behind her hands where her fingers massaged her temples. "You don't understand…I would have never left him in that hotel room if I'd had any other choice. Fact is I didn't…I still don't."

Monica's brows rose in that way Annie always recognized as a silent condemnation.

"What?" she asked, palms heavenward. "Spit it out, Monica."

She needed no further prompting. "Don't you think Martin deserves to be told that he's going to be a father?"

Annie shook her head. "It wouldn't change anything."

"For crissake, Annie…"

"—I wouldn't even know how to contact him!"

"You give me 24 hours—!"

"—no, Monica."

"Why not? You have a chance to finally be happy, and you're letting it slip through your fingers! The man should be told…"

"—I'm not gonna argue with you about this."

Monica obliged with pinching silence and the two women sat staring across from one another for several long moments before Annie finally spoke again. "I've given the hospital my notice…Dr. Clark said to take some time off but they didn't want to accommodate me. So, at the end of the month…"

"—you're gonna let the sick days you've saved up carry you out this schedule?" At Annie's nod, Monica smiled. "I'd have given anything to see Hobart's face!"

"He wasn't at all happy…said it looked to him like I stayed on part-time just long enough to make it to New York and back…"

"—the bastard. We all know he thought he should have been chosen to go instead of you…I'll bet he's had it out for you since they transferred him to personnel," Monica replied. "Wouldn't you love to hear him try to explain his reasoning for *not* granting you time off?"

"He doesn't have a legitimate reason."

"Precisely," her friend returned smugly.

Annie shook her head fretfully. "I wouldn't have ended things that way had Hobart not forced my hand; I told Dr. Clark I'd do everything she said to do and I intend to. If he'd granted my request for medical leave…"

"—it may be a blessing in disguise that he didn't," Monica interrupted. "Look, you have the insurance settlement from the airline to fall back on…it may not be a king's ransom, but you and Gramma could live comfortably for several years off that money."

Annie covered her face with her hands. "You know how I feel about that blood money—!"

"—I know, and I agree: there's no amount of money that could ever make up for losing your parents," she offered, a plaintive tone in her voice. "But don't you think if they were here, that they'd tell you to use that money to care for Gramma...and their grandchild?"

Annie's hands dropped from her face and she shook her head at Monica's words. "Please don't say any more..."

Nodding, Monica complied, reaching across the table to give Annie's hand a reassuring squeeze before turning back to her long forgotten supper: a tossed salad with a Diet Coke chaser. "Ahhh...who needs this rabbit food?" she grumbled, pushing the plate away to the farthest corner of the table. "I want strawberry pie a la mode," she announced to no one, her eyes searching the room for their waitress.

Annie's mouth dropped at her friend's flagrant injury to her diet.

"Hey," Monica offered a few minutes later as the waitress sat the luscious dessert before her on the table, "I hear fat is in this summer, for one of us anyway," she teased, "so why not the other?" Annie laughed heartily then for the very first time in weeks.

As Doctor Clark had assumed it would, Annie's spotting ceased completely within a week of her examination; and once instructed to refrain from any further heavy lifting, the cramping in her lower abdomen stopped as well making both women comfortably certain Annie had indeed suffered a simple muscle strain. She had been away from the hospital a week when she went by the break room to retrieve her few personal items from her locker. Not surprisingly, everyone on her hall was aware of her resignation and genuinely sorry to see her go. Nurse Bennett met her at the nurse's station. "I understand you're leaving us for good, Annie," the older woman offered.

"I think so," she replied evenly. "I'd hoped to someday go full-time with this staff but right now, my family must be my priority."

Nurse Bennett smiled. "You'll get no argument from me. We are all sorry to see you go, of course."

"I appreciate that..." Annie smiled. "There's a couple of patients I want to say good-bye to and then I guess I'll be on my way."

"William was asking for you just this morning."

"I suppose he thinks I've forgotten him...there was a Nolan Ryan card he wanted me to look for at the baseball card shop, and I told him I would."

Nurse Bennett shook her head and laughed. "I think I'll miss your rapport with the baseball card fanatics more than anything. I've seen you do more good with one card than a week's worth of medication."

"Hey, I've made some great swaps with my patients!" Annie emphasized smilingly. "They know my collection is as important to me as theirs is to them, and they identify with that. Every single one of them has tried to trade up for my Alex Rodriguez rookie card at one time or another."

"Whatever started you collecting?"

Annie's expression became pensive. "My dad had always wanted a son so, when he got a daughter, he indulged himself just a little by making me into a baseball nut, too…he *had* to have someone to go to Braves games with," she reasoned smilingly.

"William will be sad to learn you're leaving…you knew, of course, that there was a possibility he might be transferred to St. Jude?"

"Yeah…but I'd hoped the doctors would decide that wasn't necessary," Annie offered hopefully.

"Unfortunately his latest round of tests showed the lymphoma is growing."

"Dear Lord, no…" Annie whispered.

The older woman placed a comforting hand on Annie's shoulder. "I think it would do him a lot of good to see you," Nurse Bennett volunteered. "Sometimes a child needs to be reminded that they're a kid first, and a patient only because of a bad set of circumstances…if you've got that card with you, that little boy sure could use a reason to smile."

Several minutes later, Annie sat in a chair at William's bedside, smiling at the eight year olds' obvious delight at having been given the Nolan Ryan baseball card Annie had promised him.

"Is he really your third cousin?"

Annie laughed. "Nooo…my dad just told me that to get me started collecting. It's just a coincidence that we have the same last name!"

"The picture's even better than you said it was!"

"I dunno…I like the posed shots better than the action ones," she countered, tipping the card sideways so she might glance at it again.

"You would, you're a girl…girls always like the pictures that show 'em smiling and stuff."

"Hey, wait a minute: Bo Jackson's with him losing his ball cap diving after the ball is HIS best," she offered evenly.

"What about the black and white one of him in his football uniform where he's got the baseball bat across his shoulders? That's the best Bo!"

"Think so? Well, it's a posed shot."

William smirked and then smiled at Annie's ribbing. "Oh yeah..."

Annie laughed and mussed the tiny boy's auburn hair. "I have to get home, sweetie. My grandmother will think I've left the country, I've been gone so long!"

"Aw, man...will you come by again before they send me to St. Jude?" he asked, closing the baseball card album clumsily, his right arm in a cast and suspended in a sling.

Annie took the album and straightened the pages with infinite care. "Actually, this is my last day here...I'm leaving the hospital to spend more time at home with my grandmother."

"Your last day? You're not gonna be my nurse anymore?"

"I'm afraid not," Annie replied, moved by the anguish she saw in the little boy's face; she hadn't expected this at all. "I have responsibilities at home that have to be put before my work now, William. It's a real long story, and I can't really get into it, but I can say that I'm going to miss you and the other children more than you could ever know. Truly I am."

William's face showed that he believed her regret was genuine, and he raised huge, brown eyes to meet hers as he spoke. "I wish you didn't have to go."

"Oh, William...there are so many things we wish we could change or somehow make happen some other way, but all you can do is pray and hope the things you can't do anything about will work themselves out in the end."

"That's what my dad says..."

"And he's absolutely right."

"I wish HE liked baseball as much as you do...if it don't have to do with tobacco, he ain't interested," William offered sullenly.

"He's a farmer—tobacco is his life," Annie shrugged. "But just because he's not interested in baseball doesn't mean he isn't interested in *you*. He loves you very much...you're very lucky to have him." Immediately Annie remembered Monica's taunting words: 'Don't you think Martin deserves to be told that he's going to be a father?' And she closed her eyes against the sudden chill that shook her. Her child deserved to have a father, but could she ever tell him the truth? Would she ever even hear from Martin again?

"I'm sorry, Annie...I forgot about your dad dying and all..." William's voice brought her back to the present and Annie smiled at the self-recriminating expression on the boy's face.

"It's okay...just always be thankful you have him, as thankful as he is to have you."

"I am...Annie, can I give you something to remember me by?" William asked as he watched her move to stand.

"I doubt I'll ever forget my favorite card-swapper," she replied honestly.

William turned the album over in his lap and laid the back cover open to reveal the last page: a nine-card assemblage of Jose Canseco cards. "You always wanted my Canseco rookie card, Annie...here, I want you to have it," and with that, he removed the card from its sleeve.

"Oh no, William! Keep your rookie card! If you hold on to it long enough, you might be able to trade up for one of the other Nolan Ryan cards you want."

"I always did plan on trading it to you someday...I just wanted you to *think* I wouldn't. That way, you'd bring in better Ryan's every time."

Annie's mouth fell open at the confession. "I don't believe this! You've got a better poker face than anyone I've ever traded with at card shows!"

William smiled. "I had two of 'em anyway."

"You have two $100 cards?" Annie asked incredulously.

William nodded. "I bought one from my cousin in Greensboro: he didn't know what he had and only wanted $5 for it!" The little boy extended his good arm and Annie hesitantly took the card. "Are you sure about this, sweetie?" Though she didn't want to insult the boy by refusing his gift, she had to wonder if accepting such an expensive card was altogether correct.

"It's the $5 one...the edges are a little worn, anyway."

Annie smiled at William's reasoning and shook her head in genuine disbelief. After a moment, she hugged him and slipped the card into her purse. Taking a tissue, she dabbed a suspicious wetness from her eyes and moved to leave the boy's room. "I really didn't need the card to have something to remember you by. I have a lot already, William—in here," and she laid her right hand on her chest. "Take care, you."

"I will...g'bye, Annie."

*　　*　　*

Martin's expression revealed little. In the week since talking with Annie, he had become a recluse, leaving his apartment only when Chris summoned him to the law office and- judging from his unkempt appearance -sleeping as little as he ate. The attorney studied the hooded and distant focus of his friend's eyes, concerned that this woman, this...Annie, could weld such complete control over an otherwise strong and exuberant man as Martin Vaughn. He was wary as to what extremes the man would go to in order to find her.

"You needn't stare upon the court as if you expect her to step from a motorcar at any moment...Martin, do you hear me?"

Back and forth, tracing the curved part between his lips with the knuckle of his thumb, Martin's movements had been unconscious. And yet, he went completely still at Chris' question. "I'm neither deaf nor insane, Christopher...and your comment is ludicrous, uncalled for. I have had very nearly every freedom taken from me by my...by Claire. Am I to be robbed of the right to think as well?" he implored, turning to meet his counsel's eyes with his own fiery ones. "Am I no longer myself?"

Chris' chin came up and he held his friend's stare evenly. "You are indeed. And yet, you are still only a man, not a sorcerer or wizard; you cannot want for something and have it appear..."

"—no, dammit, I can't!" Martin bellowed, standing as if to do so might bolster his words. "But I can go to Annie and convince her to return with me...she'll not be able to deny us once I make her face me, I'm certain of it!"

"And if you lose your son in exchange for this woman, what then?" the counselor implored. "Would she ever be able to live up to such an exchange...could **any** woman?"

"I will not lose my son," Martin proclaimed emphatically, his voice suddenly even and calm. "Stuart is mine by blood; Claire cannot undo that fact and by God, I will fight her through every court in this country if I have to."

Chris closed his eyes and drew a steadying breath. As he let it go, his eyes opened again to stare at the antique Bible on his desk. "Claire can fight you indefinitely. She can keep this custody dispute in the courts until your son forgets he ever had a father. And everything you do, everyone you see has the potential to make it easier for her, Martin...if Ann-Elise has anything in her past that a judge might deem improper..."

"—I would swear on my father's grave that she doesn't," Martin broke in, drawing Chris' stare from the Bible to meet his own. "Get me to the States,

Chris…somehow, there must be a way to get me out of this country without Claire knowing…some kind of disguise and a passport that wouldn't be questioned…"

Again, Chris' eyes dropped to the Bible upon his desk, followed seconds later by Martin's. As the two men stood in measured silence, the bells of Westminster Abbey pealed through the sound of traffic outside the window facing Marsham Street, and Martin realized in an instant what it was that Christopher had in mind for him to do.

*　*　*

Annie rolled over onto her back and breathed as deeply as the nausea would allow. Never before had she felt so physically ill; never had the worst case of flu made her feel she would have to die to feel better…there was nothing worse than vomiting, she could stand anything but that!

But ten minutes later as she wiped her lips and face with a cold bath-cloth, she realized that mind over matter meant very little when her body was determined to give in. After she had drawn a few easy breaths, Annie had to admit that throwing up had actually made her feel somewhat better: her stomach was actually growling for food! Shaking her head, she stood up slowly and eased herself away from the bathroom basin. In the mirror, her face looked pallid, bloodless, and her hair was tangled beyond belief. "I look like I've fought with a cat and the cat won," she murmured, raking her tussled mane off her brow with her fingers.

"Annie? You up yet?" came Monica's voice from the bottom of the staircase. Wincing, Annie stepped out of the bathroom and walked toward the top of the stairwell. "I'm…here…what time is it?"

Monica's mouth fell open at her friend's appearance and she shook her head at the woman's tortured image. "Time to find a new hairdresser…" Monica replied sardonically.

"Thanks a lot."

"Sorry, but girl, you look like hell."

Annie's expression was incredulous. "Well at least I look as good as I feel! I can always count on you to make my day, Monica…"

"I've just never been around a lot of women with morning sickness…it is NOT a pretty sight…" Catching Annie's venomous glare, Monica winced. "I mean, it makes you wonder that humanity continues to reproduce itself generation after generation…can you make it down alright?"

110

Annie gripped the banister with one hand and held her hair out of her eyes with the other as she slowly, resolutely led herself down the staircase, a nod her only reply.

"What is it now…six weeks?" Monica asked as her friend paused on the last step, her hand trembling suspiciously as the back of it pressed against her lips.

"Almost seven…Dr. Clark said this should stop by the end of the first trimester…"

"—though some women are sick the entire nine months," Monica broke in and then silently chastised herself. "Of course, that's…a pretty rare occurrence…"

"I know all the stats by heart, Monica. I've done little more than read for the last three weeks…well, read and throw up." Monica smiled. "And plant bulbs. Gramma is adamant about getting all her bulbs in the ground before the month's out; how am I supposed to argue with her? I can't let her know I'm pregnant!"

"You're not gonna be able to keep it from her forever! Mrs. Adams will notice eventually and then everyone will know."

Annie sat down at the kitchen table and laid her head upon folded arms. "I know…I guess I'll just have to sit her down one evening and tell her the whole, sorry story…I'd rather move to Siberia."

Monica hugged Annie's shoulders and laughed, reaching into the dish drainer for a juice glass. "Think you could keep down some orange juice?"

Annie didn't say anything for a moment. Then, raising her head just a few inches off her arms: "Was Gramma in the house when you came in?"

Monica finished pouring the juice into the glass and put the pitcher back in the refrigerator. "I didn't see her…I'll bet she's out back already, bulbs and watering can in hand!"

Annie took the glass of juice her friend had offered and set it on the table, cocking her head to one side as if to listen toward the rear of the house. "Wound you go check? We should have heard her cussing a cat or something by now…"

"Sure," Monica nodded, her own sense of hearing queerly piqued as well. As she left the kitchen, some sixth sense led her the two or three steps down the hall to Annie's grandmother's bedroom. When she opened the bedroom door, she found Gramma lying face down and still on the floor by her bed.

CHAPTER SIX

It had been three days since Monica found Emma Ryan unconscious on her bedroom floor…three days since Annie had been home and slept in her own bed. It was close to nine o'clock in the evening and Annie still refused to go home. "I drove home and showered and changed at noon so I wouldn't have to go home tonight," she argued as Monica knelt before her. "I told you—I'm alright…I get plenty of rest sitting in this damned chair all day!"

Monica's shoulders dropped as she shook her head in frustration. "You said you'd do what Dr. Clark told you to do: if she tells you to go home, will you go?"

Annie cradled her grandmother's frail and bluish right hand in both her own, unconsciously rocking back and forth in her chair like an anxious child. Were it not for the sparks of anger Monica saw in her friend's eyes, she might have wondered that she heard anything at all.

"I can't leave her," Annie whispered at last, taking her eyes from her grandmother's face. "What if she wakes up and I'm not here? When she wakes up, she's gonna be so scared…"

"Annie, the doctor told you she may be like this for several days, if she even wakes up at all! You can't be expected to sit by this bed day in and day out, waiting for something that might never even happen…"

"—don't say that!" Annie hissed, turning full about to face Monica squarely. "She **will** wake up! I know she will!"

Monica looked away, unable to bear the new rush of tears that streamed down her dearest friend's cheeks. "At least talk to Preacher Wilson, will you do *that*? You've always respected him…and Gramma won't even listen to anybody's sermons but his…"

"He's here?" Annie asked surprised. "At this time of night?"

"I called him about an hour ago," Monica replied. "And no, I didn't tell him about...about you. But maybe you should."

"I can't think about any of that right now, Monica," Annie whispered, turning back to her grandmother.

"Annie, you can't NOT think about it! If Gramma should die..."

"—Monica—!"

"—if she should die, and you lose your baby, what will you have then?" Monica pressed, turning Annie's face to look at her. "What will you have?"

Preacher Wilson sat alone and deep in thought inside the hospital chapel praying for both Ryan women, members of his church since each was born. He had stood with them at the funeral of Emma Ryan's husband, and again when Annie Ryan buried her parents' remains nine years ago. Comforting his parishioners in a time of illness or death was something it seemed, he did much more often than celebrating a new life or the joining of two lives. And never was it harder, he decided, than when a death in a family meant someone else was left completely alone. He prayed that God would walk beside Annie Ryan and that she would look to Him in faith for the spiritual strength she would need in the coming days should Emma's stroke prove fatal.

Hearing the chapel door open, the elderly preacher straightened where he sat in the second pew, turning about when he heard someone speak his name. "Preacher Wilson?" a younger, bearded gentlemen whispered at his side. "I'm Jonas Wilson."

"I apologize for disturbing you..."

"—ah, you haven't disturbed me at all! I would appreciate the opportunity to stretch my legs," he replied as he stood and extended his right hand in greeting. "Forgive me if I should recognize you and don't. I could blame the lack of lighting in here," he offered, waving his other hand toward the podium. "But if I'm honest, I'd have to say my memory's goin' 'bout as fast as my hair."

The younger man couldn't hide the smile that reached to light his eyes as well and Preacher Wilson laughed outright at the other man's chagrin. "Your memory, sir, is just fine" the younger man replied, a sharp Georgia accent almost preceding his right hand as he reached to return the greeting. "I'm sorry to say we've never met before. My name is...Nathaniel Rodgers," he stammered. "I'm doing Baptist missionary work up here in the Triad and was told by Whitey Hawkins that your church in Rural Hall might welcome..."

"—want me to let you in on something?" Preacher Wilson broke in, and then didn't wait for Nathaniel's reply. "You 'bout have to take anything Whitey says with a grain of salt. Hear him tell it, he knows a little about…just about everything," he finished soberly.

Nathaniel was taken aback. "I see."

"Well, go ahead," Preacher Wilson offered after a few seconds. "Think you'd like to stay a spell, then?"

Nathaniel stroked the stubble of his bearded chin at the older man's disjointed dialogue; it was at once amusing and frustrating! "Yessir, but I sure wouldn't want t-to put you out in any way…"

"—oh, Lord no! I can't think of anything I'd welcome more right now than another good set of ears. I've got four hospitals I visit on a regular basis and all the nursing homes in between…sick people at home…you from Georgia, son?"

Turning, Nathaniel moved to join Preacher Wilson as they walked from the chapel. "Northern Georgia, sir…are you here tonight to visit a sick parishioner?" Nathaniel asked in turn, having managed at last to follow the older man's conjunctive manner of speech.

"As a matter of fact, I am. One of our oldest members Emma Ryan, a widow woman, had a stroke just three days ago and the doctors aren't expecting her to make it…"

Emma Ryan. Nathaniel stood alongside the older gentleman and stroked a bearded cheek with the back of one hand as they waited for the elevator to arrive.

"…her grand-daughter Annie, was all the family left to Emma after the plane crash…Annie's folks were such good people. And her being an only child, she was the only one left to take care of Emma. Things only got rougher when Emma lost her sight four years ago…"

"—then I reckon you're really here to see *Miss* Ryan?" Nathaniel interjected as they stepped into the elevator, only bits and pieces of the preacher's story having penetrated his conscious mind.

"If Emma dies, Annie is gonna have to rely on her faith in God more than ever…"

Slowly, Nathaniel allowed himself to relax against the elevator wall. After nearly two months of searching over hundreds of miles, he—or rather, Martin Vaughn—would finally see Annie Ryan again, perhaps in only a matter of moments…

Following Christopher's call to McDougall, Martin's attorney had recalled the detective home the next day and both he and Martin had listened in amazement to the stories of investigative misadventure McDougall related to them. The detective's log of time spent in Germanton had proven a goldmine for Martin as, was his usual procedure, McDougall had noted not only dates and times during his investigation but names—or as was the case with several of Germanton's residents—personalities. Given McDougall's profiles, Martin was able to go into the community, playing the part of a Baptist missionary from Georgia, and approach certain people for certain information without drawing undue attention to himself.

Whitey Hawkins, the owner of the small town's only store, proved to be the self-appointed 'town-crier,' knowing the marital status, occupation and general disposition of every resident within a five mile radius—and anyone beyond if given the chance to make a few calls! It was from Whitey that Martin learned of Mrs. Adams, Annie and Emma's neighbor. And from Mrs. Adams, Martin was practically granted a verbal accounting of Annie's life history, including the rescue squad's blaring arrival early Saturday morning to take her grandmother to the hospital, the victim of a stroke.

That was three days ago, he told himself. He had managed to monitor the Ryan home through the locals, learning that Annie had been home only twice, staying less than an hour each time—just long enough he reasoned, to shower and change. He had yet to catch so much as a glimpse of her, and now as Martin (under the auspices of Nathaniel Rodgers) followed Preacher Wilson down the corridor toward the Intensive Care waiting area, he felt as if his chest was constricted with steel bands. The growing apprehension he felt was fed not only by his concern for Annie's well being, but by his fear that she might see through his beard, longish hair, brown contacts, glasses and *very* Southern drawl before the crisis with her grandmother was over…before he was granted the opportunity to convince her that theirs was a relationship worth fighting for.

Approaching the nurses' station, Preacher Wilson was stopped in mid stride by Monica Holt as she exited Emma's hospital room and called out to him. "I was hoping I'd run into you, Preacher Wilson," she began. "Have you been waiting very long?"

"No, dear…I stopped by the chapel before coming up—we were just headed to the waiting area," he explained, turning to include Nathaniel in their conversation. "This here's Nathaniel Rodgers and he's up from Georgia doing some Baptist missionary work in the area. Nathaniel, this is Monica

Holt: she's a good friend of Emma's grand-daughter and another member of our congregation."

Nathaniel extended his hand in greeting and Monica accepted it smilingly. "It's nice to meet you Mr. Rodgers; I'm sorry it's not under happier circumstances."

"So I understand, ma'am," he replied.

"Has there been any improvement in Emma's condition? How's Annie holding up?" the preacher asked anxiously.

Monica shook her head no, her expression alone making Martin want to step past her and into the elderly patient's hospital room to see for himself how well Annie was coping. She had left him behind in New York because of her devotion to her grandmother, so he could well imagine the fear she must feel at possibly losing her only remaining relative.

"Gramma is barely hanging on, which makes Annie a basket case," Monica replied at last. "She'd already been strung out for weeks before this even happened..."

"—strung out?" Preacher Wilson interjected.

"Worried, aggravated...you know, over that 'American Star' article."

Martin's eyes looked guiltily away, his left hand coming up to comb his hair away from his brow.

"Ah, yes...Annie is such a good and decent young woman, it's a shame that a tabloid can actually run such an outlandish article..."

"—shame, hell!" Monica broke in. Then, "Um, sorry Preacher Wilson...you just have no idea what Annie's been going through the last couple of months. I've tried to get her to talk to you a dozen times, but you know how stubborn she is!—thinks she can handle everything by herself."

"Takes back after her father's side of the family—Emma's the same way," the preacher reasoned. "But a soul can only be expected to bear so much...the good Lord knows when to intervene and when he does..."

"—would you please just talk to her?" Monica interrupted, realizing the beginning of a sermon when she heard one. "I'm going down to the cafeteria and get her a sandwich...she hasn't eaten in days. Besides, they only allow two visitors at a time in the Intensive Care unit."

Hearing Monica's words, Martin's hopes of finally seeing Annie evaporated. She was on the other side of a hospital door and yet, he felt just as cut off from her as when they were separated by the expanse of an ocean.

"Of course I'll talk with her, Monica. I'm glad you thought to contact me: I wasn't aware of Emma's illness until you called, or I'd have been to see her sooner," Preacher Wilson explained.

"I'm surprised Whitey missed somebody," Monica commented wryly, and the pastor had to feign a cough to hide his smile.

"Only because I'd been in Salisbury with my wife and her family all weekend," he offered with a wink. "Would you like to sit in the waiting area while I visit with Annie and her grandmother?" he asked Nathaniel at last.

"I think I'll walk around a bit instead. I may have to leave before your visitation is over, anyway, so if I'm not here when you're ready to leave…"

"—come by the church tomorrow and I'll introduce you to my wife," Wilson offered with a nod. "She'd have my hide if you got away before she had a chance to meet you."

"I'll certainly try, sir. It was good meeting you Miss Holt; I'll pray for your friend and her grandmother."

"Thanks…it's good to meet you too," she replied, her eyes studying him outright. "Though, you know…I'd almost swear I've met you before."

Martin straightened his glasses nervously. "I'm certain I would have remembered," he insisted smilingly, then nodded one last time to Preacher Wilson before turning toward the far end of the corridor.

Annie sat alone again, the tick-tick-tick of the heart monitor and the buzz of the respirator assaulting her senses as they echoed against the walls of the room. Gramma's doctor had come in as Preacher Wilson was about to leave and his comment that it was "simply a matter of time" had sent Annie into a verbal furor. She chastised the doctor for being so callous, ordering him from the room; and when Preacher Wilson had tried to "help her accept the Lord's will," she had angrily asked that he leave as well. Monica, having heard the exchange from the hallway, simply laid the sandwich she'd gone for on Gramma's bedside table along with a cup of coffee and left Annie to be alone with her grandmother for whatever time might be left to them. There were arrangements to be made with the funeral home, and Gramma's best dress to press, and Monica knew Annie would be in no condition to do either: she hadn't yet found the strength to simply let go.

Martin had walked the corridors of the seventh floor until he felt his mind would literally leave him if he were not allowed at least a glimpse of Annie before the night was over. He had already watched Preacher Wilson and a doctor leave, and now Monica closed the door behind herself as she turned in the direction of the nurse's station across the hall.

"This is my number, or you can probably reach me at Annie's," he heard her tell a nurse. "Annie needs to be alone, and someone has to take care of the arrangements…call me Beth, when it's over."

Call me when it's over…dear God, Martin thought as he watched Monica enter the elevator, Annie can't go through this alone! Closing his eyes, he saw a similar corridor on a similar night and recalled the feelings of desolation and desperation he had felt as he watched his father die. Even after ten years, the hurt was as raw and the loss just as devastating; he had not been alone, and he wouldn't let her be alone either. "After tonight, Annie," he whispered as he walked toward Emma Ryan's room, "you'll never be alone again…I swear it."

Pushing the full length glass door open just wide enough to pass through, Martin drew a deep breath as he stepped into the tiny, half-lit room, wincing at the dramatic contrast between it and the well-lit corridor. Immediately the colored lights of the various machines leapt out at him, and the ticking and the buzzing…and in the shadows beside the bed itself, he found Annie bent forward in a straight-back chair, her hands clasping her grandmother's free one as she rested her cheek upon it, her eyes closed.

The door clicked closed behind him, and Martin's heels on the terrazzo floor fell in step with the tick-tick-tick of the heart monitor. He watched for some acknowledgement from her, but she never moved. Dear God, he thought as he stood only a couple of feet away, might I simply stand and look at her a while?

And then his eyes began to truly see her. Even in the half-light, she appeared pale: gone was the pink blush of shyness her cheeks had held as she stood before him, offering her hand in the receiving line, too nervous to speak. In their place, sallow planes showed with dark circles upon their crests. The tangled mane he'd combed in awe with hands too large to be gentle, too small to gather it all in one grasp, was bound with a red rubber band—the kind he had so often stripped from newspapers and thrown away. No ribbon, no clasp; she had thought of nothing but the necessity of having her hair out of her eyes.

Her eyes: once they had held and caressed him, unabashedly cherishing him in such a way that he had wanted to give back to her every possible joy. Were they still blue as cobalt beneath eyelids now wet and swollen from endless crying? Would they open for him? Would she know him? His own filled and brimmed as he studied her, waiting for her…waiting.

*   *   *

Annie ran into her house as fast as her tiny feet would carry her. She swiped at a tear on her cheek and once inside her bedroom, slammed the door behind her. Crossing her arms upon her chest Annie stomped to the window seat and sat down hard on its padded bench, drawing a huffy breath and releasing it with a stifled sob.

At that moment, her bedroom door opened and her father slipped silently in. He had to hide his smile behind a work-roughened hand, pretending at that moment to scratch at an imaginary itch on his cheek. "Slamming these doors made enough noise to wake the dead," he offered tentatively.

"I'm so mad, I could spit nails!"

"Now you sound like your Gramma Ryan…"

"Tammy Majure is so mean, Daddy! I wish she'd never come to my school!"

"Just yesterday, she was your new best friend."

"No she ain't! She made fun of me today and I hate her for it!"

"You don't hate anyone, Annie…that's a sin," her father chastised. "Whatever she did or said, I'm sure she didn't mean it."

Annie looked up at her father's solemn face. "She DID mean it! She made fun of me and Daniel and now he won't play with me anymore!"

Stephen Ryan sat down on the window seat beside his daughter and gathered her close. "Tell me what she said, sweetheart."

Annie pouted a moment longer and then offered the teasing sing-song offense in muffled sobs: "Annie and Daniel sittin' in a tree, k-i-s-s-i-n-g…first comes love, then comes marriage, here comes Daniel with a baby carriage…"

Annie's father shook his head at the familiar children's rhyme and hugged the tiny girl closer. "Honey, that little song has been around forever, even longer than I have…Tammy probably heard it somewhere and just repeated it 'cause she thought it was cute."

"Well Daniel didn't think it was cute: 'cause of her, said he wouldn't ever kiss me again!"

Stephen Ryan's brows rose in surprise. "You been lettin' that little Martin boy kiss you?"

Annie lifted her face to meet her father's surprised expression. "Uh-huh..."

"What's he kissin' you for?"

*Annie let go a frustrated breath. "Aw Daddy, you know the Prince **has** to kiss Sleepin' Beauty to break the witches' spell! That's th' only thing that'll work! The book says so!"*

*Her father's expression showed immediate recognition. "You are absolutely right, sugar...I swear, I don't know **how** I could've forgot that...guess I'm just getting' old."*

*"You ain't too old, Daddy...just **kinda** old."*

"Gee, thanks."

"You understan' now why I'm so mad?" she continued just as matter-of-factly.

Stephen's expression became solemn. "Yes ma'am, I do. Tell you what, honey: take your Sleeping Beauty book to school tomorrow, read the story to your friend Tammy and show her the picture of the Prince kissing Sleeping Beauty. I bet you she'll wanna play Sleeping Beauty next time..." At that moment, Annie's father handed her the worn storybook.

Instead of Disney characters on its cover however, Annie saw the picture of Martin and herself from the tabloid and came suddenly and fully awake. "Martin?"

Blinking, he swallowed back her name because he could not speak. They simply stared at one another.

"I'm sorry," she murmured after a moment, lifting her head and squinting in his direction. "I imagined you were someone else," she whispered, realizing at last she had been napping. Annie turned to look at her grandmother in full then, her hands clasping and unclasping the one she still held as she dismissed the man as another doctor come to tell her that her grandmother was dying. Her eyes flicked to the monitors and, hearing a movement behind her, Annie turned about to face the man again. "You're welcome to check Gramma's vital signs, doctor. She's moving into her fourth day: that's four days longer than ya'll believed she would live."

Martin stopped in mid-stride, raking his hair off his brow as he heard the determination in the woman's voice. Hurting as she was, she still had the will to fight; how he longed to hug her to him and give her his strength as well!

"I uh...you've mistaken me for someone else, ma'am," Martin began, intoning the slow Georgian drawl he'd practiced with Christopher for almost three weeks before leaving London. "I'm Nathaniel Rodgers...I was here earlier with Preacher Wilson."

Annie shook her head dubiously. "I don't remember your being here before—are you a friend of Preacher Wilson's?"

Silently Martin cursed Claire and the necessity of façade. Were it not for he and his attorney being made to create a false identity in order to get Martin out of Britain, and then continuing that falsehood in the event Claire was having Annie watched by a private investigator in hopes of catching the two of them together again, Martin would be free to make her aware of who he really was. And free to take her into his arms...

"I'm up from Georgia visiting the Triad, Miss Ryan," he began, the growing lie already bitter on his lips. "I'm a Baptist missionary and Preacher Wilson has been kind enough to allow me to serve with him in the Germanton and Rural Hall communities for a while."

Annie nodded thoughtfully and turned back to her grandmother. "Preacher Wilson is a good man—Gramma thinks there's no one else in the world like him."

Martin stared enviously as Annie's hands gently stroked her grandmothers' frail one and immediately he chided himself for his selfish thoughts. "He certainly thinks the world of you and Mrs. Ryan," he offered sincerely.

"He has a wonderful way with people, but I somehow managed to run him off..."

Martin's brows drew together at the helpless admission. "I'm sure Ann...Miss Ryan..."

"—that's all right," she interceded smilingly as she turned to face him, and Martin's heart all but leapt from his chest. "Annie's fine, really."

"Annie: is that short for, something else?"

Her eyes darted from his to stare at the wall behind him as if studying vast nothingness. "No...it's just Annie..."

Martin closed his eyes against the chill that washed over him and when he opened them, her eyes had once again focused on his face.

"I'm sorry," she began, a shy smile lifting the corners of her mouth. "Something...something about you seems very familiar, Nathaniel?"

Martin's stomach turned over at her words. Dear God, how he longed to tell her who he really was! "Uh, yes...of course, please call me Nathaniel."

Annie nodded again before turning back to her grandmother. "They tell me she's dying, Nathaniel…all the doctors: they've said it's only a matter of time…that I need to 'prepare' myself."

There was a long pause. "Yes."

Annie's eyes looked to the cardiac monitor and she seemed to study the numbers that flashed, yellow, blue, and sometimes red. "I've watched the readings go down day by day, always down…"

Another pause. "Yes…"

Annie sat silent for several moments, her eyes going from the monitor to her grandmother's face and back again. "I'm a nurse…I know what the monitors are saying, and the numbers don't lie."

"No they don't," Martin agreed, "but as long as there are numbers, you can hold her to you just a little while longer."

Annie jerked about with eyes wide and glistening, her right hand lifting to stay the trembling of her lips. "Yes…that's it exactly…" she whispered in awe as fresh tears trailed down her cheeks.

"You don't have to let her go until you're ready: don't let anyone tell you different," Martin began, the memory of his father's death suddenly clearer to him at this moment than it had been in years. Slowly, he stepped to stand at Annie's side, pulling an empty chair alongside the one she sat in. "May I sit with you, Annie?" he asked after a moment. "I'd like to stay with you if you don't mind my being here." *Please don't ask me to leave,* he added silently.

Though she couldn't bring herself to look at him again, Annie nodded and whispered, "Yes…please stay," and felt Nathaniel's nearness as he sat down beside her. Stroking her grandmothers cheek with the back of one hand, she seemed oblivious to the ticking of the wall clock as the moments passed them into the morning hours; she had been granted another night, and for that she was so very grateful.

At a quarter of six, just the slightest hint of daylight began to filter into the hospital room, and it threw such a luminescence across Annie's face that the weariness and worry Martin had seen earlier seemed magnified tenfold now. She sat slumped forward in her chair, her head resting upon her arms where they lay crossed upon the mattress, sleeping fitfully, brows drawing from time to time as if in conflict with her dreams.

If Martin had harbored any doubts before concerning Annie's reason for leaving him in New York, proof of the woman's love and devotion to her grandmother was etched clearly upon the contours of her face. So pronounced were the dark circles beneath her eyes and the sunken hollows in her cheeks that he feared she might literally be ill. She barely resembled the bright, fiery beauty he once held in his arms during their early morning ferry ride.

At the memory of those few precious hours, his mind was taken back to when he learned of the story in the 'American Star' and the anger he felt at Claire's exploitation of it. Monica had damned the publication's effect on Annie calling her reaction to it worried, aggravated—"…she'd been strung-out for weeks." Closing his eyes, Martin winced at the hell Annie must have gone through: living in such a small town, the whispers of speculation alone would have been enough to make her 'strung-out;' her grandmother's illness had only served to compound the torture.

Looking for what seemed like the hundredth time at the monitors, Martin realized with a start that Emma Ryan's condition had faltered considerably in the last half hour. Though he felt it must have been nearing the time for a nurse to look in on the patient, an inner voice told him to call on someone himself; once having reckoned that Annie was still asleep, he slipped quietly from the room and walked to the nurse's station.

"Excuse me," Martin entreated as he approached the nurse Monica had earlier addressed as Beth. "Mrs. Ryan's blood pressure has dropped quite a bit in the last half hour—would you please check on her?"

Beth nodded hesitantly. "We are monitoring her from the desk as well, sir…because she's a DNR, all we can do is continue the comfort measures ordered by her doctor."

"Comfort measures? I don't understand…"

"—Mrs. Ryan has a living will that states her desire for a natural death. Her status is Do Not Resuscitate," the nurse explained haltingly. "You didn't know?"

"No…I had no idea."

"I'm sorry…I wish Annie didn't have to go through this, but I'm grateful she has someone with her," Beth sympathized. "Is she in with her grandmother now?"

"Yes," Martin murmured. "She's refused to leave her side."

Beth nodded as she reached for the desk phone. "I thought as much. Let me call for someone to relieve me here and I'll join the two of you in a moment."

"Thank you," Martin replied unconsciously as he tried to wrap his mind around the concept of a 'natural death.' ER doctors and nurses had fought for hours to save his father's life the night of his heart attack and yet, Emma Ryan had chosen to let her life slowly ebb away. Turning in the direction of the elderly woman's room, he wasn't aware of the alarms that sounded until he was within inches of the door. As he stepped into the room, he realized immediately that something was very wrong: Annie was kneeling and crying by her grandmother's bedside.

"Annie! What…?"

"—she's gone! Oh God, Nathaniel, Gramma's gone!"

Instantly, Martin's eyes darted to the lights on the monitor and the warning "ASYSTOLE" in bold red letters. There was no blood pressure reading, only the eerie constant buzz where there had earlier been a heartbeat. Reacting with the impetus of one in grievous confusion, he threw open the door to the hospital room and bellowed, "Nurse! We need a nurse in here now!" before frantically turning about to Annie again. In the span of a breath, he was kneeling beside her, his arms wrapped tightly about her as he rocked and comforted and murmured. "It's going to be alright…I swear, Annie, I swear…" over and over into the wisps of hair at her temple.

Within seconds, Beth had entered the hospital room followed by a doctor and a second nurse, their attention focused immediately on the monitors and their patient. Though all three responded instinctively and professionally to the situation, they were similarly struck with genuine compassion for the mournful young woman and appreciation for the efforts of the gentleman trying to console her; neither was aware that the gentleman was crying as well.

When after a few moments the monitors were at last shut off, the hateful buzzing ceased and Beth kneeled at her friend and coworker's side, shaking her head sadly at the childlike eyes that beseeched a miracle. Annie's mournful, seemingly endless sobbing interspersed with the doctor's murmured instructions to the nurses, Martin feared, was a grim memory he would carry to his own death. But as he continued to hold and mourn with the woman he suddenly realized he loved more than his own life, his only prayer was that God would allow him to live long enough to take away Annie's pain entirely and in it's place, give her peace.

By the time Monica arrived at the hospital, it was nearing nine o'clock and the sun had warmed the mid-May morning to its springtime high. As Martin stood alone by the window of the Bereavement Room, he wondered that the sun shone at all: why were the skies not purple and gray, and raining in mourning for Annie's loss? This woman who had given her life to her family and her faith, and who had chosen nursing because of her love of people, deserved at the very least benevolence from her God; the bright, cloudless day seemed to him a cruel act of irreverence, and he silently cursed the skies.

"Nathaniel?"

He did not answer.

"Nathaniel?" the voice beckoned louder, and Martin turned about to stare mutely in the direction of the voice. In an instant, he realized Monica had been speaking to him and he turned fully to address her.

"I'm sorry, Miss Holt. I…was a million miles away just now. What did you say?"

Monica did well to hide the surprise in her expression, for Nathaniel's stance and his silhouette against the sunlit backdrop so resembled another mans' at another place and time that she felt a chill rack her entire body. "I…I wanted to know if there was something I could get for you from the cafeteria—coffee or a sandwich? If you've been here with Annie all night, I'm sure you haven't eaten, because she hasn't."

Martin smiled at Monica's reasoning. "I would **love** a hot cup of coffee. And bring Annie one as well; I'll get it in her if I have to force-feed her myself. There's no way she can continue in her condition without taking in some kind of nourishment."

"In her condition?" Monica's face blanched. *Has Annie finally talked to someone about her pregnancy*, she asked herself incredulously.

"It's obvious she hadn't eaten in days, probably not since her grandmother took ill," Martin replied shaking his head. "But she must drink something or else become dehydrated. She's a nurse…she should be able to recognize that even in herself."

Monica's expression was equally disdainful. "Annie is hard-headed, and stubborn, and the last person who'll admit she needs or wants anything from anybody—medical care included. And they say **doctors** make the worst patients!"

Martin knew there was no way he could argue with her.

"If you can make her drink something, Nathaniel, I'll bring you the entire pot of coffee!" Monica vowed, studying the man now with keen eyes. "She should be back in here in a bit…there were some papers she had to sign but they won't keep her long. If she gets back before I do, hog-tie her to a chair 'cause the first thing she'll want to do is start taking care of funeral arrangements," she stated matter-of-factly, watching Nathaniel's face for some familiar nuance or tick. "If I can get in contact with her doctor, I'll see if she has any suggestion for calming Annie; she can't continue much longer at the rate she's been going."

A band of hurt constricted his chest for Martin knew that he was responsible for a great deal of what Annie had been going through. His notoriety as an actor had been the basis of the tabloid's story, and Annie simply an innocent in the wrong place at the wrong time. "I agree," he murmured at last, "and I'm genuinely afraid for her." Recalling how Annie had remained kneeling and crying upon the cold terrazzo floor until her grandmother's body was removed from the room made Martin close his eyes as if to do so might shut out the horrible memory.

Monica watched then as 'Nathaniel' swept an unruly lock of hair from his brow and for one of the few times in her life, she found herself completely speechless.

"Nathaniel, Monica..."

Immediately, Martin spun around to face Annie, her having appeared behind him as he'd been thinking of her completely unsettling him. "Ann...Annie! Come have a seat..." he insisted as he led her to a chair. "Miss Holt is going for coffee and I've been given explicit instructions to keep you here until she returns with it," he insisted gently.

"Monica, please," Annie's friend corrected in her usual catty tone, keeping knowing eyes skewered on his. "I'm not your teacher."

Martin's brows rose and he smiled at the woman's candor. He'd never known a more outspoken breed of people than Southerners! "My apologies, Monica."

"None necessary," she corrected, infecting too casual as air to her voice; she might as well make this fun! "It's just that hearing 'Miss Holt,' or in Annie's case 'Miss Ryan,' at our age tends to make us sound like spinsters..."

"—Monica—!" Annie admonished incredulously.

"—you can't be serious!" Martin interjected with equal disbelief.

"Hey! You think I'm touchy, just wait till you've known Annie a while. At least I will *discuss* the prospect of a mate."

Annie turned to face Monica wide-eyed. "Monica, please!"

Instantly, Martin stiffened. "I look forward to getting to know Annie, in due time," he murmured so low Annie felt herself blush. "For now however, what she needs most is the support of her...friends?"

Monica recognized the critical undertones in Martin's comment: he was being protective of Annie. She liked that. "Annie is going through a lot right now, emotionally...physically...she needs someone that she can confide in who won't be judgmental. Unfortunately, I'm not that liberal: I know what she wants and needs but she's too damned proud..." Monica's sermon stopped abruptly and she gestured widely. "Sorry, Nathaniel. I suppose I shouldn't cuss in front of you, even if you're **not** a full-blown preacher yet."

Annie had to smile at her friend's frankness; it was Monica's way of lightening the mood, after all. Turning in Nathaniel's direction, she saw a half-grin soften his mouth and she felt herself relax somewhat for the first time in days.

"All I am is a man with a tremendous amount of will," he offered at last, relieved to see a semblance of a smile on Annie's weary face. "I'm not altogether certain yet just who guides my hand, if you want to know the truth," he offered earnestly, and Annie smiled at the admission.

"Is the truth too much to expect from a Baptist missionary?" Monica prodded undaunted, her arms crossing defiantly upon her chest. She *wanted* him to know she knew the truth.

He turned about to face Monica again and their eyes met; her defiant answer unnerved him. "Are you testing me?" he returned evenly.

"Do you always answer a question with a question?" she volleyed just as evenly.

"Monica, please!" Annie gently scolded as both heads turned in her direction. "Nathaniel was very kind to stay with Gramma and me last night but I know he must be exhausted...you're getting bad as Whitey, wanting to know so much about somebody!" Slowly her eyes turned back in Nathaniel's direction and she offered a tired, wan smile. "I do appreciate everything, Nathaniel. I think your coming with Preacher Wilson last night must be credited to some higher source...who else could have known that Gramma w-would leave us this morning?"

Monica stepped forward and brushed a loose tendril of hair off Annie's tired brow. "I think Nathaniel's arrival should be considered...timely. Yeah...timely," she murmured, chancing a glance at him over her shoulder as she spoke.

Martin felt his throat close and nerves prickle throughout his body. He glared at the smile Monica offered and felt an uneasy heat in the pit of his stomach: she knew who he was. "I would say that circumstances worked to create an odd coincidence, Monica," he defended without preamble, his eyes not wavering from hers. "I'm glad that I was able to be here for Annie; I know from my own experience that no one should be made to go through something this painful alone."

"Care to share?" Monica asked a little too casually, still piercing him with knowing eyes. *Or shall I relate the story of how you spent the last few days of your father's life by his bedside after he suffered a massive heart attack,* she wondered to herself. She never imagined that a "Star-Profile" in 'People' magazine could provide such a wealth of information!

"I really don't think an explanation is necessary," Annie interjected, Monica's boldness embarrassing her somewhat. "I'm sure that Nathaniel's missionary work has provided more painful situations than you or I might know in a lifetime, Monica. Besides," she offered as she began to walk toward the door, "I need to meet with the funeral director so will you drive me there on our way home? With Gramma's burial insurance and...and the arrangements she's already made, there shouldn't be a lot left to do..."

"—absolutely not!" Monica broke in angrily. "If I take you anywhere, it'll be to Dr. Clark's office!"

"Monica, this has to be done..."

"—it's been done, alright? I took care of everything last night, Annie, after I left the hospital...I knew you'd be in no condition today..."

"—oh Monica!" A new rush of tears came to Annie's eyes and she looked away toward the hospital window not wanting to hear anymore. She didn't think she could bear up under much more emptiness before breaking down completely. Unconsciously, her hand went to her stomach and she realized that perhaps "emptiness" wasn't the correct term for what she was feeling. Closing her eyes, she remembered the promise she had made to follow Dr. Clark's orders where the baby was concerned; and yet, it was the first time in nearly five days that she had truly allowed herself to think about the child she carried. As she recognized this new appreciation for her baby, she remembered again how she had been made to leave Martin in New York and hot tears ran down her cheeks at the memory of his loving her...

"Why don't you do as Monica suggested, Annie?" Martin whispered as he stepped past Monica to gather Annie's right hand into his two much larger ones. "From what she has told me, I understand the past few weeks have been an ordeal for you...even before your grandmother's illness. Your doctor would probably give you something to help you relax and sleep if you asked him..."

"—no, I don't think so," Monica broke in. "Annie's..."

"—I really don't need anything to help me relax, Nathaniel, honest. Once I'm home and in bed, I'll have no trouble falling asleep." Annie turned a silencing glare on Monica before she turned back to Nathaniel and shook his hand in a parting gesture. "Thank you again for everything you've done…I will never forget it, or you."

Watching the play of emotions that had so quickly crossed Annie's face, Martin wanted to gather her close and let her know he too remembered their time New York. He had recognized the look of someone being cherished flickering in the depths of her eyes; he had recognized her memories of him. "Somehow, I wish I could have done more," he murmured slowly, returning her handshake in the manner that was expected of a religious man. Then, ignoring what he knew were Monica's eyes boring into his back, he lifted her hand to his lips and touched just the fingertips to his mouth. "I'll keep you in my prayers," he whispered, a part of him begging her to recognize the closing words from her good-bye letter to him.

Annie swallowed hard and allowed her eyes to be held by his for only a moment before reclaiming her hand and turning toward the door. "Will you ask Beth to give Gramma's flowers to one of the patients who doesn't have any?" she asked, turning to Monica as she stopped at the threshold. "It's been three days since the church had them delivered, but they're still fresh enough that someone else can enjoy their beauty."

Unexpectedly, Monica burst out laughing: "Annie Ryan's motto, for those of you who don't yet know, is *Waste not, want not.*" With a smile still upon her lips, she turned to address Martin in full. "Isn't that somewhere in the Bible, Nathaniel?"

Pursing his lips, Martin reached across his chest to scratch some imaginary itch upon his right shoulder and finally shrugged at the woman's attempt to usurp him. "I honestly couldn't tell you, ma'am."

Annie chuckled, from the doorway and offered Monica a raised-brow-glance that meant to say "Touché." Then, "Are you coming? I want to call Dr. Clark before we head home."

"Go ahead to my car: my cell phone's on the charger. I just want to tie up some of the arrangements first."

Turning to nod a hesitant good-bye to Nathaniel, Annie stepped from the room; once her footfalls could no longer be heard in the corridor, Monica strode petulantly to the door and closed it in a rush, drawing herself angrily erect as she turned to face Nathaniel, alias Martin Vaughn!

"I've never seen a better performance, Mr. Vaughn! Too bad the Academy of Motion Picture Arts and Sciences couldn't have witnessed it as well! Oscar-winning material, without a doubt!"

"—you don't know what the hell you're talking about, Monica."

"You certainly have the Georgian drawl goin' on…and I suppose cussing is simply a new dimension of preaching, fresh from the Southern Baptist Convention! Come off it, Vaughn! All I want to know is why—why can't you let Annie know it's YOU hiding behind those God-awful glasses and that beard and the colored contact lenses…" Her hand flicked out at his hair. "And what's up with this hair? Do you know that's what gave you away? You kept brushing it out of your eyes in that same nervous manner as when you spoke at the Oscars!"

Martin stared at her mutely.

"Well, aren't you gonna say anything? You might start with your reason for coming here—I know for a fact Annie told you not to!"

"She told you I called her?"

Monica threw her hands heavenward. "Always, he answers my questions with questions…of course she told me! I've known Annie almost all my life. We practically grew up together: going to the same church, the same nursing school. She's the closest thing to a sister that I have."

"You're an only child as well?"

"Hardly…I have four older brothers."

Martin pondered that for a moment. "No wonder you're so damned ballsy."

Monica lifted one brow then smiled at Martin's description. "Annie calls me pushy…I'm being pushy now because I care about her. That woman has dealt with more hurt and loss in the last few years than most people will **ever** know; she's at a point now where if she lost…"

Martin caught Monica's hesitancy and prodded her to continue. "If she lost what, Monica?"

Monica drew a long breath and held it for a moment before she spoke again: she would have to continue more cautiously. "If Annie were to learn that you had been here and she hadn't realized it, she would be devastated. It would be upsetting enough knowing you felt the need to hide behind this pathetic disguise…"

"—I didn't have a choice," Martin broke in defensively. "My soon-to-be-ex-wife is was having me watched so closely in Britain that I needed a disguise and a fake passport just to get out of the country. Because of the tabloids' story, I have reason to believe she may very well be having Annie watched as well—this disguise is as much for Annie's benefit as mine…her life has been disrupted enough because of me."

You don't know the half of it, Monica added silently. Still, her expression hinted that she was beginning to believe him somewhat. "Why would Claire be having you watched? After two years, I'd think the divorce was all but final!"

"How is it you know so much about me?" Martin raised his hands in appeal. "Enough even that you'd recognize a…a nervous gesture?" It still amazed him that combing his hair from his brow had given him away!

"I have your bio from 'People', I videotaped the Oscars, and I've seen 'The Misbegotten' a half-dozen times," she clicked off frowning. "Your *nervous gesture* is a given, Martin, but the thing that really clued me in was the way you stood in front of that window earlier," she offered with a nod of her head. "It was the very same stance, the same silhouette as the scene in the library when Michael Maurer is having it out with Alex, remember? He's pissed because she gave him a black eye, and she's equally pissed because she thinks he's being arrogant…which he is…"

"—I don't believe this…"

"—my favorite line of the movie comes after she says, 'I'll not stand here and have you humiliate me when I've made every effort to apologize'…"

"—'Indeed, were you a man, you'd do well to crawl.'"

"—that's it!" Monica squealed with delight.

Martin glanced toward the window frowning. "Jesus Christ."

"And that's another thing," Monica added, lowering her voice accusingly. "Why play at being some 'Baptist missionary'? You've got your slow, Georgian drawl down pat—you could've gotten closer quicker playing a doctor. Annie's only just recently resigned from the hospital."

"It was my attorney's idea. He, rather WE, sent an investigator over from London as soon as I returned there from the ceremony in New York…his notes about the God-fearing people of this area gave Chris his direction." There was a long pause before he spoke again. "It's not common knowledge but, I was born in North Carolina, too: in Mount Airy…my family moved to England when I was a small boy."

"What?!"

"I keep having these flashbacks or memories, I guess, of a little blond girl…she lived just a couple of houses from me and I'd swear she's the same Annie, the same girl I knew as a child," he began.

Monica sat down hard in the chair closest to the window; she had suddenly found it difficult to stand. "Annie was born in Mount Airy, too...she moved to Germanton after her parents died...but then, she should know you, right? Or at least remember your name if your families had ever been neighbors!"

"I changed my name when I started acting..." he offered thoughtfully. "Martin Vaughn was once Daniel Martin," he mused remembering his agent's claim that his stage name had a certain 'strength' and *worldliness* that his birth name lacked. "I guess in a lot of ways, he still is...Daniel, I mean. My Grandma Martin always said 'A man can't get above his raising,' and I understand now just what she meant." His eyes pleaded for her to understand. "I might've changed my name, Monica, but I'm still the same person inside that I've always been. And I think I've always loved Annie, ever since I was a little boy..."

Monica's eyes studied the man standing before her now in a different light, and she brushed her own long hair behind one ear. "We have to tell her, Martin. Annie needs to know...everything! About Claire's threats, about your childhood, who you really are...you cannot begin to imagine what an impact this will have on her life!" *On both your lives*, she added silently.

"I tried to convince her to let me come back with her from New York," he insisted, "in spite of the impact it might have had on Claire and the divorce. But once she left, all I knew was that she was somewhere in the Triad. When no one in Mount Airy seemed to remember her, we simply had the investigator search until he found her in Germanton with Mrs. Ryan."

"But then you found her and...?"

"—and after I called, she still refused to see me...I couldn't believe that a grandmother could be her only reason for refusing to give us a chance; I figured there **must** be something more, another man maybe...I had to know."

"You don't know Annie at all," Monica sighed. "She's stubborn as a mule sometimes...and she was completely devoted to Gramma." There was another long pause as Monica let go a frustrated breath. "I told her she was crazy to push you away; I even offered to find you myself."

Their eyes met for the first time without daggers being shot between them. "I want the chance to tell her everything, but I don't want her hurt further by the damnable press, or worse, some investigator reporting back to Claire so that she can name Annie as 'the other woman' in our custody dispute..."

"—that's the other reason for the disguise!"

Martin nodded. "She's trying to take my son away from me."

Monica eased herself out of the chair feeling as confused as she was excited, and her face showed it. She so wanted to believe Martin, for Annie's sake and for the sake of their unborn child. "Do you love Annie?" she asked him at last as she stared out the window.

Martin studied Monica's back, surprised by the silent pleading he heard in her voice; it wasn't Monica's manner to let her guard down. She cared very much for Annie's welfare, and he realized that perhaps he had a friend in her as well. "I love her with all my heart."

Monica turned then and their gazes met as she nodded her trust in him. "Then let's do something about it."

Annie was staring at the hospital exit when Monica approached her car, and it wasn't difficult to guess what was going through her mind: a young woman was being helped into an automobile by a nurse as her husband held a newborn in his arms. "That'll be you in about seven months," Monica offered as she opened the driver's side door. "Wonder what they had?"

Annie drew in an unsteady breath. "The blanket was blue."

Monica squinted in the same direction Annie was staring. "Dang, you've got good eyes!"

Annie smiled indulgently. "I want a boy, Monica…I can't imagine this baby as anything less than the image of Martin." Stroking the tip of one finger across her bottom lip, she met Monica's thoughtful expression. "You were right…Dr. Clark wants to see me in her office at noon. Will it be a problem for you, running me by there I mean?"

Monica shook her head. "Of course not. But first we're stopping by Micky D's for a sandwich. And yes, we'll take fries with that!" Her tone stated she would brook no argument from her passenger.

Smiling gratefully, Annie simply nodded OK.

CHAPTER SEVEN

Annie bit her lip as she turned the knob and slowly swung the kitchen door open. The old house was quiet, completely quiet, a sound she immediately felt distressed by and she shook outwardly from the frigid chill that hit her as she stepped across the threshold. This is ridiculous, she reasoned, aware that Monica stood just a step behind her and could sense her hesitancy. Gramma would give me a solid tongue-lashing if she knew I was behaving this way...

Then she remembered another morning, entering the kitchen's warmth from a freezing, winter rain. It had been Gramma who stood behind her on that day, Gramma's hand on her shoulder as she hesitated on the threshold, Gramma's voice urging her to go in when her legs refused to carry her any further: *There's nothing gained in questioning the Lord's will, Annie-girl...you might better thank Him for having a home to come back to, and someone to care for you, rather than questioning the rightness of Him to take your daddy and mamma...they were His to put here on this earth and they were His to call back home; you've gotta believe He needed them to be with Him more than we needed to have 'em with us...the Lord knows what He's a-doin'...*

Closing her eyes, Annie smiled at the memory of her grandmother's words and shook her head at her own weakness...to have but a portion of Gramma's conviction, she decided, would go a long way toward getting her through the coming days.

"You okay?" Monica whispered as she laid a hand on Annie's arm. "I mean, you're not gonna pass out on me, are you?"

Annie opened her eyes and turned to her friend at the same moment. "Of course not..."

"It's just, you're pale all the time now! I don't know when you're feeling bad or sad or...what!"

"It's just so…quiet," Annie said finally, and Monica's expression showed she understood. "I suppose I should change into a dress…there'll be folks coming by with food and stuff once word gets around that Gramma's…"

"Yeah," Monica murmured, her hands going immediately to clear the kitchen table of four-day-old breakfast dishes. "Why don't you take a long, hot shower, get dressed, and I'll straighten up down here before anyone comes."

"I should have thought of this already…"

"—no, you shouldn't have; you couldn't have known any more than the doctors did what would happen, or when."

Annie sent her friend a long, challenging appeal. "Didn't you think to take care of getting Gramma's best dress pressed and to the funeral home? That never crossed my mind: I never allowed myself to go but from moment to moment…"

Monica nodded reluctantly, then shrugged. "You had to let her go in your own way; and I think you did the right thing, staying with her like you did. Dr. Clark said you're no worse ·ear—except for not eating!—so there's nothing to regret, really. ⅴ ˑⅰ her just like you always have…just like I knew you would."

Annie looked at ⅼ ⅰously wet as she smiled at her friend's admissio· ˑ the best of her. "No more scolding me fo·

"For the ⅼ u go getting sassy-mouthed Gramma would have.. ⅿⅰn or so months."

" ⅰ replied, drawing her fr· ⅼhausted all at once. "I'm

"…so th· ⅼ ecided where it was he wanted to go to college, and Dↄ· ⅼnat else was there to do but sell the beach house at Myrtle?" · ⅼⅰ asked as if it were a given. "My Lord, what else *could* we do?"

"Sell his Porsche?" Mↄnica murmured under her breath, and Annie bit her tongue to keep from laughing.

"I'm sorry, Monica—did you say something?" Janie asked, her brows rising dourly.

"I…said…well, of course. I can imagine, Janie, that any parent in your…position, would do the same."

The older woman frowned and shook her head dismissively. "Of course."

The doorbell rang and Annie took the opportunity to excuse herself from the living room. How many times had she and Gramma taken food to other people's houses over the years when someone in a family had died, and how many times had she left such a gathering thinking that instead of somber and solemn the people had seemed haughty and…irreverent? Everybody talked about everybody else, and told jokes, and laughed outright sometimes…a death was supposed to be mourned. That's what a wake was for, wasn't it? Passing the group of men standing by the fireplace, Annie heard one of them comment how dry he thought Janie Calhoun's pound cake was. It all sounded like a comedic play, and a bad one at that.

Drawing a deep, uneven breath, Annie reached for the crystal doorknob she'd pretended as a child to be a huge diamond and giving it a turn, opened the heavy oak door to the next insolent lamenter.

"Good eve'nin' Annie…I hope you don't mind my stopping by."

The woman was so genuinely surprised she couldn't speak or move for a moment.

"I'd like to pay my respects…may I come in? I…I brought a cake…"

"—of course!" Annie blurted out when she finally found her voice. "Please come in Nathaniel…forgive me, I was just surprised…"

"—that I can cook?" The question was meant to ease Annie's awkwardness and was followed by Martin's gentle smile as he stepped into the parlor. "Actually, I can't take too much credit: Preacher Wilson's wife did everything but lick the bowl."

Annie's lips parted to smile and then she laughed outright, for the first time in many long days, and Martin's laughter joined her own until after a long moment, she simply stood smiling back at him, her eyes holding him so gratefully that his stomach trembled inside. He silently wished she would recognize him so he could physically hold her again; dear God, to be this close and not be able to touch her!

Annie stepped back and allowed Nathaniel to pass before her as he moved into the living room. Perhaps, she reconsidered still smiling, laughter has a place in mourning after all. "Thank you, Nathaniel," she offered, "I can't begin to tell you how much this means to me."

"I dunno...you might want to taste it first..."

"—I don't mean the cake—!"

"—I know," Martin broke in shaking his head as he carried the parcel into the kitchen. "I'm just trying to keep that beautiful smile on your face. I never knew your grandmother, Annie, but I think she would have liked seeing you smiling rather than crying."

Her heart seemed to skip a beat then. "When Gramma could see, she said I smiled just like Daddy, so you're right...she would."

"You look very much the gentleman, Mr. Rodgers," Monica commented upon noticing he had been to the barbershop as she stepped to Annie's side. "Trimming the hair definitely helps bring out the *real* you."

"Miss Holt," he murmured soothingly, extending his right hand in greeting. "Does anything escape your keen observation?"

"I hope not," she returned cheekily, smiling as he disengaged his hand from hers to sweep a lock of hair off his brow. "The barber forgot to trim your bangs, I think."

Martin smiled and glanced upward. "I have a cow-lick."

"Uh-huh."

Annie bit her lip in vexation: what was it between these two? "Monica, would you please be so kind as to get Nathaniel something to drink? I know he must be burning up in that wool suit as humid as it is tonight."

"Sure...you want something as well?" she asked, her eyes never leaving Martin's face.

Annie didn't answer immediately but waited until Monica finally turned to face her, then her bright, blue gaze hit Monica full-tilt and there was no question as to her point. "A truce."

"Ooooh-kay...a truce and two Pepsi's, coming right up," Monica replied lightly, smiling as she took three steps back before turning to make her way around the crowd gathered in the dining room.

Annie's lips thinned as she nodded in Monica's direction. "I apologize for Monica's...behavior? I honestly don't know what's gotten into her, Nathaniel...she'd never acted so contrary before!"

Martin shrugged as he recalled their earlier conversation at the hospital and shook his head dismissively. "She seems very protective of you; I respect that in a person."

Annie frowned. "She needs a good spanking."

"Yes ma'am, she does," he drawled promptly, and she heard the smile in his voice.

* * *

It was after ten before the last visitors left Annie's house. As she stood at the front door turning off the porch lights, she could just see the lights at Preacher Wilson's house across the street, two houses down. She wondered if Nathaniel was staying with the Wilson's or if he had taken a room at a motel in Winston-Salem. Nathaniel. He had been so kind to her through everything; and before leaving tonight, he had asked if she would allow him to escort her to the funeral home the following night, and to the funeral on Thursday. She could think of no excuse to refuse him and indeed, felt relieved that there would be a gentleman to stand with her through it all.

So why was Monica so testy around him? she wondered. He seems to be one of the most considerate men I've ever met, she thought silently; and he helped me get through Gramma's death, staying with me every minute as if we'd known each other forever...Annie shook her head and murmured inaudibly, "I've known him all of a day..."

And I knew Martin for barely two days, she added silently: just long enough to conceive a child with him. That fact alone all but guaranteed she would never be able to allow herself to feel anything more than appreciation for Nathaniel's kindness: to do otherwise would betray what she still felt for Martin...what she knew in her heart she would never feel for another man. *Dear God,* she prayed, *please let it get easier...please make the hurting and the wanting stop.* Never in her life did she imagine she might know the contentment and fulfillment Martin's loving had given to her; to know she would never experience it again made her almost wish she'd never known. The baby, she realized, was all that kept her from questioning that it had even happened.

Carrying Martin's baby also meant that, if she valued Nathaniel's friendship at all, she would have to be up front with him about everything. Immediately. Her intuition told her that Nathaniel would be the kind of man to put tremendous value on trust and honesty- his religious ties notwithstanding -and as such, he deserved to know of the ill-fated relationship she'd had, and of the child she now carried. "Pregnant and unmarried..." she murmured into the darkness, resting her forehead upon her hand where it lay flat against the wall.

"You gonna tell him?"

Annie turned around with a start and threw her hands to her chest. "Monica! Don't scare me like that!"

Throwing her own hands up in mock surrender, Monica was quick to make amends. "I'm sorry, Annie...I really didn't try to startle you—you just...you looked so defeated just now. You make me want to call Martin myself."

Annie shook her head as she stepped away from the door. "Just...don't, OK? I don't want to talk about Martin tonight, Monica. Please!"

There was a lengthy pause. Then: "How do you feel about Nathaniel?"

"**I** like him just fine," she returned. "Why don't **you**?"

"What makes you think I don't?"

"Everything you say and everything you do."

Monica pursed her lips. "Oh." Remembering the conversation she and 'Nathaniel' had earlier in the day, she turned about so Annie couldn't read the conflicting feelings on her face as they battled inside her head. It was a dastardly thing to keep Martin's true identity a secret from this woman and she knew it—Martin knew it. But they had both agreed that until the situation with Claire could be rectified, it was in Annie and his son's best interest to continue the charade. "I just don't know if I can..." Monica whispered aloud.

"What did you say?"

Monica turned about a shook her head negatively. "What do we know of the man?" she corrected aloud, feigning a suspicious frown. "So he's a 'student-preacher' from Georgia..."

"—and he's kind and considerate," Annie broke in. "And probably even...cute, if he'd get rid of the beard and glasses."

If you only knew! Monica thought as she rolled her eyes heavenward, amazed that Annie still had not seen through Martin's disguise. "So...do you tell him or not?" she asked after a thoughtful pause.

"Tell him...?"

Monica returned her friends innocent stare with her own peevish one. "About the impending arrival of the little one, Annie—another month or two and Nathaniel will be able to figure it out for himself." *And Martin will have figured out everything.*

Annie's expression turned pensive. "You know, he may not even be here in a month or two," she reasoned, more to herself than Monica. "If I don't start showing before he leaves, what would it matter if her ever knew or not?"

Monica's face was doleful for that was one thing she hadn't stopped to consider. Martin wouldn't return to Britain before she was able to make him aware of the pregnancy—would he? "Maybe Nathaniel could offer some advice where Martin's concerned. You know, the best way to tell a man he's gonna be a father again, from a man's point of view."

"I wouldn't have any problem telling him," Annie answered dryly, "if I really thought there was a future in it. But there isn't—he has a wife and a son already: if they loved each other once, and there is no one to interfere, he should do everything in his power to make it work again."

"He would want to know about the baby," Monica countered stiffly.

"It's not open to debate! Just let it go!"

Not a chance, Annie. "So what do you do with this Baptist missionary who just happened along at the most devastating time in your life? You know I don't trust anybody, but Annie...what if it's divine intervention?"

"Divine intervention?"

"Well why not! Especially if you're intent upon sacrificing a future with Martin..."

"—Monica, please!"

"If you refuse to let Martin come to you and Nathaniel is here..."

"—Nathaniel could leave tomorrow..."

"—but what if he doesn't?"

"I don't love Nathaniel! For crissake, I hardly know the man!"

Monica chose to be blunt with her argument, as always: "Do you want your baby to grow up without a father?"

Instantly, Annie turned away from her friend, and the truth, and felt a tremor of fear shake her from the inside out. The intricacies of her present situation were made so much more complex when she was forced to consider raising a child alone. She had known a father's love and dared not imagine what her life would have been like without him in it: how could she, or any woman, deny her child the right to know his father?

* * *

Martin whirled toward the night table, screaming into the telephone receiver as if the party on the other end must be deaf. "Dammit, Chris—get every scrap of information you can dig up on the bastard! Anything! If Claire is allowing that son-of-a-bitch around Stuart—"

"—Martin, please..."

"—I swear to God, she will *not* get my son! I am his father! That should account for something in your damnable courts!"

In his office in London, Christopher Taylor sat on the edge of his chair, his right hand grasping the telephone receiver while the other flipped through the latest dispatch from the investigators who had been assigned to monitor Claire Vaughn. "I think we should wait until Claire makes her relationship with Eric Nielson public before moving on this. She's still trying to keep their relationship secret at the moment, because of the custody suit; but all she has to do is be seen with him once or twice, then she doesn't have a chance in hell of successfully denying what we have on her."

"In the meantime, what if he harms Stuart? That man is a walking time bomb, I tell you! I've worked with him—I know!"

"Duncan is watching Stuart every minute that McDougall is not. And with Betsy at the townhouse with him, there is very little chance your son will have any contact with Nielson whatsoever," Chris' voice was placating. "If nothing else, we know Claire loves Stuart…she would never allow anyone to hurt the boy."

Martin laughed mirthlessly. "You don't know what that man's capable of," he said finally, closing his eyes against flashes of memories that truly haunted him now. "When he's drunk and angered, Nielson is uncontrollable. I've watched the man demolish a stage set in a matter of minutes simply because he was told to run through a third take on a scene! It doesn't matter to him what or who he hurts…hell, the next day, he'll deny he ever did anything because he can't remember doing it!"

"Rest assured Martin, the premises and the child are being monitored 24 hours a day. Should Nielson become the least bit unruly, whether the child's around him or not, we can have a bobby on the scene in a matter of moments. Indeed, so long as Stuart is unharmed, such might prove the final nail in Claire's coffin, as they say…I realize she's still your wife by law, old boy, but she truly is the most despicable creature…"

"—she and Nielson are like-animals," Martin broke in wryly. "In time, one will destroy the other. I just don't want Stuart in their path when it happens."

"I understand your concern for your son, but everything that can be done is being done…I fairly doubt you could guard him as well were you in London yourself."

"The only reason I'm not is because I can't be in two places at once!" Martin countered. Then, a bit calmer: "I trust you explicitly, Chris…just keep me updated on Nielson's comings and goings where Claire and Stuart are concerned. With the suddenness of Annie's grandmother's passing, I've been granted an idyllic opportunity to present myself to the community without very many questions being asked. I think I may even have an ally in Annie's best friend, Monica Holt." A smile etched itself across Martin's face. "Now **there** is a spit-fire, Christopher! She is easily the ballsy-est female I've ever met; you, my friend, would be appalled by the woman's candor and irascibility! She has the vocal capacity to circumvent the very best arguments from lawyers and preachers alike…"

"—Dear God, Martin, you sound as if you're…impressed!"

"I am. I haven't met a man yet who would pick up the challenges that have been thrown at her for the sake of anyone less than his own brother. Perhaps that's what impresses me most about Monica: though Annie is no blood relation to her, the woman would lay everything on the line as if she were. Such is the nature of Southerners and thankfully, the law tends to follow…those who follow strict propriety in Britain, be damned!" Martin drawled, intoning the slower speech he now soliloquized at will. "You and your English cronies would do well to open your minds somewhat where child custody battle lines are drawn, for a woman isn't automatically a good mother simply because she's borne a child."

* * *

The funeral for Emma Ryan was mercifully brief; the afternoon was unbearably steamy from humidity values past 80 percent and temperatures hovering in the low 90s, and Annie welcomed the coolness of the limousine when Nathaniel handed her into it. "Your service was wonderful, Preacher Wilson. I think you read every one of Gramma's favorite passages," she offered once the four of them were settled within the vehicle and headed away from the churchyard.

The elderly preacher squeezed Annie's left hand and turned about with a smile. "Your grandmother had made a point of letting me know several times over the years just which passages she felt the congregation needed to hear and when," he recalled fondly, his brows raised, "and I have to admit, she was usually right."

"Gramma was like that," Annie nodded. "She never was one to mince words, even the last couple of years when her health worsened."

"Are you absolutely certain then, that Monica is no relation to you?" Martin taunted smilingly. "If I didn't know better, I'd think the two of you were just describing HER!"

"I'll take that as a compliment," Monica offered.

Annie nodded and smiled into his face. "No relation, Nathaniel, I swear!"

"Do you know, I've often thought the very same thing?" the preacher concurred. "Annie's always been the odd-man-out, even when her parents were still living. I've known this child ever since she was a little thing, and she's always been just quiet, unassuming Annie. Her daddy...now there was a spitfire!"

"Gramma always said the apple didn't fall too far from the tree!" Monica offered.

"—and 'Cling, swing, spring, sing—swing up into the apple-tree." Annie sing-songed.

"Your grandmother quoted T.S. Eliot?" Martin mused incredulously.

"And Harper Lee, and Abraham Lincoln, and Carl Sandburg..."

"Don't look so surprised, Nathaniel," Monica teased as she nodded in Annie's direction. "You should read some of **Annie's** poetry..."

"—no, he shouldn't, Monica," Annie broke in shaking her head. She had shared with her friend some of her writing since meeting Martin and she was certain that was the direction of Monica's thinking.

"I didn't know you're a poet," Preacher Wilson offered.

"There's a lot you don't know..."

"—can we please change the subject?" Annie interjected heatedly. "Let's...let's just remember Gramma, okay?" Her voice was almost pleading as the car pulled into her driveway.

"Gramma's everywhere in this house, so that shouldn't be too hard," Monica offered soothingly as she squeezed Annie's hand apologetically.

After a long silence, Preacher Wilson cleared his throat. "Um...if y'all don't mind, I think I'm gonna head home...Mrs. Wilson wants me to drive her to Madison this evening to see her sister."

"Thank you for everything Preacher Wilson," Annie murmured as she stepped from the automobile. "I don't think I'd have gotten through this without your support and kind words."

"Me either," Monica admitted and then met Martin's knowing look with a smirk.

"Let's go inside ladies and fix us some lunch," Nathaniel offered as he closed the car door behind the women. "And then I want a full tour of Emma Ryan's home..." His eyes met Annie's. "I think it's time I met this wonderful soul."

* * *

Annie and Daniel sat beneath the huge, old oak tree and listened to the soothing sound of water as it trickled over the creek rock. This had become their secret place and even as young as they were, their appreciation of the quiet beauty was palpable. "Cover your ears, Annie! Here comes another dad-burned plane..." Daniel offered in a raised voice, his tone damning.

"You'll be ridin' one of them, Daniel, when y'all go to Englan'..."

"Yeah, don't remind me..."

Annie put a sliver of grass between her thumbs, linked her fingers together, and blew upon the knuckles of her thumbs as if blowing on the mouthpiece of a saxophone. There was a slight squeak and then nothing; she took another deep breath and blew a second time with similar results.

"Here, silly, let me look...your piece of grass is too thin!" Daniel stroked the palm of his hand back and forth across the tips of some nearby grass and broke off one tall blade close to the earth. "You picked yours too close to the top," he explained matter-of-factly as he pinched off all but one full inch of his blade of grass. "The bottom of the grass is wider and makes a louder whistle," he offered, and then proceeded to repeat the play of Annie's fingers, creating a high-pitched 'squall' when he blew upon his knuckles. "See? Piece of cake."

Annie tossed her useless whistle aside and picked a wild daisy to study instead. "Daddy showed me *how to make a ring out of a flower," she taunted, twirling the neck of the bloom between her finger and thumb as she studied it intently. "'wont me to show ya?"*

Daniel watched her for a moment and then picked a purple bloom from some nearby clover. "Yeah, if you want to..."

Annie took the stem of the daisy, made a circle with it, and then drew the bottom tip through the loop. She slid her middle finger through the loop and drew the ring tighter though not tight. "You hafta allow some slack 'cause the stems' 'sposed to go around and through the loop a couple more times..." Her one-handed weaving movements were stealth and measured, as she glanced upon Daniel's creation. "That's right, you're doin' good! Only thing: your ring's gonna be smaller 'cause your stem's a lot shorter."

Daniel gauged his creation against Annie's and then tossed the smaller ring aside. "I don't care...ain't like I was gonna wear it or anything."

"But it was pretty!" Annie countered as she stretched to retrieve the item, bracing her left hand on the ground as she reached to pick up the flower Daniel had tossed aside. Instantly, the pressure of her weight upon her hand and fingers caused the stem of the daisy to snap in several places and then fall off her finger. "Ohhhhh! I broke my daisy ring, Daniel!" she wailed, picking up the bloom and realizing the stem was broken beyond repair. Huge tears began to stream down her cheeks.

"What in the world are you cryin for?" Daniel asked incredulously.

Annie turned away as she tried to hide the proof of her girly offense in the crook of her arm. "I ain't cryin'," she denied in a huff. "I'm just mad is all..."

Annie's tears had been totally unexpected and the boy felt an odd need to console her. "Well look: you've got mine, Annie! It'll probably fit alright...here—let me have it and I'll show ya..."

Slowly, Annie extended her right hand in Daniel's direction and opened it to surrender the ring. She still wouldn't look at him, and he took advantage of the long moment to measure her fingers against the size of the ring's opening. Finally, he slipped it gingerly upon her pinky finger taking great care to not pinch the tiny purple bloom. Turning about then, Annie's eyes lit upon the creation and she held out her hand as if admiring a perfect diamond rather than a little boy's first attempt at jewelry making. "Thank you, Daniel," she whispered in awe. "It's beautiful, and I'll keep it forever and ever..."

A slight smile tipped one corner of Daniel's mouth as he shrugged off her compliment; it was suddenly painfully clear to the little boy that he never again wanted to see Annie cry. As he stood, Daniel recognized the sudden feeling of protectiveness he felt for the tiny girl and frowned because it was alien to him. He swallowed hard before he spoke again. "Aw, you'll probably lose it before we even get home," he taunted almost hopefully.

"Oh no I won't!" Annie argued as she too got to her feet, holding her right hand protectively near to her body as if it were injured. "I'm gonna take it home and put it right in my jewelry box...some day when you come back from Englan', I'll show you how good I took care of it!"

Daniel was glad at that moment that his back was to Annie because he felt the hot sting of his own tears threatening to spill from his eyes, and he blinked hard. "What if I never get to come back?" he murmured as if to himself.

Annie saddled up beside her friend and hugged him against her with her left arm. "Then I'll come see you!" she replied with the simple sincerity that only a child contains. "You're my best friend in the whole world, Daniel and

*you're gonna be my 'husbin' someday!" she stated matter-of-factly, loving
the boy as much as one child could love another child.*
*"Huh-uh! I ain't never getting married!" he countered as he jerked free
from Annie's embrace.*
*Annie's expression was suddenly dark as she stared at Daniel's retreating
back. "I hate you...you meanie...!"*

*　*　*

Annie woke with a start and realized the ringing phone was the culprit.
Reaching across the bed, she lifted the handset from the cradle. "'ello?"

"We missed you at church this morning," Monica offered from the other
end of the phone line. "And Nathaniel actually seemed worried...I think he
has a thing for you."

"For heaven's sake, Monica, would you stop imagining things?" Annie
returned evenly. "Last week it was a 'school-boy crush' and the week before,
'divine intervention.' Next he'll be asking me to marry him, right?" Instantly,
Annie found herself recalling the dream she'd been having and she was that
sad little girl all over again.

Monica smiled into the receiver and turned to glance in Martin's
direction. He sat expectantly on the couch and traced the line of his mouth
with the back of one thumb as he was wont to do when waiting on something.
When he saw her glance his way, he lifted his index finger against his lips as
if to say, 'Shhh—don't let her know I'm here.'

"Actually Annie, I could think of a lot worse fates."

"You are so whacked..."

"Don't'cha ever wonder what he looks like minus the beard? He might be
a real babe!" Monica taunted, and Martin's eyes rolled heavenward.

"Did you stay for dinner after preaching?" Annie interjected, trying to
change the subject. "You said yesterday you were going to..."

"—YOU said yesterday you were bringing a squash casserole, too, but
when you didn't show, I didn't stay. Where were you?"

Annie shook her head wearily. "I was sick on my stomach all morning...I
made the mistake of waiting 'till this morning to fry the chicken I'd planned
to take and my stomach objected fiercely. I did finally get it all fried and the
gravy made, but by the time my stomach settled enough to get a shower, it was
already 11:00 so I didn't figure there was much sense trying to make it to

church after all. I hope you're still coming for supper, though…I've got two hens and all the fixin's to be eaten."

"Of course I'm still coming; I intend to have some of that casserole one way or another!"

"Macaroni and cheese, too."

"Oh God!"

At Monica's exclamation, Martin leapt from where he sat and was at her side in an instant. "What's wrong?" he mouthed anxiously.

"Um, hold on Annie—someone's at the door," Monica murmured as she read the alarm in Martin's expression. Then, placing her palm over the receiver: "She had a stomach virus or something this morning and didn't feel like going to church."

"Then why did you say 'Oh God'?" he asked in frustration.

"Stepped on your toes, did I?" she teased. "Sorry, I couldn't resist! I have a weakness for inside jokes, and you've gotta admit, Martin Vaughn posing as a missionary—especially after the 'American Star' fiasco!—has to be the best yet!"

Martin's expression was anything but amused. "She's alright then?"

"She's fine; just making sure I'm still coming for supper tonight by waving macaroni and cheese under my nose—**that** and squash casserole."

Martin made a face that spoke volumes.

"You don't like squash?!" Monica asked incredulously. "Oh man, THIS I have to fix!" Returning the receiver to her ear, Monica winked at Martin as she spoke: "Annie…Hey, that was Nathaniel at the door—he says 'Hello.'"

"Is he still there?"

"Yeah, he stopped by on his way from church."

"Why don't you see if he'd like to join us for supper," Annie offered, realizing as the words left her mouth that, in her role of Cupid, Monica would have a field day with the invitation. "I have so much fixed, you and I could never eat it all," she added reasonably.

"Nathaniel, Annie would like it if you'd join us for supper at her house tonight," Monica began, the receiver still at her ear. "Her squash casserole will simply melt in your mouth…does that entice you or what?"

"If he doesn't want to come, Monica, you don't have to twist his arm!"

"I don't think twisting his arm will be necessary, Annie," Monica paused for effect. "Just the mention of squash casserole and his face lit with dis—belief! I'll bet it's one of his favorite dishes, too!"

Martin's grimace smoldered with dread.

"Well, tell him to come on about six, but YOU better be here by 5:30!"

"I'll do that."

"Alright then, I'll let you get back to your company."

"Yeah, I probably should…I'll see ya in a bit, though. Bye."

"You missed your calling, Monica…you should've been a comedienne," Martin remarked once she'd hung up the phone.

"Hey! You should be thanking me! I just got you a six o'clock invite for the best supper you'll ever eat!"

"I refuse to eat ANYTHING called 'squash.'"

Monica's face showed her doubt. "We'll see."

"You seem to love provoking me—why is that?"

"Maybe I just like testing you…I intend to see Annie happy," Monica replied seriously, "and I have to make sure you're the one who can do it for her."

"What more can I do that I haven't already done?" he implored, raising his hands in exasperation. "You're NOT her keeper."

Monica shrugged and simply smiled at his aggravation. "Careful Martin, your temper's showing."

Martin shook his head dejectedly and turned about as a curse threatened to spill from his lips. Drawing a deep breath, he chose instead to broach another subject that had been bothering him for days. "Since her grandmother's death, is Annie afraid to answer the phone when she's home alone?"

For an instant, Monica was taken aback by the change in Martin's demeanor but recovered just before he turned to receive her reply. "If she is, she hasn't let me know it."

"I'd like to think there are **some** aspects of her life that you're not entirely privy to," he offered evenly.

Monica smirked, wanting desperately to say *You'd be surprised at what I know*, but instead said, "Why do you ask?"

"I have tried calling her at varying times every night since her grandmother died, and she has yet to answer the phone. I could have just left her house and KNOW she's there and she still doesn't answer. Or like last night: I tried calling from Preacher Wilson's house just after dusk…I could see her standing at the picture window in the parlor, with her arms hugging herself, staring at the phone as it rang…but she wouldn't pick it up."

Martin's expression grew so serious, Monica found herself hanging on his every word. "I'm afraid of what may be going through her mind because—as

Martin—I've only spoken to her once since she left me in New York…it's like she knows I'm trying to reach her, but she refuses to let me."

Monica's face twisted in confusion as she rested one hip against the back of the couch she stood beside. "That's ridiculous, Martin—I called her about eleven last night and she got the phone on the second ring. Why would she answer it sometimes but not others?"

Shrugging, he shook his head and simply replied, "I don't know."

"I think it's coincidence: you're either calling when she's in the shower or up to her elbows pulling weeds, or something!"

"What about last night? I SAW her stand and watch the phone ring…"

"—then she was probably giving Dr. Love the brush-off. I know he's still calling her…"

"—Dr. Love?"

"—Dr. Barry Roberts, an intern at the hospital. He started hitting on her even before the 'American Star' article. Apparently, he copied Annie's number from a Rolodex at the nurse's station and calls almost weekly to see if she's come to her senses yet and will agree to meet him for a drink. Gramma put him in his place a time or two, I think."

Bracing his hands upon the back of Monica's couch, Martin clinched his mouth shut before the string of curses that threatened were able to leave his mouth. But the agitation at learning another man was attempting to see Annie showed clearly in his pulsing temple, and Monica smiled to herself at the man's tightly controlled jealousy.

"The man's a jerk, Martin. I know for a fact Annie wouldn't give him the time of day," she consoled, "so it's not like he's competition or anything. Hell, even I wouldn't date him!"

Strangely, Martin felt his anger lessen somewhat at her confession and almost smiled when he turned his head sideways to speak to her again. "I don't think you fully understand how hard it is for me to continue this—this LIE when every morning I get up with the intention of telling Annie everything, and I go to sleep promising the same!"

"Maybe it's time you had a talk with your libido."

Martin's expression showed she had nailed him. "I can't bear the thought of her possibly being interested in another man, Monica…not even, 'Nathaniel.' Can you believe that?"

"Yeah, I can," she answered, crossing her arms nonchalantly as she continued to study him. "Too, I suppose it wouldn't do to complicate things any more than they already are by having her fall for Nathaniel when Nathaniel doesn't really exist."

"She'd think it a cruel trick."

"With good reason."

"So how do we ensure that she remains disinterested?"

Monica smiled to herself and studied him out of the corner of one eye: "We could make Nathaniel gay?"

Martin did not smile.

"Married, then."

"I've already told her he isn't."

Monica pursed her lips thoughtfully. "You have a girlfriend back home in Georgia...and you've been engaged for two years...and you're waiting to marry until she finishes at the University of Georgia! There! Simple!"

Martin nodded hesitantly before another thought crossed his mind: "Once the issue of Stuart's custody is decided and she eventually learns the truth about who I am, will Annie be able to forgive me, US, for having deceived her?"

"Oh, wow..." Monica murmured as she began imagining all the possibilities. "She's got to, Martin...she's just got to..."

Martin twisted uncomfortably in his chair as Monica smilingly handed him the platter of squash casserole; accepting it hesitantly, he stared at it as if he half expected it to bite him.

"You really do not have to eat any, Nathaniel," Annie offered, catching the look of dread that had lit his eyes when Monica passed him the platter. "Monica was teasing when she said you liked squash, wasn't she?"

Casting a furtive glance in Annie's direction. Martin simply smiled and decided to be completely honest (what he silently longed to do): "Truth is, I've never tried squash casserole...I've never been able to get past the name..."

Smiling as she caught Monica's amused expression from where she sat to the right of him Annie asked, "Do you like zucchini?"

Martin's eyebrows rose and he nodded affirmatively. "I love zucchini."

Her smile was solicitous. "Did you not know that zucchini is a squash?" she asked without rancor, her expression growing amused as she saw the look of surprise that lit his face. "Yellow squash—or crook-neck as we always called it—is even better than zucchini. And there's no sweeter way to prepare it than as a casserole…with milk, and butter, and bread-crumbs, and a little sugar…won't you at least try some, Nathaniel?"

"Yeah, Nathaniel! Eat your veggies like a good boy!" Monica teased.

"I've eaten all of mine!"

"There's plenty, Monica, would you like seconds—"

"—allow me," Martin broke in as he quickly spooned two large servings onto Monica's plate. "Your MOUTH…er, plate should never be empty," he insisted in a tone that dripped with sarcasm, and smiled when he heard Annie's low laughter. Once past his distaste for squash (which he quickly decided he liked very much!), Martin's knee nudged Monica's under the table to remind her of the conversation she was to initiate during the meal.

Within a few moments of the discussion, Martin found himself relieved that Annie seemed unaffected when he made her aware of Nathaniel's 'engagement.'

"There is no set wedding date, then?" Monica asked once the story had been laid out. "I mean, you're not planning on leaving…any time soon…?"

"Two years is a fairly open-ended span of time, Monica; but no, I…I don't really have a schedule, as such," Martin replied querulously, somewhat peeved that she seemed to be trying to pin him down to some time-table; and he couldn't for his life imagine why. His eyes bored into hers intently as if speaking solely to her: "I suppose I'll leave once my purpose here is at its end."

Monica pursed her lips and nodded in that self-satisfied way both Martin and Annie recognized. What they didn't know was her intention to keep Martin around until he could learn about the baby; since Annie had no plan to broach the subject with 'Nathaniel,' she meant to see that Martin remained in the area until Annie's condition presented itself to him.

"When you do see that you have to go," Annie offered warmly, "you'll keep in touch, won't you? I mean, I'm sure I speak for Monica when I say you've become a dear friend and we'd like for you to write or call from time to time."

At the mention of calling, Martin cast Monica a sideways glance hoping she would bring up the matter they'd earlier discussed while he was present.

The glint of recognition in Monica's expression told him she was thinking the same. "Absolutely, Nathaniel…you're irritatingly like another older brother."

"And she already has four!" Annie offered with a smile.

"Maybe that's why we get along so well!" Martin teased.

Annie laughed outright then, and Monica had the good grace to blush. "What about Martin Vaughn, Annie…has HE even bothered to call since the 'American Star' article?"

There was a long, intense silence then as both Monica and Martin watched Annie's face turn ashen in response to her troubled emotions. The mere mention of his name had set her to trembling. "Martin and I…we haven't talked but that once," she murmured finally, her whispered voice drawing both Monica and Martin to unconsciously lean toward her from opposite sides of the kitchen table. "He's called, but I don't answer the phone…"

Monica glanced at Martin then back to her friend. "If you haven't answered the phone, Annie, how do you know…"?

"—I know when it's him, Monica…I know every time…" Though Annie sat stone still, her eyes flickered across the table to meet Monica's then Martin's and finally Monica's again before she lowered them to the vase of wild daisy's in the center of the table. "I want to know that Martin's alright, and that the article hasn't hurt him or his family, but I can't…" Slowly her eyes rose self-consciously to meet Martin's again and she shook her head at his inquisitive stare. "It's a very long story, Nathaniel, and one I don't want to relate to anyone else…I hope you understand…"

"No! I mean, of course I understand, Annie, but you must know you can talk to me about anything," he offered. "I…I would never betray your confidence…"

"—you had to like, take an oath for confessions or whatnot…all preachers do, right?" Monica offered. Then to Annie, "Maybe talking with Nathaniel would help after all," she prodded. "A man's point of view might…"

"—a man's point of view won't change anything," Annie interrupted, her eyes imploring Monica to not argue. "Please…" she murmured, shaking her head when she thought Monica might begin again. "I don't want to talk about it, anymore…"

Drawing a deep breath, Monica relaxed against the chair back, shaking her head disgustedly at Annie's stubbornness. She could only imagine how frustrated Martin felt; it took every once of willpower to keep from telling the man the truth herself!

It would be several moments before anyone spoke again; as Martin slowly rose from his chair, be merely whispered his thank you for the delicious supper.

"But there's pie and coffee for dessert—" Monica offered in a final attempt to restart the conversation. "And it's early yet...not even dark outside..."

Martin never bothered to turn as he replied, "I don't want to overstay my welcome..." He was unable to even look again at Annie who had remained totally silent.

And he couldn't stay in the room a moment longer. "I know my way out, ladies...good night..."

CHAPTER EIGHT

Martin lay awake in his bed that night, unable to fall asleep as his memories of Annie seemingly tormented him at will. Her ghost had sat beside him in the rental car as he'd driven back to his hotel room, and had lathered his body when he showered; and now, as he lay naked between the crisp hotel sheets, her lips lightly brushed his chest and shoulders as he imagined her lying full upon him. And while his huge hands surrounded her head with acute gentleness and wove themselves deeper into her hair, she stroked his body in that way that made him feel protected and content and cherished. The longing just would not stop.

He rose from the bed again, for at least the fifth time, and wandered about the nearly darkened room as if to walk her off his mind. Pausing by the bathroom door, he caught a glimpse of his reflection in the mirror over the vanity and remembered how she had traced the lines and curves of his face, memorizing him in the half-light as if she knew she might have only memories of him for the rest of her life. He swallowed and cursed the bearded man in the mirror, swiping at his longish hair with both hands as if to jerk it out by the roots. Inwardly he seethed with frustration that she had not seen through the disguise, that her mind hadn't figured out the duplicity. *How could she not see?* he screamed to himself, when he knew she'd once so lovingly memorized his face.

Annie sat at the kitchen table and stared at the glass of juice in her hands. The house was completely dark, save for the lamp in the parlor she let burn all night long now, and she prayed again- for the umpteenth time this night - that if God would just let Martin call once more, she would answer the phone…she would answer this time. "I swear I will," she whispered into the darkness, closing her eyes again as she allowed her mind to envision Martin the way she had last seen him…

Such a beautiful man, she had thought as she laid beside him watching him sleep. When his features are relaxed as they are now, he looks like a little boy- vulnerable and trusting. But his chest and shoulders and arms have never been, I don't think…his skin is tanned and tight across his body, his muscles hard beneath it; and there are scars and calluses ingrained in lighter shades that she knew men got when they labored. Some of his scars had appeared to be as old as the man, and she winced at the thought of him never being a child.

When she had allowed one hand to finally touch him, her fingertips were drawn to the curve of his jaw, just beneath his ear, where she had nestled her lips as he'd moved into her body that final time. She'd grimaced at finding that her teeth had marked him and knelt above him on her hands and knees as if perhaps a kiss would make it better. And then she had tasted him again, and his sweat on her lips had been sweet in contrast to the musky scent of his hair causing her mind to spiral as she moved to back away from him. She drew her hands into fists against her mouth for they literally trembled as she held herself apart from him. But then he moved, and the sheet dropped away from his waist until he lay naked and rigid beside her, and she realized that if she did not leave then, at that very moment, she would never be able to…

The shrill, high-pitched ring of the telephone so startled her that Annie had to grasp the table's edge with both hands to steady herself before standing from her chair. By the second ring, she thought it probably just a coincidence she'd prayed for the phone to ring and then should have it happen. By the third ring, she had slowed her breathing back to near normal and closed her eyes as she lifted the receiver to her ear. "Hello?"

Sitting on the edge of his bed, Martin held his breath—he had not expected her to answer the phone, so the sound of her voice on the other end of the line startled him somewhat and he was slow in responding.

"Hello, Annie," he replied after a long moment, taking great care to not intone the Southern drawl he had come to use these last few weeks; he was Martin now.

"Martin…how are you?" she asked evenly, cradling the receiver with both hands. "It's been a while."

"Yes…it has been a while," he murmured, remembering anew the pain he had felt at her rejection the last time he had called. "I've tried calling numerous times in past weeks, but never got an answer: I even wondered if perhaps you'd changed your number after I called before," he confessed in all honesty.

Annie felt herself well chastised. "I'm sorry…I just…whenever I thought it was you calling, I was afraid to answer the phone," she replied just as honestly.

"Indeed?" He didn't appreciate hearing for the second time that night her intentional avoidance of him.

"I mean, I didn't know what I would say to you," she corrected. "A part of me wanted you to call, Martin, just to know you were alright…but…"

"—you were afraid I'd insist on seeing you."

There was a long pause. "Yes," she whispered.

Martin laughed mirthlessly. "And yet, you answered just now! Perhaps you were hoping it was someone else?"

"No, Martin…"

"Because by now, it's certainly been long enough that I must have moved on."

"I couldn't blame you if you have…I would certainly understand…"

"—that my feelings have changed? That I no longer care if I ever see you again or not?" he asked in frustration, raking his hair out of his eyes. "What should I feel for you now, Annie? What would be comfortable…what's allowed?"

Annie rubbed her eyes wearily, seeing his face behind closed eyelids and wondering the same thing herself. "I don't know what's allowed in a situation like ours, Martin…it's so complicated! I've gone through it over and over again in my mind until the only thing I'm sure of is there are no clear-cut answers. What you or I may want isn't automatically possible, you know that…not when other people are involved…"

"—like your grandmother?" he interjected heatedly, and then cursed his own callousness.

"Gramma…my grandmother passed, Martin," she murmured hesitantly, still finding it hard to put voice to the fact. "She um, she had been completely well, the best health she'd known in weeks! But then, I don't know…she just…suddenly…she suffered a massive stroke about three weeks ago and…"

Martin drew a long breath. "I'm sorry, Annie…truly I am." He cursed himself for thinking she might still use her obligations to the elderly woman, her excuse for leaving him in New York, as the reason for her continued unease. "The other people...you're talking about Stuart, now."

"Yes...I haven't heard very much about your situation: I mean were you able to resolve your differences with your wife? It must certainly be the best thing for your little boy, Martin. A child needs both his parents, especially at his young age...you *must* know that."

Standing from where he had been sitting on the edge of the bed, Martin picked up the cradle-mount telephone from the nightstand and began pacing the distance between the bed and the door. It was impossible for him to sit still. "If you mean have I dropped the divorce action, no I haven't nor do I intend to. In fact, I'm fighting now simply to hold on to at least partial custody of my son. Unfortunately, the legal system in...uh, here in Britain is notorious for dragging these things out over several months, sometimes years."

"I can't imagine what you're going through; Lord I pray I never have to...I do know how I'd feel if someone were trying to take my child away from me," she sympathized, recalling Monica's plea to make Martin aware of the child they had conceived. "I...I would do murder before I'd let someone take my baby from me," she confessed, surprising herself with the absolute certainty of her words.

"It's been hell, Annie," he murmured. "I miss him so much...I'm not even allowed visitation at this point in time, so I'm basically at Claire's mercy until the courts decide otherwise. My attorney assures me the decision will be fair; I have to hope and pray that he's right."

Annie pressed one hand flat upon her stomach, Martin's words making her face the fact that, to deny him knowledge of their child made her just as bad as Claire. *I can't think about that right now,* she told herself, and welcomed Martin's voice interrupting the direction of her thoughts. "Until something is resolved, it would seem that I have no choice but to remain in seclusion. Claire is following every newspaper and magazine lead, and is attempting to have me followed, thinking that I will give her something to use against me in this custody battle."

"How badly did the 'American Star' article hurt your case?"

"Don't even think about that, Annie," Martin countered. "You're the one who stood to lose the most because of that rag, because you've never had to deal with the crap those tabloids try to circulate; I have and I know how to handle it...well, me and my attorney, that is." There was a pause. "Are you alright, Annie...really?"

The woman ran her free hand through her hair to pull it away from her face and swiped at several strands that stuck to cheeks where her tears had fallen. "I'll be alright, so long as I know t-that someday I'll see you again..." She covered the telephone receiver with the palm of her hand to keep Martin from hearing her cry, until she heard the emotion in his voice as well.

"Dear Lord, I would be with you NOW if it were possible!" he murmured, resting the base of the phone on the bed as he stared toward the window of his room. "I never stopped wanting you, not for a minute! And were it not for that bit...were it not for Claire, I would be with you right now...you cannot know how desperately I want to hold you..."

"Oh, I think I can...I think about you every single moment," Annie smiled as she rested her forehead against the kitchen wall.

"It makes me feel better to know I haven't completely lost you...all those weeks you didn't answer, I thought..."

"I um, I was afraid if I heard your voice again and if you asked m-me again to let you come here, I wouldn't have been a-able to say no—despite knowing Gramma would never accept you." She licked her lips and took a deep breath: "I would have gone behind her back to see you, Martin...I would have lied to her, I would have lied to my friends...I would have done anything to be with you, even if it was just for one night..."

Martin took a deep breath as he returned the base of the telephone to the nightstand and sat himself down fully on the bed. Once again he closed his eyes and Annie appeared in his mind just as clearly as if she were standing before him now...her love, her desire, her need for him tantalizingly close—his again if he could only touch her. "I need you, Annie," he whispered at last, an odd note in his voice that didn't escape Annie's attention.

"I know...I know..."she murmured, swallowing hard, her body suddenly racked with a chill as she remembered how completely he had loved her. *How long must I live with only these memories?* she silently prayed to no one.

"We won't have to wait much longer," Martin enthused as if answering her and for just an instant, Annie wondered if she had spoken aloud. "This thing with Claire – it'll be resolved as soon as humanly possible. And I swear to you," he whispered, his voice husky and frightening and delicious, "once I have you again, you'll *never* be made to want for anything again...not ever."

She hugged herself as another chill shook her body, her breath raspy as fresh tears streamed down her face. "All I want is you, Martin, that's all...that's all I want..." she moaned over and over, no longer hearing his voice on the other end of the line. What she didn't realize is that he wasn't speaking; he sat in the silent darkness of his hotel room and simply listened to her cry until he swore he couldn't listen anymore...

"Your momma came by this mornin' and told my momma that y'all could go to Sunrise Services with us in Ol'Salem this Sunday!" Annie announced excitedly.

"What's Ol'Salem?"

The little girl's expression was thoughtful: "It's this place, where Daddy buys Ma'raven Sugar Cake and...Ma'raven Stars...and, where Gramma wonts us to go every Easter since we're all Ma'raven...so that's where we go!"

Daniel's expression looked doubtful. "I don't think it's allowed if you're Cath'lic."

*Annie propped her hands upon where she would develop hips one day and shook her head at Daniel's reply. "You just don't know nothin' 'bout ra'ligin, do ya? The Good Lord don't care if you're Cath'lic, or Ma'raven, or just a plain ol Baptist...He just wants you to go to church...He don't care which one," she reasoned. "This one's **real** old! And there's this cemetery...you won't believe how long some of these people have been dead!"*

Daniel swiped at his nose with the back of one hand. "Your daddy took you to the cemetery?" he asked incredulously.

"Well, yeah..."

"You think we might can go Sunday?" Daniel asked hopefully. He was forever amazed at all the neat things Annie and her daddy did together.

"I don't see why not...it'll hafta be after the preachin though," Annie added thoughtfully. "Mother said Gramma pitched a fit one year when Daddy wanted to leave early because of the cold: Gramma said hadn't nobody ever died because the Sunrise Service was too cold! Then Daddy said they wouldn't ever see the sunrise anyway because it was snowin! And then Gramma said that was beside the point."

"Must've been before you was born, 'cause I'm almost two years older than you are, and I don't remember it ever snowing for Easter!"

"Wouldn't it be pretty, though? And we could hide Easter eggs all day long and never find 'em if the snow was deep enough!"

Daniel looked at the little girl as if she were crazy. "You're just wishin, now," he countered, shaking his head.

Annie sat down in the rocking chair across from where Daniel straddled the front porch handrail and rested her chin in the palm of her hand. "You ever wonder what you wanna be someday when you grow up?"

Daniel was concentrating on seeing how long he could balance on his butt with his feet off the ground and his arms out to his sides. "I guess...why?"

"I don't know...do ya think you'll hafta stay in Englan' when you grow up?"

"Heck no!" Daniel replied. "I can guarantee you I'm comin back home just as soon as I can!" At that moment, Annie's father approached the screen door from inside and paused for a moment to listen to the children's exchange.

"You think...you'll ever change your mind about gettin married?"

Daniel's expression was incredulous. "Annie, I've told you a hundred times: I-ain't-gettin-married! So you can just quit askin!"

Stephen Ryan had to catch himself to keep from laughing out loud.

"You're a do-do, Daniel!" Annie blurted out. "All I'm tryin to 'splain is that if you and me got married, maybe your daddy wouldn't make you move away to Englan'! Ain't you ever heard what the preacher says when there's a weddin?"

Daniel looked at Annie as if she'd lost her mind. "I don't recall ever havin to go to one, thank you very much!"

Annie shook her head and rolled her eyes heavenward. "He says, 'Till death do your part.' Do you know what that means? That means you have to do everything together, EVERY thing," Annie emphasized matter-of-factly.

"Even go to the bathroom?" Daniel asked as if stricken, and Annie's father shook his head at the boy's terrified expression.

"Nooo, preachers don't won't you doin that, Daniel! Other stuff, like mowin the yard and washin dishes and working in the garden! You have to do it together, it's the law!"

"I don't believe you..." Daniel murmured.

"You ask your momma! The preacher plainly says "By the power festered in me, I now pronounce you husbin an wife...what God joined together..." Annie's expression became thoughtful. "Somethin about some man...I don't remember exactly, but I know it's the law!"

"What God hath joined together, let no man put asunder," the elder Ryan corrected as he opened the screen door and joined the children on the front porch. "You kids planning a weddin? As father of the bride, I have to know so I can start saving up to pay for it!"

"Tell him, Daddy! Tell him if we got married, he wouldn't have to move to Englan'...it's the law, ain't it?" She nodded, her mouth pursed in that self-satisfied way he'd long recognized was from his own mother.

"I'm afraid there's one small problem with your plan for Daniel's amnesty, sugar: you're a little too young to get married just yet."

Those tiny fists went back to those missing hips in a flash. "Well just how old do I have to be?"

"At least 18 I think," he replied tenderly, genuinely moved by the sincerity of his daughter's feelings for her young friend.

*"That's a **long** time from now!" Daniel interjected. "Gosh, Annie, we'll be so old!"*

"I don't think I like this at all!" she chimed in, sounding so much like her grandmother that her father chuckled.

"I'm sorry, sugar, but it's the law..."

*   *   *

Annie awakened from the dream and would have cried had the nausea not hit her first.

For eight days, she had battled insomnia and odd dreams and morning sickness and Monica's continuous flow of questions; for once made aware of Martin's call, there seemed no end to her deluge of advice.

"You need to sell this house," she announced one morning, standing in the hallway outside the upstairs bathroom as she waited for Annie to exit.

Within a moment, Annie opened the bathroom door; standing with a cold bath cloth pressed against her forehead, she murmured, "I need to WHAT?"

"Sell it!" Monica repeated as she moved away from the wall she had been leaning against. "If you put it on the market NOW, by the time Martin's able to come for you, it'll be sold!"

Annie leaned against the handrail as she carefully padded down the length of the stairs; after what seemed like an eternity, she reached the parlor and the comfort of her grandmother's wing chair. "I can't, Monica...I *won't* sell Gramma's house...I don't even want to think about it."

Sitting across from Annie in the matching love seat, Monica pursed her lips and shook her head distractedly. "How 'bout renting it out, then?"

"Why do I have to do anything right now?" Annie countered, suddenly frustrated by Monica's interrogation. "It's not like I'm on any schedule! It could be weeks or even months before Martin's divorce is finalized!" Her voice became more frustrated. "I cannot think straight as it is, okay…your berating me over and over and over does nothing but confuse me even more! I don't need it!"

"But you DO need to start making plans! You're going into your second trimester, Annie, and it's just a matter of weeks or maybe even days before you won't be able to hide your pregnancy anymore…" Monica knelt before her dearest friend and took both her hands into her own. "You know how folks are in small towns like ours: once you begin to show, and tongues begin to wag, SOMEONE will tie your being pregnant and unmarried to that 'American Star' article…how long do you think it'll take for someone to put two and two together?"

"I've thought about all that…and I know, I know what you're saying is true…but I'm not just gonna run away and hide! Everything I know and care about is right here, so many memories are here, my family home is here…my entire family is buried just a few miles down the road! Why on earth would I leave the things that are dearest to me simply because I'm going to have a baby?" she all but pleaded. "Don't you think this is the one time in my life when stability is most important? This house and all the memories that go with it MEAN stability to me."

Monica stood and walked wordlessly to retrieve her purse from where it sat upon the kitchen counter. When she returned, she opened it and removed a folded and worn copy of the 'American Star,' laying it face up upon Annie's lap. "Imagine that photograph with an inset of your baby's say, six months down the road—the headline would probably be some witty eye-catcher like 'He Has His Father's Nose: Vaughn Love Child a Christmas Surprise!'" She paused for effect. "Not enough? Then imagine some photographer camped out front in Gramma's rocking chair, or sitting on the back stoop some Sunday morning waiting for you to leave for church—what will stability mean to you then?"

Lifting tear-filled eyes from where they had settled upon the photo of Martin and her self, Annie folded the paper in half again and stared back at Monica reproachfully. "Why is it that every time in the last three months I've tried to do what I think is right, I've gotten these foreboding 'what ifs' from you that go in the exact opposite direction? You did it when I went to New York, and you did it when Gramma was dying…for a while, you even had me questioning Nathaniel's motives that I found myself sometimes doubting *his* legitimacy!"

Seeing Monica's expression turn pensive, she shook her head disdainfully, the action causing two huge tears to slip from her eyes. "I'm supposed to have a baby in little less than six months, Monica, but you have me so insecure about myself that I have to wonder if I'm capable of doing that! Am I just *that* stupid or—"

"—you are NOT stupid!" Monica broke in, shaking her head. "And I would never mean for you to think that! You are idealistic and…and naïve: you see the good in everything, regardless! Where public opinion is concerned Annie, you want to see logic and open-mindedness where others enjoy condemnation…you see and respect every person's right to the pursuit of happiness, whereas the people who are already happy doubt other folks' right to be! You should have been in the Peace Corps, for crissake, not an unmarried mother-to-be living in a small town in the Bible-belt abiding by archaic laws set forth by Jesse Helms!"

Annie bit her lip to keep from smiling. Monica's simple, forthright words tapped a sensibility she could not argue. But the question now was, what should she do to ensure what was best for her child, and Martin, and Stuart, and herself? "Should I rent an apartment, then?" she asked at last, her tone void of anger or frustration now. "Should I move to Winston…or Greensboro, maybe? How far away is far enough?"

Monica smiled and shrugged her shoulders. "You said Martin would call again in a week to ten days—why not ask him?"

"Because then I would have to tell him why it may be necessary for me to relocate," she answered tartly, more in control of her emotions than before. "With everything else he already has on him, he doesn't need another burden."

"I dunno, Annie…after hearing what he said about fighting for custody of his son, he sounds like he's a very loving father: he doesn't sound at all like the type of man who would call fatherhood a burden."

Annie smirked. "You know what I mean—"

"—I know what you should do," she bandied with a catty smile, stepping forward to pat Annie's still-flat stomach. "Don't let him find out the wrong way," Monica warned, holding her friend's gaze for a long moment.

Is there a right way? Annie wondered as her eyes strayed to the 'American Star,' and she recalled anew how learning things the wrong way could hurt those you care for the most.

Sitting at his lawyer's desk, Martin so intently studied the file the detectives had compiled on his wife Claire and her lover Eric Nielsen that, were it not for his slowly brushing the knuckle of his thumb back and forth across his lips, Chris might have otherwise believed him asleep. "Do tell me when you've gotten to the good part," he murmured.

Martin's blazing green gaze shot up. "There is no good part," he muttered angrily, not bothering at that point to continue reading any further. Flipping the stapled pages back into chronological order he all but hissed, "I take it there are photographs as well?"

Smiling smugly, Chris produced a photo album at least two inches thick and which housed both black and white and color 5x7s and 8x10s. Flipping through the pages, Martin was made to tilt his head to the left to view some angles and to the right for others; several times he had to turn the book completely when a succession of photos changed from vertical to horizontal and back again.

"As you can see, both wide angle and zoom lenses were implemented in order to capture the subjects in their, ah, entirety…" Chris offered, smiling when Martin turned the book in his direction to point out one particular set of pictures.

"You got these with a wide angle and a zoom?" Martin asked his brow arched in disbelief.

Chris studied the photos Martin held up for his perusal, pursing his lips thoughtfully as he tilted his head from side to side. "I understand no less than three cameras were used during each sitting, as it were."

Several moments passed and Martin's face twisted at times, reminding his attorney of a child who was viewing impressionist art in a gallery for the very first time. At others, a couple of photos were obviously met with utter disdain for his mouth would smirk sour and he'd flip ahead as if trying to find something less offensive. Upon reaching the final pages, however, Martin sat bolt upright in his seat and laid the book carefully upon the desk before him as if he thought he might drop it otherwise. Slowly, maddeningly so, he turned the half-dozen or so pages one by one, murmuring under his breath until upon reaching the last one, he lifted hard, hurt eyes to meet Chris'; it was all he could do to keep the tremor out of his voice.

"These are…very graphic…very disturbing photographs, Chris," he muttered acidly, seemingly awed and disturbed at the same time.

"I greatly hope the mere knowledge we are in possession of such material will deter any further effort on your wife's part to keep your son from you,"

Chris concurred, appreciating the grievous expression on Martin's face. "If necessary however, with some minor editing measures, they could be made available to the dailies: we must hope, of course, that such drastic measures will not be necessary and that your wife will not only welcome but initiate visitation between you and your son."

Martin didn't reply.

"Of course, with this kind of evidence, you may prefer to use it to its full capacity…indeed, I've already prepared the necessary documentation so that, if you so desire, we may petition the court for physical custody of the child, tomorrow morning in fact…all that's required is your signature."

Martin swallowed hard and stared for a very long while at the leather bound album, leaving Chris to believe his friend was pleased beyond words. But as the silence between the two men grew, the attorney found himself unnerved, wondering if by providing such evidence of Claire's debauchery and appalling lack of morality, he had ventured beyond the limit Martin was willing to go in order to garner court-ordered visitation with his son—that he would not go so far as to disgrace the child's mother in the public's eye.

"Tell me, Martin," he asked at last, his voice even and calm. "If the graphic nature of these photographs is such that you prefer to, how shall I say, limit the level to which they are made public knowledge, any and all sessions between our respective offices may be held strictly in judges chambers…"

"—no."

Chris paused as if expecting Martin to say more. "I'm not certain I understand…"

"—I want to sue for full custody. I want my son, Chris…" Martin replied in a low, fitful murmur. He shook his head violently, disbelievingly and angrily swiped at his eyes as his cheeks showed suspiciously wet. "Stuart's only six years old! Damn her for doing that to him!"

Though he'd known the other man since the two were young children, Chris was somewhat surprised by the fury and passion in Martin's anger. "Remember that children are incredibly resilient, Martin. We must pray that with time and the appropriate counseling, he will simply forget…"

"—how can he ever forget?" the aggrieved father exploded, grabbing the photo album and angrily flipping backward until his hand paused in a fist upon one particular photograph. "Look at his face, Chris! He's standing inside her bedroom door crying, his mouth is open, he's calling for his mommy, just trying to get her to acknowledge he's even there…she never notices him! But how could she, pressed face down upon the bed with that drunken bastard behind her!"

"—Martin, please…"

"—I want her and that son of a bitch charged with child abuse, and neglect…and whatever else your damnable courts deem 'unlawful' or…or 'a heinous act!' I don't care how much it costs," he growled. "Get my son away from Claire, tomorrow if possible! I don't care **who** knows about these pictures—you use them to save my son, even if it means you have to plaster them across the front of every newspaper in this country!"

* * *

Claire Vaughn sat at the conference table with her attorney at her side and chewed at her bottom lip; her hands shook so badly that she could barely turn the pages of the album that lay open upon the table. Across from her sat Martin and Chris, the table before them completely barren. And at the head of the table sat the presiding judge, an identical album to the one in front of Claire as well as several manila envelopes spread out in front of him. They held the necessary documents Chris had prepared for Martin to gain full, legal custody of his son.

That the petition had been heard so quickly surprised even Chris; but the greatest satisfaction came when, at the end of both lawyer's arguments, the Judge accepted Chris' motion to enter the photos into evidence; overruling Claire's attorney's objection, he cited their relevance to the case as being lawful, just, and substantial.

Now, as the group sat in relative silence while both the Judge and Claire's attorney made notations during their review of the photographs, Martin found himself particularly pleased to see his wife so completely unnerved; she wasn't one to show open expressions of emotion, excepting anger, and that she had become so upset before ever getting to the photos that included their son gave him some sense of optimism.

"I take it the child in the photographs is the subject of the custody petition," the Judge offered some moments later.

"Excuse me?" Claire's attorney broke in, glancing up at the Judge and then across at Chris. "Which photographs, Your Honor, are we referencing at this time?"

"If I may, Your Honor," Chris volunteered, 'the photos on pages 123 through 130, dated June 10 of this year, picture the minor child Stuart Vaughn as he, ah, walks in on his mother and Mr. Eric Nielson while the two are engaged in, shall we say, a rather intimate physical consortium."

Immediately, Claire's attorney flipped several pages forward in the photo album until his deep intake of breath and Claire's murmured, "Oh my God!" signaled they had found the disturbing and very damning photographs.

"It bears repeating that, included in this Court's most recent decision concerning temporary custody of Stuart Vaughn," Chris continued, "one stipulation Your Honor mandated was that at no time during the temporary custody period was a male person not related to the minor child to be allowed within the residence, dwelling, domicile or other environment in which the child must subsist with his mother…"

"—objection, Your Honor!" Claire's attorney broke in. "There can be no positive indication whatsoever that these photographs were taken at the Vaughn residence! It is quite indiscernible, given the, er, closeness of the subjects in the frames, whether Mrs. Vaughn and the gentleman were in fact in the home or in the privacy of a motel room…"

"—it is certainly the understanding of this Court that 'other environment in which the child must subsist with his mother' may very well encompass the confines of an automobile, Mr. Chase, if indeed that environment is being utilized as a vehicle for an intimate physical consortium which the child is made to witness," the Judge countered. "I daresay there is no question what has been documented with these photographs?"

There was a pause. "No, Your Honor."

"The subjects who were photographed while engaged in such an intimate…act, Mr. Chase, are they not in fact Claire Vaughn and a Mr. Eric Nielson?"

"Yes, Your Honor."

"I'll ask you again, Mr. Chase: Is the child who is pictured during this act, and who was made to witness the same, the minor child Stuart Vaughn?"

Claire's attorney looked sideways at his client; she would not meet his eyes. "Yes, Your Honor, it is."

For the first time in almost seven years of marriage, Martin saw Claire Vaughn cry.

*   *   *

Monica sat cross-legged upon her bed, applying a second coat of nail polish to her toenails, when the telephone by her bed rang. Glancing at the alarm clock that sat beside it, she winced at the lateness of the hour and hurried to grab the receiver before the phone could ring a second time and awaken her parents who slept at the end of the hall. "Hello?"

"Hello, Monica…it's Martin."

Jerking about to give full assault to the telephone, Monica murmured, "Where the hell are you?! Annie told me two weeks ago she was expecting to hear from you in…"

"—hold it, Monica! Just…chill a minute, alright?" he interrupted, using one of the phrases he'd so often heard her use. "Is Annie alright? Has something happened?"

Twisting the bottle of nail polish closed, Monica shook her head in frustration. "No…nothing's happened…Annie's fine…but she's worried SICK about you **and** 'Nathaniel!' Do you realize 'Nathaniel' has been AWOL for nearly a month now? What the hell were you thinking, leaving here without so much as a goodbye? I mean, modern-day missionaries DO use telephones!"

Martin rubbed his eyes with his right thumb and index finger, wincing at Monica's scolding. "Look, if you will give me a chance to explain…"

"Start talking."

He shook his head wearily. "First of all, when I called Annie, I hadn't yet left the States…I led her to believe that I was calling from seclusion in Britain, but in fact I was still in my room at the Zevely Inn…"

"—how convenient! Just across the road from the Old Salem Tavern!"

"Can I finish? I only decided to come back to Britain after we spoke that night. I realized before I ever got off the phone to her that I had to do something more constructive than sit in my room and wait on my attorney to summon me home. So, I flew out the next morning.

"When I arrived at Chris' office, he told be that the investigators we'd had watching Claire while I was away were compiling an extensive report and that it would be presented to us within the week. As it happened, the week ran nearly into two and I was left debating whether or not to contact Annie again, since I still knew no more than I had before I left."

"But can't you appreciate how concerned she's been for 'Nathaniel?' The two of you spent a lot of time together after Gramma died…she'd grown to genuinely care for him, er…you…" Monica stammered. "*For the person you pretended to be,* alright! You left her house after having supper that night- nearly a month ago -and then seemingly fell off the face of the earth!"

Martin smiled bemusedly at Monica's ambiguous words. "I think that in a day or two, I'll be able to explain the necessity of 'Nathaniel' to her; in fact, if things here go as well as I believe they will, I could be back in the States- with Stuart -by the weekend...Monica, after two incredibly long years, my divorce is final—and I'm finally free to be with Annie.

"And today: I was granted full physical custody of my son! Seems like I've been fighting for Stuart's welfare all his life and yet, it took barely an hour and one man's signature for me to be given back what should never have been taken away..."

Monica was speechless.

"It's hard to wrap my mind around the fact that, after being in limbo for so long, I'm free to take my son back home with me...I didn't realize how much I'd missed North Carolina until I found myself back there with Annie."

"I can understand...there's no where else I *ever* want to be."

"It still seems incredible though: that I knew Annie as a child, and found her again in New York of all places..."

Monica didn't speak for a long moment. "You might've gone the rest of your lives and never found one another again..."

"When my folks moved us to London, and my mom and dad divorced, I was so angry that I begged them to send me 'back home'; Annie and her folks were always so kind to me..."

"Your folks split up?"

"I'm surprised there's something about me you didn't already know," he teased.

"Thank your publicist: it *wasn't* in the 'People' bio," she replied shortly.

Martin chuckled. "Annie probably wouldn't remember but, I promised her that I **would** come back home when I grew up..." he began, shaking his head at the irony of it all. "It is a small world."

Monica was speechless. Only after several moments of silence when Martin asked, "Are you still there?" did she finally respond.

"It just hit me...I know who you are now."

It was Martin's turn to sound confused. "What do you mean?"

"YOU'RE the little boy she's talked about a hundred times!" she murmured incredulously. "You made her a ring out of a flower..."

"—a purple clover bloom."

"And she still has it! She still has it Martin, after all these years..."

"Are you serious?"

"It's the only thing that woman owns that she has absolutely forbade me to touch," Monica offered with a chuckle.

"Incredible."

"No, Martin, this…this history the two of you have, **that's** what's incredible. Do you know, she has loved you all of her life? Wow…**My** best friend and THE Martin Vaughn…I think I'm supposed to feel awed—or something! But it's like, yeah…it's just so cool, ya know what I'm saying?"

Martin chuckled for Monica had grown long-winded again. "I…I guess so. I'm just me, Monica."

There was a pause. "Well, no…actually, you're still you AND Nathaniel…and we've got to do something about *that* before Annie finds out through the newspaper or CNN," she warned, "or the tabloids…"

Martin winced. "Absolutely, Monica. The good thing is, there's been very little press coverage so far—local still, from what I've seen. But I expect a LOT of Hollywood press once this whole divorce and custody thing is made public…suffice it to say, the details couldn't be more lurid so naturally…"

"—Hollywood will eat it up," she finished for him. "I am sorry, Martin…how's your son handling it so far?"

"Stuart saw things no child should ever see…the Judge has recommended counseling, if that tells you anything. He's young enough though, that he should forget a great deal…however, he's also old enough to know and feel hurt from losing someone. With the exception of a dozen or so chaperoned visitations a year, Claire– as his mother –will be lost to him."

"You're right about the losing part: he's older than Annie was when you, when Daniel moved away. She never got over it."

"She could be hurt even worse by my coming *back* into her life," Martin murmured.

"Whoa, wait a minute!" Monica interrupted. "Give Annie a little credit, alright? She's tougher than she looks."

"I just—I don't want to hurt her…again. I've never loved anyone the way I love her…"

Monica shook her head derisively. "The only way you could ever hurt Annie now, would be to leave her."

Martin's heart gave a sudden lurch. "She told me the same thing once, almost word for word…though now, New York seems like a lifetime ago…"

*　　*　　*

Annie sat at her desk and listened to the morning news while she reconciled her checkbook. It never ceased to amaze her how the small things she encountered from day to day so hatefully reinforced the fact that Gramma was truly gone. The succession of checks she had written the week of her grandmother's death—she didn't remember writing any of them. Even the one she paid to the funeral home seemed foreign to her despite the fact no one but her could have written it.

Several checks later, she came across another entry: to Dr. Clark's office. Five payments into her deductible and co-pay, and she was still seeing three figures! Which reminded her of another medical necessity…she had an appointment with the dentist for a cleaning this month, so she turned to her calendar to check the exact date and time. Flipping through the weeks, her eye caught the passing image of a star drawn in red ink and she backed up to that entry: the third week in March…there on the 20th, she had noted her trip to New York with the star and several lines of times and descriptions—her itinerary. Slowly, she touched the date that followed, the 21st, and read what should have been her departure schedule, her flight number, and a reminder to send Monica a post card…

"Which I completely forgot to do," she murmured, shaking her head at the realization this was the first time she had even thought about her unfulfilled promise since before the trip.

Picking up her pen, Annie sat with it poised just above the last line within the space for the 21st, thinking how that the most life-changing day in her life had no notation saying it was so. Slowly, she put the pen to the paper and wrote 'Martin,' and nothing more. Then she started counting the days, turning the pages as the weeks became months, until she finally arrived at the date for today. Smiling to herself, she touched her slightly rounded belly: her baby was 100 days old!

As the familiar voice of the weatherman for the morning news program crept into her consciousness, she glanced up at the television screen to see the five-day forecast, highlighting the outlook for the North Carolina coast and mountains for the Forth of July weekend. *More heat, as if we should expect anything else*, she thought to herself and shook her head smilingly.

As the weather forecast gave way to 'Headlines from Hollywood,' Annie stood from her desk and started toward the kitchen for a glass of ice-cold sweet tea. She had only walked a few steps, however, when she heard the British female reporter speak a dear and familiar name, Martin Vaughn; Annie stopped dead in her tracks.

"…Martin Vaughn and estranged wife Claire escorted by their respective attorneys. Sporting rather horrid horn rims, a full beard and overly longish hair, Vaughn might have otherwise gone unnoticed had his lovely and elegant British-born wife not preceded him from the building." Annie paused at the footstool that sat to the right of the television and slowly lowered her self to sit upon it. "…according to sources who asked not to be identified, the couple was granted a divorce just one day before the custody dispute found resolution, negating rumors of a trial reconciliation and literally fueling the dailies' speculation of a third husband for Claire Burton Morantz Morgan Vaughn…"

Though Annie heard little more of what the reporter had to say, she could not tear her eyes away from the man on the television screen…the reporter was discussing Martin and Claire and yet, it was Nathaniel that she saw…it was Nathaniel muscling his way through the dozens of reporters and their cameras…it was Nathaniel being handed into a waiting limousine…it was…it was Martin Vaughn, the reporter had said…but it couldn't have been!

Unless Nathaniel was really Martin.

The scene on the television changed to a well-known American reporter standing with the White House as his backdrop, and Annie silently cursed him, she cursed the network and she struck the television screen, shaking her head disbelievingly at the pictures that remained fresh in her mind—pictures of Nathaniel, who wasn't really Nathaniel because Nathaniel didn't exist! But…he had sat at her table and shared Sunday supper with her and Monica…and he brought cake to the house during Gramma's wake…Nathaniel had stood at her side during the funeral. Dear Lord, she realized with a foreboding chill, he had stayed all night long and all the next morning after Gramma died…

Martin…with a Southerner's voice. Of course, it made absolute sense! Who better to pretend to be someone else than an actor? "He even had Monica fooled," she realized out loud. "All this time, he had been HERE…but why? Why pretend to be someone else?"

And then she felt her insides constrict, and she hugged herself to try to stop the trembling. There could only be one reason.

CHAPTER NINE

Annie's NEVER done anything like this before, Monica thought to herself as she paced the parlor floor and checked the anniversary clock on the mantle every other minute, just as she'd been doing for the past two hours. It was eight-thirty in the evening and in her mind, she imagined Annie in every worse case scenario from amnesia to zombies…"What if she's sick somewhere or, or what if she's had an accident? Oh my God: what if she broke down on Interstate 40…during Friday evening rush hour…with all that Forth of July weekend traffic headed to the beach?!" she murmured out loud, her head in hands.

"What if I've simply been out apartment shopping?" the tardy woman interjected from the doorway of the parlor as Monica turned about with a jerk.

"Annie! I'm so glad you're finally…!—where the hell have you been? Why haven't you called me? Do you know, you had me worried sick—!"

"—I'm sorry, alright—?"

Monica's expression was incredulous. "Sorry? YOU'RE SORRY?!"

"I'm so totally bummed that I forgot to check in, Mommy…Omigod! Is there, like, suddenly a curfew I wasn't told about?" she asked in her best Valley-girl voice. Then: "I've been apartment shopping—like YOU suggested—all day! Period."

Monica drew a deep breath. "Did you never once think to call and let someone know where you were, or when you might be expected home? You're just not acting like yourself!" Monica chided.

"What an ironic choice of words…" Annie murmured to no one. "Seems to be a lot of that going on…"

"HELLO! Have I suddenly become invisible—"

"—I should be so lucky."

"Have you forgotten there are people who care about you?"

Annie shook her head petulantly. "I don't have to answer to anyone anymore, or have you forgotten Monica: Gramma's dead." With that, she turned from where she had stood and walked across the hallway to the kitchen, pausing only long enough to drop her shoulder bag onto the counter by the kitchen door.

Stepping very slowly from the parlor into the hallway, Monica paused just outside the door of the kitchen: it was NOT like Annie to be antagonistic or cruel, and she was instantly struck with a sense of uneasiness. When after several moments it became obvious that Annie had no intention of furthering their conversation, Monica simply leaned against the doorjamb as if to study the other woman's strange demeanor. "Have any luck?"

Annie gave Monica a quick glance. "Did I have any luck apartment shopping?"

Monica nodded.

"Very little…"

"What made you decide to start looking today?"

Lifting the hem of her button-front blouse, Annie displayed her first pair of stretch panel maternity pants. "I couldn't get my jeans to zip this morning…I took it as a sign."

"Well it's about time!" Monica squealed as her face lit with excitement, and she stepped fully into the kitchen to pat Annie's slightly rounded stomach with the palm of her hand. "You're finally getting a belly!"

"On Monday I could zip my jeans…that was only four days ago," she murmured almost to herself.

"Well, I think it's great! Really, it is! It's something for every pregnant lady to get excited about, so don't be all down in the mouth! Goodness girl, you really had me worried for a while there—!"

"—Monica—?"

"—we'll go to the mall first thing in the morning—but first of course we HAVE to eat breakfast out, since it's my favorite meal to eat out!—and that way we'll miss the holiday rush, 'cause you know all the GOOD sells don't start till eleven-ish! We'll buy you an entire maternity wardrobe!"

"Wait a minute, Monica. There's something I need to talk to you about before…before you start planning out our weekend…"

"What on earth could be more important than shopping?" she teased with a grin.

Settling herself into one of the chairs at the kitchen table, Annie crossed her arms upon the tabletop and then rested her forehead upon them. "I um…I found out something this morning concerning Martin...actually, I heard about it on 'Headlines From Hollywood'," she corrected, turning her head slightly to glance at Monica. "Big surprise, right? I've thought about it all day, and I'm still not sure how to handle it..."

At Annie's pained announcement, Monica stepped toward the table and lowered herself into the chair nearest her friend. Her hands were visibly shaking as she meshed her fingers together and rested them palms down upon the table. Though she feared she already knew what was coming, she asked as nonchalantly as possible, "Wh-what about him?"

Annie turned her head from side to side in an effort to ease her neck muscles somewhat before she raised tear filled eyes to face Monica in full; only then did Monica realize the woman's eyes were swollen from earlier crying. "He was in London, he and Claire, and their lawyers, and the British press...and, if I heard the British reporter correctly, apparently Martin's divorce was finally granted because she said folks are already speculating who Claire would marry next...can you believe that?" she laughed mirthlessly. Annie shook her head and closed her eyes: "The one thing that should have made me so very grateful and happy, it didn't...because things aren't always as they appear...

"He had a beard, Monica...and long hair...and watching him push his way through the reporters, he looked *amazingly* like our old friend 'Nathaniel.' He WAS Nathaniel," she murmured as her eyes opened, the tears falling in full now. "Or rather, 'Nathaniel' was him—!"

"—oh, Annie..."

"And don't try to tell me that I imagined it, or...t-that maybe he just happened to grow all that hair for a part in some movie: he played a part, alright! He played it and me to the hilt—!"

"—w-wait a minute! You know Martin, and there's a very...simple...explanation! He just—he wanted to be near you—!"

"—I cannot believe you're defending him, Monica! The things he said to me when he called: 'I want to see you again...to be with you again...I want to make a life with you...' It's textbook crap, Monica! What he WANTED was to check the situation out—he had to check me out!"

"Annie, that's not how it is—!"

"—of course it is! And I'm s-so stupid for not realizing it!" she exclaimed, bringing both hands to her face and rubbing at her eyes as if ashamed to be crying. "What other *possible* reason could he have for keeping his true identity from me? NONE! The only glitch in his plan of 'I Spy' was Gramma being sick: when I wasn't home, waiting by the phone like a good little girl, he had to create this…this MISSIONARY character…Martin Vaughn, a missionary?" she laughed insolently. "You have to love his acting ability! He certainly had me fooled…and a-all those nights I laid awake, remembering h-his face…"

"—Annie, listen to me!" Monica broke in, reaching to grasp the other woman's trembling hands in her own as she watched a steady stream of tears begin to rain down upon the front of Annie's blouse. "Look at me, please…please? You have to hear me, girl, 'cause if you're upset with Martin, you're probably gonna want to **kill** me…"

Annie looked up with the most confused expression one might possibly imagine; and in turn, Monica dropped her eyes shamefully and shrugged her shoulders as if to say, *I don't know where to begin…*

"I don't understand…what, Monica…?"

"—I knew," she murmured contritely, "almost from the start, but he made me promise not to say anything…for your sake!"

"You…how did—?"

"—I thought when I saw him at the hospital the night that Gramma died that 'Nathaniel' looked familiar, or that maybe I'd met him before…it wasn't until the next morning when I saw him standing by the hospital room window that I **knew**: he was standing there and he had the same…look, ya know?" At Annie's blank expression, Monica elaborated. "He was standing there all dark and motionless…but like he was gonna explode with fury at any second…the way Michael Maurer stood at the library windows the afternoon Alex arrived, in 'The Misbegotten…' do you remember the scene?"

"The movie…? You recognized him from that movie—?"

Monica shook her head. "I recognized his stance, and the way he kept swiping his hair off his brow—his mannerisms…his habits!"

"I still don't understand, Monica…how could you have known he was here…and not tell me?" she pleaded, her eyes filled with hurt. "Especially after I found out about the baby!"

"The baby and his son Stuart are the two main reasons I **couldn't** tell you!" Monica insisted, squeezing Annie's hands even tighter. "Jesus, Annie, you have to know if I could have told you, I would have! I swear! It was just so…complicated!"

Monica drew a deep breath. "Annie, Martin had an investigator search for you *for two solid weeks* after you left him in New York, did you know that? From what he told me, he was absolutely distraught until he finally got a phone number for you...and then, then you refused to see him! Every single time he spoke about how he missed you, I wanted to tell him what YOU were going through! That was the hardest part for me—NOT telling him how desperately you needed him!"

"It still doesn't make sense...why you never told me who he really was!" Annie returned dejectedly.

"Annie, once he made me understand the necessity of his disguise, there was no way I could go against him...just hear me out, OK?" Monica pleaded, wiping away her own tears with the back of one hand.

"When Martin returned to London from New York, and after the 'American Star' article hit, Claire hired detectives to follow him—everywhere. She fully intended to catch him with you, and eventually name you in a counter suit if Martin continued to fight for joint custody of Stuart...she wanted him out of their son's life completely and, what's scary is, she almost succeeded: he was denied any visitation whatsoever at one point because the bitch and her attorney were able to convince the judge that the article was perfect documentation of what a 'womanizer' he was...that it all but proved he was too irresponsible to be given even weekend visits with his own son.

"He made me see how that being followed by those lowlife scumbags was literally like being tailed by bounty hunters! Hell, he couldn't even walk from his apartment to his attorney's office without the time and route and what he was wearing being recorded! Then too, all this time, he wanted so desperately just to see you, to see for himself that you were alright; and to make you face him and what the two of you had rather than allow you to continue denying it because of Gramma...that the three of you couldn't somehow make it work was something he could never accept, Annie. That's why he and his attorney created the false identity—so Martin could leave London without being followed to the States by Claire's detectives.

"You must be able to appreciate what a chance he took just coming here: he chanced the possibility of losing his son, Annie, because even with the disguise, there was no guarantee that SOMEONE wouldn't recognize him. And if it had gotten out that Martin Vaughn was seen with you again...you gotta know, Claire would've nailed him to the wall. As it was, his disguise was nearly perfect; and by creating Nathaniel Rodgers, the Baptist missionary, he fit into our community perfectly! You saw how Preacher Wilson warmed to him—everyone did! The only thing that didn't work for him, in the beginning anyway, was my recognizing him. You know how disbelieving *you* are right now: once I saw through the glasses and colored contacts and the beard and the long hair, I wanted to **strangle** him! All I could see was this totally conceited jerk pretending to be something he wasn't—an actor, through and through, feeling out the situation to his own satisfaction. And there you were: so in love with him you couldn't see straight, proud to busting to be carrying his baby..."

"But you said you realized who he really was the morning after Gramma died...he hadn't even been here a full day then!" Annie realized in disbelief. "How was he able to make you trust him so soon?"

"Whoa, think back a bit! I DIDN'T trust him! Not completely, anyway...remember all those times you thought I was being hateful to him? You actually called me down, and made apologies for 'my actions.' You'll never know how torn I was: wanting to believe he loved you enough to put your best interests first and yet, being scared to death you were only gonna get hurt again...

"But the way he stood by you—your not having to go through losing Gramma alone meant a lot. And later, when he realized I was watching him like a hawk, he told me more about what Claire was doing and trying to do...he showed me in a lot of ways that all he wanted for Stuart was what was best for the child; and he made it possible for me to better understand what was and wasn't real, what was hype by the attorneys and the media, and what was the truth. It took a long time, but I finally accepted what he'd been telling me all along: Martin loves you with all his heart Annie, and more than anything, he wants to make a life with you."

Annie still wasn't convinced. "Something still doesn't make sense to me, Monica," she countered, shaking her head negatively. "If you knew who 'Nathaniel' really was, why in the world did you push me toward him? What if I'd fallen in love with 'Nathaniel' only to find out 'Nathaniel' didn't really exist!"

"Oh Annie...I wasn't trying to push you into 'Nathaniel's' arms, really; I just...I wanted you to confide in him because I was afraid Martin's attorney would call him back to London before he could learn about the baby. I thought he deserved to know. And I still do!"

"So you wanted to make sure we ended up together for the baby's sake—!"

"—for everyone's sake! And now, with the divorce finalized, he's free to come home to you!" There was a long pause. "I'm sorry, Annie. Everything we did was to protect YOU from Claire's investigators, and in turn, keep

Stuart from being taken away from his father forever…if it weren't for the damned news…"

"—the news told me very little…all I had to hear was Martin's name put with Nathaniel's face…I'm sorry, Monica. I know you think you were doing what's best, but what would have *been* best was the truth. Right now, my head hurts so bad—from crying, from screaming inside my car as I drove around…I haven't eaten today. I just need to be alone for a while; can you understand that," she murmured as she rose from the kitchen chair.

"But, there's more—!"

"—I honestly don't think my brain could hold anymore," she argued as she turned to face her friend squarely, raising one hand as if to say *STOP*. "And worse, right now I need to throw-up..!" she murmured as she ran up the steps to her bathroom.

* * *

"It's a little cool this mornin' children," Gramma announced from the backseat of Stephen Ryan's car. That was her way of letting her son know to adjust the heat; Mary glanced sideways at her husband and just smiled.

"Annie! Quit pullin at your hair bows!"

"Aw, Gramma…the rubber bands are too tight! It hurts!"

"You look real funny with pigtails!" Daniel taunted. "I'm glad I ain't a girl!"

"That comment was ill-mannered, Daniel Martin! You apologize right this minute!" Gramma ordered.

"Now Mother, I'm sure he didn't mean any harm…" Stephen offered.

"I don't care if he meant it or not: children nowadays don't think before they speak…why, when I was a girl…"

Annie nudged her young friend and whispered, "Now you've done it: she'll talk all the rest of the way to Ol' Salem…"

"You know…it's a shame your folks couldn't join us, Daniel," Mary interrupted with a gentle hand to his knee, and a smile at her mother-in-law. "But we intend for you to have a real good time anyway." Then to Gramma: "I'm not sure, Mother Ryan, but which year was it we came out for Sunrise Service and it snowed on us…do you remember?"

The elder Ryan, who bristled at having been interrupted, instantly welcomed the opportunity to offer her keen knowledge to her daughter-in-law. "Why I remember it like it was yesterday! I'm surprised you don't! It was the Easter you and Stephen were expecting. We got almost four inches that day, we did."

"What were they expectin' Gramma?" Annie asked.

"Well Miss, they were expectin' YOU!"

"Wh...what were they expectin' me to do?"

"Expecting a baby, Annie! Don't you know nothin'?" Daniel interjected.

"You've got a fresh mouth, young man!" Gramma chastised. "Children should be seen, not heard!"

"...you did it again..." Annie whispered to Daniel, and he simply crossed his arms and lowered his head to rest upon them on his lap...

Annie put her arm around her friend's shoulder and hugged him tight. "It's all right...Daddy will talk to her now and we can pretend we're asleep," she whispered before she crossed her own arms and leaned forward to rest her head upon them on her own lap. Their faces were only inches apart, and it was all Annie could do to keep from kissing the boy she loved so dearly. She smiled at him and he smiled back, and she thought again to herself how she wanted this boy to be her 'husbin' someday. "You've got pretty eyes," she whispered. "They look like them marbles we played with yesterday."

"The Chinese Checkers?" he whispered back. "No they don't."

"Cause they're shiny!" she insisted. Then "...what do mine look like?"

"I dunno..." Daniel murmured, studying the girls' eyes. "They're kinda blue...and there's this black circle in the middle. Did you know sometimes that circle's big and sometimes it's small?"

"I see yours now!"

"Are they big or little?"

"I dunno..."

"We're here kids! Wake up!" Stephen announced. And instantly, both little heads shot straight up.

"Look, Daniel! That's where Daddy buys Ma'raven stars! He gets Momma one every Christmas!"

"Now, you weren't supposed to tell that!" Stephen teased. "Your Momma don't need to know everything!"

"I know all about your shopping sprees, Stephen Ryan! Remember: I keep the checkbook!" she corrected.

"And there's where we buy Ma'raven Sugar Cake!" Annie continued. "Can we take Daniel to buy some, Daddy?"

"We didn't come out here to shop, young lady! We're here to give praise to the Lord! And you'd do well to pay extra close attention, young man..." Gramma nodded toward Daniel. *"Considerin' your momma and daddy—!"*
"—weren't able to join us; I know they'll want you to tell them everything you did and saw today," Mary interrupted, casting her mother-in-law a stern stare. It was those times that Gramma would completely stop talking; Annie wondered if her mother put some kind of spell on the older woman, because Gramma's mouth would close-and stay closed!-like magic...
"We will take Daniel on a full tour, sugar," Stephen offered, glancing at his daughter in the real view mirror. *"It'll be a day neither of you will ever forget..."*

*   *   *

Martin jerked awake at the sudden jolt of turbulence. It took a moment for him to realize that he was no longer a seven year old in an automobile, but an adult on an airplane. Staring out the window of the jet, he could see nothing but the blackness of the night. Then a weight upon his lap drew his attention away from the window and, glancing down at his son, Martin realized he must have been cradling the little boy's golden head nearly the entire flight. His fingers had woven themselves into the silken mass; gently stroking, they moved of their own volition—movement as natural and constant as his lungs expanding and contracting as he breathed, or his heart steadily beating within his chest. His hands reveled in simply touching his son again...it had been so many weeks since he had last held the precious child that he felt quite like someone who had long fasted and was just now being allowed to eat again.

And his son...Stuart had run into his father's arms the moment he stepped from his mother's limousine squealing "Daddy! Daddy!" and squeezed Martin's neck with amazing strength for a six year old. Claire simply sat within the air-conditioned comfort of the automobile, never speaking or even turning her head to look out the door...she had sworn in the judge's chambers that she would have her son again, for Martin to enjoy his 'visit'—that she would make certain it was his last. As Martin had knelt on the sidewalk outside his attorney's office and watched the long black vehicle pull away, he felt a chill at the memory of her threat. So certain had she been of her promise that Claire had simply dropped the child, sans luggage or other belongings, and left without so much as a word good-bye.

Martin reopened his eyes as the voice of the pilot came over the speakers, not realizing until that instant that he had subconsciously squeezed them shut as if to shut out the memory of Claire altogether. The child, however, slept through the announcement that the Boeing 757 was preparing to circle Kennedy International; there was such a tranquil look upon his sleeping face that Martin felt envious of the innocence of a child, unable to recall his own youth except when he dreamed. Inwardly he trembled, praying with all his soul that God would grant benevolence to the child and to himself, perhaps in the form of an earthly angel...immediately his heart ached for Annie.

*   *   *

Annie crept down the stairs as quietly as the old pine step treads would allow, though a creak now and then seemed to echo in the early morning quiet and she could only hope they didn't wake Monica.

"You couldn't sleep either, huh?" came the familiar voice from the kitchen as Annie stepped inside the doorway to find Monica preparing a pot of coffee.

"Not after you told me that Martin's on his way here!"

"I probably should have waited till this morning but, I just...I couldn't keep it to myself! I had to tell someone!"

Annie shook her head in disbelief. "Your timing was lousy..."

"It's kinda hard to schedule discussions with someone who spends so much time praying to the porcelain god!"

"Monica!"

"Well...! I know morning sickness is common but you have it 24/7!"

Annie simply shook her head. "Someday, I will repay you for all the hours you tormented me during this pregnancy; what goes around comes around, ya know."

"And paybacks are hell," Monica laughed outright as she carried two mugs of steaming hot coffee to the kitchen table. Then, glancing into the parlor, she caught Annie looking out the front window. "You realize this is the Fourth of July weekend...one of the busiest travel weekends of the year...he may not get a flight to the states before next week—"

"—if he told you he was going to try to be here by the weekend, he'll do all he can to get here..."

"The Fourth of July weekend is three days long!" Monica finally interjected. "We may not see or hear anything else from him before Monday, if then!"

"I know," Annie replied with a nod, "but I've just got this feeling…"

"Yeah, right…the last time you said *'but I've just got this feeling…'* you talked me into buying a cigar box full of old baseball cards at auction at Germanton School's Fall Festival…the best card was a Gregg Jeffries rookie card: 'The Mets' '80s phenom' who had a less than mediocre rookie season; and I was out of pocket fifty bucks!"

Annie had to smile as she reached to pick up her mug from the table. "The sportswriters jinxed him…"

"Humph!"

Shaking her head at Monica's feigned furor, she pulled out a chair at the kitchen table and sat down across from her dearest friend. Spooning two teaspoons of sugar and one of Coffeemate into her mug, she stirred the still hot drink for a long while and then placed the spoon on her napkin. Reaching into her blouse pocket, she removed four prescription medications, and one by one, swallowed each with a small sip of the coffee.

"What *hasn't* Dr. Clark prescribed for you?" Monica asked as she watched Annie blow on the steaming mug.

"They're all for the good of the baby," Annie murmured in return as she studied the final one. "The pink horse pills are prenatal vitamins, and my favorite," she added before swallowing it. "…aaggh! Can't you tell?"

Monica laughed at the horrible face Annie made. "You're gonna make one heck of a mom! And I can't wait to see you around Martin's kid…I just hope he's not another Claire: imagine having to deal with THAT for the next 15 or so years—!"

"—thank you so much for putting my greatest fear into words!" Annie broke in, jumping up from the table and taking her mug of coffee with her. "The last thing I should be doing is looking for 'Claire' in Stuart! He's Martin's son, too, and because he is, I'll come to love him as if he were my own…how could I *not* when the best of Martin is in that precious child?"

"Whoa! I was just…kinda, trying to prepare you…I mean, what if he doesn't warm to you like he oughta? Six year olds are usually pretty attached to their mommies. What's worse, Claire's had him practically all to herself for several months now: what if she's filled his head with a load of crap about 'daddy's girlfriends'…wrong as that is, parents *will* do it."

183

"I know," Annie broke in distractedly. "I'm as prepared for it as I know how to be…and I'll deal with it when the time comes, if it comes. Until then, I'm going to think good thoughts…I don't even know what Martin's plans will be. I haven't spoken with him since the custody hearing; you probably know more than I do at this point."

"You know…*almost* everything I know," Monica assured her with a smile. "He got his divorce, he got custody of his son, and he wants more than anything to make a life with you—!"

"—hold it! Back up! What's the 'almost' you so cleverly skirted?" Annie asked, one hand on her hip and the other holding a near empty coffee mug.

Monica smirked like the proverbial Cheshire cat! "That my dear, is a precious, delightful secret that is Martin's alone to share. I'm not telling you what it is, so don't badger me."

Annie was speechless, and uneasy…and growing more fretful by the moment. "What have you done?" she murmured suspiciously. "You've had a hand in whatever's going on, Monica…I can tell."

Her friend shook her head and simply smiled. "For maybe the very first time since I've known you, I can truthfully say I didn't have so much as a fingertip in this surprise! And I wish I could be a fly on the wall when you find out," she added earnestly. "Because you're gonna absolutely cry yourself silly…"

The cell phone in Martin's jacket pealed a low chirping sound, and Stuart glanced up at his father's face with a huge smile. "Yours doesn't play a song!"

"Nope, I think the music tones are too loud sometimes," Martin replied with a wink, as he answered the caller. "Vaughn."

"I take it you've landed," Chris offered. "Your voice sounds quite a bit calmer than when we spoke before."

"I don't like to fly."

"You absolutely must come into the twenty-first century, old boy…it's all but second nature for most of us in today's world to utilize and embrace the most efficient means of transportation, that being air travel and…"

"—I'm pretty sure I'm on 'roam' Chris, and I don't have any free rollover minutes so if you don't mind…"

Martin was answered with a great chuckle. "You're in layover."

"I'm in Kennedy, can't BUY a flight to Greensboro, or Raleigh, or Charlotte, and I'm seriously considering hailing a cab and driving down," Martin corrected.

"What time is it there?"

Martin glanced at his watch. "Early yet. If I leave now, I could be there before dark."

"You're not seriously considering—?"

"—I don't have a lot of options. It's a holiday weekend and all the rental car agencies are booked."

"Go to the Hertz counter, give them my name and you will receive the keys to a Mercedes sedan: not **my** first choice, of course, but I took into account the child you now have in tow and…"

"—you secured a rental car?"

"As I was saying, with Stuart I'm sure there must be considerably more luggage than your usual solitary carry-on, therefore I made allowances. I hope a sedan is acceptable?"

There was only silence.

"Hul-lo? Are you there?"

"Yeah."

"Ah, I'd feared we lost our connection."

"No…I have to wonder sometimes…"

It was Chris' turn to be silent.

"You're always one step ahead: of me, Claire, the press, the courts…h-how did you know?"

Chris chuckled. "You forget just *who* was on the other end of the Colonies' fight for Independence; though we applaud your forefather's tenacity, t'was a bitter pill to swallow…still is, truth be known. We Brits loathe losing; it's not in our spirit to lose. So while you Americans celebrate the victory with cookouts and…*automobile races*," his voice was disdainful, "we drown our miserable souls at our local pub."

"Like you need a reason to frequent a pub!"

"Of course not. But then, July is an otherwise uneventful month…" he murmured. "I knew that you would have, shall we say, more important things on your mind than managing your itinerary so I simply had Maggie plan ahead in the event you found yourself stuck at Kennedy with no connection. Of course, had you allowed her to plan your visit to the states rather than choosing to, ahem, fly by the seat of your pants, you might have already found yourself well on your way to North Carolina, by way of…"

"—I know, *the most efficient means of travel*…" Martin broke in, repeating Chris' earlier words with a genuine smile. "Hug her for me, Chris…you do realize your secretary is absolutely priceless."

185

"Yes, I know…however, I daresay she'd rather receive that hug from you: she has a soft spot in her heart for strays, little children…*Hollywood actors*…" Again, his tone was disdainful. "Must be the Irish in her…"

"Don't let **her** hear you say that!"

Again Chris chuckled. "Just, go now to your Ann-Elise and…and find that happiness that's eluded you for so long. You're the closest thing to a brother that I have Martin and, well, it's bloody well time."

Martin shook his head at the other man's well wishes. "You will never know, Chris, what your friendship has meant to me. You gave me my life back, and Stuart…I…I owe you my life."

"Nonsense." Chris replied, a smile in his voice. "You owe me quite a large barrister's fee, the bill for which you will receive in short order. For now, stop dillydallying or I shall have to summon Maggie!" he threatened.

"Thank you Chris." There was a long pause as Martin stroked Stuart's golden head. "I thank you for my son."

It wasn't so very warm this Fourth that sitting on the front porch in the early evening was uncomfortable. In fact, there was a light breeze that brought with it all the smells of neighbors grilling hotdogs and hamburgers. "I'm hungry! How many dogs can you eat?" Monica asked.

Annie sat with her head flush against the back of the old rocking chair, her eyes closed. Her bare feet on the worn wooden floor of the porch unconsciously pushed the chair to and fro. "I…one maybe…I'm just not very hungry," she murmured.

"How can you sit here, smelling all these delicious aromas, and NOT get hungry?"

"Too nervous, I guess…" she replied, the rhythm unbroken. "I just…I keep running through my mind what I'll say to Martin once he arrives. I'm a little scared…"

Monica shook her head. "Yeah, you look absolutely petrified…" she taunted.

Annie smiled and kept rocking. "I mean, I don't want to say the wrong thing, especially with Stuart…I've thought about what you said this morning and, you're right: he may already resent me…" The rocking stopped and Annie turned to look squarely at Monica. "What if that little boy is never able to love me? And how's he gonna react when the baby comes…? What if—?"

"—would you stop the 'what-iffing'…jeez!" Monica interjected, "You're gonna do fine…you're all three gonna be fine; there is no child on

RUNNING TO STAND STILL

the face of this earth who wouldn't love you, Annie. You're like, a kid magnet: it's almost embarrassing sometimes..."

"What?"

"We can't ever go to Barnes and Noble's without you wanting to hit the children's section *just to see what they have.*' And then some kid will ask you to reach up for a book he can't get to, or he'll ask you what some word means in the story he's reading: you guys are on the same plane. It's a gravitational thing having to do with the cosmos...or the alignment of the planets," she offered matter-of-factly. "It's not your fault, really; it's just the way you were made."

"So I'm...cursed?" Annie asked, almost laughing now.

"I certainly wouldn't want to trade places with you!" Monica replied. "Feel better?"

Annie smiled and pressed her head upon the back of the rocking chair. "Actually, I think I want two hotdogs," she announced as she closed her eyes and her feet began the rocking again. "No onions and..."

"—light on the chili, yeah I know..." Monica smiled to herself.

"I'll go heat the grill."

"Why does Gramma hate Daniel?"

Stephen was shocked by his daughter's question. "Gramma doesn't hate Daniel, she doesn't hate anybody! What in the world made you ask such a question?"

Annie glanced up at her father from the bench outside the Moravian Book and Gift Shop where both of them sat as they waited for Daniel to return from the bathroom. "She's so mean to him; she's meaner to him than she is to anybody..."

Stephen pushed his glasses up further upon the bridge of his nose as he took a long moment to consider his daughter's words. "I'm not sure what I can say to make you see that...I don't..." he cleared is throat. "I don't rightly know why Annie but, Gramma...just between you and me, she's always been just a little bit...ornery..."

"—between you and me? Huh-uh! Everybody knows! Momma, Preacher Wilson..."

"—what I mean to say is...I agree that Gramma can be contrary at times. But she hasn't had an easy life...she lost her husbin—my daddy—when I was ten years old. And...she never got over it. She's...still...awfully lonesome for him sometimes."

"Why don't she come live with us; then she wouldn't be lonesome anymore."

"Gramma will never leave her house. And the three of us, well, Mount Airy's your momma's home..."

"—and she don't wanna leave..."

"—WE don't: neither your mother or I want to move from our home...it's grown-up stuff, sugar..."

Annie was thoughtful. *"All right...but, would you tell Daniel it's not his fault?"*

"Has Gramma upset him?"

Annie nodded. *"He won't say it, Daddy, but I can tell when I look in his eyes: when he gets sad, his eyes get real shiny...like marbles..."*

"What do you want me to say to him sweetheart?" Stephen asked solemnly, hugging his daughter close.

"Tell him that you love him too, like you love me...I've told him a million-brizillion times, but he won't listen...I swear Daddy, he's stubborn as a mule sometimes—!"

"—don't swear, sweetheart."

"Well he is! I plainly told him if he was my husbin, you'd be HIS daddy too, and then he wouldn't be sad when his real daddy never wonted to do things with him..."

"—Annie, you just shut up!" Daniel yelled from where had walked up beside her. *"You can just shut up right now—!"*

"—Daniel, come here son," Stephen broke in evenly. *"Come over here and look at me..."*

Certain he was going to be spanked for telling Annie to shut up, Daniel dropped his head and sniffed, walking the two small steps that put him in front of Stephen Ryan. *"Yessir?"*

There was a deafening silence as Annie looked between Daniel and her father and back again. *"Don't spank him Daddy...it was my fault...I'm sorry..."*

Stephen lifted the little boy and, sitting him upon his lap, put his left arm around Daniel and drew Annie close in his right one. *"Daniel, you are such a dear, dear child. If God ever sees fit to give me a son one day, I can only hope He gives me someone just like you...in the meantime I wont you to know that, even when y'all move away to England, you have another family here, and we love you...you will always be welcome in our home, do you understand?"*

Daniel nodded, and two huge tears rolled down his cheeks.

"Annie?"

The little girl turned huge eyes up to her father's. "Yessir?"
"We won't discuss Gramma's...contrariness, anymore."
"No sir."
"Now...can I talk the two of you into a tour of the old cemetery?" Stephen
asked airily.
"You mean it...Really?" the children asked in unison.
"I kinda don't wanna go walkin there by myself, but if y'all will go
with me..."

"Annie...Annie, wake up!"

Opening her eyes slowly, Annie glanced about and realized she was on Gramma's front porch; and she looked at Monica like she'd never seen her before. "I was dreamin 'bout Daddy," she whispered, her hands rising to cover her face. *It seemed so real*, she thought to herself. "I must've dozed off..."

"—uh yeah," Monica taunted, and then noticed the hint of tears in her friend's eyes. "The hotdogs are ready to eat," she offered. "Want me to bring 'em out here?"

"No! I mean, I'm sorry!" Annie apologized. "I never meant for you to do all the work!"

"Oh please...I dropped the package of weenies on the grill and the charcoal did all the work," she teased.

"I can at least come in and help..."

"—You can help squeeze some of the lemons I bought, OK?"

"You got fresh lemons for lemonade?" Annie asked excitedly. "I have been craving lemonade! Monica, how did you know?"

"You mention it every time a *Country Time Lemonade* commercial comes on."

Annie laughed with delight as she reached for the handle of the screen door and Monica followed her inside.

Both women were in the kitchen preparing to heap condiments on their hotdogs when they heard a knock at the front door. Annie drew a deep breath and glanced first toward the front hallway, and then back at Monica whose hand still held a tablespoon full of cole slaw over one hotdog. "Do you think it's him?" Annie whispered.

Monica simply shrugged her shoulders and returned the spoonful of slaw to the bowl. "I guess it could be...or, it's probably just one of the neighbors..."

189

"—they'd come to the kitchen door," Annie reasoned. Running her hands through her hair, she brushed lose tendrils back from her face as her eyes went again to the front of the house. As if on cue, the knocking sounded again and Annie's eyes shot nervously back to meet Monica's.

"C'mon…we'll both go to the door," Monica announced when Annie still made no effort to move. "It may not even be him—!"

"It is! I just have this feeling…!"

"Oh, Lord have mercy!" Monica murmured in a stammer. "If it's just Whitey wanting to borrow ice again, are YOU gonna feel stupid!"

Standing at the front door, Martin's right hand rested gently upon his son's right shoulder; his left, having just rapped upon the door for a second time, reached up to swipe his hair off his moist brow. *Stuart is so calm*, he thought enviously, as the tips of his fingers tapped the boy's chest reassuringly. A yellow porch light came on and Stuart tipped his head backward to look up at his father, grinning at the reassuring smile he was met with.

As the front door slowly opened, Stuart's attention was drawn back with a start as he watched the huge diamond doorknob being turned from within. But the instant the door was fully open, both the boy and his father looked at the woman in the simple white cotton dress and they smiled identical smiles.

"Martin…" Annie murmured, her smile seemingly pasted upon her lips. The beard was gone and his hair was once again neatly trimmed.

"Hello Annie," he barely whispered as he studied the thick mass of hair she'd gathered behind her head with a covered rubber band and clips. "You don't know how good it is to see you again…you look wonderful," he murmured, his eyes locking again with hers, his body shuddering in the heat of the early July evening.

"So do you," she replied, wondering how she never saw through his disguise. "Did you have a good trip? I hope you didn't have any trouble finding us…"

"I uh, I've made the trip once before."

"Yes," she concurred as she felt herself blush, recalling that once he had visited her as 'Nathaniel'. "Of course you did…"

"I…this is my son Stuart," he offered at last, his eyes unable to break from hers; he couldn't get enough of simply looking at her.

Slowly Annie knelt upon the threshold, tearing her eyes away from Martin's with keen difficulty as they lowered to welcome his son. Though her mouth opened to greet him, her disbelief stilled any sound from her throat for her eyes openly studied the child's face then rose to the father's for an instant before lowering again to the son's. "Y-you look just like..."

"I am pleased to meet you, Madam," the child offered in a clipped British accent as he extended his right hand in greeting and bowed slightly at the waist.

Swallowing hard, Annie lifted her right hand from where she realized it had been bracing her upon the floor and somehow took care to keep her balance. Taking the tiny one that had been offered to her, trembling as she felt the child's fingers squeeze her own quite tightly, he pumped it twice in an oh so gentlemanly manner before withdrawing it again. Annie then let hers drop like a dead weight to her lab as she watched the child return his hand to the right front pocket of his trousers. Bracing her left hand upon the doorjamb, she slowly rose and lifted knowing eyes to meet those of the boy, no, the man she had loved all her life. Both hands then went to her mouth as she caught a sob and whispered "Daniel!" so low that only the man could hear her.

"I feel like I've been away from you for a lifetime—" he murmured.

"—Dear, Dear Lord, h-how I've missed you!" she whispered between sobs.

"What am I now, a doorstop?" Monica tearfully chastised as she watched the exchange. Then: "I'm Monica," she offered, bending at the waist to introduce her self to Martin's son. "You have the coolest accent I've ever heard come from a kid!"

"I do?!" the child asked in amazement. "I rather like the way you talk, like all the Yanks did in Daddy's movie!"

At that, Monica laughed and looked to Martin appreciatively. "Though he has his Yanks and Rebels confused, the kid **has** taste...even if he does look enough like you that you might've spit 'em out your mouth!"

Martin returned Monica's teasing smile and extended his own hand in greeting. "Believe it or not, Monica, I actually missed your stinging tongue—how are you?"

Brushing away his hand, Monica enveloped Martin in a tremendous hug, standing back after several seconds to murmur, "I think we'd all feel better if we went inside out of the heat."

Martin looked again at Annie, who was still sobbing silently behind hands pressed against her face, and he drew her close against him as Monica led Stuart inside the house. "There's fresh home-made lemonade in the fridge!" she offered the little boy as she took him by the hand and walked indoors.

"Home-made?" he asked incredulously.

"What other kind is there?" she replied impishly.

CHAPTER TEN

Though the couple had been together in the dark for several hours, neither seemed aware that night was passing into another day. Martin and Annie were totally content to lay together on the sofa in the parlor, in the silence, and simply hold one another.

"Monica said, when she told me you had a surprise for me, that I'd cry myself silly when I found out..." Annie murmured.

"I had to kiss you to make you stop crying."

"I wanted you to kiss me, so I'd know you were really here...that I wasn't just dreaming again. Do you know: I dreamed about you earlier in the day? You and Daddy...I dream about you almost weekly, Martin...and when I saw Stuart earlier, I swear to the Good Lord, I saw the little boy from my dreams..."

"Only he has Claire's 'yellow' hair, as he calls it...mine was more..."

"—dirty blonde."

"Dirty blonde..."

"Why did you change your name," Annie asked almost as an afterthought. "Why aren't you Daniel anymore?"

There was a low chuckle in the man's chest. "Two syllables, two syllables."

"What?"

"My agent said 'Dan-iel Mar-tin' didn't flow...apparently, it ping pongs."

Annie rose from where she lay upon the man's chest, her mouth agape. "You're kidding, right?" she asked incredulously.

Martin shook his head and smiled. "Nope. He told me at our first meeting that a study had been done—governmentally funded, mind you—that proved

Americans like men's names that flow, rather than hop. For instance, Richard Nix-on…A-dolph Hit-ler…"

Annie was thoughtful. "So, Mar-tha Stew-art and…Tri-cia Year-wood got to keep their names because they're female?"

Martin laughed. "Guess so!"

"Then…where did Vaughn come from?"

"Don't you ever remember me talking about Gramma Vaughn?…Vaughn was my mother's maiden name…" he replied. "I really didn't like the idea of changing my name, but this guy is one of the best in the business and, I was an upstart, didn't have a clue…" Martin's face was pensive in the early morning light.

"I basically went to my first casting call on a dare, and he was one of the managers there checking out the new prospects…I didn't get the part but, Allan approached me later and convinced me I had plenty of potential; if I'd let him manage my career, he'd made **me** a star and I'd make *him* lots of money…I must admit, the man knows what he's doing. Two commercials, a small-budget movie and three tryouts later and I had the part of Michael Maurer…two syllables, two syllables but with French pronunciation, so it's allowed!"

Annie laughed then with Martin as he continued. "Allan told me to be myself, to let my drawl come on through and to let the people doing the casting know—in my own way—that there was no one else who could be Michael, but me."

"And I guess you took the same approach when you became 'Nathaniel'?"

Martin's eyes studied Annie's nervously. "Monica explained about the reason for—?"

"—she told me everything," the woman broke in, shaking her head as if to dismiss the thought from his mind. "It took a little while for it all to sink in; and I'll admit, at first I was too hurt to even want to listen…but after I learned why Claire was having you followed, I better understood the why of it. Monica helped me to realize you did the things you did because you had no other choice. I love that you wanted to be here for me; and I love you for…for wanting to protect Stuart and me."

"I'm glad," he murmured, his eyes touching her every place his lips longed to, and at her smile, his heart all but leapt from his chest.

Annie traced Martin's lips with her fingertips. "I like you **much** better without the beard: as Michael or Nathaniel or Martin…"Annie ventured smilingly. "Your face is much too handsome to be hidden behind a lot of hair!"

Martin smiled shyly and stroked his jaw with the back of one hand. "I'll admit, I can't imagine anything more uncomfortable."

"Daddy always said it felt like a cat was attached to his face!"

Martin smiled as he could picture Stephen Ryan saying that very thing. "Indeed it does," he agreed and hearing Annie laugh with him, felt a chill shake his entire body. "Do you have **any** idea how very happy I am right now?"

Sensing a subtle change in Martin's voice, Annie gave the man a nervous smile, her voice lower as she watched the sunlight flicker in his eyes. "I think so."

Martin was quiet and thoughtful for a long while. "Until this very minute, I've been so scared…so many things had to go right, so many situations had to develop exactly as they did, or I could lose everything…" he whispered. "All the way here, I kept pinching myself: I've been given my freedom AND my son! I was thanking God every other breath and yet, I was scared to death to ask Him for your forgiveness, afraid I didn't deserve even one more gift from Him…"

"You haven't done one thing to need forgiveness for," Annie interjected.

"But wouldn't I be tempting fate, asking for one more thing?"

"Then don't ask Him," Annie replied, pressing her fingertips to Martin's lips as her eyes held his like a lifeline. Feeling his breath against her hand she all but pleaded, "Ask me, darlin'…ask me…"

Slowly…slowly, Martin trailed his lips down the length of Annie's fingers and into the palm of her hand, pausing only long enough to take that hand into his own as she lowered her lips to Martin's, replacing where her fingertips had been. Her mouth met his, parted and waiting, willing him…needing him. As his tongue probed and teased, her lips stroked him lovingly, longingly, reveling in the remembered taste of him. It was wondrous, their exploration of each other: deliberate, passionate, and yet patient; a path unforgotten that no memory could prepare them for.

A ragged breath broke from the man's lips as his arms went around her and he pressed the side of her face against his shoulder. "You don't know what you're doin to me…" he murmured; and as if in reply, she only pressed closer, lifting her face to press soft, plucking kisses against his throat while his hands clung to her hair, caressing her scalp with infinite tenderness.

Somewhere a child giggled and a moan broke from Martin's throat as he turned his lips into Annie's temple. Two, three seconds longer he held her until finally he whispered, "Was that a 'yes'?"

Lifting her face from where she had pressed kisses against his throat, Annie watched the drumbeat of tension in the crest of his jaw and she felt his need for her press hard against one thigh. Lying fully on top of him, a place she had dreamed of being over and over again for weeks, she pressed tender kisses upon his chin, and jaw, and the very tip of his nose as she whispered, "You already know that I have loved you all my life…but I fell in love with you the moment I first saw you at the banquet…you have always had my heart, and I know I will never feel like this about anyone else!"

He held her tightly, immersed in the pleasure of holding her full against his chest, of having her lips and tongue tease the length of his throat; closing his eyes, he remembered the morning Annie had left tiny bite marks there and how he had wondered if he would ever again know the joy of having her nuzzle him that way. "God, I have prayed with all my heart for this…"

"So have I Martin…I have hurt from wanting you—!"

"—I thought I'd go mad when I couldn't find you—!"

"—I'd jump every time the phone rang! And each time you called…oh, darlin, did you have to let it ring two dozen times?!"

He laughed throatily and shook his head. "All I wanted was to hear your voice…to hear you say 'Hello'…just your message on an answering machine would have been something!"

"A-hem…"

From the hallway, Monica cleared her throat loudly and the couple moved to sit upright upon the sofa a scant second before Stuart bounded into the parlor and into his father's arms. "Oh Daddy! You MUST come see the old woodstove in the kitchen!" he exclaimed in awe. "Aunt Monica says they actually use it sometimes in the winter!"

"*Aunt* Monica?" Annie mouthed to her friend with a smile.

Martin drew a deep breath and hugged the tiny boy tight against his chest. "I hope you're remembering your manners, Stuart: you're not runnin' wild are you?"

"Aw, c'mon, dad…loosen up, *relax*!" Monica teased with a wink, the double meaning not lost on Martin or Annie. "This house has raised three generations of children, so I fairly doubt there's anything me and Stuart could get into, that me and Annie already haven't!"

Smiling, Annie nodded and reached to comb the child's bangs off his brow. "She's right, sweetheart. I want you to make yourself completely at home...in fact," she offered, turning to look directly at Martin then, "I'd really like it if the two of you would consider staying here indefinitely...I have plenty of room and, where I'm used to always having someone around, now that Gramma's gone..."

"—you mean madam, that we might LIVE here?" Stuart broke in, and then turned to look at his father in awe.

Martin's eyes met Annie's over the little boy's head and he stammered: "Well, I don't know...I haven't really thought..."

"—it's settled then!" Monica broke in, slapping her hands together once. "Whatcha think, Annie? Wanna give Stuart your daddy's old room?" Then to Stuart, "It has an awesome hidden passage way!"

"A hidden passage way...Aunt Monica you're jesting!"

"It leads to a playroom FULL of trains! And just wait till you see Annie's baseball card collection—!"

"—you still have the baseball card collection?" Martin murmured incredulously.

"—baseball cards?" Stuart whispered at Annie.

"My daddy and I collected for years and years" she replied with a smile, still amazed at how much the child reminded her of Daniel..."And your daddy used to try to steal my best cards!"

The child's mouth dropped as he turned huge eyes to look at his father. "Daddy, you didn't!"

Martin's brows shot straight up and he looked querulously at Annie. "I...don't remember..."

Smiling, Annie clipped the little boy under the chin. "But, he never succeeded...you know why? I'd tell your daddy that, if he didn't give my cards back, I was gonna kiss him on the face!"

"Oooh...gross!"

Martin nodded his immediate recognition. "THAT'S why I never had a baseball card collection."

"I promise madam, that I would never do anything so dreadful," Stuart enthused, as he took a safe step backward.

"I know sweetheart. But you...you are always welcome to play with the trains, or the stuffed animals, or any of the other toys to your heart's content. Maybe later today, I'll get my old ball card albums out and we can all look at them together!"

"Good deal Annie, because I've got a whole cigar-box full of baseball cards you can buy!" Monica chimed in cheekily. "Come on kiddo!" And without a backward glance, she headed the little boy up the old staircase.

"I never quite got around to giving Monica that spanking she so badly needs," Annie whispered at last.

Smiling at the shared memory, Martin's eyes returned to meet Annie's from where they had followed his son up the stairs. "This is all so…are you sure, Annie…really sure?"

"I'm sure that I love you, and that I'll come to love that precious little boy as if he were my own," she nodded, reaching out her hand to slowly caress the side of Martin's face with just the tips of her fingers. "I want to make a home for us; I want it to be everything that's good for you and for Stuart, and for **our** children…I've always wanted the kind of life my parents had, but until this very minute, I wondered if it would ever be possible." Holding his eyes with hers as her hand stole up to play into his hair, Annie brushed her fingers through its thickness lovingly, cherishing simply touching the man again. His eyes dropped closed, she saw him swallow as a childlike smile winged his lips; he shook his head from side to side as a long breath heaved from his chest.

"Oh Annie…I want to do it right this time," he murmured low as his eyes opened to meet her curious ones.

"'Do it right'?"

Martin's expression was dubious as he drew her into tremulous arms and pressed one side of her face against his chest. "I want to do things in the right *order* this time…before, with Claire, we were married because she was pregnant—with Stuart. I want you and I to marry for US rather than out of obligation…"

Annie's breath stopped and she held weakly to Martin's shoulders, certain that had he *not* been holding her she would have literally fainted.

"…I loved and wanted our child from the moment I learned of the pregnancy, but I was no more in love with his mother than she was with me…"

Closing her eyes, Annie felt her body go cold despite Martin's hands stroking up and down her back. She barely heard his words through the ocean of heat and confusion crashing in her ears; unconsciously, she shook her head as if to clear it and Martin drew back to look at her.

"I should have told you all of this before, I suppose," he shrugged and smiled coyly. "I'm surprised Monica hasn't read about it somewhere and told you already! She knows more about Martin Vaughn than I do..."

Annie winced. *'He's had a bitch of a life,'* Monica had said...and he married Stuart's mother because she was pregnant...

"Annie...you didn't know, I can tell by your expression..." Martin tipped her chin up until he was looking at her in full while his other hand played up and down her spine. She forced herself to sit upright, meeting his eyes quickly and just as quickly looked away. *I'm going to be sick,* she thought desperately...*I've got to get up...*

"I was young, and Claire was an older, very beautiful...very experienced woman..."

Stop, Martin...please don't say anything more...

"...I was taken by her sophistication, awed even that such a famous actress might somehow be interested in a nobody like me..."

"Martin...please..." Annie heard herself whisper.

"...when I learned about the baby, I wanted to do the right thing, and I guess I figured if I worked at it hard enough..."

"Martin, please!" she murmured louder, cupping her hand over her mouth as she stood from the sofa and practically ran up the staircase.

"Annie! What—?" Martin stood almost instantly and in a near run intended to follow the woman. The bathroom door at the top of the stairs slammed with a loud bang, and Monica was in the upstairs hallway and intercepting Martin as he topped the stairs.

"What the hell!" she murmured as she threw both hands up and met Martin square in the chest.

"Annie sick! I've got—!"

"—you've got to get a grip!" she ordered, shaking her head. "What were ya gonna do, run in there after her?"

"She might need..."

"—and she might not...OK? She's...skipped supper and...breakfast...geez-Louise! I'd puke too if I was living off love and lemonade!"

"What...?"

"Don't you ever get sick on your stomach when you don't eat?" Monica reasoned, listening close for some sound from the other side of the door that might indicate Annie was in fact all right.

"Not that I remember..."

"I did one time Daddy," Stuart offered as he stepped into the hallway. Looking up at his father, the little boy slipped both his hands into one of the man's much larger ones as he drew his father down closer to his height.

"What, son?" Martin asked, as he combed the child's hair back from his brow with his free hand.

"Betsy was late to the townhouse one morning...Mummy was expecting a visitor and told me to go into my room and to stay there until Betsy arrived...but, Betsy had the day off and Mummy forgot, I guess...she never told me I could come back out until that night...and then, then I ate some tarts for dinner and...and I got sick on my tummy..." he finished in a whisper, shaking his head from side to side. "Mummy was very upset...please don't be upset that Annie is sick..."

In an instant, Martin drew the child close and hugged him tightly with both arms. "I would never be upset that Annie got sick, or that you got sick...not ever. Don't you ever be afraid to tell me if you don't feel well, promise me son."

The little boy's head nodded up and down against his father's shoulder. "I promise," he murmured.

Annie had stepped from the bathroom during the child's confession and felt her heart skip a beat when she heard him finally call her Annie for the first time. She knelt behind Stuart as his father still held the child tight. "I'm all right, sweetheart," she whispered into the child's ear, "My tummy isn't sick anymore." Then, meeting Martin's eyes above his son's head, "I'm sorry that I scared you, Martin...I just didn't—I didn't want to embarrass myself in front of you..."

Martin took one arm and drew Annie against himself and Stuart. "Do you have any idea how much the two...how very much the two of you mean to me...?" he murmured with some difficulty. "I don't know what I'd do if something..."

"—I wish I had my camera!" Monica interrupted, hands on hips. "This...it's the perfect Hallmark Christmas card!"

Stuart giggled, throwing his head back to look up at Monica. "Oh silly goose! We're not a Christmas card!"

"You're not? Well, y'all look like one to me!" she teased, trying to lighten the moment for the two adults who wouldn't let one another go. "All right then, smarty-pants: what are you?" she prodded, mussing the child's hair with the palm of her hand.

Stuart wrapped one arm around his father's neck and the other around Annie's. "We are a new family!" he announced proudly; then to Monica: "And you're my new best friend!"

It was Monica's turn to require assistance. "Uhhh...wouldn't you rather have...a puppy...maybe?" she offered, looking in Martin's direction for some idea what to say next.

"I would adore having a puppy, Aunt Monica; only, *he* couldn't help me run the trains!" the child replied logically.

"Maybe we'll teach your dad how to...Or, maybe one day you'll have a brother or sister..." Monica prodded, looking in Annie's direction. *You can jump in at any moment*, her eyes intimated.

"—maybe...one day..." she murmured, glancing at Martin as they both moved to stand up. "Um, Martin and I were j-just discussing children, before my tummy started acting up," she winked at Stuart. "I think...I mean..." She shrugged. "I love children! I'd love for us to get you a little brother or sister, just, whenever your daddy's ready!"

Martin looked first at Annie and then turned to find his son's expression incredulous. "Would you like to have a brother or a sister, son—?"

"Really? Really, Daddy!?"

Martin knelt before his little boy. "I know this isn't anything we've ever discussed...there wasn't any reason; I mean, I didn't think there would ever be a brother or sister for you..."

"Because you and Mummy don't love each other anymore."

Annie pressed close to Martin and felt her eyes well with tears.

"Because...Mommy and I aren't *married* anymore," Martin corrected, as he felt Annie's tears fall on his arm. "I know that this has been...**so** hard on you..." He swallowed. "If there was any way I could have...I wish things could have been different..."

"It's OK, Daddy," the child murmured as he patted his father's shoulder. "You don't have to explain. I had a very long talk with Betsy and she told me that one day, when I'm older, I'll see that *'it is was all for the best.'*"

"I see..."

"Did you know, Stuart," Annie offered, "I never had any brothers or sisters, either...your daddy was my only playmate when I was just about your age."

"Really?"

"Uh-huh...he was *my* best friend in the whole world until he moved to England...so I know what it's like to be lonesome and to want someone to play with." Annie smiled at Martin and he smiled back. "I used to tell him that, if he'd just marry me and become my husband, he wouldn't have to move away...we were too young back then to really understand..."

"—are you old enough now?" the child implored his father.

"Old enough for what, son?" Martin asked shaking his head.

"To get married! Oh, Daddy, this is the most wonderful house; I don't want us to ever move back to London!"

Martin cocked a brow at his son. "I don't think we will be going back there except maybe to visit, but..."

"—folks don't get married because of where they live! They marry because they love one another and because they want to be a family," Annie offered.

"But we are a family," Stuart insisted. "Aunt Monica said so!"

In unison, Annie, Martin and Stuart turned to look at the other woman.

Monica shrugged. "I think I said...y'all are, like...a 'ready-made family', Stuart...it's not *quite* the same thing!"

The child shook his head dejectedly. "Mummy told Betsy there wasn't enough pounds in the United Kingdom for you to buy another wife..." Stuart announced in that innocent, offhanded manner that is so common from children; Martin winced at the comment. "But I told them that since I am six now, I shan't be needing a nanny anymore! I'm not a baby, after all!"

Both Annie and Monica smiled surreptitiously as Martin's brows rose in response to his sons' appraisal. "Did you, now?"

Stuart nodded. "Betsy is a dear, but she's such a mother hen!"

Laughing, Martin grasped the child's neck tenderly and drew him close for a hug as he asked, "Are you *really* sure that you're ready for children, Annie?"

Looking down at the little boy who was proving to be more and more like his father at every turn, she smiled and replied, "How could I *not* be?"

"Did you tell Martin about the baby?" Monica asked some moments later as she and Annie stood at the kitchen counter preparing breakfast.

"Believe it or not, I had every intention of telling him...it was like the absolute perfect time: until I found out Claire was pregnant when *they* married...Martin caught me so off guard, explaining that he wanted to do things 'in the right order *this* time' because he'd married Stuart's mother out of obligation...just hearing him relate all that, I literally got sick on my stomach!"

"I've told you about forgetting to eat!"

Annie glanced out the window over the kitchen sink and smiled at Stuart's two-fisted attempt at lifting a piece of luggage from where Martin had sit it on the gravel driveway. "I'm glad that Stuart's so positive about everything."

"I think the kid would marry the two of you himself if he could—!"

"—but now that I know how Martin feels about marrying for 'the right reason,' how do I tell him?"

"That he got the cart before the horse **again**?" Monica laughed. "Aw heck Annie, you'll marry for the right reason! And he'll get used to the idea of being a daddy again. You see him with Stuart," she offered, nodding in his direction. "So what if he can't do things in A-B-C order? He makes up for it by being real dexterous!"

Following the direction of Monica's attention, Annie again glanced out the window and laughed out loud to find Martin walking toward the back porch with two suitcases under one arm and a huge, four foot teddy bear under the other!

"...and then, once we have the bags and Winston upstairs, I'll need your help arranging everything in the armoire—!"

"—excuse me?" Monica interrupted, hand on hip. "What was that I heard come outta your mouth?"

"The uh...the chifferobe!" the child corrected himself. "Aunt Monica said that Annie's grandfather built it even before she was born! It's made of cedar, Daddy, and it smells wonderful inside...I'm sure it will do quite nicely for my things, but wherever shall we put yours?"

Standing just inside the doorway with an expression of utter disbelief upon his face, Martin felt his gaze travel from his son's face to Annie's at the kitchen counter and back again, shaking his head at the amount of authority with which his six year old son had seemingly taken the situation in hand.

"What to do with my things—you know, Stuart, I haven't given it a thought..." he replied at last, realizing for the first time that he really had not!

"You're um, you're welcome to use the guest room across the hall from Stuart's if you want," Annie interjected, shrugging her shoulders as she wiped her hands on a dishtowel. "Grandpa also made a chifferobe out of walnut; it doesn't smell as good as the cedar one, but it has plenty of room. There's also a table and a chair that he made, and a matching queen size bed that just about fills the room up," she offered, motioning for him to just drop the bags at the doorway for now. "How 'bout we get you two settled in after breakfast?"

"Eggs and sausage and gravy and biscuits and grits..." Monica offered.
"I only have the one carry-on..."
"MY bag is bigger that Daddy's!" Stuart exclaimed. "We went shopping
in Piccadilly and I have the most wonderful new wardrobe...and, he bought
Winston to keep me company since Paddington is still at Mummy's—" Stuart
stopped in mid-sentence. "What is that you just said Aunt Monica: grits...?"
His tone was disbelieving. "Yuck!"

Martin closed his eyes and shook his head again, his son's outspoken
manner making him feel suddenly very inept. "Stuart, you really should
not..."

"—you've got to chill," Monica interrupted good-naturedly, glancing at
Martin with a dour expression etched upon her face. "I mean, it's like
Dorothy said: 'I don't think we're in Kansas anymore...' *YOU'RE* not in
London anymore, kiddo. Not only do we eat grits- which happen to be
delicious, by the way, and very good *for* you -but we like our tea sweet and
over ice!" she nodded at his wide-eyed expression. "Oh yeah...don't knock
it till you try it!"

"Uh, Monica...could I talk you down from your soapbox before the eggs
get cold," Annie broke in with a smile.

Glancing from Annie's tolerant face to Martin's amused one, Monica
nodded and slipped an arm around Stuart's tiny shoulders. "I don't think
either of them appreciate comparing the vast differences in our two cultures,"
she murmured teasingly as she set Stuart in his chair. "You, on the other hand,
seem to...I appreciate that in a kid..."

Annie turned from watching Monica sit Stuart at the kitchen table and felt
Martin slip his arms around the back of her waist, drawing her into a full-
bodied hug she realized she needed just as badly as he did. "I'm starved..."
he whispered huskily.

"Well then, lets sit down..." Annie murmured against his throat, pressing
close to bask in the scent and strength of him.

"I'm not talking about for food," he whispered as his heart drummed
heavily in his chest, and Annie giggled. "I swore that I could keep from
touching you- at least through breakfast -but it's all I want to do..."

Awed by the throbbing urgency of his heartbeat beneath her fingertips,
Annie drew back far enough to look at him, smiling then when their eyes met
and she saw his love for her reflected in their clear, guileless depths. "I'm
glad," she breathed appreciatively, "because I'll never get enough of simply
touching you...not ever..."

Wordlessly, Martin bent to touch his lips to hers and was met with a soft smile, a teasing smile that made him happy...simply that. "What are we gonna do?" she murmured low as her eyes held and adored him.

"You're going to marry me, Annie Ryan."

Oh, Martin, Annie thought to herself, *how I long to be your wife...I want to be Stuart's mother and make a home for us with all the love I knew as a child. I want you to know what it's like to have a **real** family to come home to, and a wife who cherishes the memory of your touch every moment of the day...* "Mr. and Mrs. Martin Vaughn," she murmured aloud, tracing his lips with her fingertip, "I want that someday as well..."

"—no Annie, not someday," he broke in as he withdrew to look at her in full. "Right away, just as soon as we can arrange it...just as soon as Preacher Wilson can perform the ceremony."

Monica's attention went from spooning sausage gravy over her biscuit to the couple standing in the doorway between the kitchen and the front hall. "Did I hear someone say 'ceremony?'" she asked outright.

Immediately, Stuart turned in his chair to face his father and Annie. "What type of ceremony, Daddy?"

The couple seemed oblivious to anyone else but themselves. "Right away...Martin, are you sure? It's only been a few days since your—?"

"—is there a waiting period I don't know about? Some legality?"

Annie studied his expression for a long moment, her brows screwing up. "I—I don't think so..."

Monica tried again: "Hel-lo...? Earth to the love-birds...!"

"How soon could we get a license...with the holiday—?"

"—our county offices are closed Monday..." Annie shrugged.

"We'll drive to Danbury first thing Tuesday, then."

"HOLD IT, you guys!" Monica interrupted at last. "Could you let the two of us in on the plan?" she asked, motioning back and forth between Stuart and her self. Then: "You've uh, piqued our interest," she added, pointing both index fingers directly over the child's head. The couple had been so wrapped up in one another that they weren't aware they had an audience.

"Are you going away again, Daddy..." the child whispered, his chin trembling, and then there was a long, empty space of silence.

Martin walked across the kitchen floor and lifted his son straight up from the chair he'd been sitting in; he wrapped the child in his arms and turned back in Annie's direction whispering "I will never leave you; I will never, ever be made to leave you again, Stuart." Then, more vehemently: "The last thing in this world you will ever have to concern yourself with is not having your family...because from now on," Martin drew Annie into his embrace, "we *are* a family: a daddy, a mommy, and you."

The little boy wiped a tear from his cheek. "But...you said we're going to Danebury...that's in Addington...that's where Mr. Nielson lives..."

"—oh no, son," Martin contradicted, "not...not England!" he stammered. "There's a Dan-bury here...it's about twenty minutes away..."

"—so you won't take me back to England?" the child persisted.

Martin cupped the child's face. "I don't plan on letting you out of my sight!"

"WE," Annie corrected, as she pressed a kiss upon the child's forehead. "You will never have to go away, and your daddy will never have to go away...you are home, sweetheart, this is your home now, forever and ever."

"You promise...?"

Annie cocked her head to one side. "I swear, with all my heart...I will never lie to you and I will do everything I know to do, to make you feel like you've always lived here. In fact: in just a few weeks, you can start school at Germanton Elementary; I will drive you there every morning and come back for you every afternoon."

"Do you know how cool that is—?" Monica interrupted. "Getting to be a 'car-rider'...I always had to ride the school bus!"

"—one of your brothers was always DRIVING a school bus!" Annie countered.

"Yeah well...that's beside the point..."

"How far away is Tuesday?" Stuart asked his father as the man sat down with the child upon his lap. "Is it a very long time?"

"Just a few days...why son?"

Stuart picked up a round of the alien breakfast food that Monica had called sausage: "May I go to th-the 'ceremony'?" he asked tepidly, smelling the round, flat piece of meat before he chose to take a tiny bite.

Hugging his son close, Martin replied: "Of course...you and Aunt Monica are expected to be in attendance."

"You just try to keep me away!" Monica taunted, smiling at the pleased look on the child's face as she spooned grits onto Martin's plate.

"I'd likely have better luck keeping that...stuff...off my breakfast plate..." Martin murmured.

"Probably!" Annie offered, realizing she would remember this moment for the rest of her life. And she smiled.

As the afternoon wore into evening, and as the last of Stuart and Martin's things were placed in their respective rooms, Annie found herself physically exhausted; after relaxing into her grandmother's wing chair to simply catch her breath, she literally dozed off for a little while. It was Monica who woke the woman and Annie found herself unnerved that she could drift off to sleep as if Martin were nowhere in sight.

"You know exhaustion is to be expected—pregnancy takes a lot out of a woman!" Monica rationalized.

"But this is not like me..."

"From here on out, you'd do well to pace yourself more; it'll get worse, ya know, before it gets better."

Annie shook her head. "I can't just MAKE myself slow down, especially now that there's a six year old in the house!"

"Well, you *can* make yourself tell his father why you're draggin...I hope sometime before Tuesday!"

"I...uh...I know...and you're absolutely right—"

"—of course—!"

"—but it's not as simple as you think! Every time I'm ready to broach the subject..."

Monica shrugged impatiently. "What...? Sit him down and tell him: 'Martin, that baby brother or sister we talked about earlier—it'll be here about the first week of December!' What's so hard about that?"

There was a pause. "You are no help."

"So, you want *me* to tell him?" Monica shrugged.

"Of course not...I really am anxious, and excited—he'll probably be ecstatically happy..."

"—and the only reason he might not be, is if he finds out in some manner other than being told by **you**," Monica finished succinctly.

Unconsciously, Annie nodded as her mind pictured the scene her friend had just suggested; she agreed he had to be told immediately. "Tonight..." she murmured under her breath, "I'll tell him tonight..."

* * *

As Martin sorted through the few belongings Stuart had been allowed to carry from the townhouse in his preschool backpack, he came across a 3x5 framed photograph of a younger version of himself, proudly holding his infant son at the child's christening. Slowly, reverently, his thumb stroked the glass under which the photograph lay pressed beneath a baby blue matte and he smiled at the tiny sleeping face, just as the man in the photograph did. *You slept through the entire ceremony,* he thought silently as his eyes held fast to the infant's face. *What a good baby you were...* Turning the frame about, Martin extended the hinged brace that was attached to the back and set the photograph upon one of the cedar shelves he stood in front of. "Thank you, Betsy" he murmured aloud, realizing that Stuart's nurse had obviously been the one to help his son pack the small bag; Claire would have never shown such consideration as to forward the cherished photograph—just the opposite, he realized: she would have taken tremendous pleasure in destroying it.

As his eyes moved to look upon other photos placed on the shelves, Martin found himself studying the numerous black and white pictures. They had been placed in simple, inexpensive frames and each sat upon aged crocheted doilies. Two of the pictures, he realized, had been hand-tinted with color and he smiled to recognize the man and woman in the larger of the two...she wore a 'pink' dress, coat and hat and smiled through lips touched with blood-red lipstick, and rouged cheeks the exact same color as the flowers that she held. The gentleman stood tall in a 'brown' suit and tie—the same color brown as both their pairs of shoes, and his hat and her purse...the photo was of Annie's parents, Stephen and Mary Ryan, probably taken on their wedding day.

The other hand-tinted photograph was that of a child of about two wearing a 'blue' dress, holding a 'brown' toy train engine, and whose cheeks and lips blushed a pale 'rose' color against aged Kodak white. Touching the photograph, Martin's fingertips strayed to the child's cherubic face and 'green' eyes and he smiled. "Her eyes are blue..." he murmured to no one, shaking his head at the obvious mistake.

"And the train was pink," came a voice from the doorway, and Martin turned about with a start to find Annie standing there. "Daddy sent away to Grandfather Mountain for it...said it wasn't proper for a little girl to have any other color..." Walking into the bedroom, she moved to stand alongside Martin, reaching up on tiptoe to retrieve something from the very highest shelf.

"Even at our house in Mount Airy, I kept it up high so other children couldn't get to it," she murmured low as she held the precious item out for Martin to take. "It's the only toy I ever really refused to share with other kids—even you Martin: because Daddy had looked so hard to find it, I knew it couldn't be replaced."

Martin turned the faded rubber train engine over in his hands as reverently as Annie had handed it to him, smiling at the tiny teeth marks upon the molded wheels and bell.

"If you squeeze it, there's a...a whistle in the bottom that's supposed to sound like a train whistle..."

Martin squeezed the toy and winced at the high-pitched sound it made.

"But it sounds more like the 'peep' of a very large mouse, doesn't it?" Annie asked smilingly and Martin nodded, not daring to break her train-of-thought by speaking. Taking the toy once again into both her hands, she sat it beside the photograph of herself as a baby and shook her head at the child in the picture. "Except for that spit-curl on top of my head, I was practically bald 'till I was two and a half...that and the fact I was never without my train made people think I was a boy, much to Mother's chagrin! But she said Daddy was the one that always set folks straight, which I still find peculiar, considering how badly he had always wanted a boy..."

Shrugging, Annie let the remainder of her thought go unspoken as her eyes suddenly noticed the photograph of Martin and Stuart. Swallowing hard, she studied the picture from where it sat, smiling first at it's image and then up at Martin; but for whatever reason, she never made a move to touch it or move it from it's place on the shelf. Martin sensed the woman's trepidation and glanced from her to the photograph and back again before he was able to understand her obvious reluctance to do anything more than simply look upon it. Without taking his eyes from her face, he reached out to grasp the framed photograph: "I'll go to a store next week and buy another frame, Annie," he whispered almost apologetically.

"Buy another...but why?" she asked incredulously, her eyes leaping to his face at once as if to dispute him.

Cradling the heavy marble frame in his left hand, Martin seemed to study how its inlaid 24-karat gold border encircled the oval shape to create a cameo-like casing. And for the first time since he and Claire had received the frame as a wedding gift, he saw the opulent creation as over-bearing, intimidating, hauntingly oppressive...not at all the type of frame to hold a picture of a baby. "It doesn't go with the others," he offered at last, handing off the obese bit of enclosure to Annie who grasped it with both hands to keep from dropping it.

"But Martin, this..." her eyes drifted downward. "It must be worth..."

"—it's completely worthless. It doesn't belong...here," Martin interrupted in a tone that told he would brook no argument.

Annie lifted wary eyes that showed her obvious confusion, but once she realized the man had no intention of elaborating, she simply replaced the framed photograph to the shelf and turned about with a gentle smile to say, "This is your home now, Martin. You do whatever makes you most comfortable, and happy."

Pulling her into his arms, Martin drew a long, cleansing breath and let it go as he rested his chin upon the top of her head. "THIS makes me happy... YOU make me happy. Marry me and let's have a dozen brothers and sisters for Stuart... and I'll buy every one of them a squeaky rubber train!"

Closing her eyes, Annie smiled at the man's loving words and silently thanked some unknown patron for having provided the much hoped for opportunity to broach the subject of having babies. "I want a house full of children, Martin, just as soon as possible..."

"Ummm," Martin began thoughtfully, leaning back just far enough that he could look at her: "And when do you propose we begin work on this project?" he teased with one brow cocked seductively, nipping at her lips with gentle love bites.

"Daddy, Annie! There you are!" came the excited voice from the open doorway and in an instant, Stuart had bounded into the bedroom seemingly oblivious to his father's and Annie's embracing forms. "Mine is the most fantastic room in the entire house, is it not?" he bellowed, his arms spread wide as if to embrace the entire space.

Annie drew a long breath for she felt almost as if it had been knocked out of her, so surprised was she by Stuart's sudden appearance; she winced at the realization she'd just lost that ideal opportunity of only a moment ago...

"I'm glad you like your new room, Stuart, but you really must stop being quite so boisterous," Martin urged in stern but gentle words. "You've got a lot of time to enjoy your new home...many, many years I hope."

Annie forced a smile.

"Your dad's right, sweetheart...settle in with Winston and play safely; every single toy in this room has missed having someone to play with, and if you're careful and take good care of them, they'll last you a long, long time...maybe until you're as old as your father!" she winked.

"Yes ma'am, thank you," the child murmured with a half bow. Then: "I don't understand why Mummy didn't want me to come here with Daddy," he offered point-blank, "for you've been nothing but kind..."

Annie's mouth open to reply, but no words would come. She felt Martin's arm around her shoulder and welcomed his support: "What do you mean, son?" he asked as casually as possible.

"I've seen Mummy's photographs of Annie..." he murmured shaking his head. "She doesn't like Annie at all," the child stated matter-of-factly.

Martin's grip around Annie's shoulders tightened and only she knew the fury he withheld from his voice. "What photographs are you talking about, son...I bet they were in a newspaper, huh?" he asked slowly, carefully so as to not allow the child think he was anything more than a little curious.

Shrugging, Stuart turned about and walked toward his beloved Winston, propping him more upright in the center of the bed. "They're just pictures...of Annie and Aunt Monica, of her and quite an older woman...there's some with you, Daddy, before you shaved your beard—just a lot of photographs in a box."

Both adults studied the child's expression when he turned back around to face them; he appeared genuinely unmoved, though maybe just a little bit curious if only because his father had been. "They're in the townhouse, Daddy, if you wish to see them: I know which closet Mummy keeps them in," he offered casually.

"Naaah, we can take some new pictures of Annie and Monica," his father reasoned as convincingly as possible, hoping his 'disinterest' would curb any he might have stirred in the child. "But I am curious about something else: why do you think your mother would dislike Annie?"

Once more the child shrugged, though his eyes went to Annie: he seemed to measure her from head to toe, and he shook his head from side to side. "She's nice, and really quite pretty...maybe Mummy is *jealous* again, like she was before."

Martin's expression showed his confusion: "Before?"

Stuart turned back to face his father squarely. "You know! Like you said she was after the movie...you called Mummy 'jealous' when she was yelling at you about the lady you kissed!"

Wincing, Martin nodded and let go a long, hard breath. "I never knew you heard us that night..."

"Oh heavens, Daddy—really! Betsy said it was for certain the dead in St. James' Park could hear you as well!"

Covering the threat of a smile with the back of his free hand, Martin pretended he was deep in thought, casting Annie a tolerant wink before continuing with his son. "Don't you think it odd that the uh...the *dead* in St.

James' should be able to hear our yelling, Stuart?" he asked as evenly as possible.

The child appeared to study his father's question very intently. Then: "How silly of Betsy to think they might hear you and Mummy at St. James," Stuart nodded at last, his expression showing he too saw the absurdity of his nurse's statement. "They're on one side of the River Thames and the townhouse is on the other!"

CHAPTER ELEVEN

Annie listened as Martin's footfalls sounded on the old pine step treads as he neared the bottom of the stairway. Once upon the landing, she heard him pause then step into the kitchen; his "Ummm..." from smelling the strawberry cobbler she had just removed from the oven made her smile. "I haven't had strawberry cobbler since the filming of 'Misbegotten,'" he murmured as he joined Annie on the old Queen Anne love seat.

"I always bake a cobbler for church on the first Sunday," she replied smilingly, unable to conceal her genuine happiness at having Martin so close again. The day had flown by, she realized, with hardly any opportunity for them to be alone...she relished his nearness now.

Martin wrapped his arms around the woman's shoulders and drew her back against him. "I have a horrendous sweet tooth: strawberry cobbler, cheese Danish, chocolate éclairs, *lovely necks...*"

Feeling his lips nuzzling the sensitive skin behind one ear, Annie giggled, "You have a horrendous appetite PERIOD, Mr. Vaughn," as she let her head roll slowly forward to accommodate his delightful play.

Closing his eyes, Martin drew in a deep breath as his lips followed his nose down the length of her neck. "I love the way you smell..."

"Ummm..."

"I think I've imagined doing this a thousand times..."

"Uh-hmmm..."

Enjoying the way she went limp in his arms, Martin smiled and teased: "You're not going to sleep on me, are you?"

Instantly, Annie turned fully about to cradle his face in both her hands. "Oh darlin', not a chance..." she murmured as she kissed him softly, wistfully, slowly—her love for him felt so right and it came so naturally for her, she wondered aloud that it could ever be improved upon: "I don't think I'll ever want for another thing as long as I live…"

Martin smiled and nipped at the tip of her nose with his lips. "I have imagination enough for both of us…where shall I begin?"

Annie smiled and traced the shape of his mouth with one finger. "Perhaps, in bed?" she whispered. "There is a little boy in the house…"

"—and thanks to no nap today, that little boy and his BIG bear are down for the count, curled beneath crisp, air-dried cotton sheets…I nearly crawled into the bed with him!" he smiled.

Annie laughed. "There's fresh sheets on your bed as well, sir…"

"My bed…how about **our** bed?"

"Is that an invitation?"

"Absolutely!" Martin enthused as he moved to stand up.

"I need…we need to talk about something first," Annie murmured as she held his hands and drew him back down beside her. *Lord, help me to say this the right way,* she silently prayed. Then: "It seems like every time during the last day or so that I've tried to get you alone, to tell you…" she paused and looked Martin in the eyes. "There's just no perfect time, I guess…no right way…"

"—what is it, Annie. You're scaring me."

Annie shook her head and brushed his hair off his brow. "Oh sweetheart…it isn't anything bad. I promise…"

"Has Stuart done or said something—?"

"—no! No, Martin…that precious child has been a joy! He is so much like you…like Daniel, the way I remember *him*…I even caught myself almost calling him 'Daniel' at one point!"

Martin's expression relaxed somewhat. "Then what is it, Annie? Something obviously has you on edge…I can feel it…your hands are shaking…"

Looking down at where she had drawn Martin's hands into her lap, she shook her head and squeezed his hands tightly to try and stop hers from trembling. "Monica would laugh her head off if…"

At the ring of the telephone, Annie jumped nervously and whatever else she might have thought to say died on her lips.

"You had to say her name…" Martin scolded.

Annie smiled apologetically. "Surely, she wouldn't call this late…"

The phone rang again.

"I really should get it…"

"—just let the damned thing ring," he countered, upset now by the intrusion.

"I don't want it to wake Stuart," she murmured at last, standing from the seat and walking the short distance to her desk before it rang in full a third time. "Hello," she all but whispered, "you better have a good reason..."

Sitting with his head against the back of the love seat, Martin stared at the ceiling and vowed to get an unlisted number for Annie's phone. A quick glance to the anniversary clock on the mantle showed it was 1:45 in the morning and he shook his head in utter disbelief.

"Yes...yes, I'll hold," Annie muttered as she turned about to answer Martin's incredulous stare. "It's an overseas call: the operator asked for you," she added, extending the receiver in his direction.

Realizing in that instant the call must be from Chris, Martin took the receiver and wrapped his free arm around Annie's shoulder. "I'm sorry...I gave this number to my attorney, in case he couldn't get through on my cell..."

"—it's all right," she whispered, actually relieved that it hadn't been Monica after all! "Take your call and I'll go check on Stuart," she offered, pressing a tender kiss upon his lips.

Martin cradled the side of Annie's face and in turn, placed a long, longing kiss against her temple, smiling as she drew away to walk from the room. After a moment, he heard his name being spoken from the receiver where his hand held it at his left thigh and he lifted it to his ear. "Hello...Chris?"

"Ah, Martin. Yes, hello! I gather you and Stuart arrived at Miss Ryan's without incident," he offered.

"Yeah, just...just a little after dark last evening."

"And your son—what does he think of your new venture?"

Martin smiled. "He's accepted all the changes of the last week extremely well, especially his new home."

"Bear in mind, Martin, that a child as young as Master Stuart has no true concept of what has transpired these last days," Chris warned. "The trip with you, the change in accommodations, having new people in his life...he may believe this to simply be a vacation with his father than the permanent change that it is. You should be prepared for the inevitability of him asking for his mum."

Martin drew a long, thoughtful breath. "I know...I've thought about all of that, and I'm trying to look at this situation from the same perspective a child would...I just want him to be happy. So far, he really seems to be."

"I'm certain he shall—the boy adores you."

"You know, having him with me this week, I see that I've missed so much with my child that other fathers probably take for granted: small things like waking me in the mornings with his bear hugs...and showing me how well he's brushed his teeth every night before crawling into bed...I feel like I need to make up for all the time Claire kept him from me and yet, I don't want to overwhelm him."

Chris smiled. "You've been granted permanent physical custody—enjoy your son and simply allow him time to adjust to having a full-time father again! You can only live one day at a time, anyway..." Chris paused thoughtfully. "You haven't said how Miss Ryan has received your son..."

Martin chuckled. "She's upstairs checking on him this very minute. Her first thought when the phone rang was keeping it from disturbing Stuart...your timing, by the way, couldn't have been worse."

"My apologies, old boy, but you did say to call if anything new concerning Claire came to light."

"Of course..." Martin nodded to himself, "but couldn't it have waited till later in the day?"

"It IS later in the day—here."

Martin grimaced. "I'm sending you a clock set on Eastern Standard Time, Chris...just as soon as a store around here reopens..."

"Ah...the anniversary of the Yanks divorcement from Mother England cramping your style, is it?"

Martin chuckled. "Not really...I'd just forgotten how the folks here in the South truly celebrate...everything shuts down: stores, businesses, government offices—no one goes back to work until Tuesday."

"Quite an egalitarian concept," Chris teased.

"Enough about holidays: you said there's something concerning Claire that I should know about?"

"Actually," Chris began soberly, "it more concerns Miss Ryan."

"Annie?"

"Yes...and her condition."

"What condition?" Martin asked, turning at that moment to find Annie stepping into the room. Upon hearing his words, she hesitated in mid-stride, silently praying they weren't discussing her.

"What condition...?" Chris' own confusion was evident in his lengthy pause. "Er...perhaps I've misspoken...I assumed...forgive me, Martin. You and I shall talk at a later time..."

"—wait a minute, Chris! What condition…what the hell does Claire have to do—?"

"—Martin," Annie broke in abruptly as she laid a hand upon his arm, "could you tell your…your attorney that you'll call him back later? I need to talk to you…"

"Is something wrong with Stuart?" the man asked apprehensively.

"No, no Martin he's…he's sound asleep. I…please," she whispered, her tone strangely conciliatory in the long silence. "There's something you need to know…something I should have already told you, about me…"

Martin was silent a long time, growing numb from the same eerie sense of apprehension he'd felt in New York when she had told him there could be no more for them than their one night…that she could not stay with him. He lifted the receiver to his ear. "I have to go, Chris…I'll call you sometime later…" he murmured in a near whisper, not waiting for a reply before he returned the receiver to its cradle: his eyes never left Annie's face.

What seemed like an eternity actually lasted only a few moments; but during those moments Martin stood waiting for her to speak, Annie saw more pain in his eyes than she ever wanted to cause him in a lifetime. Her first thought was how Martin's attorney could have learned of the pregnancy. There had been some mention of Claire during the men's conversation: and then she reasoned if Claire had obtained a box of photographs of her, Monica, Gramma, and Martin, the woman's detective must have found out about the pregnancy as well. For Chris to be calling his client meant Claire's attorney had contacted *him*: she must be attempting to use the information against Martin somehow.

Suddenly, Annie felt nothing but anger, for wasn't this the worst-case scenario Monica had been alluding to? *How did I not see this coming*, she thought silently, *given the underhanded things Claire has done to hurt Martin in the past*…Though she felt Martin's eyes upon her, Annie still could not speak: it was as if someone gripped her throat with an iron-like grasp, so tight that she could barely breathe…

"You know what Chris was calling about…don't you?" Martin asked finally in a low mumble, his eyes pleading. Annie could only nod in reply. "This…condition, whatever it is…are you…?" Martin swallowed, "is it really serious, Annie?"

"Oh, Martin…no…NO!" she shook her head almost violently, stepping toward him at that instant to cradle his face in both her hands. "I don't know what…what Chris told you but…" her voice trailed off into silence, grateful that whatever had been discussed between the men, the attorney hadn't told Martin about her pregnancy; she silently thanked God for allowing her one more chance.

"I'm not sick, darlin, I swear it…" she whispered, pressing trembling lips against his cheek. She found his skin cool beneath hers that was flushed and warm, and she grimaced at having scared him so. "I know I should have told you before now…and I've tried! God knows, several times today, I tried but …" She drew back to look at him in full, nervous and excited all at once, with just the merest smile alight in her eyes. "I'm…pregnant, Martin…I'm gonna have, a brother or sister for Stuart…" she whispered, her eyes welling with happy tears.

Slowly, Martin's brows drew together over once-tortured eyes, his expression at once gratified and incredulous as Annie's words seeped into his conscious mind. He lifted his hands to her shoulders and squeezed them in such a way that she felt reassured, and she smiled at the gesture. "When Chris asked about your…your condition, I immediately thought…" The man's words were wrenched from his throat leaving it raw and aching, and he paused and swallowed as if to do so might relieve the pain. But there *was* no relief, there was no easing of the putrid burning that now also stung his eyes; there was no sense of regained equilibrium that should have come at learning she was not ill, only greater confusion and a sudden, dreadful suspicion that quickly set an angry muscle in his temple throbbing in time with his labored breaths. His hands still gripped her shoulders, only painfully now, and he felt her tense beneath his fingertips.

"You're not…sick…you're pregnant…"

And suddenly the silence exploded between them, exacerbated when Martin slowly, purposefully set her away from him with churlish hands, backing away a step as if he could no longer bear to be near the woman. Annie's hands dropped from where she had so lovingly held the man's face and she was left to let leaden arms fall to her sides. Suddenly cold, she began shaking all over, drawing her hands into fists, shuddering as the skin on her scalp crawled and prickled as if touched with a thousand tiny pins. "This isn't how I intended to tell you," she whispered, her voice contrite. "There just…trying to make Stuart feel comfortable, getting the two of you settled in, there just never seemed to be the right moment…" she shook her head fretfully as tears rolled down her cheeks. "I'd planned to tell you tonight, I was trying to tell you before Chris called, but then the phone rang and…" Annie let her words break off in a whisper once she realized Martin still had

217

not moved, had not spoken. He stood erect and menacing, overpowering her with his cold silence; she felt like a cornered animal, as if she were falling backward into blackness. "Please Martin...say something...tell me you understand—!"

"—understand, Annie?...What?" he bellowed low and with hateful insolence as his mind remembered another place and another time...another woman. "What do you want me to understand? How a woman can use her body to draw a man into her bed? How she can offer him one...incredible night, and nothing more? How she can hide her pregnancy from him until she decides how SHE wants to use it to get what she wants!?"

"No!..."

"I understand all too well how it's done...my God, I've been fool enough to fall for it TWICE!"

Annie took a timid step toward the man, "I swear...Martin, it's not what you think!"

"Then what? WHAT?!" he goaded, an odd note in his voice. "Tell me what it IS, then, if it isn't what I think!" The man's cruel suspicions stabbed clear through to her soul: he was comparing her to Claire. That hurt worse than anything. "What happened in New York was as much a surprise to me as it was to you," she murmured as if talking to herself. "I wouldn't...I *didn't* plan any of it, no more than you did...and becoming pregnant, knowing I was already caring for Gramma...you have to know t-that isn't something that I would have planned..." she stated matter-of-factly, shaking her head.

"Our meeting was *accidental*, our affair was *accidental*, our baby was *accidental*..." His expression showed his disbelief and he laughed hatefully. "THIS, from the most organized person I know!"

Annie felt a sense of emotional betrayal. "I have never lied to you...I swore to you that I would not."

"Then why, Annie, did it take a phone call from Chris to compel you into telling me the truth? Lying by omission is still a lie," he accused through gritted teeth, remembering how many times he'd dealt with the same from Claire.

This faithlessness, this imperious pose was a side of the man Annie had never seen before, outside his role of Michael in 'The Misbegotten,' and she didn't know to relate to it, how to defend herself against it. There was a hesitation in her reply for her words seemed futile now. "I never intentionally lied to you, Martin...I was attempting to tell you when Chris called. I don't...know what more I can say."

Martin studied her features as his mind dueled with the memory of her lying beneath him, loving him, giving all of herself *to* him, as she unknowingly received his seed...then leaving him because she swore the needs of her grandmother came before his and her own...again, he resented it. "What did your grandmother think of your pregnancy? How did you convince her to accept an illigit—?"

"—Gramma never knew!" Annie broke in angrily. "I was...somehow able to keep our affair from her!"

"And you were able to keep your pregnancy from me." Martin sat down hard on the love seat, bracing one arm on his knee as he pressed his face fully into his palm. "The tabloids alone will have a field day with this...the editors are ruthless bastards who'll pay millions for something they want badly enough." There was a long pause. "You need only name your price, and they'll pay it..."

Annie swallowed back a burning lump in her throat, horrified at what Martin seemed to insinuate.

"But Claire, knowing what she does, is far more dangerous...she had this information before Stuart and I left...he saw pictures of you in a box..." His voice trailed off. "She knew at the custody hearing and she didn't say a word..." he whispered to himself. *Enjoy your visit: I'll make certain it's your last...*

Martin ran his hands across his eyes, his gut sick from fear because he knew what Claire was capable of. Across the room, he watched as Annie stood stone still and silent; angry as he was at her, he still wanted to hold her, and he wanted to shake her...he wanted to believe her, and yet he refused to. He loved the woman for keeping their unborn child, and yet he hated her for keeping his child from him..."Just like Claire..."

Slowly, grimly Annie lifted her eyes back in the direction of his voice. "I'm not...'just like Claire'! I'm *nothing* like Claire..."

Martin's eyes locked with hers, hardened by the years lost to him and his son that could never be called back, and he completely shut out all common sense: "I've had one child stolen from me," he murmured grittily, "and I'll not go through that again, I promise you!"

Annie's heart broke in two then as the realization hit her: there was no understanding, no forgiveness, no emotion left in the man but anger...there would be no going forward: the finality of it felt as if time had stopped. It felt like an eternity before she was able to speak again. "I have no intention of keeping your child from you," she stated at last, clearly and firmly, clinching her teeth to keep from crying—she wouldn't let him see her cry again! "This child deserves to know the love of his father, just as I did...just as *you* did. No matter what you may think, I would *never* use a child as a means of gaining anything. I'm not like Claire...I could never be like Claire.

"I don't...I don't know what your feelings are for me now: you may despise me, you may loath the very sight of me...but this child, Martin, was conceived in love, and he'll never be made to want for love from either of us...in spite of what happens to you and me."

Martin looked at her, considered her words, allowed them to seep into his subconscious. A part of him wanted to believe her, because the taste of her was still on his lips, the scent of her hair and skin was all around him...he remembered her passion—the wanting still hung in the air between them, drawing him to her like a tether. And yet his mind flashed memories of Claire: refusing visitation with his son, taunting him with the threat of a scandal, Claire and her lover and the photographs that would forever haunt him. His elbows braced tremulously upon his knees as his hands curled into fists, and he dropped his head at the same moment, closing his eyes tightly as if to do so might clear his mind of her memory.

Annie had read the varied emotions as they crisscrossed Martin's face; she realized the tortured expression that left him bent was from his memories of Claire rather than his feelings for her. But he also questioned **her** motives...doubted **her**. Hard and derisive, intentionally hurtful, his silence was shutting her out and his damning words pushing her away. Even so, that part of her that wasn't ready to give in to the old ghosts, the deepest part that still ached for the man's touch and his understanding, impelled her movement from where she stood by Gramma's old wing chair. Barely feeling her legs beneath her, for her body had bourn up to all it was capable of for one night, she stepped slowly toward where the man sat- where the two of them had sat barely an hour before -and knelt slowly to sit beside him. Weary from no sleep and from the hurting the man had inflicted upon her emotions, Annie drew her knees close to her chest as she wrapped trembling arms around herself.

If he knew she was there, Martin didn't acknowledge it; and though she longed to touch him, to lay her head upon his shoulder and simply feel his warmth again, Annie took care to *not* touch him, to not even look at him again. She barely spoke above a whisper: "I'm sorry that you hurt so very deeply...I thought that with time, you might get past it or that at least you'd be able to put it behind you. I know now that's not gonna happen...at least not completely. Too much has happened to you...you've lost *too* much...

"I've loved you all my life, and I waited twenty years for you to come back to me," she winced and corrected herself, "for *Daniel* to come back...only, Daniel doesn't exist anymore, does he?" She laid her head upon her knees and closed her eyes, realizing then that she had stopped trembling, her body had become sickly still. In that moment of growing calm, she became accepting...resolved...she was prepared to let him go.

Martin more sensed than felt the woman sitting at his side. He turned his head just enough to find her nearly drawn into a ball: her cheek rested upon her knees, her eyes were closed and her hair fell in one long wave against her legs until it touched the cushion she sat upon. The crocheted shawl that had once draped across the back of the couch now lay in a heap on the floor in front of her, a reminder of the few precious moments before the telephone rang and interrupted their loving. Martin felt his traitorous body respond again and angrily shook his head at the irrefutable truth: as hurt and confused as he was, he still wanted her. "I need some time to think," he stated as if speaking to himself.

"I think we both do," she murmured, knowing only time could exorcise the pain from his soul...and from her own.

He moved to stand from where he had been sitting, albeit awkwardly because he too was so completely exhausted, and walked to the staircase in silence. He took each stair step slowly, deliberately...never saying another word. And he never looked back.

*   *   *

The ring of his cell phone woke Martin and he sat bolt upright at the noise, having conditioned himself for many months now to the sound that almost invariably signaled an incoming missive from Chris. For just an instant, he was disoriented, wondering absently what hotel and what city he had slept in last night. And then he saw the walnut chifferobe against the wall by the bedroom window, and he remembered precisely where he was, the repeated ring of the phone a slap in the face for his awakening. He rose from where he had lain and reached the menacing instrument in one abrupt lurch. "Yeah!"

The other party cleared his throat. "Bad timing again, old man?"

"Uh, no...no Chris..." Martin pinched the sleep from his eyes with his thumb and index finger. "W-what time is it?"

Chris chuckled. "Here or there?"

"Here...my time..."

"Well past noon...did I, interrupt something?" he quipped, his voice overtly bright.

"No...I was asleep," Martin returned, cognizant now. He opened his bedroom door and listened into the hallway; the house was silent, no television or other voices...it seemed completely empty except for him. He listened for another long moment then stepped across the hall to Stuart's room only to find the bed made and the child nowhere in sight. "Stuart? Where are..." His brows furrowed in immediate concern until he found a note lying on the child's pillow, his name written across one folded side in Annie's now familiar hand. His gut then twisted in eerie apprehension. His voice had been so oddly coarse, that Chris implored, "Martin, is something wrong?"

"Hold on a minute," he murmured as he dropped the phone onto the bed and retrieved the piece of paper in the same movement:

Monica and I went to church. Stuart seemed so eager to go once he found out I'd cooked that I didn't have the heart to refuse him. I hope you won't be upset, but he doesn't know about what happened last night and I didn't think you would want me talking to him alone about it. We should be back home about 1:30.
Annie

Martin read and re-read the note then retrieved the phone from the quilt to hear Chris' "Have you forgotten me?" before the phone ever made it fully to his ear.

"No Chris, I haven't forgotten you," Martin murmured, raking his mussed hair off his brow as his eyes studied the note. "I just found a note from—from Annie...she's taken Stuart to church."

"To church...ummm, and why are you not with them?"

Martin sat down upon Stuart's bed and let go a long sigh. "My plans have changed."

There was a moment's hesitation before Chris spoke again for he had recognized the terse tone of Martin's voice; the lawyer in him sensed the necessity for tact and patience. "What happened after I called before?"

Martin closed his eyes and laughed a short, bitter prelude that in itself was another question: "Tell me, Chris, how it is that Claire's investigator should be able to learn about Annie's pregnancy, and McDougall didn't?"

"Extraordinary luck, damn her eyes...During these many weeks we've been having Claire and her lover monitored, Duncan, I'm afraid, only just yesterday came upon the information concerning Miss Ryan's pregnancy...information Claire has been hiding for weeks..."

"But how did she keep it—?"

"—it has been physically with her every moment of every day. Indeed, she had it with her at the custody hearing."

"But, Stuart saw pictures, Chris—a box of pictures of Annie, her grandmother, Monica...me when I still had the beard..."

"The photographs were quite a cleaver diversion, actually," Chris confessed. "When Duncan went through the townhouse, he found the photos straight away. And a notebook, telephone records...Claire kept them in her closet, hidden but not concealed..."

"—she expected someone would be looking." Drawing an unsteady breath, Martin closed his eyes and ran the palm of his hand across day-old stubble. "What has Duncan found?" he asked at last, his voice dangerously calm now.

"There is a file, Martin, that Claire's investigators compiled," he began stoically. "It documents everything about Miss Ryan's life...from the day she was born up through, her application for an apartment in...in Greensboro on the first of July—just a few days ago!"

"Apartment? Are you sure—I mean, she owns a house: whatever would she want with an apartment?"

"I haven't the foggiest idea," Chris admitted in return. "The home has been in her family for numerous generations; why leave now that it belongs entirely to her? I don't quite know what to make of it all." There was a pause. "Are you aware of the tremendous tragedy which befell Miss Ryan some years back, and later when her grandmother became an invalid?"

Martin swallowed roughly. "I know about her parent's deaths AND her grandmother's illness...Annie hasn't had an easy time of it...but nothing justifies hiding her pregnancy from me!"

"Then...you *didn't* know."

Martin's temple throbbed angrily. "No."

"I...I'm sorry, Martin...perhaps if I had not called..."

"—if you hadn't called, I probably still wouldn't know," the man reasoned. "It's too coincidental, Chris…so very similar to Claire's becoming pregnant with Stuart."

"Really, Martin," Chris countered, "you can't honestly mean to compare the two! Claire as much as admitted that she conspired to become pregnant whereas Miss Ryan…

"—is pregnant with my child and seemingly all but conspired to hide it from me!" Martin broke in. "She's no better than Claire if she means to begin our relationship with a lie!"

Chris considered his friend's rationale for a moment: given Martin's history with women, he could hardly blame the man for being jaded. But he found himself recalling the evening in his office when Martin had broken down during his initial telephone conversation with Miss Ryan—never had he witnessed such hurting in a man…not to mention the mournful woman on the other end of the phone line. That evening, in addition to all the drastic measures over many weeks to find and protect someone he so obviously loved, led Chris to wonder if his friend had given Annie a fair opportunity to explain why she kept her pregnancy from him, or if he had come to his own conclusion based on suspicion and Claire's previous deceit. "Tell me, Martin: what excuse did Miss Ryan give for having not already told you of the pregnancy?"

"What difference does it make?" Martin returned distractedly. "Bottom line is, she didn't."

Chris' voice was propitious: "I'm a lawyer; I'm required to hear both sides."

Martin shook his head as he rose from Stuart's bed, left the room and headed down the staircase. "She said something like, there was never the 'right moment'…that she was trying to tell me when you called…I don't remember a whole lot of talking between us just before the phone rang!"

"Then, you can't say with absolute certainty that she *didn't* try to broach the subject, only that you can't recall…"

"—we kinda got carried away with other things—!"

Smiling, Chris expected that was probably an understatement. "Very well…how often *were* the two of you completely alone during the, ah say, 25-30 hours following your arrival to her home?"

Martin sat down hard at Annie's desk. "I don't know! A couple of times…why are you harping on this?"

"I'm simply trying to establish that, it's entirely possible there *wasn't* an opportune time for much intimate conversation…Consider for a moment the possibility that this first time mother *did* in fact desire a special opportunity in which to announce to the man she has been in love with all if her life that they are going to have a child together. Would you consider that a reasonable desire on her part?"

Tilting the desk chair back on two legs, Martin smirked at his attorney's question. "That is **not** the point—!"

"—it is absolutely the point, for wasn't Stuart almost certainly in tow, *and under foot*, throughout the lengthy settling-in process?"

Martin didn't bite at the attorney's attempted play on words.

"And as for the ever-present Monica: when did she finally take *her* leave? I should think you able to nail *that* moment down…"

"—I get your point, Chris, but it doesn't change the fact that Annie hid something so important from me—!"

"—nor does it prove it," the attorney interjected rationally. "I think you've grown a bit paranoid, Martin, if only because Claire has done such a splendid job of nurturing that vexing seed…what a shame that you might allow it to cripple you emotionally, especially now when you seemingly have everything you've worked so dearly for. Do you remember why I called last evening…or did we even get that far before you hung up on me? Oh well, I called because it was my concern that Claire was planning to use the information concerning Miss Ryan's pregnancy to destroy your new relationship. Sadly, she could *not* have played you any better had she literally been standing in the room pulling your strings. Tell me: have you *once* during this brooding process paused long enough to consider that, yet again, Claire is getting exactly the result she desires…and at *your* hand…"

"—you've made your case, Chris."

"Have I?" A long pause: "Then, you realize you have a minute window of opportunity in which to plead temporary insanity…perhaps, even plead for mercy. And I am NOT being facetious, old man…done correctly and with just enough aplomb, and you could come out of this debacle smelling like the proverbial rose."

Martin swallowed, hard, and set the chair back on all four legs; his voice was sedate when he spoke again. "You don't know all the things I accused Annie of…I can't even remember all that I said; it was senseless…"

"—you were hurting. You jumped to the wrong conclusion. You were undoubtedly close-minded and positively cruel. However, if you *were* stupid enough to even once bring up Claire as a comparison..."

"—I was real, real, real stupid...I don't think she could ever forgive my doing that."

"Then you have no other option *than* to beg...seriously; women love that, it's empowering for them." Chris temporized. "The moment your Annie steps foot back within the home, one: apologize for being such a veritable ass, two: take back every cruel, senseless thing you accused her of, three: assure her that you're thrilled that you're to be a father again..."

"—I am thrilled—!"

"—and four: promise her that there will NEVER again be any comparison between she and Claire," Chris implored. "Isn't a woman alive deserves that kind of insult!" And then he had the good grace to be silent.

*   *   *

Sunday services for Annie and her young charge proved an ideal learning opportunity for both of them for Stuart's intelligent and unending string of questions concerning the Moravian faith surprised both she and Monica. Initially, Annie had questioned even trying to attend church after the events of the previous evening; but once the child woke her, already dressed and so very eager to spend the morning with her, she couldn't bring herself to tell him no.

"The Protestants and Catholics where I live are always fighting one another," the child commented as he watched the congregation spill out onto the front lawn of the large brick church. "Mummy would never believe that I had been welcome here."

Annie smiled at Stuart's awestruck expression. "A lot of the Pilgrims who settled here from Britain, Ireland and Scotland came because they were tired of being told they couldn't worship the way they wanted...they were tired of the fighting, too, and figured they'd just start a whole new country where folks could respect each others beliefs."

"There's a Catholic church in King," Monica offered. "Maybe your dad and Annie can take you there next week."

At the little boy's eager nod, Annie saw for the umpteenth time a glimpse back at Martin as she remembered him from their childhood. She swallowed hard and glanced down the long road that led to her house: *He's probably been up a while now,* she thought cheerlessly, *and he's probably packing his and Stuart's things so they may leave once we return.*

Monica caught the look of hurt and dread that crossed Annie's face as they walked toward the church's picnic tables. Recalling all her friend had told her about the previous evening's discussion, she offered a sympathetic smile as they began setting up for the outdoor dinner: "Ya know, given time to think about everything, Martin's probably already realized he over-reacted...he knows you, and he knows in his heart you'd never do anything to purposely hurt him."

Smiling at Stuart's beautiful, expectant face as he watched the various platters of food being placed upon the tables, Annie simply shrugged her shoulders wearily and murmured, "I pray to the Good Lord you're right...if you could have heard him last night, though..."

"The man's not stupid; and given a little time, he'll realize how wrong he was to accuse you of the worst."

"But what if he doesn't?" Annie insisted in a whisper, her face only inches from Monica's. "He honestly accused me of being just like Claire...he said I plotted to hide this child from him...!"

"It wasn't so long ago that he DID plot to keep something from you: when he hid his true identity to protect you and Stuart! I know both sides of the story, remember?"

"I fairly doubt you could convince him the two situations are even vaguely similar," Annie countered in frustration. "He's beyond believing anything I say, even when I swear to him it's the truth...he is always gonna compare anything I do to *everything* Claire's done..."

As she poured Stuart a tumbler of sweet iced tea, Monica watched Annie spread a napkin upon the child's lap, her gentle sweep of his blonde bangs bringing a smile to his face. "Are you enjoying yourself, sweetheart?"

"Aye...I just, I don't know anyone but you and Aunt Monica..."

"I promise that you'll have new friends before you know it! It's confusing though, wanting to meet the other boys and girls but not sure quite how?" Stuart simply nodded. "I'm confused too...I've never had a little boy to care for; and as badly as I want to do everything right, and help you, I know I'm gonna make mistakes...it would really make me feel better to know you're willing to overlook my mistakes, and tell me when I need to do something different. Will you do that for me?"

Again he nodded and Annie smiled, extending her right hand and accepting Stuart's smaller one into hers. "We have deal: you will always know that you can come to me about anything, and I will always do everything in my power to help you. Okay?"

Pumping her hand in the same gentlemanly manner as when they had first met, Stuart replied, "Yes ma'am...Annie..."

The woman heard his hesitation. "Are you comfortable with calling me 'Annie'?"

"Yes...I guess," he murmured hesitantly. "Mummy said that I'm to not call *anyone* 'Mummy' but her...I promised her that I would not..."

Swallowing hard, Annie smiled at the boy's strained admission: "Your mother...is absolutely right. No matter what happens, ever, Claire will always be your mother...you are too special a little boy for me or her or your dad to ever want otherwise."

"Are we ever gonna eat today?" Monica broke in as she took a tiny sip of Stuart's tea.

"Hey, that's mine!" he fussed, and Monica handed it to him with a wink.

"I think he's a little lonesome for home," Annie murmured as she placed small amounts of several dinner items on the boy's paper plate. "I don't even know what he likes to eat...or if he has allergies...I hope he's not a vegetarian," she fussed as Monica added a spoonful of chili beans and a fried pork chop to the assortment.

"Trial and error...and if he *is* vegetarian, he won't be for much longer!" she teased. Then, more seriously: "Just be patient! There's going to be a certain amount of uncertainty early on: you have it in any relationship. But how Martin could watch you with his son and even think of doubting your sincerity and your devotion..."

"You're up on your soapbox again," Annie broke in teasingly as she removed the twist cap from her diet soda. "Go ahead and fix yourself a plate; I'm gonna sit with Stuart so he doesn't get lonesome."

"Lonesome...?" Monica asked as she nodded in the child's direction.

Turning about, Annie smiled as two little girls in their Forth of July dresses sat down on either side of Stuart, becoming quick friends as he charmed them with his "accent." Motherhood, she decided would prove very interesting indeed!

Upon returning home, Annie was gratified when Monica suggested taking Stuart to Germanton Park for a while; once he learned of the jungle gym and the creek that so many children seemed to enjoy, there was no need for persuasion. Stepping from Monica's Volkswagen with the left over dinner items in her picnic basket, Annie smiled her appreciation for the few precious hours of privacy Monica was granting Martin and her self, silently praying it would somehow be time enough for the two of them to try and talk things through…if it wasn't already too late.

When Martin heard the familiar purr of Monica's car as it pulled into the driveway, he absently swiped at his still damp hair and nervously tightened the cuffs of a fresh white shirt where the sleeves had been turned up to his elbows. He had hurried through a quick shave and shower after finishing his conversation with Chris, wondering all the while if it would be his first and last in Annie's home…a home she had so graciously and lovingly welcomed he and Stuart to share. The man shook his head at his own incredible stupidity…would she be able to forgive him, he continued to wonder now or—hurt too deeply by all his cruel doubts and accusations—would she simply ask him to leave?

A moment went by, then two, and Martin found himself glancing out the kitchen window to see if he had mistaken what he thought to be Monica's car for someone else's. But no—Annie stood on the gravel drive with a basket in her hand, waving goodbye to Monica and Stuart as they headed back onto the road and north out of town. When Annie turned toward the house, he stepped away from the window and walked purposefully back toward the parlor, placing himself on one end of the couch the two of them had sat upon only hours earlier.

The same eerie silence Annie had come to dread whenever she entered her home since Gramma's death, was magnified now by the knowledge that Martin might at this very moment be packing his and Stuart's belongings in order to leave her life forever as well. Pausing upon the threshold as she slowly opened the kitchen door, she listened in the direction of the upstairs rooms but heard nothing; *he's had plenty of time*, she reasoned…*he's probably finished packing by now.*

Martin felt himself tense at the sound of the woman's footfalls upon the kitchen floor, and again when the basket was placed upon the counter and he heard the sound of her placing glass bowls upon the shelves of the refrigerator. The lengthy, absolute silence then told him she had stilled, hesitating to continue further, dreading the moment when she had to confront him and the probable continuance of his earlier anger and accusations. His fear that there might be no forgiveness, no feeling for him at all left within the woman, impaled Martin where he sat.

I should let him know I'm home, Annie reasoned as she stepped toward the stairs…

Sweet Jesus, I love her...how can I ever expect her to forgive what I've done?
Ask her.

"Annie?"

She jumped, startled at the voice: Martin's, but *not* Martin's.

"I'm...in the parlor," the gravelly voice spoke again, and she trembled at the hesitant invitation. Literally willing her legs to move, she crossed her arms before her now to still their trembling but found little relief; the July afternoon was warm, but her whole body felt deathly cold.

Martin sensed the moment she moved into the room and stood from where he had been sitting, his own nervousness causing one of the throw pillows to fall from the love seat to the floor by his feet. Annie welcomed the momentary distraction, taking the opportunity to step to her grandmother's wing chair and leaving Martin standing by the couch alone. Replacing the pillow back from where it had fallen, the man swallowed nervously and lowered himself back upon the couch, lifting his eyes to meet hers across the room. "Did Monica forget something before?"

Annie's face went blank; his question completely confused her.

"I mean, she headed back in the direction of town..."

"—oh. No, she...she and Stuart, she offered to take him to the park for a while; I hope that's alright."

"Of course. It'll...give us some time alone..."

Annie nodded.

"How did he do, at church...?"

A smile gently curved the corners of Annie's lips and the man felt his breath catch at the beauty of it. Just to see her smile again...

"Stuart was a delight...the entire congregation adored him. He was perfectly behaved, and just as friendly to everyone as he could be," Annie offered, still smiling. "I think he really enjoyed himself, though he was awfully surprised that he could be comfortable in a Protestant church. He made a point of telling us that his mother would never believe...he had been welcome there..." The woman's voice trailed off when she realized their conversation had brought them back to Claire: she placed the tips of three fingers upon her lips and shook her head. *It always comes back to Claire*, she realized sickly.

"Last night..." Martin swallowed hard, realizing the direction of her thoughts. "Last night was...absolutely the most disgraceful behavior...to compare you to Claire is probably the most irresponsible thing I've ever done..."

Annie dropped her eyes, unable to bear the piteous expression on the man's face.

"You, Annie...you're nothing like her—at all! I am...I'm disgusted with myself," he murmured, balling up a fist at his side and then bringing it to his lap to be met and massaged by the other. Annie heard the popping of his knuckles across the room and looked back up at him. "My anger at what happened in the past, it...it's this vile *thing* that still eats away at me. And, like Chris said, it's Claire's way of continuing to control me, as pathetic as that sounds...she's on the other side of an ocean, and she's still..." he shook his head at the disgust he felt for his own weakness, roughly massaging the back of his neck with one trembling hand. "I'm sorry that I allowed it to hurt you: I'm sorry that **I** hurt you, that I **doubted** you...with God as my witness, Annie, I will never treat you that way again."

"I never want to be like Claire," she heard herself think aloud, and then put her hand over her mouth when she realized she had.

"You have no idea how UN-like her you truly are," he stated solemnly, remembering the dozens of times she had stood over him with her finger aimed within inches of his face, one lengthy blood-red fingernail dancing in time to the proper English enunciation of every syllable of every word she shrieked.

"I should have found a way to tell you about the baby sooner...even if it meant I had to lock us both in a closet," she admitted. "Monica warned me to NOT let you find out the wrong way...she was right. Again."

"She said the same thing to me when we were discussing how to explain Nathaniel to you," Martin murmured, shaking his head at the ironic similarities.

Annie lifted her eyes to meet Martin's, their brightness conciliatory and hopeful. "Keeping the truth from someone, no matter how good your intentions might be, almost always causes problems...I promise: I'll never keep anything from you again..."

Martin drew a long, calming breath. "Nor will I..." There was a long pause then as he stood from the couch and walked to where Annie sat in the old wing chair; kneeling on one knee, he took both her trembling hands into his own and willed her not to turn away. "I know, I have no right to expect it...God knows, I don't deserve it...but I'm...I'm asking you to put what happened last night out of you mind, to forget every despicable thing I said because I didn't mean it; give me the time and opportunity to make all this right...I cannot begin..." He felt Annie's hands squeeze his and it sustained him, it strengthened him. "I can't tell you how sorry I am…I could say it a million times, and it wouldn't be near enough…"

"—then don't say anything else," Annie whispered, as she placed trembling fingertips upon his lips. "We're both sorry and it's over: it's like it never happened…" she added vehemently, tilting her head to one side as Martin leaned toward her and pressed his lips lightly upon her own. He murmured words she couldn't make out as his lips pressed kisses down the length of her throat, to the hollow of her throat, and then drifted upward again; he took her mouth in full as he coaxed and teased her with the sweetest desire she had ever known until she was moaning his name. "Martin…oh darlin'…" Suddenly weak from his kisses alone, she vaguely realized how that his hands seemed everywhere at once, lifting her, stroking her, pulling from her every bit of control until she thought she might drown in the thick delicious sensations he caused within her. "What are you doin' to me…?" she whispered as she realized she somehow lay beneath him now, his weight resting on his elbows as he tangled his fingers deep to remove the covered rubber-band from her hair. But the question had been rhetorical and remained unanswered in words as his thumbs traced the line of Annie's jaw and her throat for as far as her tangled mane would let him reach, further with his lips and tongue once she cupped his head to guide him lower.

"Oh Annie…just the taste of you," he whispered, his voice raw and pleading. "So many nights I laid awake thinking I'd dreamed you…tell me I'm not dreaming now…"

"Please Dear Lord, please don't let this be a dream!" she prayed aloud. "I couldn't bear it, I couldn't bear…"

As Martin's lips hovered just inches above hers, he felt her breath catch and knew she was crying. The back of one of his hands lay tangled in her hair against her temple, and the wetness when it touched him was like punishment. He turned that hand until his fingertips settled on her lips, and he traced their line, tantalizing her with the callused texture and musky scent of just his fingertips, pressing them gently inward until she tasted him. Feeling the man's roughened fingertips against the tender pink flesh just inside her lips, she lifted her head to take them more fully into her mouth, sucking first one then another until he literally trembled in his gut.

"No dream Annie…" he murmured as he slowly withdrew his fingers to settle them upon her lips, tracing her perfect pout with his eyes as well. She turned her head to kiss his wrist and the palm of his hand, and then welcomed his lips again upon her own with a low, pleading moan.

"I need you," she whispered, bowing beneath him as if pressing her body against his might somehow tell the man what her voice couldn't. "Please, Martin…I hurt from wanting you…"

The man slipped his hands beneath her hips and drew her even closer. "My beautiful Annie…tell me what you want…tell me—!"

"—I need you, inside of me!" she groaned, grasping his face in both hands now to make him look at her. "I need you, I need to feel you…" she whispered until his mouth closed down upon hers again. Feeling him moving above her, she grasped fists full of his hair to keep him close until she thought her lungs would explode from drawing in such deep, hungry breaths. And then his hands moved to her waist, his fingers slipping inside the width of lace that circled her hips to slide the wisp of material down past her thighs.

"Are you sure? That it'll be alright—?"

"—oh God, Martin, yes…yes, it's alright! It's perfect…" she murmured, and then gasped as she felt him fill her. "Ohhh…oh, oh yes…it's perfect, oh Martin…" Her hands opened and fisted in his hair and opened again to drag down the back of his neck and grasp his shoulders with all her strength. For a long, long moment it was as if he read her thoughts, just pressed fully, deeply within her was all she wanted then. She hadn't forgotten, and she hadn't imagined how this felt…over and over she made low, whispered sounds that Martin finally realized was her crying again, and he lifted his head from where his lips had pressed her brow.

"Annie, what's wrong?" he pleaded. "Look at me!"

Opening her eyes and then letting them drift closed again, she shook her head: "Can't talk…not now…please…" She bowed upward and thought she would die from the incredible fullness as the slight movement pushed him deeper. "Martin…oh God…" she whispered as she wrapped her arms around the man's neck and lifted even higher. "Ohhh…please, please!" she wreathed, her head rolling side to side, "I can't wait any more…"

Closing his own eyes, Martin slipped the palms of his hands under her hips and lifted her even higher, moving his body as he lifted hers to meet him, slowly, tantalizingly slow again and again until he had drawn her body into rhythm with his. It had been so long, the weeks of waiting and the nights spent hurting to feel her beneath him again, as she was now, her hands holding him hungrily, fisted and yet pleading to feel the release that they both sought. "Annie…how…how have I lived?"

"I can't…I can't ever be without you again…"

"No…no, never—!"

233

"—don't stop! Oh darlin', don't ever stop..." she whispered, over and over, until she tensed suddenly, her nails digging painfully into Martin's shoulders through his shirt as she lifted her head to press her open mouth hard against his throat. The man's moist, hot skin muffled her cry until it finally echoed through his chest and became his voice, deeply wrenched from somewhere between both their bodies. His movements then were like thrusts of anger and elation and deliverance, again and again and again until his body ceased it's convulsive release and his head-heavy upon his spent body - finally fell forward in exhausted relief.

Annie's death grip upon his shoulders gradually eased and he felt her breaths against his chest deepen somewhat as they finally slowed.

When he felt her begin to go limp, Martin shifted his weight to one side, braced on one elbow as he placed his right hand behind her head, and lowered the woman gently down. He just looked at her for a while then: her eyes closed with beads of tears still clinging to the tips of some eyelashes, she might have been asleep were it not for the low, whispered moaning sounds she still made long minutes after their loving. His hand remained behind her neck as Martin lowered his mouth to press light, gentle kisses to her eyes, silently pleading for her forgiveness again and praising her with the same touch. Though his ministrations were met with just the barest hint of a smile to acknowledge his nearness, Annie sensed when Martin would have drawn away and turned just slightly until her body was flush again with his. Pressed close against his side, she grasped the front of his shirt with both hands as if the say "Don't leave me" and finally, reluctantly gave up to exhausted sleep in his arms.

CHAPTER TWELVE

It was some time before Annie finally awoke. Her sleep had been endless, complete, and she was disoriented when her eyes opened to focus on a man's face. "Martin...?"

"Welcome back," he smiled, leaning forward to place a chaste kiss upon her nose.

She realized it was still daytime. "What time is it?" she murmured groggily.

Glancing up at the anniversary clock on the mantle, Martin replied "A little after four."

Looking around, she also realized they were in the parlor, and lying side by side on the loveseat...*How did I get here?* she wondered to herself. "How long have I been asleep?"

Martin shook his head. "Not long..." The man was too quiet, and he looked at her as if he'd been let in on some secret that he wanted to share but couldn't. "What is it? You have the strangest expression..."

Again he smiled, and shook his head slightly. "You really don't know?"

Annie's eyes widened and she shrugged. "Know what...?"

Martin lowered his mouth to hers and kissed her deeply, long and intimately, teasing her with tiny bites to her chin and neck before returning tenderly to her mouth; when he drew away, Annie realized she had wrapped her arms around him and wasn't letting him draw back but so far. "Do you remember *now*?" he whispered.

Her face felt flushed and her mouth tingled from where his lips had been; her whole body was tense, and the centermost part of her was heavy and throbbing as she looked at him thoughtfully. "I didn't dream it? It really happened?"

"Oh yeah, it happened…and I probably have the scars to prove it," he taunted, smiling at her look of disbelief.

Her eyes went wide then. "Dear Lord…I thought I'd dreamed the whole thing…" she whispered as she drew in a deep breath; her hands went to her mouth and she closed her eyes as if in silent prayer. After a moment she opened them again, and again took in her surroundings. "On the loveseat?" she whispered incredulously, her hands still pressed in the shape of a prayer against her lips and Martin nodded. "And then you redressed us," she thought logically, to which Martin surprisingly shook his head no. "We were never undressed, at least not very much…"

Annie's hands fell away from her mouth and her expression showed she was trying to picture exactly how dexterous Martin must actually be! "I'd never…I mean, on the loveseat…?" she asked again.

Martin finally had to good grace to laugh then. "…it was the closet thing to the wing chair. I considered the floor, but I didn't think the braided rug would be very comfortable."

Annie smiled tenderly at the sincerity of his expression. "All I remember is wanting you…"

"Ummm…you were terribly demanding, and impatient, and incredible…" he whispered, as he placed his palm on the slight roundness of her abdomen. "You're sure it's alright," he asked more seriously then.

Annie placed her hand flat upon his and gave it a gentle squeeze. "Yes, I'm sure…I'm a nurse, remember?"

Martin smiled and rubbed his hand in slow circles as if measuring the child within her. "He must have thought you were doing jumping jacks earlier…"

"Probably!" Annie laughed then and cupped his face with both her hands. "I have an appointment this week for the first sonogram—will you go to the doctors with me?"

"Of course," he replied without hesitation. "I want to meet the guy who's been lucky enough to touch this body when I couldn't!"

"SHE!" Annie corrected laughingly.

"Oh yeah? Maybe I'll get her to check me out while we're there—I swear, you've grievously wounded me…"

"Dr. Clark would no doubt enjoy examining you *very* much, Mr. Vaughn, but I'm not so sure I would like her doing it!"

Martin smiled shyly and kissed Annie's lips tenderly. "And I was just thinking how relieved I am your gynecologist **isn't** a man!"

Annie shook her head at his infuriating teasing. "The last thing in the world you will ever have to concern yourself with is my being interested in another man. There's not another person on earth I could ever love as much as I love you...I swear that, Martin, with all my heart."

"You say that now," he offered tepidly, "but wait 'till you've lived with me for a month or so...you may feel like kicking me out!"

"Why? Do you snore?"

Martin smiled tolerantly. "Not that I'm aware."

"Don't you put your dirty socks and underwear in the hamper rather than on the floor?"

Grimacing, Martin nodded slowly. "I'm...getting better..."

"Which part of the Sunday paper do you grab first?"

Thoughtfully, the man cast Annie a wry smile: "The entertainment section, of course—why?"

"Then you're a keeper!" she shrugged with a huge smile. "Had you said the sports section, we really would have had a problem!"

Hugging her to him, Martin lifted her chin and kissed her deeply, longingly—awed by the woman's ability to make him feel so loved. "Lord, how you make me want you...!"

"You have me, Martin...for the rest of our lives," she whispered in reply against his lips. "But you know: if you keep holding me this close, it's gonna be hard for me to make myself presentable before Monica returns with Stuart..."

"—oh sweetheart," he murmured against her temple as his fingers stroked deep in her hair, "it's already hard."

Barely an hour passed as Annie showered, dried her hair, and slipped into another sleeveless cotton dress; the looseness was much more comfortable in the July heat than the stretch-panel maternity pants she had purchased and, as the previous events of the afternoon had proven, more easily accessible as well! She drew a long, deep breath as she recalled those incredible moments and wondered that her day had begun with any doubt whatsoever as to Martin's love for her. Standing before the full-length mirror, she placed her palms flat against cheeks that had blushed and thanked God again for Martin's repentance, his understanding and for the miracle of the day.

Hearing the phone ring, she turned to step out of the bathroom and then slowed: *this isn't just my home anymore,* she reasoned, and smiled when she heard Martin's deep "Vaughn" from the bottom of the stairs. She took her time as she walked down the old staircase so that he might know she wasn't rushing to intercede; as it was, the call appeared to have been for him anyway for he was sitting at her desk and listening to the caller very intently. As she stepped toward him, she smiled at the memory of their early afternoon spent in the parlor and wrapped her arms around him from the back with a gentle hug.

Martin's left hand grasped both hers where they clasped just beneath his chin and he gave a squeeze that held tightly as his voice simply replied "Of course you have…" to the person at the other end of the line. His tone sounded terse, strained and then he shook his head and let go a long, tortured breath. "There's nothing else you *can* do," he added after another lengthy silence. Then: "Of course I'll tell her…she's right here with me…just, let me know as soon as you can, Chris. I don't want this to drag out…yeah, good-bye…"

Annie held her breath as Martin replaced the receiver on the phone and then pulled her around to face him. His eyes lifted from the phone to meet hers as he circled her waist and drew her to stand between his legs. Leaning forward in the chair, he laid his head upon her chest and simply held her close, drinking in the scent of the woman, feeling her heart race beneath her breast as her breaths became more shallow. Annie cupped the back of the man's head with both hands, pressing her lips to his crown to force her self not to speak as she waited for him to share the conversation with her: if it was Chris, then it must have to do with Claire, and her body began to tremble.

"Did I tell you, I spoke with Chris earlier, while you were away this morning?" Martin began after a moment, his head still resting against Annie's body.

Recognizing a haunting somberness in the man's voice, Annie closed her eyes and stroked the man's head with trembling fingertips, her lips barely an inch from his scalp…she needed his nearness, the smell of him to keep her focused. "I guessed he would call today…after last night. That was Chris again," she murmured.

The woman's fear was palpable, as well it should be concerning how his attorney's call the night before nearly destroyed them; she would welcome his latest even less…he started slowly: "Do you remember when Stuart mentioned the box of pictures…? Chris—started to tell me last night that Claire had investigators following you."

Annie's face went ashen. "Monica said you had feared that she might…"

Martin nodded as he murmured, "She actually found you before I did." Tilting his head back then, he locked eyes with Annie as he tried to prepare her for the worst. "She apparently thought it would help her to retain custody of Stuart if she could name another woman in a counter-suit…at least, we believed that was her plan."

"It didn't do her any good, though…I mean, you have Stuart! And with the divorce, it doesn't matter now who you see…right?"

Martin winced as he drew in a frustrated breath, silently cursing Claire for continuing to disrupt his life; he had to wonder if it would ever end. "She's aware of your pregnancy, Annie; she's attempting to blackmail me with what she knows, and for no other reason than to hurt **you**…"

Annie took a step back and broke the connection with Martin, turning from him so he wouldn't see the hurt and anger that threatened to suffocate her. He rose from the chair and moved to stand in front of her, grasping her shoulders to make her look at him, but he felt impotent for she was crying as desolately and desperately as a lost child.

"Oh Annie, this…THIS is the part of my life I'd always hoped to shield you from! You and Stuart, you don't deserve the kind of hell Claire can wield in her attempts to hurt me—!"

"—NO! **We** don't deserve it, Martin!" Annie broke in vehemently. "Stuart doesn't deserve to have his life disrupted any more, and you shouldn't be made to defend your relationship with me with a damned payoff! Oh Martin, our baby doesn't deserve to have his conception pasted across every tabloid in the world…that's what she's really threatening, isn't it…?"

At Martin's own pained expression, Annie broke down completely then, the rage deep inside her chest rumbling forth in great heaving sobs until her throat ached…he recalled her crying this way when her grandmother had died, and reached out to her—to draw her close and comfort her. "I can't tell you how I know, but I swear to you, I can keep her from going public with the information she has—I won't let that bitch hurt you, I promise!"

"C-can't you see h-how she's using it a-already?" the woman beseeched between sobs. "She w-won't stop until she's c-completely destroyed us…until she's b-broken us…" Her face wet from tears and her nose so stuffed she could barely breathe, Annie pulled away from Martin and stepped to her desk for tissues, brushing the back of her hand against a framed photograph with the movement. Though she grabbed for the frame with both hands, it slipped from her fingertips to land with a crash upon the oak floor, shattering glass as far as five feet in every direction.

239

The sound of the crashing glass in the late Sunday afternoon silence seemed as loud as gunfire, and Martin spun about to find Annie kneeling over the broken frame, huge sobs jarring her entire body as she brushed the slivers of glass off the photograph. Tiny droplets of blood began to appear and then smeared as splinters of glass embedded in the palm of her hand. But she seemed unaffected by pain, simply cried harder as tears mixed with blood to wash the photograph in a pink stain that was literally destroying the image.

Martin saw Annie's frantic attempt at salvaging the photograph and knelt behind her to take her right wrist into his hand, turning it palm up so that she might see the damage the broken glass had done to her skin. "Stop it Annie! You're cutting yourself!" he murmured against her shoulder as she tried to pull away.

"Let me go!" She demanded in a quavering voice, making a fist of the hand he grasped as she jerked to dislodge his hold. "Gramma's picture...it's the last one made before she died!" she murmured as she continued to try and wrench her arm free.

"It's ruined, Annie—you *can't* save it!" Martin insisted as he grasped her other wrist in the same vice-like hold. "Look at your hands—look at them!"

Not strong enough to break his hold and too distraught to do much else, Annie finally stopped resisting Martin and slowly followed his instruction to open her fists. When she saw the bloodied gashes and splinters protruding from her skin, her hands began to tremble and she flexed her fingers outward in hopes of stilling them. Closing her eyes, she finally let go her resistance and collapsed weakly back against Martin's chest as he cradled her in his arms. "She's hurting everyone Martin..." Annie whispered. "Claire's even taken Gramma from me..."

"No she hasn't sweetheart," he whispered as he pressed his lips against her temple. "I promise you, I **will** deal with Claire...in time you'll see that I was right...oh sweetheart, go ahead and let it out...I'll hold you all night if you need me to..."

Hearing his whispered endearments and feeling the warmth of his breath now upon her neck, Annie turned and pressed her lips against the curve of his jaw and throat. "I do need you Martin, always. Please don't let me go."

*   *   *

Monica returned Stuart home within just a few minutes of Annie's injury from the broken glass and reacted to remove the splinters and bandage the woman's hands with such skill that Martin was all but awestruck. Though she fretted over Annie's physical pain and pretended for Stuart's benefit that the woman's tear streaked face was simply the result of the pain from the cuts and the loss of a cherished photograph, there were silent, knowing exchanges between the two women which told Martin that Monica understood more. For the first time since she confronted him as 'Nathaniel' and questioned the reason for his duplicity, Martin didn't resent her intimate knowledge of his relationship with Annie; indeed, he had come to depend on it.

"Aunt Monica? May I tell Annie our surprise now?"

Both women looked in the direction of the child and Annie smiled. "I would welcome a surprise, Stuart! Is it a good surprise?"

"Most certainly! I have found a new best friend!"

"Really?" Martin mused.

"It was destiny, I swear," Monica enthused shaking her head. "Do you remember little William, the fella we sent to St. Jude's a few months back?"

"William? He's home?"

"He has the most wonderful adventure to tell," Stuart exclaimed once he realized Annie did remember. "He was once very, very ill and then traveled to a magic place that made him well again! Quite like the Wizard of Oz, it was!"

"Where did—?"

"—he was at Germanton Park, of all places!" Monica exclaimed. "He recognized me right away, and asked for you, Annie: he wanted to know where **you** were and why you weren't with us!"

Annie's expression became serious. "Is he well, really?" she murmured to Monica.

Monica shrugged. "His father said the doctors gave him a clean bill of health…he's been completely released!"

Annie drew a deep breath and smiled at Stuart. "You've made my day, sweetheart! And you couldn't ask for a better *new* best friend!"

"He's quite a bit taller than me, though…" Stuart mused. "*He* could reach the first limb of the massive oak we climbed whereas, Aunt Monica had to give **me** a hand up…"

"You were in the tree?" Martin asked Monica incredulously.

"William's about a year and a half older than you are," Monica reasoned, ignoring Martin completely. "You'll catch him eventually!"

"He told me all about the wonderful baseball card collection you have, Annie…he said the two of you traded cards all the while he was at the Baptist!"

"At Baptist Hospital," Monica corrected succinctly. "Why do foreigners always call it *'the Baptist'*?" she whispered for Annie's ears only, and she had to laugh.

"Would you like to look at my albums," Annie asked and laughed even louder when Stuart jumped to attention. "Please, Monica, take this child upstairs to my room and get him my Atlanta Braves album; that's as good a place to start as any."

"Might I look at it in my room, Annie? I've spent but a tiny amount of time in there all day…and I rather miss Winston…"

"—of course! You can lay the book on your bed, snuggle up beside Winston, and look at it however long you want to. Take your time…"

Standing from where she had been sitting across from her friend, Monica stepped within inches of where Martin was sitting: "He's had no nap all day…he'll be out like a light within the hour—" she murmured in a matter-of-fact tone for Martin's ears only.

"—I'm counting on it!" Martin finished with a knowing smile, and winked at his co-conspirator.

* * *

"How are your hands?" Monica asked nearly a week later as she and Annie walked through the aisles of the local drug store.

"I don't think but one of the cuts will need a Band-aid anymore," Annie replied holding up her hands for Monica's perusal.

"As clumsy as you are, and with a little boy in the house, I'd invest in another box of Band-aids if I were you," Monica teased as they walked up the aisle with bandages and first aid items on it.

"You're never gonna let me live this down, are you?"

Monica laughed and plucked a box of 'assorted sizes' from the shelf. "If you could have seen Martin's expression while I was doctoring on you, you'd have thought the situation required a call to 9-1-1; Stuart was calmer about it than Martin was."

Annie glanced down at the various items stacked in Monica's basket as she placed it on the counter. "Don't you make it to the drug store more often than once a month?" she asked teasingly.

Monica's face lit with a knowing smile. "I'll have you know, Martin gave me a list of things to get **and** a hundred dollar bill to pay for it all—the bulk of this stuff is his!"

Annie's brows drew together in question. "Why on earth didn't he just have me get everything...he gave me a hundred dollars, too!"

"Because you spent the entire trip picking over baseball cards for Stuart...the important stuff, just like he knew you would!"

Annie lifted her eyes heavenward. "Every time I turn around, the two of you are in cahoots about something! I can buy baseball cards and medicinals and...keep it under a hundred..."

"And...how much of *your* hundred do you have left?"

Annie's expression was thoughtful. "That's not the point! Had I known I needed to budget..."

"—you wouldn't have bought Upper Deck—right?"

Annie shrugged. "Topps are good cards, too..."

"But...?"

"I want Stuart to have the best...and, I just incriminated myself, didn't I?"

"It's okay...you'll learn not to argue with me one of these days..." Monica replied with a shrug.

As the two women waited for the clerk to finish adding up Monica's purchases, another clerk approached the counter and handed Monica a large envelope with her name and telephone number written on it. "It came in day before yesterday, Miss Holt. I called your number and left word with your mom."

"Yeah, mom took the message and then put it in her jeans pocket," Monica concurred dourly. "She didn't even think of it again until she started the laundry this morning and happened to check her pockets."

"I hope you're pleased with the results," the clerk offered.

"I'm sure we will be," Monica replied, casting a sideways glance at Annie as she handed the first clerk the hundred-dollar bill Martin had given her. The rack of tabloids to their left however, had captured Annie's attention, and Monica shook her head at the look of frustration and worry on Annie's face.

"You look as if you half expect to see your picture on one of them again...didn't Martin assure you that Claire couldn't use what the investigator learned against you?"

Annie nodded absently. "I don't know what he's basing his certainty on, though; my heart trusts him implicitly, but my head remembers all the trouble the 'American Star' article caused. And this time, it's not just he and I who are being threatened: there's an innocent baby's future to be considered."

"Well, if whatever Martin had on Claire was damning enough for the court to award him custody of his son, I'm certain he wouldn't hesitate to use it again if it meant protecting you and the baby."

"I'll just feel better once Preacher Wilson marries us; not that it's anyone else's business but..."

"—folks will try to make it their business...I know, but you can't let it get to you...you can't let **Claire** get to you! The marriage license is bought, the ceremony is tomorrow and this time next week, you'll have forgotten what you were so worried about!" Monica concluded as they walked to the parking lot and put the numerous bags in the back seat of her car.

A couple of minutes later as they started the drive home, Monica reached into her handbag and retrieved the envelope she'd been given earlier. "Here Annie...this is for you," she offered smilingly as she laid the parcel on the woman's lap.

"What's this?"

"Why don't you open it up and see?" Monica teased, a half-smile playing upon her lips.

Lifting the gummed flap of the envelope, Annie shot the other woman a querulous look as she removed a white gatefold enclosure which read 'Your Cherished Photographs Enclosed—DO NOT BEND.' When she opened the white folder, her breath caught in her throat for inside was a 5x7 reprint of the photograph she had thought to never see again: she and Gramma in front of the Christmas tree during their last Christmas together. "Oh Monica...the picture!"

"Yeah, well...it was Martin's idea, so I can't take too much credit," she replied coyly. "You know what a pack rat Mom is—she never trashes ANYTHING she thinks she might need again or that *would be nice to have.'* For once, I'm glad...even if I DID have to look through a whole cigar box full of negatives to find that one."

Annie took Monica's right hand into her left one and gave it a squeeze. "Do you know how special you are to me? That picture meant an awful lot, but your doing what you did to replace it means even more—I'll never forget it."

"Well, it was Martin's idea, I just supplied the negative. And, I was given explicit instructions to drop the print by the Germanton Gallery on the way back home: remind me to ask what their best Germanton Vineyards wine is too 'cause Martin wants several bottles to celebrate with."

"Martin, you, Preacher Wilson, Mrs. Wilson..." Annie counted off the adults who would be present for the ceremony. "How many bottles could he possibly expect to be consumed by four people?" Annie teased.

"Maybe he's planning on putting a couple back for *future* celebrations! He's already looking toward upcoming anniversaries, Annie...not many guys around who even remember a wedding anniversary much less plan the wine menu a year ahead! Thoughtful, and he's gorgeous, too! Boy, did you luck out!"

"One day, Monica, you'll find someone as special to you as Martin is to me...I just know it."

"Humph! I think I'd just as soon wait on Stuart to grow up. The trick is to get 'em young and train 'em the way you want them to be!"

Shaking her head, Annie smiled indulgently. "You are bad."

"Well...it's not like I have anything really pushing during the next twenty years!" Monica teased.

But Annie knew Monica's self-mocking remarks held more truth than not. And she set her mind at that moment to help change the direction of her dearest friend's life; everyone, she thought gratefully, should be as happy as she was...especially Monica!

*   *   *

The moment Annie returned home, she was greeted by a rambunctious Stuart and an ever-resilient Martin: the elder's brow beaded with perspiration from trying to keep up with his son's exploration through the wooded area behind Annie's house. "I see you found the creek," she commented as she focused on two sets of muddy knees.

"Annie's gonna have both your butts!" Monica added as she rolled down her car window. "Don't you boys know better than to get in the creek with your good pants on?"

"Aunt Monica sounds quite like Betsy, doesn't she?" Stuart asked his father laughingly.

"Worse."

Monica smirked. "Yeah well, you'll learn quick enough...just wait till Annie waxes the floors again..."

"—yeah, yeah…the wrath of Chelsea all over again," Martin broke in tauntingly, recalling one of the more colorful characters from 'Misbegotten.'

"All right you two," Annie interceded as she closed the passenger door of Monica's car. Then to her friend: "Thanks for driving me into town…and for everything."

"Lucky for Martin I like you so good," Monica replied wryly, handing Annie the drug store bags through her open window. "Tell him the receipt's in the bag and that I charge 15% for my time."

"Don't forget about tomorrow!"

"Hel-lo! **How** long have I had this in the works?" she taunted. "I'll be here first thing in the morning!"

Martin grimaced. "But the ceremony isn't until three…I was wanting to sleep in…Sunday's the day of rest…"

Monica shook her head at Annie's amused expression. "Are you sure you wanna go through with this?"

"Absolutely!" Annie replied with a laugh, waving as Monica drove out of her driveway. Smiling inwardly, she could imagine Monica's chagrin at having her earlier joking prophecy fulfilled, for with Stuart standing up as his father's Best Man and she as Annie's Main of Honor, Monica was going to walk down the aisle with Stuart Vaughn after all!

EPILOGUE

"Isn't he beautiful?" Martin asked for at least the third time as he and Chris stood before the glass at the nursery, Martin's day-old son lying in a Plexiglas bassinet before them.

Rolling his eyes heavenward, Chris smiled his indulgence of his friend thinking there was absolutely nothing 'beautiful' about a wrinkled and pink newborn. "Aye, Martin...he looks just like Stuart did." (It was the kindest thing he could think to say!)

"I can't wait for you to meet Annie," Martin continued. "It's hard to believe that in all these months, the two of you never had the opportunity to meet."

Chris placed a reassuring hand on his friend's shoulder. "We have not had the best of circumstances these past months..."

As Martin watched the tiny boy yawn and stretch, his mind ran through the many battles Chris had fought for Annie and himself during the past nine months, circumstances that might have proven fatal to any other relationship given similar situations. Resting his forehead against the glass that separated them from the infants, Martin released a long breath, and murmured "Annie and I couldn't have gotten to this point without your help...not to mention the fact, you have saved my ass more than a few times!"

"So long as you keep paying the bills..." Chris teased, then grasped his friend's shoulder reassuringly. "You said the doctor would allow us a visit with Miss Ry—, er, Annie, by seven...I think it would do you good to see her, Martin. Come," he prodded smilingly, "introduce me to your wife."

"My wife..." Turning about thoughtfully, Martin smiled at Chris' words. "I've had little time to be any kind of husband to her and yet, she never lets me forget how proud she is to *be* 'my wife'."

"You've been well blessed," Chris offered as they walked toward the nursery entrance.

"Blessed...given that Claire still attempts to destroy us at every turn, that's *not* the first word that comes to mind when describing my life this last year," Martin mused aloud.

"So long as Claire believes she has any hope of getting Stuart back, she will fight you. But you can't let fear of the unknown dominate your existence," Chris warned. "You can't stop living for once you do, Claire will have won."

* * *

Monica led Stuart into Annie's hospital room and smiled as he carefully set the vase of carnations on her bedside table. "These are from Aunt Monica and me! She let me pick out the colors and everything!" he boasted proudly.

"Oh sweetheart," Annie began, leaning over the bedside somewhat and opening her arms for a huge hug from the little boy. "They are the most beautiful carnations I've ever seen! Who'd have ever thought of putting all those different colors together in one arrangement?"

"I told you: the kid has incredible taste," Monica offered. "The florist didn't want to listen to him at first, but once he explained why he wanted one of each color, side by side..."

"—and a big white ribbon, because Annie's house is white!" he chimed in.

"OUR house, sweetheart...and it makes absolutely perfect sense to me," Annie concurred smilingly. "I suppose Daddy's already told you all about your new baby brother, huh? Did Monica take you to see him?"

"Not yet. Daddy said he shall bring the baby from the nursery in a bit, for we are all to meet him together."

Annie raised her brows in question, but Monica simply shrugged, "That's what he said, word for word."

"Well then, why don't you scrunch up here beside me 'till your daddy comes?"

"May I really?" the child asked in surprise, inching closer to the hospital bed once Annie opened her arms to him.

"Sure! There's plenty of room, and the nurses are friends of mine: they won't mind you keeping me company for a while," Annie explained as Stuart followed her instruction; sitting upon the mattress, he reclined into the crook of his step-mother's arm and crossed his legs at the ankles atop the bed linens.

"I missed you last night, Annie," he confessed after a moment and the woman hugged him closer, pressing a lingering kiss upon the crown of his head.

"I missed you too…that's the only part about having a baby that I really, really hate: having to be away from the people you love for even one night!"

"What about the hated morning sickness, and the hated vitamin taking, and the hated maternity clothes…" Monica contradicted as she counted the items off on her fingers.

"—alright, alright! So…there's a few other things to DISLIKE," Annie replied, sticking out her tongue at Monica's impish teasing and getting the same in return.

At that same moment, Martin walked into the room pushing the bassinet and found himself in the middle of the exchange. His smiled inwardly to find his wife in such good humor, whereas Chris' attention went immediately to Monica. "I rather hope Stuart didn't see that juvenile display," he demurred for Martin's ears only; Monica however heard it as well.

"Excuse me: would you care to speak up? I don't think the folks at the nurse's desk heard you," she scolded, pointing toward the hallway.

"Monica, please!" Annie murmured.

"'Monica please' my eye! Who **is** this guy?" she murmured in return.

"It's just Christopher, Aunt Monica…daddy's barrister," Stuart offered, rolling his eyes.

"Shall I return later, Martin?" Chris offered defiantly. "I can certainly understand if this is a bad…"

"—of course not," Martin interjected, casting Monica a censuring look. Having come to realize after months of knowing her that it was useless to try reasoning with someone so bent on having the last word, he addressed her head on. "If you could please refrain from starting an all out duel with my attorney **and** dearest friend, I'd like to introduce Stuart to his baby brother."

"Hey, absolutely Martin! I mean, that is what we were all waiting on," she affirmed with a saccharine smile.

"Please bring him over, Martin," Annie entreated with a loving smile. "Stuart's my bed buddy this evening, and I think he can hold the baby if you lay him on his big brother's lap."

"Oh yes, Daddy! Please let me hold him!"

Reaching into the bassinet, Martin lifted the tiny bundle and stepped toward the bed that his wife and son shared. "Hi sweetheart…how are you feeling tonight?" he whispered before pressing a tender kiss upon her lips.

"Better…rested," she replied smiling, touching his face with the palm of her hand. "I have missed you terribly…"

"I've missed you…"

"Daddy!" Stuart broke in impatiently, "I want to see him!"

Martin lifted the thin blue blanket from where it lay across the newborn's face and head, and placed the infant carefully upon Stuart's lap. The child's face lit immediately with awe and disbelief, his eyes scouring over his baby brother's face, body, hands and legs, touching one tiny foot with precious reverence and tenderness, stroking the tiny toes until the infant flinched and Stuart drew his hand away laughingly.

"I think he's ticklish, sweetie!" Annie whispered, hugging the older child closer. "Feel of his hair," she instructed with her fingertips, and Stuart followed suit just as gently as he'd watched Annie do it.

"You must always be careful with the baby, Stuart…be very gentle," Martin coached as he stroked the older boy's golden head.

"Hey—whoa Martin!" Monica interjected as she stood from where she had been sitting by the door. "Y'all can't keep calling that child 'the baby' indefinitely! When me and Annie were talking before—"

"—Ahem…"

A precariously uneasy silence followed Chris' feigned throat clearing as Monica turned slowly about to face him. "Well, you have everyone's attention…so, were you wanting to say something?" she prodded, hand on hip.

"I am sorry, Miss Holt…"

"—MS. Holt, please."

"Miss Holt, I mean no insult but, my old *tutorial side* simply flares when I hear grammatical slips…it's…it's 'Annie and I'…" he offered, clearing his throat for real this time as his eyes circled the room; his smile fading as his eyes met Monica's again.

"I'm sorry, I must have missed the formal introduction, *'Barrister Christopher'*—!"

"—Taylor, Chris Taylor," he further corrected.

"**My** *old cinematic* side simply bristles at disjunctive speech patterns," she enunciated perfectly. "Bond, James Bond may get away with it, but you sir, are NO James Bond…bless your heart," she offered oh too delicately.

Chris turned beseeching eyes toward his old friend: "Martin, I really was not…"

"—Mr. Taylor, please," Annie broke in, hiding a smile behind fingertips pressed upon her lips. "I don't think you and I have been properly introduced," she offered, extending that hand now in greeting.

Martin stepped in on cue and urged his friend to his wife's bedside. "Forgive me, Chris...I don't know what I was thinking about!" *Other than strangling Monica!*, "This is my Annie."

"I'm pleased to finally make your acquaintance," she offered warmly.

"As I am, madam. I congratulate you on the birth of your son and, if I may say, Martin is quite the luckiest of men: you are as lovely and as charming as he said you were."

Annie's face blushed at the compliment and she looked at her husband with adoring eyes. "I feel like I am the lucky one...I didn't think it was possible for one person to give another such happiness."

Holding her stare, Martin leaned over his sons and touched his wife's lips with the softest of kisses. "I love you so much," he whispered before slowly drawing away.

"What happiness they've known wasn't handed to them," Monica proclaimed from her chair by the door. "There were times even **I** wondered if they would end up together."

Chris arched one brow imperiously. "You speak as if you rather consider yourself responsible—the helmsperson, as it were."

"Or a demagogue?" Martin teased with a smile.

"I'd like to think I helped!" the woman defended, her arms crossed before her defiantly. "You were NOT the most agreeable person to conspire with, Martin Vaughn!"

"She has me there."

"She does indeed," Chris concurred. "Some of the stories that I could tell!"

"Oh please! Don't get me started!"

"I should love hearing the tales from this side of the ocean," Chris teased his friend. Then: "We shall have to compare notes sometime, **MS**. Holt..."

"Yeah, like *that's* ever gonna happen," she returned petulantly, her eyes looking to Annie for agreement. Annie's expression, however, spoke volumes for her brows were drawn in reproof, and she shook her head ever so slightly as if to censure.

"What?" Monica mouthed with a shrug.

Biting her lip thoughtfully Annie's next words were tinged with an air of persuasion. "Having come here straight from the airport, Chris, I can imagine you must be nearly famished...why don't you show our friend to the cafeteria, Monica?"

"Aye, madam...I would welcome a spot of hot tea," Chris replied wearily.

"You want ME to show him?" Monica murmured incredulously, then caught Annie's eminent smile and mischievous wink. After a moment's pause, her own eyebrows rose thoughtfully and she found herself hesitantly offering, "I...suppose, I could do that...it would be the...the *neighborly* thing to do..."

"Oh yes! Absolutely!" Martin chimed in after getting an elbow in the side. "The...the food is actually quite...good?"

"You're a terrible liar, Martin," his friend teased. "A wonderful actor, but a terrible liar."

"OK...well, the tea is good and the coffee's strong..."

"—look, let's be up front here," Monica interjected. "You want a really good, late supper? Ryan's, hands down."

Martin's eyes went back and forth between the two, an eerie sense of foreboding making him somewhat uneasy.

"Sounds delightful! Very well then, shall I call a hackney, Ms. Holt?"

Monica just stared at Chris. "A what?"

"A taxi," Martin murmured, feeling as if he'd somehow missed a step.

Monica rolled her eyes. "Why can't he just speak English?" she murmured to Martin. Then to Chris: "I have my car, if you don't mind riding in a VW?"

"Indeed, I should welcome a ride in a vintage automobile! Ah well then, shall we?" Chris offered, taking her heavy winter coat from where it lay across the back of her chair and placing it upon her shoulders.

Monica glanced over her shoulder and drew her brows together at Annie's satisfied smile. "I'll come with Martin in the morning and help with Stuart, and your things..."

"Fine...whatever," Annie replied still smiling.

Feeling Chris' hand beneath her elbow, Monica glanced at him to find him smiling with not only his lips but with his eyes; she had to admit, when he wasn't critical and arrogant, he was actually, surprisingly, quite attractive...

"It has been a pleasure meeting you, Annie," Chris offered in parting. "Martin—I'll call if I hear anything."

Nodding, Martin couldn't take his eyes off Monica's dumbfounded expression, which pretty much was a reflection of his own! "Have a good evening...?"

"We shall indeed," his friend replied for both Monica and himself as he opened the door that led to the hospital corridor: "After you, madam."

Monica swallowed. "Uh, yeah...thanks," she returned in a near whisper as the door shut with a click behind them.

"That was weird...wouldn't you love to be a fly on the interior of her Bug?"

Annie shook her head at her husband's statement. "I'd say Chris was quite taken with her..."

"Taken?! Not hardly. Overwhelmed maybe; appalled, definitely! She is NOT his type sweetheart, trust me."

Pursing her lips in that thoughtful way Martin had now come to recognize, Annie dipped her chin to her chest with a coy smile she couldn't hold back. "Nor was I yours."

Martin looked at her reflectively then, recalling for a moment the little girl who had followed him so adoringly when they were both children. The little boy and the infant she now held so lovingly slept in secure peace within the woman's arms and he nodded, more to himself, that she had always held his heart as well—even when he didn't know it.

"Strange how things like that work out," he conceded as he stroked the woman's hair tenderly.

"How very fortunate for us," Annie whispered in reply a scant instant before touching loving lips to her husband's.

DESTINY OF A WAR VETERAN
by Sal Atlantis Phoenix

Destiny of a War Veteran depicts the life of a conscientious veteran. The subject matter of thestory is serious and tends towards the realistic side of the aftermath of war. The story is about the analysis of the human soul lost in fantasy and in reality, about submission and rebellion, and about philosophy and tyranny. The story is vivid with images, and complex and rich in characters. It is an intriguing tale that defines the socio-political scenarios.
Vietnam War veteran Joe is tempted to participate in Middle Eastern and international politics, compelled with insinuated illusion of establishing freedom and democracy. The subsequent effects of the human tragedies engulfed from the political scenarios devastate him, and he seeks refuge beyond the realm of humanity.

Paperback, 188 pages
5.5" x 8.5"
ISBN 1-4241-8005-8

About the author:

Sal Atlantis Phoenix, a veteran of life and a conscientious citizen, is a playwright and fiction writer. His lifelong experience convinced him that "...with all its sham, drudgery and broken dreams, it is still a beautiful world. Be careful. Strive to be happy."

THE ASSASSIN WHO LOVED HER

by Janet M. Henderson

In *The Assassin Who Loved Her*, journalist Jennifer Long wants two things: to become a great writer and to fall in love. Her dreams come true when she writes about a serial killer called the Assassin who stalks, threatens, and torments her for exposing his motives in the media.

Tim, the pilot, brings Jennifer financial security. Jason, the actor, brings her fame and fortune. John, the former FBI agent, brings her protection and intrigue. But Jennifer must survive murder, deceit, heartache, and grief before she finds true love, happiness, triumph, and relief.

From Chicago, to Washington, to Hollywood, to Portugal, Jennifer fights for her life and career. Her story will make you laugh and cry. It'll make you believe in love. It'll make you hope and pray she wins. With a fairytale beginning and a Hollywood ending, it has everything a good novel should have! Read it and love it!

Paperback, 276 pages
6" x 9"
ISBN 1-60610-424-1

About the author:

Janet M. Henderson teaches English in the City Colleges of Chicago. She was born in Chicago and, as the daughter of a U.S. Marine, grew up in Virginia, North Carolina, California and Hawaii. Her first novel, *Lunch with Cassie*, received excellent reviews from Writer's Digest. She lives in Chicago.

also available from publishamerica

THE SCARLET "P"

by Ron Sullivan

The Scarlet "P" is a novel centered in the affluent town of Paradise Valley, Arizona, a bedtime community of Phoenix where business professionals, sports figures and captains of industry reside. The peace and security of the town is shattered by the death of four young ladies out jogging or playing tennis. They are savagely murdered and their bodies mutilated.

Detective Don Graves of the Paradise Valley Marshal's Office leads the multi-agency investigation to identify and arrest the monster that was responsible for the killings. Amy Brady, an assistant DA working the case, becomes romantically involved with Graves and helps with the identification and capture of the monster.

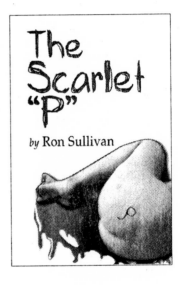

Paperback, 163 pages
5.5" x 8.5"
ISBN 1-60474-392-1

About the author:

Ron Sullivan was born and raised in White Plains, New York, and has lived in the Phoenix, Arizona, area for over thirty years. The father of six children, he has recently retired from residential real estate and has now fulfilled his lifetime ambition to become a novelist.

ABYSS OF INSANITY

by J. Michael Beck

John Thomas Parker is a man pushed to the edge of sanity. He has just discovered his wife is cheating on him and he is hurling down a dark path that will change his world forever. He begins looking for a companion in the wrong place at the wrong time. He meets Marcy, a lovely woman apparently working the streets as a prostitute. However, Marcy has a secret that will pull John into an abyss of evil, where murder and ruined lives surround him. His and Marcy's fate may rely on others to figure it out before it is too late.

Paperback, 335 pages
6" x 9"
ISBN 1-60610-092-0

About the author:

I have thirty-three years of law enforcement experience, beginning with the military, state and city police and twenty-one years of federal law enforcement. I have a bachelor's degree in criminal justice and currently work as an investigator completing federal background investigations. I have worked alongside men of honor and had the misfortune to be associated through my work with some men so filled with evil I could never create a character who could live up to the real bad guys. I put my years of law enforcement into this novel. The best and worst of mankind are represented in these pages. —J. Michael Beck